Into Something Good

by

Stanalei Fletcher

*The Special Something Series,
Book 1*

This is a work of fiction. Names, characters, places, and incidents are either the product of the author's imagination or are used fictitiously, and any resemblance to actual persons living or dead, business establishments, events, or locales, is entirely coincidental.

Into Something Good

COPYRIGHT © 2020 by Kim Finnegan

All rights reserved. No part of this book may be used or reproduced in any manner whatsoever without written permission of the author or The Wild Rose Press, Inc. except in the case of brief quotations embodied in critical articles or reviews.
Contact Information: info@thewildrosepress.com

Cover Art by *Tina Lynn Stout*

The Wild Rose Press, Inc.
PO Box 708
Adams Basin, NY 14410-0708
Visit us at www.thewildrosepress.com

Publishing History
First Sweetheart Rose Edition, 2020
Print ISBN 978-1-5092-3089-1
Digital ISBN 978-1-5092-3090-7

The Special Something Series, Book 1
Published in the United States of America

Indecision crept into her eyes, tinged with a touch of fear and sadness too.

That protective feeling washed over him. "Or how about this? How about we tell your brother the truth—that I foolishly jumped in with both feet to rescue you from Peters by announcing our engagement. And after discussing it over tonight, we realized this is a good thing for both of us. It may have started out as a fake, but it's real now."

Her gaze swung to his face. A tiny light of hope—of gratitude—gleamed in the depths of her blue eyes.

Stepping closer, he captured her shoulders. She quivered under his touch. He wanted to wrap his arms around her and shield her from every single worry in her world. He couldn't do that, but he could offer to bear some of her burdens. "Say yes, Cayme."

Kudos for Stanalei Fletcher

Finalist in the
2018 Desert Rose RWA
Diamonds in the Desert

Dedication

This book is dedicated to the men and women
of our military who commit their lives
in the service our country.
Thank You to you and your families
for your dedication and sacrifices
in service to others.

Acknowledgements

A special thanks to ELF for her dedication and commitment to venture forward with a new series with me. And a huge shout out to my critique partners—Steve, Kent, Lyn, and Mary—for their time and input to help me make my stories better.

Chapter One

"Caaymeeee!"

The shout came from Sherry Jackson, Cayme Foster's best friend. Her one-volume voice echoed over the entire Blakely, Idaho neighborhood.

Right after that, a couple of car doors slammed shut—not a moment too soon.

"I'm around back," Cayme answered, her voice breathless as she gingerly returned her cell phone to her back pocket. That dratted acrophobia had her paralyzed on the ladder. "Hurry! I'm stuck up here." The only place she could go was straight down, and she wasn't quite ready to do that.

Now that she was level with the gutter, all she had to do was work up enough courage to scramble onto the roof. Except, she'd left all her sanity and bravado at the bottom of the ladder, and it looked like neither would join her anytime soon.

Sweat pooled on her palms and a chill ran down her spine when she realized how far it was to the ground. How was she supposed to keep her promise to her mother to take care of the house when obviously she hadn't outgrown her fear of heights?

"What do you think you're doing?" A deep, disgruntled voice shouted from the foot of the ladder.

Willing herself to peer down, she swallowed a groan. Of all the people to witness her foolish attempt to fix the roof, why did it have to be Rick Morrison? Despite him being Sherry's older brother, she'd not interacted with him much in the month she'd been back in their hometown. She certainly hadn't expected her best friend to enlist his help.

"I'm looking for a leak." She intended to sound defiant, but her words came out whiny. "Where's Sherry?"

"She's getting little Rachel out of the car seat. You know you need to be on the roof to find a leak."

"I know." Her words were barely a squeak.

"Is it really that hard to ask for help?"

"No… Yes." She conceded defeat.

"Where's Ben? Why isn't he up there?"

"Ben's on his way to Boise. It's his therapy week." No matter how scared she was, she wouldn't let Rick accuse her brother of not helping. Ben had enough on his plate without tackling house repairs, too.

"Fine. Climb down. I'll take a look at the problem."

Even from her fifteen-foot perch, she heard Rick's disapproving grumble. A bubble of hysteria threatened to escape. "I can't."

His expletive was much more audible. "Don't move." He dropped his tool belt. "And stop looking down and focus on something pleasant."

Nothing was pleasant about being this high up. She tore her gaze from the ground, took a deep breath, and concentrated on the amazing view of Hawk's Peak. The mountain, which was part of the lower Sawtooth Mountain range, loomed over the Blakely River that ran alongside her family's property. Several feet of snow still covered the close-enough-to-touch northeast face and sparkled in the late May sunshine—beautiful but ominous.

As Rick ascended, the ladder vibrated.

She gripped the rung even tighter. *I'mnotgoingtofall. I'mnotgoingtofall. I'mnotgoingtofall.*

Just like she had when she was ten years old and fell out of that old cottonwood tree, she would crash and burn. Forcing her mind away from imminent doom, she focused on the mountain again.

The last storm had dumped several more inches of snow on the peak. If not for the prediction of another blast of late-winter weather, she would have gladly left the ladder in the old shed, ignored her e-mails, and gone for a hike around the small community. Instead, she'd convinced herself that this rare warm spring day was the perfect time to fix the leak threatening the boxes in the attic.

The vibrations slowed as Rick stopped just below her.

"I should toss you over my shoulder and carry you down."

"It's too dangerous." He wouldn't follow through with his threat, would he? "I got myself into this mess. I can get myself out. Just give me a moment."

"Take your time." His deep voice was calm, as though he had all day. Then he moved and the ladder rattled again.

"And don't leave me!" Stupid phobia. Ugh, and even worse, Rick had a front row seat to witness it.

"I'm not leaving. I'm climbing closer to guide you down." Rick reached for the rail next her waist, his arm brushing her calf.

She gasped. As his body blocked the spring breeze,

the cold that had clutched her middle was suddenly gone, replaced by a heat that arrowed straight through her.

"You're safe now."

His low reply was almost gentle, and no three words had ever meant more.

"We'll be on the ground in no time."

Warmth from his breath penetrated the thin material of her T-shirt, making every one of her senses come alive. "I don't think I can move."

"You can. I won't let anything happen to you."

His tone was reassuring, almost pushing away the terror of falling to the ground. Tears burned her eyes at his generosity. She blinked furiously to keep them from spilling over. "Okay." That stupid squeak again.

"I'll guide your foot to the next rung. Ready?"

She shook her head. She'd never be ready.

"Relax. Here we go."

A large hand closed over the side of her thigh. "No!"

"Cayme, you can't stay here. You have to climb down."

He said it more patiently than she deserved.

"Now come on." He prodded her leg.

Nodding, she took several breaths before stretching for the rung below, but her hands clung to the rail. "I can't." The memory of that fall from the old cottonwood tree came rushing back. How stupid to believe she could take care of things on her own.

"You can do this."

His tone was stern this time, penetrating her fear and commanding her to move.

"You climbed up. You can climb down." He

gripped the side of her jeans and gave a steady tug.

Panic filled her. She was frozen on this stupid ladder, never to move again.

"Trust me."

Cayme'd never had a problem trusting Rick. Even when they were kids playing ball, she knew he would never intentionally hurt her. She willed her racing heart to slow and put her life in his hands. Okay, she would do this. She couldn't stay there forever. Cautiously, she followed his coaxing to the next rung. Her foot found the step and he patted her leg.

"See? That wasn't so hard."

"That's only one step."

"And there's only eight more to go." He singsonged the words.

Too bad she couldn't see his face. Maybe his smile would make this whole ordeal easier.

"Now your other leg."

One rung at a time, she eased down the ladder.

Rick stayed with her until he reached the ground. Then he grasped her waist, lifted her off the last rung, and lowered her to the grass.

She turned to thank him, and her heart did an unfamiliar double tap—probably from hyperventilating. It couldn't be because of his rugged features, or the scruffy...make that...*sexy*, five o'clock shadow. Nor was it because of the warm span of hands resting at her waist sending pools of heat where there should be none.

A hard glint filled his chocolate brown eyes. "You could've been seriously hurt if you'd fallen. Why in the— Why didn't you ask for help?" His husky tone belied his expression.

"I really wanted to make the repair myself. I was

sure I'd lost my fear of heights."

His gaze softened.

For a moment, it looked like he would dump a load of pity on her. Her chest tightened, ready to fend off his sympathy. Then a teasing light appeared in his eyes and his hands tightened on her waist.

"You and I both know better. Don't you remember a certain tree?"

How could she possibly forget? After finding her flat on her back all those years ago, Rick had wisely not moved her. Instead, he'd made a pillow from his shirt then raced back to the house for help.

When she'd returned from the emergency room sporting a bright-pink cast on her arm, he'd drawn a stick figure wearing a sling on it, whispering so no one else could hear, "Don't ever do that again, you scared me half to death."

That day, and all the days of unrequited love that followed, rolled through her oxygen-deprived brain like runaway railroad cars. Despite the lower-than-normal spring temperatures, heat crept up her neck. "You're such a gentleman to remind me." Hopefully her tart reply masked those old feelings.

"I'm no such thing. But I am impressed you got the ladder out." He gave her a crooked smile.

Her stomach lurched. Silhouetted against the springtime sunlight, he was her knight in a leather tool belt, with no clue how she'd felt about him all these years. "You haven't changed at all. Still coming to my rescue."

"It's what I do best." He leaned closer, lowering his voice. "Never scare me like that again."

She reeled under a touch of déjà vu.

Just then, Sherry rushed around the corner of the house with her eight-month-old daughter bouncing on her hip. "Sorry…I had trouble with the latch on the car seat…" Her gaze darted between Rick and Cayme. "Are you okay?"

Rick took a step back.

Cayme gave her friend a weak smile. "I'm fine." She pulled her cell phone from her back pocket, waving it. "Thanks for coming when I called."

"Of course." Sherry pulled Cayme into a one-armed hug. "Thank goodness we got here in time."

Cayme returned the embrace then faced Rick. Whatever tenuous moment they'd had was gone—not that it had been anything more than her imagination. She tucked the phone back in her jeans and pointed to the roof. "I think the problem is in a seam over the attic."

He searched her face, his dark eyes seeing through her false bravado. "No more climbing for you. I'll check it out." He retrieved his tool belt off the lawn, swung it over his shoulder, and started up the ladder with the ease of having done it hundreds of times.

She watched him climb until he stepped over the rain gutter onto the roof before letting go the breath she'd been holding. Oh well, the important thing was fixing the leak before the next storm, not who fixed it. If it saved the eighty-year-old house from more damage, she'd let Rick save the day and endure these awkward schoolgirl feelings in silence.

As he disappeared from view, she wiped clammy palms on her jeans, pushing away the scare, as well as the disconcerting allure of Rick Morrison. She was way too old to let a teenage crush, in addition to her fear of heights, turn her into pudding.

Tossing her ponytail off her shoulder, she looked over at Sherry. She owed her friend for a timely intervention. "Thank you for coming over. But you could've warned me you were bringing Rick."

"Hubby's busy with the boys and it's just me and the baby." Sherry pursed her lips. "I don't know…maybe I should have sent Rick over here alone. What was that I walked in on?"

"Nothing. He was just helping me past my stupid phobia."

"Hmmm. Didn't look like nothing. But I guess you'd know." Sherry turned and headed toward the worn wooden steps to the back porch, the late afternoon sunlight making her chin-length hair look more auburn than brown.

Thank goodness, Sherry didn't push for an explanation, which Cayme couldn't have provided anyway. That interaction with Rick was…unexpected and had left her heart pounding. She straightened her shoulders and followed her friend up the porch steps.

The previous day's spring storm had scrubbed the sky and left it a deep azure. The air was so clean that the scent of damp cottonwood and fresh pine wafted up from the sun-warmed ground where robins marched across the back lawn in search of an afternoon snack.

Once on the porch, Sherry bounced her daughter on her hip and received a toothless grin. "I still can't believe you were up there. What were you thinking?"

"I needed to find the leak."

Sherry snorted. "What you *need* is to stop doing everything yourself. Let someone else help."

"I'm doing fine." Cayme crossed to the old wooden

railing and stared at the rushing water a few yards from the edge of her property. "Regardless, thank you for bringing Rick."

Sherry laughed and rolled her eyes. "Don't overstretch that gratitude muscle. It might snap."

Cayme turned away from the rising river and sat on a folding lawn chair that had seen one season too many. "I really wanted to make the repair on my own."

"For Heaven's sake, Cay." Sherry sat on the other chair and scowled. "You may think living alone in the big city qualifies you for 'Miss Independence of the Year,' but you're back in Blakely now. You're part of the community."

Cayme grunted. "The jury's still out on whether the community wants me."

"Nonsense." Sherry shifted little Rachel on her lap. "You're letting those old insecurities take over. You're right where you need to be, and you know it."

"Maybe." Did the insecurities her friend spoke of stem from wanting to stay home, or the tug of her job in Seattle? Lately, she seemed to have a foot in two different worlds.

Putting it all aside for a moment, she grinned goofily at the baby to mask the turmoil churning in her stomach.

The little cutie was named after Cayme's mom, who thankfully had lived long enough to spend time with her namesake. At the end, those visits brightened her mother's day when little else had.

Sherry gently bounced the baby on her lap making the lawn chair rattle. "It's so peaceful here. I could listen to the sound of the water forever."

Peaceful didn't describe Cayme's feelings. At the

moment, her life was much like the rising river, rushing headlong through the valley, ready to spill over the banks at any moment. The difference was sandbags could hold back the river, while she struggled to find any defenses to protect against the encroaching floodwaters of her current circumstances.

Leaning back in her lawn chair, she surveyed the yard, her gaze drawn to the old cottonwood tree that stood close to the water's edge. It still had the wooden planks nailed into the trunk. She didn't think anyone had climbed the tree again since she'd fallen out of it.

Dragging her mind from the past, she focused on all the things she still had to take care of. The house, the garden, her mother's store, and of course, her brother. After a full month home, she still couldn't tell if her presence made a difference—either for herself or for Ben.

Sherry was over there holding her young daughter as though she'd been born a mother. Her best friend had always known what she wanted and never deviated from that path. Cayme envied that single-mindedness. At twenty-eight—almost twenty-nine—she still hadn't figured out where she belonged.

Growing up, she'd always believed she'd live in Blakely after graduating from college. She'd wanted to marry, have a family, and raise her children in this small community. Indulge in the passion of her youth and finally write that novel.

Instead, a broken engagement had her looking to the city for a fresh start. Even though she loved her job, Seattle no longer had the appeal it once had. Sometimes she felt she was marking time, waiting for something momentous to open a path to the rest of her life. If only she could put aside her past failures and let the mountain air clear her mind.

Little Rachel reached out a chubby hand.

Cayme smiled and offered a finger.

The baby latched on and immediately brought it to her mouth.

"Oops." Cayme gently tugged free. "Shouldn't have done that with these grubby hands. Let's go inside so I can wash up. I want to hold her."

Sherry stood and led the way to the back door. "You can hold her all night if you want to. She's teething."

"Ah. She can't be that bad." Cayme cooed at the angelic face. "A little slobber never hurt anyone." When she opened the screen door, it creaked on rusted hinges, then banged closed behind them. The scent of the bacon and egg breakfast she'd cooked for Ben before he left for Boise lingered in the kitchen. She hadn't told Ben about her plan to check out the leaky roof. The fact that he hadn't noticed all the boxes strewn about the living room proved his attention was on the 2-1/2-hour drive for his weekly therapy session at the VA hospital. The sessions were critical for his recovery and she hadn't wanted to distract him.

"Ben won't be home tonight, so if you're serious about tending, I'd love to take the baby." As she washed her hands in the kitchen sink, her mind fast-forwarded to Monday's schedule. "Oh, shoot! I can't. It's my turn to open the store tomorrow."

After her mother died, Cayme had extended her leave of absence from her job as an assistant editor for a small publishing firm in Seattle. She'd needed to deal with Rachel's affairs and manage Books, Bytes, &

Brews, the combination bookstore and Internet cafe Rachel and her partner, Skeeter Burke, had started a couple of years ago.

Sherry settled in a chair and propped Rachel on the table. Leaning nose to nose with the baby, she crooned, "That's just like your Auntie Cayme. Always promising something then reneging." She looked over at Cayme. "It's a good thing the store is closed on Sundays, otherwise you wouldn't have taken a single day off in the last month."

"It helps to stay busy." Cayme dried her hands, tossed the towel on the counter, and joined her friend at the table. She held up a hand to stop the inevitable objection. "Before you say anything more, it's my choice. I need at least another month to determine if the store can afford to hire more help." Without waiting for a reply, she grabbed Rachel and pulled her into her lap. "How's my little goddaughter?" She breathed in the sweet baby smells. Chubby little fingers curled around Cayme's thumbs as she played pat-a-cake. Gentle warmth settled in her chest and she grinned at the baby's delighted laughter.

"You know—" Sherry gave her a quizzical look. "—when you smile like that, you almost look relaxed. Since Ben's gone, why don't you come over for dinner tonight?"

Cayme glanced over the baby's head. "Can't. I have more of Mom's boxes to go through. I could catch up on some reading and my backlog of e-mails, too."

"Come on. It's dinner. You have to eat."

"Does your hunky husband know you want to bring home strays?" When Sherry had introduced her husband, Ken Jackson, Cayme couldn't help but be a bit envious of the tall handsome man.

"You're not a stray." Sherry waggled her finger. "More like a prodigal. Besides, even though Ken won't admit it, he's really flattered you think he's a hunk."

"Can I take a rain check? I really ought to go through the rest of those boxes from the attic." Cayme settled the baby on her hip and stood.

The other woman glanced out the kitchen window at the blue sky dotted with fluffy clouds. "If you don't come over tonight, you'll *have* to take a rain check. This is the first decent weekend we've had all month." She stood, a crease marring her smooth forehead. "I hate that you're working so many hours almost as much as I hate these constant storms."

Cayme sighed. "I know. Except, I haven't even opened my work e-mail today to see what's waiting there." She had agreed to read some of her boss's slush pile and handle nitpicky details on smaller client accounts remotely. Right before she'd left Seattle, he'd hinted at an opportunity for her to groom her own authors. That would be a huge step up the career ladder—one that didn't involve heights—and would keep her close to the industry she'd grown to love. At least today being Sunday, she tried not to feel too guilty for ignoring work.

"For crying out loud, you're supposed to be on bereavement leave." Sherry's lips thinned. "Work can wait until tomorrow. If there'd been a crisis, you'd have gotten a phone call, right?"

"Yes…but—"

"You're just not happy unless you have too many irons in the fire." Sherry placed her hands on her hips and gave a hard stare much like the one that Rick had given earlier. "It's no different than this leak. Other people can help. You need to let them."

Cayme held the baby tighter, taking comfort from the warm little body curled against her. Sherry was right, of course. But sometimes Cayme was sure that if she let go, she'd let down everyone who needed her.

Chapter Two

From his perch on the roof, Rick heard the screen door open then bang closed, signaling Cayme and his sister returning to the porch.

"What you need is stress relief." Sherry's voice floated through the crisp spring air like a helium balloon freed from a child's grip.

"Like what?" Cayme's question followed in a quieter, more cautious tone. "I don't have time to drive to the resort for yoga classes."

Ignoring a spurt of conscience at eavesdropping, Rick eased toward the edge of the roof overlooking the backyard and porch. Not that his sister's words were hard to hear. She'd been born with an outdoor voice and had never learned to curb it.

"There's a Lamaze class starting at the community center in a couple of weeks. They have great breathing techniques. I'll go with you and leave this grouchy little teether with her daddy."

Sherry's comment broke Rick's concentration, making his step slip. An innate sense of balance and self-preservation saved him from tumbling over the edge. Lamaze? Cayme Foster? An image of her, soft and round with a belly full of baby, popped into his head. No. Wait a minute... They were only talking stress relief, right?

He craned his neck for a glimpse of her on the

porch below.

She jostled his niece, a soft grin gracing her features.

Even from that height, he saw the worry lines around her full lips ease. She should smile more often. The baby's laughter carried on the same breeze that tugged at Cayme's ponytail, making the strands of red hair look like ribbons of new copper in the early afternoon sun.

He didn't think she was pregnant, yet something about her looked different. Maybe the way she held Rachel gave her a maternal glow, or maybe the baby's infectious laughter had relaxed her. Maybe he should stop gawking and get back to the project that brought him here in the first place.

"I'm not invading a class for expecting mothers just to ease my own stress." Cayme's words held a rebuke, but she smiled at the baby as though that was all the stress relief she needed.

Sherry folded her arms. "Fine. You should still do something. What about your writing? Have you ever submitted your book to the publisher you work for?"

Cayme wrote? Rick could imagine her bent over a computer, hammering out the next bestseller with that funny frown between her eyes.

Just then, little Rachel spat up, sending some of the baby's lunch down the front of Cayme's shirt.

The women hurried back inside, and Sherry's laughter drowned out Cayme's explanation about the book.

How was it he never knew she liked to write? In a town the size of an abandoned mine tailings pond, it wasn't hard to know everyone's business. Just because

Cayme had been living in Seattle for the last five years, didn't make her exempt from hometown gossip. Ben never said much about his sister at the monthly poker game. Granted, Ben never talked much these days. Even less since their mother died.

When Cayme had returned to Blakely, Rick seemed to know exactly when she was in the same vicinity, making this strange attraction to her hard to ignore. Even more difficult was reconciling the image of the girl he'd tackled playing football, with the woman who'd filled out in places he'd like to tackle in bed. He didn't like it messing with his head.

Turning his attention back to the roof repair, he found the problem with a ridge cap. He clipped it down and sat back to check his work. The quick fix should hold for now, but the entire roof needed to be replaced. Of course, if Cayme and Ben sold the property, his company would be leveling the house to make way for the new park and bike trails.

He hated thinking about his friends losing their home. But a job was a job, and his company needed the work. A project in town instead of those long drives to the other side of the county was something he'd been looking forward to for several months.

With the roof fixed, his mind wandered back to Cayme. Even though this wasn't the first time he'd considered dating since his divorce, getting involved with a potential client was something he never did—no matter how tempting. The bid on the Fosters' property was still on the table waiting for Cayme to agree to the sale. Tangling with her, not only as a client, but his sister's best friend, was a complication he didn't need.

Once down from the roof, he unbuckled his tool

belt and dropped it on the bottom step of the porch. Then he collected the ladder and hauled it to the old shed Cayme and Ben's dad built the year before he died.

When the four of them were young, they had used the old shed as their secret fort. Cayme's mom used to call them the "fearsome foursome." When he thought of Rachel Foster, a small ache filled his chest. Her death had hit him as hard as his own mother's passing two years earlier.

Their families had always been close. Each woman had lent a hand to raise the other's children as though they were her own. The four kids grew up together, almost like siblings. Only they weren't. Rick was acutely aware of that today.

He'd loved playing at the Fosters', especially during the summers. The backyard was an acre and a half of some of the most prized land just inside Blakely's city limits. Part of the property was undeveloped and butted up against the woods near the river. The place was a young boy's adventure playground. His son Adam would love to play on the river sandbars shaded by the old cottonwoods as much as he had at that age. Except with this year's runoff, those old cottonwoods offered the only protection between Cayme's home and the rising river. No way would he let Adam play there this spring.

"Rick!" Sherry shouted from the porch. "You about done? I need to pick up some groceries for the barbecue before the boys get home from the ballpark." She turned to Cayme. "Ken's been teaching them to catch pop flies."

"Just finished." Rick jimmied the shed door closed.

Maybe he'd come by later in the week and fix that, too. Just because he didn't want a romantic complication, didn't mean he couldn't be neighborly. Then again, he couldn't ignore that little matter of the development bid.

Sherry and Cayme came down the back steps.

Cayme hadn't changed her shirt after little Rachel's spit up. Somehow that made her seem more like the girl he remembered who didn't care about appearances.

"Can the leak be fixed?"

Her detached tone bugged him—as did her too-polite expression. Despite the fact that he hadn't seen much of her for five years, she was no more a stranger to him than his own sister. How many summers had they spent playing cowboys, or army, or sleeping outside on summer nights in clothesline tents? "It's all done." He tried to keep the annoyance out of his voice.

"How much do I owe you?"

"No charge."

"I can't let you fix the roof on this old place and not pay you. It's money out of your company's pocket." She lifted a stubborn chin.

"I promised your mom I'd take a look at the roof as soon as the snow stopped." His answer was more of a growl than he intended.

"But it never stopped." Cayme finished his thought. "Mom e-mailed about the constant storms even before she got sick." She glanced at the mountains and swallowed. "I can't believe there's still so much snow up there this late in the year. I know I've been away for a while, but even this weather's been unusual, right?"

His gaze dropped to the curve of her throat then jerked back to her face. "Unusual is one word for this year's crazy weather. Even the resorts are reopening for Memorial Day weekend skiing. But it'll melt soon enough."

Sherry draped an arm over Cayme's shoulder and leaned her head close. "We're just hoping it will melt gradually or we'll have the flood of the century."

They walked around the side of the house between two old lilac bushes that had served as a border between the front and back yards for as long as he could remember. The blossoms' fragrance, one of his favorites, wafted on the warm sunshine and followed them into the front yard.

Cayme stared at the river, pulling her lower lip between her teeth. "I noticed the change in the current. I heard the city dredged the river north of town a couple of years ago to protect those expensive homes."

"Can't stop progress," Rick pointed out.

Part of that progress was the town's offer to buy the Fosters' place, the neighbor's property next door, and all the surrounding undeveloped land parcels. Ben had apparently left the decision to Cayme. Since her mother passed, she'd been sitting on the contract and the council wondered if they'd have to cough up more cash for the purchase. The delay had also caused old Mrs. Jones next door to waffle in her decision to sell.

Why wouldn't Cayme sell? The offer was more than fair and would make a nice little nest egg for her and Ben to live on without the upkeep of this old place. Especially if she wanted to quit her day job and write books. Or have a family someday. He glanced at Cayme's flat stomach, oddly relieved she wasn't pregnant. Then, he averted his gaze. He didn't want to think about her carrying another man's child.

He'd had his chance at marriage, and now he had his son, Adam. If he wanted more, his sister and her family, as well as Dad, were just a block or two away. They were all the family he needed for now. No. They were enough. Period. He tugged his sister's arm. "You ready to go?"

Sherry gave Cayme another hug. "Don't forget what I said about your writing," she reminded. "I'll be happy to read for you. Or even go to those classes if you want."

Cayme's smile looked more like a grimace.

Rick frowned. Why was she working herself so hard? She was young, attractive, and should be dating— *Nope, not going there.* She could have all the *special someones* she wanted. He walked to the minivan and waited for Sherry to buckle his niece into her car seat.

"Thanks again for fixing the leak." Cayme gave another small smile and waved.

Sherry finished securing the baby in her seat then opened the driver's side and waved in return.

Rick climbed inside and slammed the passenger door, scowling at his inappropriate thoughts.

"What's the matter with you?" Sherry pulled onto the street and headed toward her house. "You're acting like a grumpy badger. You volunteered to fix the roof. I didn't drag you over."

Rick shifted his gaze to his sister and rubbed the back of his neck. "Sorry. I just don't understand why Cayme and Ben are hanging on to that old place."

Sherry's eyebrows disappeared under her bangs. "You spent as much time over there as I did. You love that house and yard as much as they do."

"And if the house was mine, I probably wouldn't sell. But Cayme hasn't visited for more than a few days at a time over the last few years. And Ben…" He swallowed. To a certain extent, he understood what Ben was going through. They'd stood side by side during the swearing-in ceremony at the recruiter's office. The difference was Ben had deployed three times to Rick's one. Ben hadn't had a kid right out of the gate, either. "Ben needs to focus on recovering. Put his life back together. Not deal with an old house crumbling around his ears."

"You think it's foolish for Cayme and Ben to hang on to the only home they've ever known?"

Rick swore under his breath. His sister sure knew how to spin things. "No. Not when you put it like that. You're a pain when you're making a point. You know that?"

Sherry grinned. "That's what sisters are for." She turned the van into her driveway and parked.

Rick climbed out and headed around the back for his tools. If he didn't put them in his truck now, he'd be chasing them down for work the next day. He stared at the empty spot on the floor of the van where his tool belt should have been. "Of course," he muttered.

"What's wrong now?" Sherry was unbuckling the baby.

"I left my tools in Cayme's backyard." He'd dropped them on the back steps and then got distracted by a pretty redhead.

"Must have been a Freudian slip." Sherry grinned. "Now you have an excuse to go back over there and convince her to come to the barbecue."

"I don't think so." Rick slammed the back of the

van closed. "I'll get my tools, but I'm not talking her into anything."

"Please?" His sister pleaded with those golden-brown eyes. "She's all by herself this week until Ben comes home."

"Why is that? It's like she's hiding from something." The words rushed out before he realized how judgmental he sounded.

"What?" Sherry's eyes grew round then narrowed. "You were eavesdropping on our conversation."

He shrugged, ducking his head. "I was right over the porch while you were talking. It's not like you were whispering."

She frowned. "Cayme's got a lot on her plate. I don't like it either, but she's a grown woman who needs to figure it out on her own."

Rick pictured all the womanly parts that tugged at him, and heat warmed the back of his neck. His reaction was ridiculous. She was a friend—someone he'd known all his life. As kids, how many times had they planned a raid on the Wilson's raspberry patch or strategized a football play? Why on earth were those memories so strong?

His sister gave him a speculative look. "Are you really that pissed about her situation?"

"What Cayme does is her business." Ready to move on to another topic, he fished the keys out of his pocket. "I'll grab my tools and be right back."

"Not without Cayme." Sherry stood her ground. "Bring her back here with you."

"What if she won't come? She's not a social nutcase like you are."

"Now you've gone too far, big brother." She

marched up to him, shifted her daughter to her other arm, and poked him in the chest. "You go over there, and don't come back without her, or you can go without dinner tonight."

"You won't let my son starve."

She turned her back on him and headed into the house. "Oh, I'll feed Adam," she called over her shoulder. "Just not you."

Rick stared at the house long after the front door closed behind his sister. The sun dipped lower, but the spring temperature felt as if it had risen ten degrees. He ran a finger under his T-shirt collar and sighed. Sherry was such a pain—especially when she was right. He had to get his tools. And if he wanted dinner, he'd put on the charm to coax Cayme to join them—even if her womanly features messed with his mind. He was man enough to handle it.

Chapter Three

Cayme entered the house, took off her shoes, and placed them next to the door so she wouldn't track in mud. The old wood floor was cold on the bottoms of her bare feet, and the chill caught her off guard. She wanted to go back into the sunshine, to feel the earth coming to life and enjoy the rebirth of spring. Anything to avoid facing the emptiness.

Having Sherry and Rick over had been a nice diversion from the routine she'd fallen into. She eyed the ceiling and gave a shudder. If Sherry hadn't dragged her brother over, the next storm might have leaked all the way through to the main floor. The damage might have been irreparable, forcing a decision she wasn't prepared to make yet.

She rubbed her palms along her arms. Mom had only been in the ground a few hours when Councilman Peters showed up on the front porch waving the house sale papers she'd promised to sign. He'd been brash and ornery—almost worse than he'd been five years ago—making Cayme glad she'd never married his son despite the humiliation she'd suffered from cancelling the wedding.

Peters' attitude had unearthed all the pent-up emotions she'd been holding in since returning home. She'd sent him packing with the agreement unsigned. Her emotions were too raw to make such an important decision while standing in the same dress she'd worn to the funeral.

A few days later, Cayme had found the courage to review the papers. She was stunned to learn that Rick's general construction company had bid on the plans to build a park on her family's property. Had her mother known about the bid when she first entertained the offer? Did she think that by selling she was helping Rick?

Cayme would never know. With her dying breath, Rachel extracted a promise that Cayme wouldn't sell the house. Of course she promised. Why wouldn't she? At the time, she hadn't known her mother had all but turned the house over to the community. Those papers had blindsided her.

She still didn't know why Ben had never said anything about their mother wanting to sell the house. And because he'd never mentioned it, Cayme never told him about her promise to their mother. Since coming back from Afghanistan, his challenges were beyond her ability to comprehend, and she didn't want to add to them. Now, after a month of keeping her promise a secret, she didn't know how to tell Ben without fear of upsetting him.

Crossing to the window, she studied the garden plot that had fed most of the neighborhood in previous summers. Where tomatoes, zucchini, beans, and corn had thrived was now overgrown with weeds, as if the same cancer that invaded her mother's body possessed the land. Could the illness be why her mother decided to sell? If so, then why change her mind at the last minute?

The questions raced through her brain and gave her

a slight headache. She turned away from the window and wandered over to the worn, faded couch. With a sigh, she plopped on the cushion and picked up a brightly colored throw pillow, hugging it to her middle. Almost everything in the house needed repairs, but it was clean and tidy. The leak over the attic was fixed—thanks to Rick—but she had no doubt the entire roof needed replacing.

The only thriving part of her mother's legacy was the venture she'd bought into a couple of years before she got sick. Books, Bytes, & Brews was *the* hotspot in Blakely and the first stop for tourists on their way to the resort a few miles north.

A preliminary review of the store's accounts the week before confirmed the business was in the black. In another month, Cayme would know if they had enough profits to hire help to take her place in the store. If Ben could manage on his own, maybe she'd return to Seattle. Maybe she would crack open that novel again and polish it for publication.

Or not.

For now, she had just enough money to pay the property taxes. The salary from her job covered living expenses. She didn't have much in savings to make major house repairs, but the bookstore provided a steady income to pay for Ben's therapy expenses not covered by military benefits.

He'd been steadily improving until their mother took ill. When she died, he seemed to dive into a tailspin of despondency.

Cayme worried about him. Regardless of everything else on her plate, she wasn't leaving until she knew her brother would be okay on his own.

And she had to admit, being home was different this time—like she was supposed to stay.

A breeze stirred, and the sweet aroma of lilacs wafted through the screen door along with a rush of spring air. Cayme stood and crossed the room for another look at the front yard. At the edge of their property, the river flowed fast and cold. It looked as if it had risen another couple of inches since this morning. Not quite at the bank-full stage, but this late in the year, the weather would get warmer, melting the snowpack quickly. It was not a matter of *if* the river flooded but *when*.

Just one more thing to worry about.

She kneaded the back of her neck, wishing away the knot of tension. Maybe Sherry was right and it was time to pull out her writing, to revisit that love of creating stories, spinning plots, and letting the characters take over her mind. Where had that passion gone? Had she lost it like the other parts of her life she'd failed at?

For now, she'd deal with the anxiety the same way she had since returning home—work until she couldn't keep her eyes open any longer. Then she could at least sleep without worrying.

With a sigh, she turned away from the deceptively beautiful scenery of the yard, river, and snowcapped mountain and closed the door with a mournful squeak.

She padded past the boxes stacked next to the couch—more reminders that she was too late to make amends for being an absent daughter—and focused on her mental to-do list.

After Ben left that morning, she'd carried the last of the boxes from the attic and placed them in the living room to go through that night. Several more boxes were stacked in the kitchen, out of the weather, waiting to be donated. She'd take care of those later in the week.

First, pans of dirty roof water needed emptying. She retrieved them one at a time from the attic, dumped the water in the upstairs bathtub, then carried the pans to the kitchen.

The kitchen was her favorite room in the entire house, and she was grateful that her mom had used a portion of Dad's life insurance money to tear down the wall between the kitchen and living room, making one large room. Off the kitchen was the laundry/mudroom and half bath. A short hallway led to her mom's office and a guest bedroom where Rachel had stayed those awful final days, too sick to climb the stairs to her own room.

Cayme had only gone into the guest room once after her mother died, to strip the bedding for washing. It was too hard to go back in again. Maybe when she finished with the boxes in the attic, she'd find the courage to face that room. Or maybe she'd look at the next manuscript on her computer. Someone else's story, not hers. Neither task held any appeal.

As she rinsed out the last pan, a loud knock at the door echoed through the empty house. Startled, she dropped the pan, spattering water on her shirt to join the baby's spit-up stain. Grabbing a towel, she wiped her shirt and hands and then crossed the living room. She opened the door, surprised to see Rick standing on the small front porch. "You're back. Is everything okay?"

"Hey, Cayme." He shifted his feet.

A lock of unruly black hair curled against his forehead making him look boyish and dangerous at the same time. It seemed weird that he'd knocked when, as a teenager, he used to walk right in. As kids, she and Ben had done the same when they visited the Morrisons' house. Strange how the day had brought out all these recollections from her childhood.

She pushed the screen door open and he stepped inside. Instantly, the living room seemed to shrink. Rick glanced at her T-shirt and she followed his gaze to where the water had molded the material to her chest. Heat rushed to her cheeks. "I was rinsing out the pans that caught water from last night's storm. It spilled."

He blinked—his gaze jerking to her face. "Oh. At least you and Ben don't have to worry about that leak anymore." He shifted his feet again, as if he was ready to bolt out the door.

"So…are you okay?" *She* was struggling with this uncomfortable tug of attraction that wouldn't go away but what was up with him?

"Oh. Yeah."

He looked like a kid caught with the ball that broke the neighbor's window.

"I came back because I left my tool belt on the porch. And Sherry insisted I bring you back for dinner."

Cayme opened her mouth to decline, except Rick was talking again.

"Look, I know you probably have a lot of things to do. I told Sherry I couldn't make you come with me." He shoved his hands in his pockets. "But if there's one thing I've learned, it's not to cross my sister when she sets her mind on something."

"You're a grown man. Can't you handle your sister?" She felt a little sorry for Rick because she'd been on the receiving end of Sherry's cajoling. In fact,

Sherry had talked her into that first date with Chase Peters. Another memory best left in the attic with the broken engagement and all her other past mistakes.

Rick held out a hand. "Come on. You know how she can be. Besides, from what Sherry's said, you need a night off. Will you join us for dinner?"

So, Sherry shared her concerns with Rick. Cayme supposed she couldn't be too mad at her best friend who simply had her welfare in mind.

Eyeing the boxes, she inwardly grimaced. No thanks. Not ready to face the task of going through more of Mom's things. And another evening alone, with another manuscript she'd probably have to reject? Not appealing either. Why not take a break? The sudden lightness of that thought eased the burden off her shoulders. Glancing at Rick, she said, "I guess I can spare a couple of hours."

He smiled his relief as though she'd saved him from a flogging. "Thanks! That'll keep me out of hot water with the little pest."

"What if I told Sherry you said that?" *Do NOT stare at his dimples.* She was over her silly crush, right?

"I'll deny it with my dying breath."

"Your word against mine. Who will she believe?"

Shrugging he said, "I'm sure she'll believe you."

"Smart man." Cayme laughed. "Go get your tools. And give me a minute to change." She gestured to her wet shirt and then pointed to the stairs. "I'll be right down."

"Meet you back here in a minute." He headed straight for the kitchen and the back door just like he'd done hundreds of times as a kid.

She reached the top of the stairs, breathless and

flushed from a conversation that had been much less strained than the one earlier. Maybe things between her and Rick didn't have to be so stiff, even with his company bidding on the demolition of her home—if she sold.

Hurrying to her closet, she pulled out a pale blue sundress. As an afterthought, she grabbed an off-white sweater. The calendar might say May and the day had been the warmest of the month, but the evenings cooled down quite a bit.

Stripping out of her T-shirt and jeans, she pulled the dress over her head then tugged the band free and let her hair fall around her shoulders. She applied some lip gloss and brushed her hair. A quick glance in the mirror confirmed she'd transformed the gawky tomboy look of her youth to that of a woman. After slipping on a pair of brown sandals, she grabbed the sweater and her purse, making sure her phone was inside in case her boss called, and headed downstairs.

She reached the bottom step at the same time Rick came in from the kitchen.

As he spotted her, his eyes widened. "Wow."

Heat warmed her face. "Is this too dressy? I can change again."

"No." He cleared his throat. "I mean, you look fine. I can't remember the last time I saw you in a dress, that's all."

"Well, I wore one at the funeral, but before that, it was at your Senior Prom," she replied without thinking. "Sherry and I went stag, hoping to score a few dances." They'd been sophomores, and Cayme had hoped for at least one dance with Rick. But it never happened. Thank goodness she'd kept *that* little secret.

"Really?" He shook his head. "I don't remember seeing you at the prom."

She swallowed the sting his statement caused. "That's because you had tunnel vision for Amy Wells." Amy, who'd been on the varsity cheer squad, had a family now and was happy with her life as a stay-at-home mom.

An ache gnawed inside Cayme's chest. Silly, envying another woman's family. She was still young. The right man was still out there…waiting. After she figured out a direction for herself.

"Right. Amy." He made a face. "What I do remember is how expensive that night was, and then Tom Showalter ended up taking her home. I wanted to bust his nose."

"It's a good thing you didn't. He played right-tackle that year."

"That's right! Great memory." Rick grunted. "Tom had fifty pounds on me back then. Now he outweighs me by at least a hundred—none of it muscle."

Cayme winced. "Ouch. Poor Tom. I guess we've all changed since high school."

"You can say that again." Rick gave a tight nod, staring a bit longer.

His brown eyes seemed to melt like dark chocolate in the sun and her breath hitched in her throat.

He looked away first, his gaze landing on the boxes next to the couch.

Thankfully, he missed seeing the blush that warmed her face.

"Are you packing up already? Did you decide to sell?"

Was that panic or hope she heard in his voice?

"Um—no, not yet. I'm clearing out the attic. That's how I found the leak." Should she talk with him about the house sale? No, it would probably put him in an uncomfortable position.

Peeking inside the top box, he said, "Ben and I used to hide up there sometimes when he didn't want to clean his room. It made a great clubhouse before your dad let us use the shed."

She gave a small laugh. "Ben does a better job on his room now." Although, she'd still gathered a pile of his laundry this morning. "From the two-inch layer of dust I found, I'd say you guys were probably the last ones up there."

"I believe it. I can't imagine Ben wanted to go through the attic after…he got home. I'm sure Rachel didn't go in there much. She would've rather puttered around the kitchen or in her store." Rick's smile was one of remembered fondness as he began digging through the box.

Cayme couldn't find her voice for a moment. While she'd been hiding in another state, Rick had been in town—in this house—offering support to Ben and her mother.

He lifted out an old photo album and started flipping through pages. "Look at this."

Curious, she stepped closer.

The blunt end of his finger pointed at a picture of the four of them. They wore rodeo hats and held popsicles, their lips a bright shade of red. "Look how young we were. You and Sherry look about…eight?"

"Probably. You and Ben would have been ten or eleven. Looks like summer so you might have had your birthday by then."

His eyes widened. "You remember my birthday?"

"It's the same month as mine."

"Oh, yeah. I guess it is."

So, he hadn't remembered how close their birthdays were. So what? It's not as if he should have. When they were kids, he'd never paid attention to the way she'd followed him around or watched everything he did, either. She *really* needed to bury this stupid crush deep enough that it would never find the light of day.

He turned another page. "Hey, there's a picture of me and Ben with the Little League trophy we won that year." He looked up as though lost in the memory. "I wonder where mine is? I should find it to show Adam. He'd get a kick out of it." Rick kept browsing. That same lopsided smile stayed on his face as he mentally strolled through their shared childhood memories.

Having Rick in her home felt comfortable. Familiar. Part of her didn't want to stop his reminiscing, but his sister was waiting for them. "Rick?"

He glanced at her. "Yeah?"

"You've gone to all this trouble to follow Sherry's orders. Shouldn't we be going?"

"Right!" He closed the photo album and placed it back in the box. "Ready?" He started toward the front door.

Maybe I am *ready. Ready for something different, something good.* She forced a bright smile and followed him outside.

****

Rick reined in his appreciation of those long, shapely legs and the way Cayme's coppery hair softly framed her blue eyes, making them look like two sapphires. When she'd descended the stairs—that first glimpse of her had stolen his breath. She seemed to glow. Did that glow have anything to do with escaping the worries of that old house, even for just a few hours? He was glad he'd followed his sister's orders to bring her to dinner. Still, he'd have to be cold and in a grave not to appreciate the sway of her hips as he followed her to his truck. A stab of lust gripped hard, and he shoved it back down.

When they reached the passenger side, he opened the door for her before tossing his tool belt in the truck bed. He turned back to help her up, except she'd already hopped into the cab and was reaching for the seatbelt. He curled his fingers into his palm. Just as well he didn't touch her and end up doing something he shouldn't—like seeing if she tasted as good as she looked.

Hurrying around to the driver's side, he jumped in. The scent of fresh honeysuckle wafted toward him—very different from the little boy smell of baseball mitts and muddy shoes that typically filled his cab.

He glanced at the floor mats. Sure enough, part of the ball diamond filled the grooves of the truck logo. "Sorry for the mess. It's usually only me and Adam. I don't clean out the truck much."

She gave a wry smile. "Hey, it's me, remember? I tracked in just as much dirt as you and Ben. I'm sure Mom hated the wear and tear on her vacuum."

He chuckled and started the truck. "Nah. Your mom didn't mind. She loved having us around."

Cayme's sweet laugh, the one he'd not heard in over five years, joined his. "We were pretty inseparable back then, weren't we?"

"The Fearsome Foursome. That was us."

"Yes, we were."

He drove to the end of the short block, all of two houses—Cayme's and her neighbor, old Mrs. Jones'—then turned onto the street where his sister lived.

The roads were just wide enough for two cars to pass each other but had no painted dividing lines. The posted speed limit was twenty-five miles per hour. Most residents crept along much slower, keeping an eye out for kids who used the street as an extension of their yards for ball diamonds or football fields.

Both he and Ben had done the same thing once they'd outgrown the yard and needed more space to catch fly balls. They were fortunate none of their errant baseballs had broken any windows.

A couple of minutes later, Rick slid the truck to a stop in front of Sherry's house.

Adam and Joey, Sherry's son, were playing catch in the front yard. They were almost as inseparable as brothers, and neither kid got enough of playing ball.

"Is that your son?" Cayme gasped and nodded toward Adam.

Rick couldn't help the swell of pride every time he looked at his boy. He had a few regrets in his life but having Adam wasn't one of them. "That's Adam."

She smiled. "He looks just like you did at that age."

The yearning on her face caught him by surprise and something tugged on the tightly wound ball of wire around his heart that had been there since his divorce. He swallowed at the sudden rock in his throat. They were old friends, and he shouldn't have kept his distance once she'd returned home. Helping her out didn't necessarily mean things would get complicated, right?

Chapter Four

Cayme watched the boys playing catch, the hardball flying back and forth through the crisp spring air. Too bad she hadn't worn her jeans and brought the old mitt she'd found in the attic. What she wouldn't give to be out on the freshly mowed grass with those boys. Wow, she'd been so wrapped up in work—between her editing and the store—she'd forgotten how to play.

Her previous visits home had been quick trips for Christmas, Mother's Day, and birthdays, rarely staying longer than a weekend. Sherry had posted hundreds of pictures of her kids on her social media page, but a few months had passed since Cayme'd last seen Joey in person. He was the spitting image of his father but with Sherry's reddish-brown hair instead of Ken's blond locks. Given how tall Joey was now, he'd probably inherit his father's height.

There was no mistaking Adam and Joey were related, but Adam clearly took after his dad in the looks department. Lanky and lean, even for an eight-year-old, his dark brown hair curled on his forehead, just like his father's.

Cayme had been watching the boys and hadn't noticed Rick climb out of the truck until he opened her door. The spring breeze brushed along her arms, making her glad she'd brought a sweater for the evening.

"Come on." Rick tilted his head toward the house. "The barbeque is in the backyard and I'm sure Sherry's back there pacing. Her patience disappeared after little Rachel was born. She's gotten quite bossy."

"That's not entirely true, she was bossy before the baby." Cayme smiled and unbuckled her seatbelt. "And she's my best friend, so don't tell her I said that."

"My lips are sealed, only because I'm hungry and want dinner."

"You'll have a tough time eating with sealed lips."

Rick's gaze strayed to her mouth. He grinned and held a hand out.

She hesitated.

"I don't bite." He wiggled his fingers. Then he made a show of sniffing the delicious scent wafting on the late afternoon breeze. "Unless you make me wait much longer for my food."

Her stomach fluttered again. This was Rick. Someone she'd known all her life. Surely, she could get through the evening without making a fool of herself. As she took his hand, his thumb skated across her knuckles, and a tingle of contact raced up her arm. Stepping out of the cab, she found herself staring right at his mouth and that dangerously sexy smile. *Oh my!* Her breath hitched and she quickly looked away. "Thanks." The word came out in the same breathless rush as when she'd been on the ladder.

He squeezed her hand as though he knew exactly what she was thinking then let go. "Come on. I'll introduce you to Adam before we go around back." He closed the truck door and led the way across the lawn. "Adam!"

The boys stopped tossing the ball and ran over. Adam glanced at Cayme then his father. "Hey, Dad."

"Aunt Cayme!" Joey threw his arms around her middle. "You're here!" He leaned back and looked up at her. "Mom said you might be too busy."

Cayme tugged Joey's ear. "I found some time." She threw a grateful look in Rick's direction. It seemed her reputation for avoiding gatherings had filtered down to the younger generation. She made a mental note to never let Sherry's kids think she was ever too busy for them. She was their godmother, after all.

The miniature version of Rick stared curiously at her. "Are you my aunt, too?"

Cayme glanced at Rick with a raised eyebrow. Did she want to be Adam's honorary aunt?

"No way!" Joey said with a laugh. "Cayme's not related. That's just what we call her because her and Mom are best friends."

"Oh." Adam looked between Rick and Cayme as if determining their friend status and what he should call her.

"If it's okay," she said, "I'll be your Aunt Cayme, too."

Adam gave a shrug. "Okay with me." With a grin, he held out his hand. "Nice to meet you, Aunt Cayme."

She shook the small hand with solemn formality, ignoring the patches of dirt and grit on his palm. "Nice to meet you too, Adam."

"Cool, bacon beans!" Joey parroted a favorite saying of his mother's. Satisfied he'd cleared up the relationship issues, he tugged Adam's arm. "Come on. Let's show her my fastball." He raced off.

"Bye!" Adam hurried to join his cousin.

"Watch me, Aunt Cayme," Joey called. He waited for Adam to crouch behind a cardboard home plate. After a moment, he bent over to stare across the lawn. Adam gave a hand signal that was quickly dismissed by a shake of Joey's head, followed by another flash of fingers and a nod.

Cayme couldn't contain a burst of laughter.

Rick joined in. "They are a pair, aren't they?" Pride oozed from his deep voice.

"Yes." The word came out strangled, and she cleared her throat. "They make a great team." She sighed inwardly at the twinge of longing. She and Sherry were the same age. Had things turned out differently, she might have had a child about the same age as these cute little boys.

Joey straightened, brought his hand and mitt together, and started his windup. A moment later, the ball whizzed through the air and landed with a satisfying smack in Adam's mitt. Joey looked over with a grin as wide as the bend in the river near her house. "See that, Aunt Cayme?"

"Bravo!" She clapped. "A perfect strike."

Joey punched the air. "Yeah!" He ran to Adam and grabbed his arm. "Come on. Let's go tell Dad what Aunt Cayme said."

Rick chuckled, watching the boys race around the side of the house before turning his gaze back to her. "That's a special power you hold. My approval never carried that much weight."

Something suspiciously like sunshine bloomed in her chest. She curtseyed. "Just call me Princess Cayme."

Rick bowed and offered his arm. "Your highness.

Dinner awaits."

She took his arm. This bubble of happiness was worth leaving all her worries behind. Even for just a little while.

****

An hour later, Sherry's backyard was a scene of barely contained chaos. Sherry's dad, Gary Morrison, presided over the barbeque like the patriarch of the family that he was. He, Rick, and Ken, Sherry's husband, were in deep conversation about their next fishing trip.

The younger boys had finished eating and were playing a game that looked like horseshoes with colored hoops tossed over pegs on a stand.

Little Rachel was in her walker, pounding the tray with a teething ring, singing gibberish at the top of her lungs while maneuvering closer to the boys.

Cayme couldn't remember the last time she'd laughed so much. She barely thought about her job and not once did she check her phone for messages. She'd even forgotten for a moment that Ben was at the rehabilitation center in Boise and her mother was in a grave.

Grown-up problems seemed to melt away under the laughter of playing children. Adam patiently tried to keep the baby from interfering with their game. Joey whined to his mother to get his sister out of the way so they could play. Through it all, little Rachel babbled and slobbered and wormed her way further into Cayme's heart.

She was in awe watching Sherry manage the kids' enthusiasm and her husband's subtle hints for another beer, all while handing a plate of brownies over to

Cayme to pass around.

"Give a brownie to Rick, first." Sherry popped the tops off three beers and passed them to Ken. "They're his favorite. If he doesn't get one, he gets really grumpy." She found the baby's bottle, scooped up her daughter, and settled into a lawn chair.

"Now you're talking!" Rick rubbed his hands together.

"Seriously?" Ken said, interrupting his conversation with Gary. "You'd rather have a grumpy husband than a grumpy brother? By all means, serve Rick first. I'll just get my dessert later." He winked at his wife.

"Too much information for this old man." Gary took a pull on his beer.

"Not for me. I earned my brownie points today." Rick glanced at Cayme with raised eyebrows.

Her cheeks grew hot. Not only had he fixed her roof, he'd saved her from a fall that might have killed her. "That you did, Rick." She showed off the plate filled with the delicious, gooey goodness. "But there's plenty to go around," she added, to ensure Ken would get a chocolate treat, too. "At least once."

Sherry glanced up from feeding the baby and shook her head. "Grown men fighting over a little cocoa and eggs. You'd think they were three years old."

Just then, Adam and Joey stopped their game and ran over to Cayme. "We want some brownies," they chimed at the same time.

The grownups laughed and even little Rachel stopped sucking on her bottle and grinned.

As she handed Adam a large brownie square, Cayme caught an odd gleam in Rick's eyes. Even if she wanted Rick to notice her as someone other than Aunt Cayme or the gangly kid who fell out of trees, she wasn't sure she was ready to explore a relationship. A month before, she was positive she'd head back to Seattle. And now here she was still attempting to get a grip on the changes at home—but for how long?

****

Two hours later, Rick pulled his truck to a stop in front of Cayme's house.

"Thanks for the ride," she said.

"Is this where you live?" Adam asked from the back seat.

"Yup." She turned to face him. "This is where I grew up."

"Wow." He pointed across the yard, his eyes growing wide. "How cool is that? Your house is right next to the river. Do you go fishing a lot?"

"I…um…" She glanced at Rick who merely raised his eyebrows. No help there. "My brother fishes sometimes," she told Adam. "But I really don't like to."

"Me and my dad love to fish. Right, Dad?"

"That's right, buddy."

Rick winked at his son, and then gave her a lopsided grin that should be outlawed in all fifty states.

"If I remember right, Cayme doesn't like to touch the bait."

She made a face. "I certainly don't, especially if they're worms."

"That's because you're a girl," Adam said.

"I'll take that as a compliment, I think." She grinned.

Adam bounced forward in his seat. "As soon as school's out, Joey and me are gonna stay up late every night and catch night crawlers. Last year, Dad showed us how to sneak up on them with a covered flashlight. We caught lots of 'em. This year, we're gonna catch even more and sell them."

"That sounds very…enterprising." Hopefully her encouraging tone wouldn't get her in trouble with Rick. Maybe he didn't want his son up all hours of the night filling buckets with worms. "I'm sure the local fisherman will love knowing they don't have to catch their own bait."

"Do you think your brother would buy some?"

"Adam," his father warned. "You don't have any to sell yet."

"I know, but Joey says if we have customers first, we'll make lots of money."

"That sounds more like Uncle Ken talking." Rick turned back to Cayme. "Sorry for the sales pitch. If I'd known my son was peddling worms to unsuspecting redheads, I'd have left him at Sherry's house."

Cayme laughed. In spite of being a bit rusty in the fun-times department, it felt good. "I think you have a budding entrepreneur." She looked back at Adam. "I'll talk to Ben about buying some worms."

"Yes!" Adam punched the air. "Our first customer." He held a fist toward his dad and Rick gave him the obligatory knuckle bump.

A smile tugged at her lips at the father-son ritual.

Rick reached for his door handle.

"Oh, stay put." She raised a hand. "You don't need—"

"A gentleman always sees a lady to the door." He eyed his son in the backseat. "Right, buddy?"

Adam's head bobbed like a float on calm water.

"Right."

She glanced between father and son. "Far be it from me to come between a young gentleman and his training." She unlatched her seatbelt but remained inside the truck until Rick opened the door. She waved at Adam. "Good luck with your worm business."

"Night, Aunt Cayme."

Rick helped her down from the truck.

When he took her hand, that same tingle of awareness scurried up her arm. And like before, she tamped down the urge to give in to the feeling. Rick was simply showing his son the proper way to treat a woman. He couldn't possibly know what his touch did to her. "I had a great time," she said. "Thank you for following your sister's orders tonight."

"I'll give her the credit, but I'll take all the pleasure," he said in a low voice and seemed to lean closer. "I'm glad you came."

"Me, too." Her stomach pitched and she placed her hand over it.

Rick's gaze dropped to her lips, then he cleared his throat and drew back.

Was he about to kiss her with a curious eight-year-old looking on? A kiss from Rick had been at the top of her "things she wanted most" list all through high school. But right now, her life was in too much flux. When he pulled back, a mix of disappointment and relief engulfed her. This was the wrong time to start a new relationship—any relationship. Especially one that involved an adorable, precocious little boy.

"Shall we?" Rick gestured toward the house. "I, uh, we—should get going. Adam has school tomorrow."

"Me too. Well, not school but work." She tugged

her sweater closer around her as they walked toward the front porch.

He looked across the overgrown lawn to the trees at the edge of the river. "I love this yard."

"Then why…" She left the rest of the question unasked. Did she really want to hear Rick's reason for bidding on the plans to level her home?

"Why does the town want to tear down your house?"

She shivered at hearing the truth put so bluntly but didn't back away from the question. She couldn't continue to ignore the offer to buy her family's property. At some point, she'd have to face the fact that everyone in town wanted her home torn down. "I guess I want to understand."

He buried his hands in his pockets. "The old park isn't big enough anymore." He stared out over the river. Even in the dark, white caps from the high runoff were visible near the bank's edge. "There've been a lot of close calls with kids straying too close to the river. If we expand the park over in this area, we'll be able to build a large berm and fence it in. It'll function as a levee to hold back the water in flood years like the one we're facing now. We're also planning a skateboard park that we hope will keep the kids away from the river. There're even plans for a skating rink during the winter."

It sounded ideal—a place she'd love if she were a kid. "And if I don't sell?" Cayme had to ask. She'd promised her mother she wouldn't sell, but she also needed to understand all the consequences.

Rick's shoulders slumped a little. "The town will go ahead and upgrade the old park. Though, it'll be a lot smaller without some of the amenities they've planned. They'll reroute around your property and you'll be forced to build a fence to separate your property from the park boundaries. And the town can't do anything to prevent the river from flooding your land in the future."

A hard knot filled her stomach at the image of water filling her backyard. Would she lose the house anyway? She glanced at Rick. "What does it mean for you—for your company—if I don't sell?"

His expression grew serious. "My company will revamp the old park, except the project will be dramatically reduced."

"I'm sorry." She *was* sorry it affected his livelihood, but she couldn't break her promise. If she did, where would Ben live? For that matter, if she decided to stay in town, where would *she* live?

"I have to admit I'd love to close this bid." Rick shrugged. "But you have to do what you feel is right. Don't sell on my account."

"I…I'm not sure what to do." Everyone believed she was holding out for more money. Not even Ben knew what she'd promised their mother. She looked over at the garden and along the side of the yard where large cottonwoods stood like sentinels guarding her home. "Since Mom died, everything feels like it's in upheaval."

"You have a little time to make the decision, Cayme," Rick said. "Take that time to think it through."

"By then it may be too late."

He lifted a shoulder. "The timing's got to be right for you. That's all that matters."

She shook her head. "You don't understand. No

one seems to understand it's not just about me. I have to think about Ben's future, even if he doesn't want to."

"Ben will be fine."

They reached the front porch and she looked over at Rick. "How can you be sure?"

"Trust him," Rick said. "I know he's been through a lot, but he's strong."

That was easy for Rick to say. He'd served overseas, too and had somehow learned to deal with the horrors of that awful war. How was it that Rick seemed to have come out relatively unscathed, while Ben had to fight demons at every turn?

How was she supposed to believe her brother would get well when he didn't want to get out of bed some mornings? Not once had he mentioned what he wanted to do with their home. Most of the time she wondered if he even cared.

As relaxing as this evening had been, she had to face reality. She started up the steps, feeling the dark night close in around her.

Rick touched her arm. "Wait."

She turned.

He was staring at the ground, shifting in that same uneasy manner he'd shown at her door earlier tonight.

"What is it?"

"When I was storing the ladder, I noticed the hinges seemed rickety on the shed door. Would it be okay to come over sometime this week and take a look at it?"

She rubbed her temple in confusion. "You want to tear the place down. Why would you want to fix the shed?"

He tilted his head slightly. "I want to help you and

Ben. Let's go with that."

She studied him in the growing dusk. Behind him, the first stars peeked over the northeastern skyline. This entire night had that twitchy, magical quality she remembered long ago as a kid. Maybe these feelings were a sign. An omen to slow down a little and take things as they came.

"Sure." She shrugged. "I'm usually home from the store around seven."

Rick gave her another one of those smiles. "I'll be over later this week then." He turned and with his long, lean gait, quickly reached the truck and climbed inside. With a wave, he started the engine.

Then he and his darling son drove away.

****

Cayme sensed something was wrong the moment she shut the front door.

"Where the hell have you been?"

She flipped the light switch beside the door. "Ben?"

Light glowed from the lamp in the corner of the living room. Her brother sat in one of the old recliners, his guitar off to the side. He wore the same T-shirt and jeans he'd put on that morning. His square jaw was dark with unshaved whiskers. His close-cropped reddish hair looked like he'd run a hand over it until it was flat against his skull. The constant worry lines around his hazel eyes were deeper than usual.

Where Rick was lean muscled, Ben was broad across the chest. Solid, without an ounce of spare fat.

The first time Cayme had seen his boot camp photo, she'd been in awe at the change in him. His neck was thicker, jawline more defined. More like a man—

more like Dad. Even in his disheveled state, she had to admit his classically handsome face was so much like how she remembered Dad.

"Well?" he demanded. "Where were you?"

"Not that it's any of your business, but I was over at Sherry's. She invited me to a barbecue."

Cayme hadn't been home long before learning the best way to answer Ben was as straightforward as possible. He'd always had a sixth sense about dishonesty. Since his return, he didn't tolerate half-truths—said it felt like being coddled. She didn't know if that was part of the PTSD paranoia she'd read about or something deeper. When he asked a question, she gave a prompt, truthful answer. Regardless, he didn't know all her secrets. He didn't know what she'd promised Mom. And now wasn't the time to tell him.

"You don't ever go out." His accusatory tone set her back.

"I've gone out before."

"Not since you've been home." He folded his arms across his chest in a defensive posture. "You were with Rick."

A hot-cold flush of guilt raced over her skin. "Rick's your friend and Sherry's brother. He was there for dinner and gave me a ride home."

Sitting on the couch across from him, she tried not to stare at the acoustical guitar. What did it mean that Ben had taken it out of the case? How long had it been since he'd played? "Why are you home? Are you okay? Your therapy was supposed to be first thing in the morning."

"I'm done with therapy." He leaned back in the chair, his eyes bloodshot and weary. "I'm not going back to that place."

A jolt of fear shook her at Ben's announcement. How could he refuse the help he needed for his PTSD? Did that mean he'd never get better?

She swallowed her anxiety, attempted to calm her racing heart, and gave him a chance to explain. "What happened?" she asked softly. Ben sometimes clammed up if she prodded him with questions but tonight his look of resignation, mixed with a bit of fear, wrenched her heart. "What is it, Ben?"

Her brother took a long breath. Then another—as if preparing to dive into the deep end of a pool. "I was standing in the foyer, like always. Just waiting to check in." His voice was barely a whisper. "Everything was like every other time. Then a large van pulled up. One from the base. Three guys got out. Something about them…I could tell they were fresh from the zone." He stopped, swallowing hard.

The zone. That's what Ben called his time in Afghanistan. Cayme never pressed him to share exactly what happened over there. She wasn't sure she wanted to know. Maybe someday, if he wanted to tell her, she'd listen, no matter how hard.

"I saw their faces, Cay." His eyes grew dark. "I saw their empty, blank stares. Their dependence. Their helplessness. I-I saw myself." His hands fisted, the knuckles turning white. "I'm done being like that." He stood abruptly and started pacing beside the chair. "I'm done being treated like some washed-up shmuck who can't wipe his own—who can't tie his own shoelaces." He stopped in front of her and nearly shouted, "I'm not going back."

Cayme froze, afraid any reaction would stop this

spill of emotion—more emotion than she'd seen from her brother since before their mother died.

He collapsed into the chair, bumping the guitar. It teetered and started to slide onto the floor. Ben's quick reflexes caught it before it crashed. A string twanged in protest at the rough handling.

Cayme couldn't help wincing. She stared at the instrument—the very thing that had brought so much joy into their lives growing up—that had been abandoned after her brother joined the military.

Ben's hand tightened around the neck to stop the sound. Surely, he could feel the frets under his fingers, the texture of each string, and remember what it was like when he played.

She held her breath, afraid he would hurl the instrument across the room, smashing it into a million splinters.

He didn't. Instead, he just sat there and stared at it.

The guitar was a masterpiece as well as a musical instrument. The smooth blond body had an ivory inlay rosette around the sound hole. In the right hands, it produced the sweetest sounds. But more than that, the guitar was precious to both her and Ben. Their father had played it, long before they were born and through their years growing up. He'd filled their home with music and joy, teaching Ben to play before he could read. On Ben's fourteenth birthday, Dad had given him the guitar because his arthritis had become too painful for him to keep playing.

For a while after Dad died, the music had stopped. But Ben cherished the guitar, and it wasn't long before the music started again, to the delight of both Cayme and their mother. In his wilder days when Ben, Rick, and two of their buddies had formed a band, they played at high school dances, weddings, and community picnics. Ben always made sure the guitar was secured before he took it anywhere.

At that moment, Cayme would have given everything she owned, including the house, just to hear Ben play again.

He stood and walked to the corner where the case lay open and gently placed the guitar inside. When he closed the lid and flipped the latches with a snap, it sounded as final as the last nail in a coffin. "I'm off to bed," he said, facing her.

"Ben…" Cayme didn't know where to start. How could she get back to the uninhibited conversations they used to share?

The corners of his mouth turned up so briefly that she might have imagined the smile. "I'm tired, Cay. We'll talk more tomorrow after you get home from the store."

He crossed to the staircase but paused without looking back. "I'm sorry I yelled. Rick's a good guy." Without waiting for a reply, he started upstairs. Instead of the heavy, lumbering steps she'd heard almost every night since their mother died, his tread was lighter, as though some previously unseen burden had suddenly lifted off his broad back.

The guitar case was still propped in its place of honor in the corner of the living room. Something told her this was the first time Ben had touched it since his return from the Middle East.

Whatever happened today at the rehabilitation center triggered something remarkable and scary in her brother.

Was it a sign he'd found a way out of the darkness that had imprisoned him?

Chapter Five

Two nights after dropping Cayme at her house, Rick was winding down from a busy workday. He'd yet to make it over to the Fosters'. What had he been thinking, to invite himself over to fix the broken shed? As he climbed the stairs to check on his son, he reluctantly admitted he was more than a little attracted to the pretty redhead. As much as he tried to talk himself out of it, thoughts of her snuck into his mind at odd times of the day, which was not a good thing. If she sold the property and he got the bid, then he'd be the one tearing down her childhood home. He'd feel terrible if the shoe was on the other foot, and that bothered him.

Cayme was a nice woman. Well, maybe the word "nice" was a little tame for what he'd been thinking recently, but still, she deserved some smooth sailing for once. Maybe to find a husband, settle down, and have a family. He hoped she'd make a better go of marriage than he had. After stepping up to marry the mother of his child, he'd been left high and dry. He knew firsthand how hard it was to be a single parent, and he wouldn't want that for Cayme.

Rick scrubbed a hand down his face. Here he was again, spending way too much time thinking about her. Time to focus on his own family.

He stuck his head inside Adam's bedroom where

his son was putting together his latest superhero toy set for the third time this year. Watching Adam focused on locking the blocks together made moments like this worth all the heartache he'd endured after the divorce.

Their small house was the perfect size. A couple of bedrooms upstairs with a full bath. The spare bedroom downstairs was Rick's office. They didn't need more than that for the two of them. Adam's room was smaller than Rick's but had a window seat that overlooked the front yard. The space under the window seat was perfect for storing all those small pieces.

Rick stepped into the room and looked over his son's shoulder. "Hey, bud. It's about time for bed, don't ya think?"

"Hang on." Adam took a moment, his tongue working the corner of his mouth, to click the last block into place before he looked up. "Done." He held up the masterpiece. "Isn't it great?"

Rick studied it as though examining blueprints for his next project. "It's perfect."

Adam beamed.

As his son grew, it would take more than admiring a toy to keep him happy. For now, Rick was grateful his little boy was easy to please. Especially, when Rick wasn't home as much as he'd like to be.

"I want to show it to Aunt Cayme," Adam said. "Do you think she'd like it?"

Whoa, where had that come from? Rick cleared his throat. "What made you think of her?"

Adam shrugged. "Dunno. Just did." He put the toy on his desk next to the lamp. "She's nice."

Rick smiled. Hadn't he just been thinking the same thing? "She is nice." It seemed attraction to pretty redheads ran in the family. Was Adam starting to feel the absence of a maternal figure in his life? Sherry had done a great job of filling that role, except it wasn't the same as having a mother tuck him in every night. "Maybe you can show Cayme later this week. Right now, you need to get ready for bed. Go clean up."

"'Kay." Adam ran into the bathroom and turned on the water. The nightly ritual began. Brush teeth, wash face and hands, unless it was bath night. And thank goodness that wasn't a battle. His son had enjoyed baths from the time he was a baby, even keeping him out of the water was a challenge. Last summer, he and Joey started swimming lessons. Rick planned to sign him up again this summer. They didn't live right next to the river like Cayme and Ben did, but he wanted his kid to know how to swim. Just in case.

While Adam got ready for bed, Rick closed the window shutters. He sort of envied his son for the fun bedroom. As a kid, Rick would have loved something this great.

After he first bought the house, he'd given Sherry a budget, and she'd created a light, open space for Adam to call his own. White-framed bunk beds were on the wall next to the door. A desk sat under the window that overlooked the north side of the house. A large rug, made of primary-colored square blocks, covered the oak wood flooring. At some point, Rick figured he'd have to open his wallet again to update the decor. Maybe something with a fishing or sports theme. For now, he appreciated the simple and entertaining tones his sister had created.

"Ready!" Adam bounded into the room, pajamas on and face scrubbed clean on one side, a smudge from the night's dinner at the other corner of his mouth.

Rick smiled. "Good job." Instead of making Adam climb the ladder, he lowered cupped hands. "Come on. Up you go." He hefted his son onto the top bunk.

The bottom bunk was reserved for the occasional sleepover with school chums. Adam and Joey traded every other Friday or Saturday night for a sleepover. They'd started the tradition once Rick completed his military service and had permanently settled in Blakely to be near his family.

Adam scrambled under the covers and rolled to face Rick.

"Scoot closer, bud. You missed a spot." He wet his thumb and rubbed the fleck of gravy off his son's face, an automatic gesture for the last eight years.

"Yick, Dad." Adam tried to jerk away, but Rick kept at it until the spot was gone.

"It's that, or wake up with sticky food in your hair for school."

When Rick finished, Adam slid back on the bed. "I was looking at the calendar tonight. There's only two more weeks left," he said. "Then we're out for the whole summer. I can't wait."

"I hear ya, bud. But you still have to get up when I call you in the morning." It had been a challenge that morning to get Adam going. Normally, his son loved school, except after the nice weekend with the sun unexpectedly bright over the snowcapped mountains, they'd both battled spring fever. Rick couldn't blame his son for not wanting to go to school. He wanted to play hooky himself.

"I will, I swear." Adam held out his pinky.

Rick's heart tugged a little. He hooked his pinky

over Adam's. "Pinky swear."

Adam grinned. "Night, Dad. Love you."

Rick kissed his son's forehead, hating the thought of his little boy growing too old for this nightly ritual. "Love you too, bud."

After turning out the light, he hovered in the hallway for a moment, listening to the sounds of Adam settling down to sleep. Too bad sleep wouldn't come easily for Rick. The hours just before he went to bed were when loneliness crept in. To fill those tough hours, he'd gotten into the habit of bringing work home. He certainly wasn't about to leave his son with a sitter on a weeknight to party around town looking for companionship. Even if he had the urge sometimes.

As he closed Adam's bedroom door, his cell phone rang. The caller ID didn't look familiar, but something told him to answer it. He hurried downstairs so he wouldn't disturb his son. "Rick Morrison."

"Of course, it's you, silly. Who else would answer your phone?"

Rick froze on the bottom step at hearing Roxanne's voice. He hadn't heard from his ex-wife since December when she called to wish them—mostly Adam—a Merry Christmas. The calls were her biannual foray into their lives since leaving before Adam was even three months old.

Twice a year, Adam got a call and a card with money. One for his birthday and one for Christmas. Sometimes postcards arrived showing far-off places Roxanne had visited.

Rick got the fallout of answering questions about an absent mother and why they weren't together any longer.

"Rick? Are you there?"

"Yes, I'm here." He kept his voice low and glanced upstairs. He hurried into the kitchen, the room farthest from Adam's. "Why are you calling? Adam's birthday isn't until September."

A husky, sexy laugh came through the lines. One of the things he'd loved about Roxanne was how she made him feel when she laughed—as though he was the only one in the world who could make her smile. He wasn't. Still, his gut tightened in response.

"Just because you have full custody, doesn't mean I don't know when my own son was born," she said. "I was there. Remember?"

"Yes." Rick remembered other things too, some not so bad. Other recollections he could live without. "Why are you calling?"

"Is Adam there? I'd love to talk to him."

"Of course, he's here. But he's asleep. It's a school night." If this had been one of those "special day" calls, he might have considered waking Adam so he could talk to his mother. But he sensed there was more to this call than an obligatory check-in. "What do you want?"

"Straight to the point. As always." She sighed. "Would it hurt to talk to your ex-wife for a few minutes?"

He rubbed the bridge of his nose to ease the headache starting behind his eyes. They'd been married less than twelve months when she'd left—not a lot of time to really know a person. But having Roxanne for an ex the past eight years had taught him some of her tactics. She was delaying telling him something he didn't want to hear. "Fine," he said, wearily. "Just tell me why you're calling in the middle of a school week?"

"Fine, yourself," she snapped. "You haven't changed much."

Odd that Cayme had said almost the same thing to him after he'd saved her from falling off the ladder. At the time, he'd considered it a good thing.

"I'm hanging up, now," he said. "That would be different."

"No, Rick. Please."

He paused, holding out the phone to stare at it. *Please?* That was new. He waited a beat.

"Rick?"

Bringing the phone back to his ear, he said, "Still here." He heard another sigh—of relief this time, if he wasn't mistaken.

"I want to see Adam." The words came out in a rush, almost as if she couldn't get them out fast enough.

Rick's *ex-alert* radar pinged. For the last eight years, Roxanne had been content to be the absent mother. Why the sudden change of heart?

They'd met while serving in the army—a chance meeting at the Post Exchange—and had clicked right away. A date for coffee morphed into a couple of young adults enjoying a bit of freedom away from their small-town roots. The pregnancy shocked them both.

Rick thanked Heaven every day that she'd agreed to carry the child to term. Then, of course, he did the honorable thing and married her.

Right after Adam was born, Roxanne had re-upped for her next duty tour. Rick had decided he'd rather find a civilian job and be a full-time father. He didn't want his son growing up moving from post to post. The divorce was finalized on their first wedding anniversary.

"What's going on, Roxanne?" Whether he wanted to know the answer or not, he had to ask. Although he had full custody of their son, he'd generously allowed her contact with Adam. It seemed only right since she was his mother, and Adam wanted to know about his mother even if she was a long-distance one.

"I have some leave coming soon." Again, the words came out in a rush. "I was thinking it was time for me and Adam to get to know each other better."

"Why?" For the life of him, Rick couldn't begin to guess what she was up to.

"I'm his mother." She nearly shouted it through the phone. Very un-Roxanne like. "Does there have to be a reason?"

"Yes." Rick swallowed. Something was definitely up, but he'd give her a chance to explain.

She rambled on about her motherly instincts.

Rick didn't buy it and started to argue. She launched into another "maternal responsibility" discourse that left him seething. The acid in his stomach burned all the way up his throat. But since she hadn't completely relinquished her parental rights, he listened until she finished. "When were you thinking about coming out?" he asked cautiously.

There was a telling silence on the other end.

"Roxanne?"

She cleared her throat. "I was actually thinking of having Adam with me for the summer."

"No." The response was as automatic as if she'd asked to take their son to the moon. "You can't just jump back into his life like that. The only thing he knows of you is from phone calls and greeting cards." His voice grew harsh. "You're little more than a stranger to him."

"I want to rectify that, Rick." Her voice grew softer, less assured. "I want to know my son."

Funny, he had just been thinking that Adam might be longing for a mother. And now, here was his son's biological mother, wanting to step back into that role. But for how long? Would she break their son's heart just when he began to trust she'd stay in the picture? Rick wouldn't let that happen. But he couldn't deny Adam the right to know his mother, either. Still, he needed to protect his eight-year-old boy, and sincerely hoped Roxanne wasn't planning a custody battle in court. A bit of compromise might go a long way.

"Adam's out of school in a couple of weeks. He has a full schedule with baseball and swimming lessons."

"Oh." So much disappointment came through in that one word. "I wouldn't feel right taking him away from all that."

The last thing he wanted was Adam out of his sight. Maybe if Roxanne saw firsthand everything that went into raising a kid, she'd go back to playing army and forget about her maternal responsibilities like she had the first time she'd abandoned him and Adam. "If you want to see him, you'll have to come here. That's the only way I'll agree to this. I'll make sure he wants to be with you—get to know you, first." Rick wasn't about to let Roxanne take his son away, even for a little while.

"Thank you, Rick." Another long silence. "You're more generous than I would be."

"Yeah…well. Just remember he's a little boy." They talked a few minutes about a time frame she could visit, and although her schedule wasn't set, she'd let them know. He wasn't looking forward to seeing her again. Too much time had passed and whatever love they might have developed after having a child together evaporated the moment she signed a contract that took her overseas and out of their lives.

In some ways, he couldn't blame Roxanne for her choices. They'd been in the military, young, and alone. She'd turned twenty-one right before Adam was born. Rick was a couple of years older. They'd had their whole lives ahead of them. But that's where their similarities ended. Rick had taken his turn in the Middle East before they'd married. He'd seen enough war and horror to know he wanted to walk through the front door every night to see his son. So, he'd brought Adam home to Blakely once his enlistment was over. With the help of his sister, and Mom and Dad, he'd provided a family for his son—minus a mother.

He didn't want Roxanne to interrupt or destroy his family. She had never been a part of it, and never would be—as her eight-year absence confirmed. Hopefully she would come, fulfill whatever motherly duty she felt she needed, and leave without causing lasting pain in anyone's heart—especially Adam's.

Chapter Six

Cayme stood in the upstairs bathroom, staring in the mirror at the dark circles under her eyes. A zombie looked back at her. Pale flesh drooped at the corners of her mouth and her chin was splotchy from sleeping on her face. It didn't take much imagination to picture pieces of skin falling into the sink, making ugly, brown stains. She was one hot mess. Not that she should expect anything different after three nights straight of hardly any sleep.

When Rick wasn't reaching through her fogged brain with large, warm hands to pull her closer for a kiss, she'd had nightmares of Ben smashing his guitar against river rocks and tossing the mangled pieces into the raging current. Little wonder she'd wake in a cold sweat, breathing hard. When she closed her eyes again, worry about her job, or the promise she'd made to Mom, chased through her mind, denying any sleep.

Another worry was that she hadn't heard from her boss in over two days. No e-mails, no phone calls. She'd wished for space, at the same time, wondered about the silence and what it meant for her job. The second month of her extended leave of absence started that week. She'd have to make a decision about returning to Seattle. And soon. Her job didn't pay all that well, but she liked it. She stayed crazy busy, most of the time—busy enough to keep from thinking about the might-have-beens. Those might-have-beens had been creeping through her brain way too much lately. The alternative to going back to Seattle was to stay in her hometown, a place filled with responsibility and heartache.

What scared her more was not being sure she was capable of fulfilling either option.

As she climbed into the shower, a third choice occurred to her. She could always move away—start over where no one knew her. Except she'd already done that five years ago, and she hadn't succeeded as well as she'd hoped. Besides, she was tired of hiding, tired of shuffling through her days, like the zombie in the mirror. Time to stop being an observer and accept the risks of becoming a full-fledged participant.

The decision made, she squirted shampoo into her palm and worked it into her hair. She wasn't leaving Blakely anytime soon. All she had to do was convince her boss to give her more time, without firing her. Then she could figure out a way to make the store, Ben, the house, and her job work, and hope it didn't all crumble around her feet.

She was toweling dry when a pounding sounded at the bathroom door.

"You done in there?"

"Ben?"

"Who else lives here? Of course it's me." His rumbly voice was muffled by the door. "Are you done?"

"Give me a minute." She wrapped the towel around her damp hair and pulled on her robe.

Since his decision not to return to therapy, Ben's mood had improved from dark and brooding to one of purpose. Every morning that week, he'd been up around the time she left for the store. He was up even earlier that day.

She didn't kid herself into thinking he was cured or even close to the same brother she'd known before the war, yet she hoped this change was an improvement for him.

Opening the door, she let the steam waft out. "It's all yours."

"Smells girly in here." He brushed past her, wearing the camo T-shirt and plaid boxers he'd slept in.

That fun sense of humor was coming back, too.

"That's my special shampoo. Don't use any of it." She smiled and slid past him in the doorway. "Maybe while you're off this summer you can get the downstairs shower working and stock your own manly products."

"About that…" He turned, his face shadowed by the bathroom light behind him.

His unshaven jaw gave him a rogue appearance and Cayme caught an unsettling glimpse of her big brother the scary warrior. She cleared her throat. "What? You don't think we need another shower?"

He shrugged. "We've done fine so far. But that's not what I meant. I'm…" His gaze landed somewhere over her shoulder, his expression nervous. "I'm planning to talk to Rick about a summer job."

"Really?" That was good…she hoped. Ben had never been physically incapacitated by his condition, but he'd struggled with sleep and had been unable to work a regular forty-hour week. The part-time job he'd found with the high school athletic department had been a perfect fit, allowing him to help with the baseball and track teams and still take time if he needed space.

If he worked for Rick, he'd be around heavy equipment. Combined with lack of sleep, it could be dangerous.

"Don't look like that, Cay. I'm taking things slow. Rick understands."

She nodded. "You're right. Rick would be the first to understand. I'm glad you're talking to him." Should she talk to Rick, too? Maybe he could provide insight into Ben's condition. On the other hand, asking might tread on memories from Rick's own time in the Middle East he'd prefer not to relive.

"Be happy for me, okay, sis?" Ben almost smiled. "I'm doing better."

Cayme swallowed the lump in her throat and stepped back inside the bathroom to give her brother a hug. "I'm happy for you, Ben. I really am."

Ben wrapped his war-hardened arms around her and squeezed, giving her the first hug since she'd been home—he hadn't even hugged her at Mom's funeral.

Cayme clung to him, feeling as if sunshine had burst through a thunderstorm. "I could stay home today," she whispered. "Make Mom's special pancake recipe. We could talk." She was willing to skip work. A rarity since she'd taken over for their mother.

Ben let go, held her at arm's length, and then gently shoved her out of the bathroom. "Not today. I have an early morning appointment and you have a store to run."

"Okay. But maybe you can stop by the store later and tell me how your interview went."

"Deal."

He closed the door, leaving Cayme standing alone

in the hallway. A surge of love washed over her, tumbling her like a boulder in the rising river. Was her brother back? Would he really be okay? She'd read everything she could to better understand his challenges. Her brother's struggles were so distant and unconnected to the reality she faced every day. She'd never fully comprehend what had happened to him.

Regardless of Ben's assertion that he was doing better, she wanted to be vigilant. Just because he said he was ready to handle life without therapy, didn't mean it was true. In fact, even if he was completely healed, he could never be the same. If she left town now, she could destroy the fragile progress he was making.

Like a novel coming to a conclusion, her decision was made. She was staying in Blakely—for as long as it took. She'd find a way to make it work. And if she lost her assistant editor job, so be it.

****

All the way to the store, Ben's conversation bounced around in Cayme's brain. She really wanted to help him on his path to recovery. She just needed to be patient.

As she unlocked the rear entrance to the store, she realized her decision to stay in town made her entire body buzz with a combination of dread and excitement, as if some invisible switch had turned on, sending her down a path for which she had no road map or steering control. Regardless, she was determined to make it work, for both her and Ben's sake.

A quick peek out the big front windows revealed clouds gathering for the next storm, but she refused to let the dreary day dampen her mood. Arriving at dawn, before customers stopped in for their first cup of coffee and morning news—whether from the paper delivered in the predawn hours from Boise, or via headlines on the web—was something she looked forward to.

The combination bookstore/coffee shop was located on Main Street, six small-town blocks from Cayme's house. Far enough away to be safe from flood danger and close enough she could walk on nice days, which she'd done the last two days with the break between storms. Even with the day's unsettled weather, warmer May temperatures were returning to the Rocky Mountains. Which meant the snowpack was melting and the likelihood of flood was greater.

Cayme stowed that worry for another day and shoved her purse and jacket in the same cubby her mother had used. When she first started at the store, she couldn't bring herself to use the sacred spot until Skeeter Burke, her mother's best friend and business partner, insisted she take ownership. Now, tucking her purse in that special place was as much a habit as checking her phone for messages before leaving the house.

Still no word from her boss on her last message check. Maybe that wasn't a bad thing since she'd decided to stay in town.

After turning on the lights for the main store, she headed outside again to retrieve the bundle of newspapers stacked on a shelf protected from the weather outside the back entrance. Rick's handiwork, no doubt. He'd probably made the shelf for her mother right after the store opened.

He'd always been one of the good guys like that, which made his charm all the harder to ignore. Not that she would do anything about this unwarranted attraction. For the moment, she had enough challenges without adding a relationship into the mix. Obviously, lack of sleep was throwing her imagination in all sorts of inappropriate directions.

She dropped the bundle of papers with a satisfying thud next to a display case near the counter. For the first week or so after the funeral, the store had been an escape. Now, a month later, it was not only a safe haven, full of her mother's personality, but something she could hold on to. The loneliness that sabotaged her at inopportune times wasn't as frequent. Who would have guessed that she'd enjoy being a barista instead of a desk jockey? Even the food-handlers course had been mildly interesting.

Grabbing some scissors, she cut the string on the stack of papers and set to work, once again admiring the store's quaint decor. The interior looked more like someone's living room than a shop on Main Street. The homey style was undoubtedly what her mom and Skeeter had intended.

An angled wall blocked off an area along the side of the store, offering a cozy reading nook with overstuffed chairs and lamplight, rather than overhead fluorescents. At the front of the store, a built-in counter stretched underneath the large windows facing Main Street. It provided a place for customers to connect their own devices to the Internet, sip lattes, and watch the activity outside, while perched on comfy bar stools. Recently, that activity consisted of people running from their cars into the building to stay out of the constant storms.

The counter continued with a ninety-degree turn and ran half the length of the adjoining wall. Four flat screen monitors, with keyboards, sat along this wall for those who didn't have their own computers. Three small, rectangular tables, with two chairs each, sat in the center of the store. The main counter took up the back end of the store. They served both hot and cold drinks, pastries from the local bakery, and homemade scones and sandwiches.

The muted sage-colored decor contrasted nicely with the pine paneling on all the walls and matched the bookshelves placed throughout the store. The ambiance was deliberately laid-back. The first time Cayme saw what her mother and Skeeter had created, she loved it and felt immediately at home.

The rear entrance chime sounded.

"Cayme, girl!" Skeeter called in her husky tenor voice.

"Out here," Cayme shouted back. "I'm setting up the newspapers."

Skeeter breezed in. "It's so good to be home. You have no idea how much I've missed you and the store." Dropping her purse and keys on the counter, she came around and gave Cayme a hug, surrounding her with the exotic scent of sandalwood.

Razor thin, standing a couple of inches taller than Cayme's five-nine, Skeeter expended so much energy that it was probably how she'd gotten her nickname. Blonde streaks ran through her long brown hair. On any other woman her age, the highlights might have looked like she was staving off the next decade. On Skeeter, it looked sexy and attractive.

"You were only gone for a four-day weekend." Still, Cayme was glad Skeeter was back from visiting her brother in Denver.

"Two days too long," Skeeter replied. "I love my brother, but he's so structured."

Cayme laughed. "Is that a bad thing?"

"Boring. He had my entire visit planned down to the last minute. We didn't do a single spontaneous thing."

Sunday flashed through Cayme's mind. She'd scheduled her entire weekend too. Was she structured and boring? Then Rick's cajoling changed all her plans and she'd ended up at Sherry's barbecue.

"So, tell me about your weekend." Skeeter straightened the magazine rack next to the newspaper cubby.

Had Skeeter read her mind? "Nothing much to tell." Cayme focused on her task and hoped the inner turmoil from the sleepless nights didn't show on her face.

"Nothing?" Skeeter's tone was skeptical. "I heard you had company on Sunday and actually got out of the house."

Heat burned Cayme's cheeks. Blakely's gossip mill must have been burning up the phone lines if Skeeter already knew about her weekend. "Sherry dragged Rick over to fix the leak on the roof then invited me to her place for a barbecue." She glanced up. "Did Mom ever mention the roof leaked?"

"The roof leaks?" The change of subject seemed to work. Skeeter shook her head. "Rachel never mentioned it to me. Where was it?"

"Over the attic." Mom probably hadn't looked up there all winter. And after she got sick…well, she couldn't even climb the stairs to her bedroom.

"That explains it." After straightening the last

magazine, Skeeter rearranged the rack of beaded bracelets next to the register. Not only were the bracelets there for an impulse purchase, it was a way their little shop supported the town's local craft store. "She probably didn't know anything about the leak."

"Maybe," Cayme said, recalling that Rick mentioned her mother had wanted him to check out the roof. "I wouldn't have known about the problem myself, except I'd put off going through Mom's things long enough and started digging through the attic. Everything up there could have been ruined if I'd waited longer. I'm glad the water damage wasn't worse."

"When a door closes, a window always opens." Skeeter gave a sage nod. "Think of all the special things you might have lost if you hadn't found the courage to start looking."

"I guess." If Mom hadn't died…if she hadn't been home…all those boxes of memories—things she hadn't seen or thought of for years—might have been lost. And yet, she would trade every one of them to have a few more months with her mother.

"Deep down inside, I'm right, and you know it." Skeeter poked at a spot over Cayme's heart.

A shudder of longing burned Cayme's throat. "Do you honestly believe that Mom's illness was a blessing?"

"'Course not, baby." Skeeter swallowed hard. "Not in the way you're taking it." She gathered Cayme in another bony-armed, sandalwood hug. "She was my best friend. I'd give all my world to have her back."

"I'm sorry." Cayme hugged her back. "I know you miss her, too. And I know I need to look for the good."

She laid her head on the other woman's shoulder. "It's just so hard."

"It takes time, baby." Skeeter gave her another squeeze. "Time will make it better…and some of my scones, of course." She patted Cayme's back and then stood. "I'll bet you ran out while I was gone."

Cayme nodded.

"I knew it! The fresh batch is in the car. Finish up, now. We need to open those doors in a few minutes, and we're not even ready." The woman rarely sat during the workday. Forget lazing around during the store's rush hours, especially in the morning. The only time she hesitated was if a customer had problems with the Internet. Technology eluded Skeeter like a pesky fly.

Cayme snapped out of her gloomy mood. Skeeter was right, and the woman always found something positive to focus on, no matter how bad the day got. No wonder she and Cayme's mom had been such great friends. With the last of the newspapers on the rack, she gathered the brown paper and string to throw in the recycle bin.

"Thanks for doing the papers, girl." Skeeter nodded at the rack. Nothing fancy, just a display next to the counter within easy reach while ordering a cup of morning coffee. "I hate getting the black print on my fingers."

Cayme showed off her ink-covered digits. "I'm getting better at it, and at organizing the books after they come in. I'm lucky to have you show me the ropes."

Skeeter had done more than show her the ropes. She'd taken Cayme and Ben under her wing and guided them through those horrible, dark days after their mother passed. She owed Skeeter for that, and for being her mother's stalwart friend and partner because Cayme hadn't had the courage to come home for more than a brief visit. She took a breath. That was all in the past. At least she hoped so.

After washing her hands, Cayme unlocked the main door and switched on the OPEN sign. A few minutes later, the usual customers, along with a few new faces, trickled in for their morning caffeine fixes. Tourists were getting a jump on the upcoming Memorial Day weekend and some late spring skiing. If the temperatures dropped as predicted, there'd be snow on the valley floor as well as the slopes, and a good weekend for the store.

****

Cayme cleared paper plates and cups off a table and tossed them into the trash. The lunch crowd had been light, which was typical for the middle of the week. When she first looked at the store's commodities, she realized the genius behind her mother's venture. By offering Internet and free Wi-Fi, they were taking advantage of a need in the community. These days, it seemed people couldn't live without virtual worlds at their fingertips. The café was a natural draw to keep customers using their services. By adding the side business of the bookstore, it encouraged patrons to make Books, Bytes, & Brews a regular hangout.

As she finished wiping down the last table, the entrance chimed. She glanced up and her heart gave a little bump at seeing Rick's son, Adam, step inside. He looked so much like Rick had at that age that her stupid crush rose to the surface.

Adam paused beside one of the tables and stared uncertainly at the computers along the wall. He crossed to a station, dropped his backpack, and eyed a monitor. After a moment, he settled onto a stool and wiggled the mouse to the side of the keyboard.

Cayme glanced at the clock. Three-thirty. School must be out. But why was Adam in the store instead of at home? She finished straightening the coffee flavors, reminding herself it wasn't any of her business what Adam did with his after-school hours. Surely his dad or Sherry knew where the boy was.

After returning from the backroom with a replacement flavor, Skeeter motioned her over.

"He has some questions." She nodded to Adam. "Can you give him a hand?" With Skeeter's aversion to the tech stuff, helping with the Internet had naturally fallen to Cayme.

"Sure." Cayme crossed to the bank of workstations. "Hi, Adam. How are you today?"

He turned and his face lit up at seeing her. "Aunt Cayme! I didn't know you worked here. I'm doing good."

"Glad to hear it." His greeting certainly brightened her day a notch. "Is this the first time you've been in the store?"

"Um…no, I was in once with my friend, Devon. A few months ago." He glanced back at the computer with a sheepish grin. "I was wondering if I can use the Internet."

"You don't have Internet at home?"

He looked away and scuffed at the floor with his shoe. "I do, but I'm looking for a present for my dad's birthday. I don't want him to know. We have parent controls at home, so he might figure out what I'm looking for." He glanced at her, eyes alight with excitement to share his secret. "I was thinking I could find him that fly rod he wants, only I can't remember the brand. Mr. Anderson, at the sporting goods store, didn't have time to help me today. If I don't get it soon, it will be too late. His birthday's next month."

"A fly rod." She lifted her eyebrows. "That's a pretty cool gift. Wouldn't your dad be one of your worm customers, though?"

"Yeah. He uses worms too, but he really likes to fly fish."

Hmm. Rick standing in the ice-cold river, waders to his thighs, wearing a hat pinned with imitation bugs, whipping his line back and forth, those powerful shoulders rippling under a chambray shirt.

Back off, girl. She pushed the image aside. Here was a boy who just needed a little help, and she was getting all tingly thinking about his father. She took a deep breath and refocused. "Okay then. Have you asked your Aunt Sherry what kind of rod he likes?"

"I want it to be a total surprise."

He looked so earnest in his quest.

"That's why I didn't bring Joey with me. If I told him, he'd tell his mom and she'd probably tell my dad."

"I see your point." It seemed the gossip mill wasn't only reserved for the older generation.

His eyes grew round with excitement. "Could you help me? You'd keep it secret, wouldn't you?"

How could she deny those hopeful brown eyes? So much like Rick's and so full of excitement to surprise his dad. She'd never seen Rick come into the store, so he wouldn't have to know she'd helped Adam, would he? Besides, that's what a friend would do. If she was sticking around town, she had to stop acting like a stranger.

"I suppose I could," Cayme agreed. "I think we can keep it a secret until his birthday." Funny how she was just talking about Rick's birthday the other day. "That doesn't leave much time. We'd better start looking." She logged onto the computer and opened a browser.

"How much will the Internet cost?" he asked. "Since Christmas I've been saving my allowance and some of the money my mom sent me."

When Adam mentioned his mother, her smile slipped a little. Rick had been married, and according to Sherry, the woman was a mother in name only. Such a shame, because Adam was a great kid. "We don't charge for using the computer. We just ask customers to respect the time if there's someone waiting." She glanced around the mostly empty store now that lunch was over. "It's pretty quiet for the moment."

He nodded solemnly. "Okay. I'll make sure I'm not on too long."

Cayme winked. "We'll be fine for a while."

"Thanks." He grinned. "I'm glad you're helping me. I wasn't sure how to do this."

That same cute dimple on Adam's smile was just like Rick's, and she couldn't quite ignore the quiver in her middle. "My pleasure." Time to stop worrying about 'what-ifs' and help Rick's son. "Let's get started."

She keyed in a search for fly rods and several links displayed. Goodness, this could take weeks. Was there any way to narrow down the parameters?

"There," Adam exclaimed, pointing to a link on the

screen. "That's the name. I knew it was something simple, I just couldn't remember."

Cayme clicked on the site and a list of rods displayed. "Which one?"

"That one." Adam pointed. "For freshwater. He likes to fish the river during the summer."

She clicked on the image and the price list came up. Oh, dear. No way would an allowance cover those prices.

"Does that say six hundred and twenty-five dollars?" Adam's shoulders slumped.

"I'm afraid it does." She felt his disappointment in the pit of her own stomach.

"No wonder he keeps saying he'll have to wait until his lotto ticket wins big. I didn't know for sure what that meant." He pointed at the price. "Now I do."

"What's something else he might like that's related to fishing?"

"I don't know." Adam worried his lower lip with his teeth. Then his eyes lit up. "Yes, I do! I saw Mr. Peters' new blow-up raft in the trunk of his car last week. I think he takes that fishing. My dad might like one of those." He turned back to the computer. "Can we look?"

This time, she typed in a search for inflatable rafts.

"Wow," Adam said. "I didn't know there were so many different kinds." He pointed to the screen. "How much is that one?"

She clicked on the picture and brought up the product site.

He sulked. "That costs more than I have, too."

Cayme's heart melted a little. Even if she had the money, which she didn't, she couldn't buy the gift for the boy. The price tags stepped well beyond the realm of friendship and into totally inappropriate territory. "Tell you what. Since your dad likes to fly fish, what do you say we look at some of the books we have for tying flies?"

Adam frowned. "He won't like a book the same as a new rod or a raft."

"He'll love the gift because it came from you." She tapped the little boy's chest. "It'll be something that you give him from your heart."

He perked up. "You think so?"

His eagerness to please struck hard, and a tiny voice urged her to watch her own heart. "I know so." The Rick she remembered hadn't cared much about material things. Hopefully, he hadn't changed too much over the years

Looking at Adam, in his not-so-new yet serviceable tennis shoes, clean jeans, and jacket, she guessed Rick's values held true. The boy wasn't wearing expensive, trendy brands, but he was clearly well cared for. Yeah, Rick was still practical. Seeing how Adam reacted to the price of the fly rod, he'd obviously raised his son the same way.

Cayme logged off the computer. "Come on over here." She led him to the fishing section in the bookstore and pointed to a shelf filled with different topics. Some books were by local authors who'd spent most of their lives fishing the Blakely River that ran through the valley. "Why don't you look through these? You might find something that will interest your dad."

"Okay." Adam ran his finger along the book spines.

"I'll be over behind the counter. Would you like a

root beer?"

He looked at the fountain drinks and his eyes brightened. Then he shook his head. "No, thanks. I better save my money."

"How about a drink on the house this once?" she asked. "It's not too close to your dinnertime, is it?"

"Okay." He gave her a smile that showed big front teeth. "Dad's doing a side job for the mayor, so we won't eat until later."

Cayme gave an inward groan. She didn't want to think about the mayor. He was the man heading the campaign to buy her property and wasn't one of her favorite people right now. However, she couldn't fault Rick for taking jobs when he could, especially with such a terrific kid to support. "One root beer coming right up."

Chapter Seven

As much as Cayme loved the early mornings at the store, her absolute favorite time of the day was the afternoons. The lunch rush tapered off and the lull lasted until just before they closed around six p.m. It gave her time to reflect on the day and stretch the soreness out of her muscles. As an assistant editor, she sat all day at her job. Coming home to sit again didn't really feel like resting after a long day's work. Not in the way it did when she got home from the store.

A short while later, she waited on a couple of teenagers who came in to use the Wi-Fi and study. Students were given a discount on the soft drinks, which made the store a popular hangout after school. However, with summer break just around the corner, fewer students stopped by to study these days. Cayme wasn't sure what the summer crowds would be like, but if everything went well with her request for a longer leave of absence, she would soon find out.

She checked her phone again. Four-thirty. And still no word from the senior editor. Maybe she should have turned in her resignation instead of requesting more time. It would save her boss the task of firing her. But she wasn't quite ready to give up on Seattle. Besides, hadn't she already proven she could do her job remotely?

After waiting on the teenagers, she checked on

Adam. He took his time browsing the bookshelves, sipping his root beer, occasionally cocking his head to the side to read a title.

His leisurely perusal reminded her of the time she and Sherry had made a trip to the library to find books for their fifth-grade book report. At twelve years old, they'd figured they were old enough to go alone, but Sherry's mom insisted Rick take them. For a seventh grader, he'd been patient with two girls trailing in his wake. Not once had he rolled his eyes while Cayme studied book titles before selecting *Island of the Blue Dolphins*. He hadn't told her it was the same book he'd picked for his fifth-grade book report. She'd known anyway, thanks to Sherry. The book was still one of her favorites.

She'd almost forgotten that buried memory until she watched Adam showing the same interest in books as Rick had back then. He stopped beside the fly-tying section, placed his drink carefully on the floor, and reached for a book. Turning it over, he gave a little grin then picked up his drink, wandered to an empty table, and began looking through it.

Cayme joined him and sat in the opposite chair. "What did you find?"

He showed her the cover—*The Complete Guide to Fly Tying.*

"Nice." She smiled. Sometimes a title said it all.

"It's got some really great pictures and tips." He bounced in his seat and grinned. "Look at this one." He scooted around the table to show her the page with an intricate fly and step-by-step instructions on how to make it.

"That's pretty cool. I think you made a great

choice."

Adam's lips turned down. "It's still not the same as a fly rod."

"That's true. But I knew your dad growing up. I'm positive he'd rather have a gift like this from you, than some fancy fishing pole any day."

"You knew my dad when he was a kid?" His eyes grew round. "I'll bet that was weird."

Not as weird as having this conversation with his son. "Your dad was a very nice boy, just like you."

Adam gave a shy grin and dropped his gaze to the book. "Do you really think he'll like this?"

"I know so. He likes doing things himself, right?" Even during Rick's wilder teenage years, he never strayed far from his home values. That was one of the things she'd always admired about him—right up until he'd joined the army fresh out of high school without ever asking her out on a date. She wondered what in the wide world had steered him off the course she had envisioned for the two of them. Not that he'd known her plans for their future. Those were a closely held secret.

"Yeah, Dad likes building all kinds of things." Adam's beaming smile brought her back to the present. "I guess I'll buy it." He stared at the book. "I can't take the book home, though. He might find it before his birthday and spoil the surprise. Do you think I can keep it here?"

"Absolutely. I'll show you my secret hiding place." She led the way to the counter.

Adam grabbed his empty cup and tossed it in the garbage, then he picked up the book as if he was holding a prized trout. He carefully placed it on the counter.

Cayme rang up the sale and told him the amount, less her employee discount.

He frowned. "That's not the price on the back cover."

"It's on sale." She winked.

His eyes lit up. "Wow! That's even better."

She held back a smile while he sorted out dollar bills and a handful of coins from his pocket.

"I learned to count money last year in school." With a final look at his allowance, he slid it over to her. "I'll even have enough left over to take Dad to dinner at the frosty stand."

"Dinner and a book. That'll be the best birthday ever," she said.

As Cayme closed the register drawer, the front door chimed. She looked up with a smile for the new customers. There stood the one person she could have gone the rest of her life without seeing.

Chase Peters. Her ex-fiancé.

Cold infused her cheeks as though all her blood drained to her feet. Her smile froze and she clutched the side of the counter for balance. Her irrational fear of running into him—his very presence in Blakely—was the reason she'd left home and barely saw her family during the last five years. Her self-imposed absence was shallow and childish, but she had built up the ugly situation so much in her mind that she'd found it easier to stay away.

Chase stood in the entryway, as head-turningly handsome as he'd been on the day she'd handed back his ring. He wasn't quite six-feet tall, but tall enough she hadn't towered over him—unless she wore heels.

His blond hair was sun streaked, and the tan he sported confirmed he still spent more time on the slopes or the golf course than managing his father's five-star resort hotel.

"Aunt Cayme. Are you all right?"

Adam's worried voice penetrated her brain. Her gaze dropped to her young customer and she drew a steadying breath. "I'm fine." She was over Chase, wasn't she? She'd left town, moved on, and had the scars on her heart to prove it. However, seeing him again didn't prevent those old feelings of humiliation, anger, and a hint of regret from bubbling to the surface. She may have had a crush on Rick, but at one time, she'd loved Chase. And Chase had shattered that love in a single selfish act.

Adam glanced over his shoulder at the newcomer. "Oh, that's Mr. Chase. He runs the hotel where Uncle Ken works." Adam leaned over the counter and whispered. "He doesn't like me and Joey to visit. But Uncle Ken told us it was okay, so we just stay out of his way when we're there."

Cayme doubted that Chase would appreciate two rambunctious little boys running around his father's hotel. How she'd failed to see his up-town snobbery while they dated, she'd never know. She looked back at Adam. "You and Joey can visit my store any time you like."

Adam grinned.

"Well, if it isn't Cold Feet Cayme," Chase said from across the room.

Heat flared on her face. Everyone in the store would've heard the snide comment. Had she really loved this man at one time?

A girlish twitter floated from behind Chase as he sauntered toward the counter. He wasn't alone.

The girl was six inches shorter than Cayme, with shiny hair that draped in a chestnut curtain down her back. Dressed in a chic parka and fur boots, she followed in Chase's shadow like a snow bunny chasing a ski god. That was something Cayme had refused to do—among other things.

A twinge of jealousy caught her unawares, until she remembered she'd been the one who'd called off the wedding—allowing the town to believe she'd gotten cold feet. A misrepresentation then, and too much water under the bridge to rectify now. "Chase." She hissed his name like a warning and pointed to a sign that said customers were served at the privilege of the establishment.

Apparently, Chase didn't want to look foolish in front of his latest conquest by getting kicked out of the store by his ex-fiancée, so he had the grace to look apologetic. He owed her for not giving away his dirty little secret five years ago and he knew it. "I was sorry to hear about your mom," he said in a more civil tone.

"Thank you." Cayme hadn't really expected him to show up at the funeral and he hadn't. "Was there something you needed?" She schooled her voice to sound polite, professional, and totally neutral.

"I'm showing Joy around. She's new in town. We came in to check out the store and grab a couple of lattes to warm up."

At that moment, Skeeter sidled beside Cayme and glared at Chase from her domain behind the counter. "I'll take care of the customers, Cayme girl. You finish up with Mr. Morrison here." She winked at Adam, her face softening instantly.

Adam stood a bit straighter and grinned at the use of his proper name.

Cayme gave Skeeter a grateful smile. "Thanks." She leaned toward her friend and whispered, "Adam's buying a secret birthday gift."

"My lips are sealed." Skeeter made a zipping motion then looked at Chase and his girlfriend. "Two lattes coming up." She turned her back and whispered just loud enough for Cayme to hear, "I'll try not to spit in them."

Good ol' Skeeter. A friend indeed. Cayme suppressed a smile and waved Adam over to the other counter. "Let's gift wrap this, and then I'll show you my secret hiding place."

Adam followed Cayme, a puzzled look on his face. "How come your feet are cold?"

"It's an expression." She didn't really want to explain to an eight-year-old why she'd cancelled her wedding.

"Sort of like 'saved by the bell'?" he asked. "My dad says that one a lot."

Cayme laughed. "Sort of. I like your expression better." It might not have been a bell, but with time and distance, she'd come to realize she'd been saved from making a terrible mistake. Marrying Chase Peters would have been an all-out disaster. What stung more was failing at the relationship. She'd tried, and what she'd thought was love hadn't been enough.

She focused on wrapping the book, acutely aware that Chase and his girlfriend hadn't left after paying for their drinks. Instead, they wandered over to one of the store computers and clicked onto some social network site. They laughed and pointed at a video flashing across the screen. It took all her concentration, but she never gave the two another glance.

After tying the perfect bow on the gaily-wrapped gift—the book was for Rick, after all—she took Adam into the back room to stow it until the special day.

He peered into the cupboard that held paper and plastic products for the store. "That's a perfect spot. I'll come in the day before Dad's birthday and pick it up, if that's okay."

Rick's son was so polite, proving once again that he'd done a great parenting job. "Sounds like a perfect plan." She closed the cupboard that now held the prized birthday present. With her hand resting on Adam's shoulder, they walked out of the back room.

He stopped short in the doorway. "Oh, no." With a quick turn, he ducked under Cayme's arm.

She looked at him hiding behind her. "What's wrong?"

Slipping farther into the shadows, he pointed and whispered, "My dad. Why is he here? He said he was working late. Like until six. Is it six?" Panic crept into his voice, making it squeak a little.

"No. It's almost five, though." Cayme glanced over her shoulder. Rick had propped a hip against the counter and was talking to Skeeter. Had he seen them? If he hadn't, maybe she could sneak Adam out the rear door and his secret would be safe.

Adam tugged on her arm. "What should I do? I don't want him to know I'm buying his present. It'll spoil the surprise. And my backpack is in there."

Cayme was torn. She didn't want Adam to lie to his father. On the other hand, she wanted to help him keep his secret. Her gaze landed on the broom leaning against the wall and an idea formed. "How would you like to earn some money?"

"Huh?"

"We could use a little extra help in the store. You know, take out garbage and tidy up after our lunch rush." She pointed to the garbage bags waiting beside the door to go out later.

"We can tell my dad that I'm here to earn money for chores?" Adam's eyes widened.

"What do you think?"

"This isn't a fool, is it? You're really offering me a job?"

"No fool. We can use the help, and right after school is the perfect time. Another boy used to come in and help sometimes."

"That was Devon," Adam said. "He's my friend I told you about."

"Right." Adam had mentioned a friend. "He stopped by a few weeks ago and talked to Ms. Skeeter. I didn't have the chance to speak to him. Do you know why he didn't want to work here anymore?"

"Ummm…" He shrugged. "Not really."

Adam looked as if he knew something but didn't want to say. "Is Devon sick?" Maybe she should have investigated the boy's reasons instead of assuming he wanted afterschool playtime.

"No. He's not sick," Adam said. "I just think he doesn't want to come here anymore."

"Then it won't hurt his feelings if you take over the afternoon chores?"

"I…don't think so."

"Good. Are you in?"

Adam beamed. "I'm in."

"Okay." Now to sell the job to Rick. "Let's get your dad's permission." Cayme kept a hand on Adam's shoulder while they walked out of the back room.

The store seemed darker and Cayme saw through the front window that slate-colored storm clouds hung over the mountains, creating a dreary shroud to the late afternoon. The two students gathered up their laptops and left. Glancing around, she didn't see Chase or his girlfriend, so they must have left, too. Thank goodness for small favors.

Adam rushed over to Rick. "Dad! Guess what? Aunt Cayme said I can help out at her store."

Skeeter glanced at Cayme with one eyebrow raised.

Cayme mouthed, *I'll explain later*. "So, Skeeter. Looks like we'll have our afternoon help again."

Adam tugged on his dad's arm. "Can I?"

Rick's unreadable gaze landed on Cayme before shifting to Skeeter and then back to Adam. "What's this about?"

Adam turned to Cayme, excitement shining in his brown eyes.

She squared her shoulders and hoped she was doing the right thing. "I've asked Adam if he could help with our after-lunch clean up. Right after school, and of course if it's okay with you, and—" She sent Adam a meaningful look. "—all your homework is finished. Right?"

He scrunched his nose at the homework qualifier then nodded vigorously. "Right." He tugged on Rick's arm. "Can I, Dad? I can earn money to spend during the summer. I'll save up for school clothes and stuff like that. I won't have to bother you for extra chores."

Rick gave his son one of those indulgent looks that Cayme remembered getting from her father at that age. A lump lodged in her throat, forcing her to swallow hard. Her own dad had been such a softy. It looked like Rick was too.

"What about your worm business?" Rick asked.

Adam's brow crinkled, then his face cleared. "That won't interfere. Joey and me will work on that at night. Besides, we can't hunt for worms until it gets warmer. And I can start here tomorrow. Right, Aunt Cayme?" He looked expectantly at her again.

"You bet, kiddo," she said. "*If* your dad says it's okay."

"Please, Dad?"

Rick's face softened even more.

Cayme could tell he was inches from giving in. Her chest bloomed with a sudden desire for him to look at her in that same soft way.

He cleared his throat. "Tell you what, bud. Let's talk about this later tonight and you can give Ms. Skeeter and Aunt Cayme your answer tomorrow. Deal?"

"Would that be okay, Aunt Cayme?" Adam's tone was so polite and earnest.

"Absolutely. We'll look forward to your answer."

"Yes." He fist pumped the air.

"Whoa, there," Rick said. "Nothing's settled. Now, why don't you head out to the truck. I want to talk to these fine ladies for a moment."

"Okay." Adam headed for the door, waving. "Thanks Aunt Cayme. Bye, Ms. Skeeter. See you tomorrow." The bell chimed and the door shut behind him.

Rick turned to Cayme, his indulgent expression replaced by suspicion. "What's this all about? Did Adam come in here asking for a job?"

"Of course not!" She quickly came to Adam's defense then realized she'd need to tread carefully or she'd give away his secret. "He—"

"I think he was looking for a book." Skeeter jumped in to save Cayme from an outright lie.

"Book?" Rick looked skeptical.

"You know, for school. But he didn't find what he was looking for, did he?" Skeeter glanced at Cayme for confirmation.

"Uh…no. He did mention his friend was the boy who used to come in. We offered Adam the job because we can still use the help."

Rick searched Cayme's face as though he was looking for an alternative motive.

She returned his look, heat creeping up her neck. Movement at the front of the store caught her eye and she looked over Rick's shoulder.

Chase and his girlfriend came around the corner from the book nook.

Cayme's face went from hot to icy in an instant. She hated that she reacted every time Chase came into her space. Couldn't he just disappear down a sewage drain or something?

Rick turned to see what had grabbed Cayme's attention.

Chase and Joy sauntered toward the counter where Rick, Cayme, and Skeeter stood.

"Rats," Skeeter whispered. "I thought they'd left."

"It's okay," Cayme whispered back. "I'm a big girl

now. I can deal with him. I think."

Rick's expression hardened, overhearing her and Skeeter's words.

"So…Cayme." Chase walked up to the counter, still holding his latte.

He was close enough for Cayme to pick up the scent of his expensive cologne. The scent she believed she'd love forever now made her stomach churn.

Chase offered a pompous smile to his captive audience. "Nice store you have here. I'm impressed. Your mom did a good job. Is it making a profit?"

"We're doing fine." She tamped down a rise of panic at the question. The last thing she needed was Chase or his father sweeping in and making investment noises. "And this isn't just my mother's store, Skeeter and Mom are…um…were partners."

"Of course," Chase said. "I meant great job to you, too, Ms. Burke."

"Nitwit," Skeeter muttered and stalked behind the counter.

He stiffened and his smiled slipped but he recovered quickly and turned to Rick. "Oh, hey, sport."

Chase had a way of pretending to notice others as though they were an afterthought. Just one more thing about his ego and arrogance Cayme should have seen while they dated yet somehow missed. She was an idiot to believe she was once in love enough to marry him.

"Peters." Rick's voice was low with cautious civility.

Joy wiggled her way to stand almost directly in front of Cayme and inadvertently upstaged Chase. "You didn't introduce me." Her big green eyes ogled Rick, then she unzipped her parka and stuck out a petite hand.

"I'm Joy. Chase's girlfriend."

Cayme had no problem looking over the top of Joy's shiny hair to see Chase's scowl at the woman flaunting her wares in front of another man. *Payback's a bugger, isn't it buddy?* She swallowed a hysterical laugh. Chase deserved whatever he got. However, she wasn't ruining her own karma by wishing it on him.

Rick's hard gaze shifted from Chase to Cayme.

No way could he miss seeing the same panic that had been on her face when he'd rescued her from the ladder.

Then he glanced at Joy and shook her hand. "Nice to meet you. I'm Rick Morrison." He released her hand a bit more quickly than she expected based on her frown.

A sudden gleam entered Rick's chocolate-brown eyes, and he stepped closer to Cayme.

Before she could register that he had moved, his warm breath puffed near her ear.

"Sorry." His arm slipped around her shoulders.

Pulling her into an unexpected hug, he placed his lips against her cheek. The kiss was quick, evaporating any response to his apology. His firm, warm mouth grazed her skin and nuzzled her neck, sending a tingle down her spine and a tremor to her thighs. She had no idea what he was doing and didn't care as long as he kept doing it.

He lifted his head and gave her shoulders another hard squeeze before looking at Chase and Joy. "I'm Cayme's fiancé."

Chapter Eight

If Rick lived to be a hundred and ninety years old, he would never understand what made him tell the most outlandish lie of his life. The moment the words, *I'm Cayme's fiancé*, left his mouth, everything inside the store slowed to a snail's pace. Even his own heartbeat seemed to stop. Maybe the situation wasn't real, just some bizarre aberration his imagination had conjured up.

Then Cayme stiffened and emitted a strange little squeak.

Not an aberration. Everyone had heard his words. His gaze dropped to her face, hoping the apology was clear in his eyes.

She stared up at him, her blue eyes wide. Her mouth was slightly open, and the tip of her tongue darted between those kissable lips. Two spots of color flagged each cheek.

He had to admit that he was a little stunned, too. His impulsive announcement was foolish, to say the least. What if she was involved with someone? And if she was, why wasn't he there to save the day? He blamed Chase Peters for these contradicting emotions that made him itch to break the guy's perfect nose— maybe knock out a few teeth while he was at it.

Instead, he placed a finger under Cayme's jaw and gently pushed her mouth shut. The touch was electric.

The bookstore and people fell away, leaving only the two of them, wrapped in a private cocoon.

His finger lingered on the smooth silk of her skin. He was tempted, beyond what any man should endure, to slide his palm up the side of her face and pull her close. He liked the way she smelled of fresh honeysuckle—the way she shivered under his touch. He couldn't ignore the protective swell in his chest. With sudden clarity, he realized that this urge to protect her was exactly the reason he'd blurted out the insane announcement.

Rick swallowed the unexpected punch of desire that drove through his chest, making him want to kiss her fully on the mouth. That would be a monumental mistake because he'd probably never stop.

He pulled his gaze from her face.

Outside the big front window that overlooked Main Street, rain had started to fall. Huge drops pattered against the glass, interrupting the silence that had fallen like a curtain inside the store.

Joy slunk over to Peters who glared at Rick as if he'd managed to steal away both girls. Which made no sense. Rick had no interest in the skinny girl. And why would Peters care if Cayme was engaged? According to Sherry, Cayme had dumped him two weeks before their wedding. Rick didn't know the particulars, only that he was sure Peters had done something to hurt her. The girl he'd known growing up kept her promises. Peters was damn lucky both he and Ben had been in the Middle East at the time she called off the wedding, or they would've taken him behind the shed and given this pretty boy a "a talking to."

"Rick Morrison! You never could keep a secret."

Skeeter broke the silence and rounded the counter to stand on Cayme's other side. Now both Rick and Skeeter flanked her, presenting a united front. "Cayme said you wanted to wait to announce your engagement." She nudged Cayme. "That's what you told me this morning, right, baby?"

All eyes zeroed in on Cayme like a swarm of hungry mosquitos.

Another surge of protectiveness filled Rick. He wanted to beat everyone back with a baseball bat so they'd leave her alone.

Skeeter glared at Rick. Her eyes narrowed to slits as if she were ready to skin him alive.

Cayme looked at the others, another little squeak making it past those kissable lips, then she stared up at Rick again.

He winked and offered an apologetic smile. "Sorry," he said, sounding contrite for spilling a secret that didn't exist. "I know it's still too soon after your mother passed…" He gave a sheepish shrug. "I don't know what came over me."

Cayme blinked and some of her color was returning, making her look more like the resilient woman Rick knew.

"I hope you have an explanation, because I can't think of why you…" She swallowed, her voice little more than a croak. "We're not—"

Before she could contradict his outrageous statement, he leaned in and pressed his lips to her soft mouth. The kiss was quick, whether to protect her or him, he didn't know, but it was suddenly the right thing to do in more ways than one.

Her supple lips were warm, melding to his. He

struggled against deepening the kiss. When he pulled back, her warm breath mingled with his. "We're not supposed to say anything, I know. Sorry…I guess I couldn't wait." His gaze dropped to her soft mouth again. Maybe another kiss to continue the charade.

"So," Peters said, letting that single word shatter the moment.

Rick and Cayme looked at Peters, whose gaze bounced between them then settled on Cayme with a you-could-have-done-better-than-this-schmuck smile. "Congratulations!" He reached out as if to give Cayme a hug.

Rick intercepted the other man's hand instead, preventing him from touching Cayme. He squeezed hard, barely controlling the urge to break every finger, making Peters wince. Message sent—and received.

Pulling free of Rick's crushing grip, Cayme's ex-fiancé stepped back and straightened to his full height, which was still several inches shorter than Rick's. "Well, we should be going." He wrapped an arm around his girlfriend and drew her close.

Joy's pouty gaze speared Rick with a last-ditch effort to draw his attention, but she let Peters guide her to the door. "Nice to meet you," she called over her shoulder. "Congratulations."

The door chime echoed through the silence left behind. Five seconds passed before any of them moved. Rick still had his arm around Cayme, afraid of what might happen if he let go. Would she crumple at his feet or attack him like a wildcat?

Cayme jolted free. "Are you out of your mind?" Her face was now an intriguing shade of pink, and her eyes burned like a blue flame.

Yup. Wildcat. He'd forgotten how pretty she was when she got angry. "That man's lucky he still has all his teeth. I don't know what you ever saw in him."

"What I saw in him is my business." She waved a hand at the door. "Why on earth would you tell him we're engaged?"

"I was helping you out of a tight spot." Yeah, that sounded lame. Maybe he should have let her fend for herself.

"You call that helping?" Cayme poked him in the chest. "The next time I need help with Chase Peters, I'll call a dump truck!"

"Rick Morrison. Cayme Foster." Skeeter's tone warned them to remain calm.

Cayme froze and looked at Skeeter.

Right then, the door chime sounded again. "Hey, Dad. I think I left my backpack in here." Adam walked over to the chair. "Yup. Here it is." He plopped down, the backpack at his feet. "Can I wait in here? It's getting cold in the truck."

Rick had forgotten about Adam waiting outside for him. That never happened. It showed just how messed up he got around Cayme Foster. Little wonder he'd steered clear of her since she'd been back.

"It's okay, bud. We're leaving now." He turned to the women. Cayme's face had turned a deeper shade of pink that made her look even more kissable.

The combination of Skeeter's glower and his son's curious stare stopped him from planting another kiss on Cayme's luscious mouth. "Sorry," he said for the third time. "We'd better go." He hesitated, wanting to say something—anything to make things better but only managed to say, "We'll talk about this tonight."

His purpose for stopping by the store in the first place had been waylaid by his impulse to rescue Cayme. She'd find out soon enough about his plans to help Ben. He placed a hand on Adam's shoulder. "Come on, bud." Together they hurried out the door and through the rain to the truck.

****

"Can you believe that?" Cayme gestured to the closed door, feeling like someone had just tossed her in the churning river. She touched her lips, still feeling Rick's kiss, and heat rushed to her cheeks.

"He's a man." Skeeter's voice had lost some of that sharp edge now that Rick was gone. "Nothing they do or say surprises me." She gently squeezed Cayme's shoulder and offered a long-suffering sigh before returning to her place behind the counter. "I do have to admit I didn't see that one coming. You must have made quite an impression for Rick Morrison to pop the question at Sherry's barbecue." She gave a teasing wink. "And you said nothing happened this weekend."

"Rick didn't propose." Cayme wrapped her arms around her middle and turned away from the door, wishing she could ignore the whole mess. "What just happened wasn't a proposal." She looked at the closed door again with a scowl. "I have no idea what possessed him to announce that we're engaged. And to say it to Chase Peters, of all people!" She tugged the band out of her ponytail and ran a hand through the strands before tying her hair at the base of her neck. "I'll bet Chase is texting his father right now. The news will be all over town before midnight."

Skeeter started mixing a couple of lattes. "I don't think I'd worry about what Councilman Peters or the town thinks."

Cayme's stomach dropped. Skeeter was right. She had a bigger problem than back-fence gossip. "Ben." Her brother hated lies. Here she'd been worried about lying for Adam, and Rick had just gone and told a whopper to beat all whoppers. How would she explain this to her brother?

She looked over at Skeeter. "I never told you…Ben came home early Sunday night. He said he's not going back to therapy anymore. I'd better call and tell him what happened."

"You don't want to deliver this news over the phone, baby." Skeeter handed a hot drink to Cayme. "Maybe you and Rick can tell him together. Rick dumped the marbles all over the floor. He should help clean them up."

Cayme groaned. "This is a nightmare." She cupped her hands around the warm container and inhaled the stimulating aroma of coffee and chocolate. Even that didn't ease the dread creeping into her stomach. "I left five years ago to avoid the humiliation of a failed engagement. How can I face the town once they find out this one is a fake?"

"Make it real." Skeeter brought her coffee cup to her lips.

Cayme jerked at the suggestion. "You can't be serious. Rick was just doing some sort of white knight thing, saving the day, like in third grade. He punched Tyler Davidson for pushing me around." She moaned. "This'll hurt Rick as much as me."

"You're defending him after what he just did to you?" Skeeter lifted a skeptical eyebrow. "Maybe you secretly want to be engaged."

Cayme sputtered for a comeback.

Skeeter continued, "Rick Morrison isn't in grade school anymore. He must have some idea of the floodwaters this announcement will create."

"Right. He was so sure of himself that he couldn't wait to hightail it out of here, holding his little boy in front of him like a shield."

"You're overreacting." Skeeter wagged a finger at her.

"I don't think so." Cayme crossed to one of the tables and sat, grateful no other customers had witnessed her meltdown.

Skeeter joined her in the other chair. "Give him a chance, baby. He said he'd talk to you tonight, and he'll keep his word." She looked over at the clock hanging on the wall behind the counter then outside at the rain that was coming down harder now. "We'll close up early. You go home and talk to your brother. Then you can wait for Rick to walk through the door… just like you did in high school."

"Oh, no." Cayme moaned. "I refuse to go through that again." She caught Skeeter's smug expression. "How'd you know?"

"Your momma wasn't blind, baby. You think she didn't know about that crush of yours?"

How much more humiliation could she take? Cayme wanted to run and hide, never show her face again. "Who else knew?"

Skeeter patted her hand. "Relax. Your mother only told me. As far as I know, your secret is safe. The problem you've got now is telling Ben the truth."

****

Thirty minutes later, Skeeter and Cayme had

cleaned up, prepped for the next day, and closed the store a few minutes before six. Cayme climbed in her car and backed out of the alley. Clouds darkened the sky and the deluge of rain matched her mood perfectly. The one thing that didn't weigh heavily on her mind was the leak over the attic. As ridiculous as Rick had behaved earlier, she was grateful he'd given up part of his Sunday to fix the roof.

She parked around the side of the house and climbed out of the car, catching a glimpse of the river. Whitecaps of angry water tumbled over the river boulders. Maybe she should put off talking to Ben and start filling sandbags instead. They had some bags filled and stockpiled on the other side of the house near the river, but if it started to flood, she was afraid it wouldn't be enough.

Movement on that side of the house caught her attention, and she headed over. Rain soaked into her jacket and plastered her hair as she rounded the corner toward the shed. She stopped at the sight before her.

Adam and his cousin, Joey, stood in the bed of Rick's truck handing sandbags to Rick and Ben. A new pile of sand, soaked with rain, was nearby. The original stack of filled sandbags had grown and stood at the ready beside the riverbank.

Her talk with Ben would have to wait. She had work to do, and now wasn't the time to discuss what Rick had said, especially with little boys listening. She crossed the soggy lawn and approached her guys. Well, maybe not literally *her guys*, but the thought they could be chased away the rainy-day chill.

Rick glanced up and stabbed his shovel into the sand and then met her halfway across the lawn.

"Hey."

His soft voice sent a tingle through her.

"I'm sorry about what happened at the bookstore. I stopped by this afternoon to let you know Ben wanted help with more sandbags. And then… Well, things just got out of hand." He glanced over his shoulder. "Adam doesn't know. And I haven't said anything to anyone. So, can we just keep it…um…what happened between us?"

Cayme brushed a drop of rain off her face. "It" being his glib announcement they were engaged. "You blabbed to Chase Peters. The first person he'll tell is his father. I may not have lived here for the last few years, but I'm pretty sure the news is all over town by now." She was as exasperated with him as she was with herself for not saying something before Chase left the store. "I won't say anything in front of the boys, but I have to tell Ben tonight. You know what he's like if he thinks someone's lied to him."

"I know." Rick heaved a sigh. "I'm sorry to put you in this position. Maybe you could hold off for a couple of hours? Just until we're done here?" He gestured at the sandbagging project behind him.

Near the riverbank, Ben eyed them curiously. At least he didn't look upset. And he was outside working. He'd even asked Rick for help. That was a good sign, right? "As soon as we're done, I'm telling him. He has to hear it from me first."

"Let me help you out. I put you in this predicament." A muscle in Rick's jaw jumped. "When we're done here, I need to take Adam and Joey home. But then I'll get a sitter and come back so we can talk to Ben together."

Cayme hesitated. She didn't like waiting, yet she really didn't want to face her brother alone. If she wanted Rick's help, she had no choice. "Fine. I'll go change and be right back out to help."

Rick frowned. His gaze dropped to her mouth much like it had earlier.

As warmth filled her middle, the cold rain went unheeded. Surely, he wasn't thinking of kissing her. Especially with Ben not more than twenty feet away. As much as she might want that, it would make matters more complicated. "What's the matter?"

His gaze jerked up. "Um… nothing. It's just…never mind."

She wondered if Rick was losing his mind. Skeeter had been wrong about him knowing what he'd done. It appeared he had no idea how to handle this situation.

****

They bagged sand for another half hour, until the rain finally let up. Cayme had sent Adam and Joey into the house to dry off and warm up a bit, giving them permission to watch TV. The cable service was Ben's account. If he was feeling down, he could plant himself in front of the TV and watch whatever he wanted to keep his mind off his problems. She tried not to worry about the shows the boys might find. If she and Rick were really engaged, setting up parental controls would be one of the first things she'd change.

Whoa, there. She wasn't a parent. The rain must have soaked her brain to be thinking like that. She dug her shovel into the sand and focused on filling the next bag.

Cayme slid in the last shovelful and then Ben tied it off.

He tossed the bag onto the stack as though it weighed next to nothing.

Wet, achy, and cold, all she wanted was to soak in a hot bath, and then wrap up in a downy comforter with a cup of hot tea and a book. She wanted to forget the river and the impending flood that could destroy her home, the lack of communication from her boss, and most of all, that scene with Rick and Chase at the store.

Instead, she needed to make dinner and wait until Rick returned to help her talk to Ben. She faced a long night ahead.

"That's the last of it," Rick said, tossing his shovel into the back of the truck. He arched his back and rubbed his neck.

Cayme wished she could do something to ease his tiredness, except that was the prerogative of a real fiancée. Not her.

"Thanks for your help, man." Ben slapped a hand across his buddy's back.

Oddly enough, her brother seemed unaffected by the rain or the hard labor. In fact, he looked invigorated—ready to tackle another pile of sand.

"I can't believe I'm shoveling this crap after leaving that sandbox last year." He gazed out over the river. "The difference is I'm not doing it in a hundred and fifteen degrees and dodging bullets."

Ben sounded as if he hadn't minded all that backbreaking labor. In fact, he almost sounded like he was joking about his time in the Middle East. Maybe this was another sign he was coping better.

"I know what you mean." Rick gestured to the stack. "I hope these bags are enough." He looked up at the clearing skies. "I can get more sand tomorrow if we need it. By the looks of the clouds, this will be the last of the rain tonight."

Cayme followed Rick's gaze to the parting clouds that let a hint of sky peek through.

The setting sun had turned the clouds to a dusky rose. It did indeed look like the storm was done for the night. The air hadn't warmed up much, which meant the snowpack might melt more slowly. The slower the snow melted, the less likely the river would flood. The forecast called for clearer skies but cooler than normal temperatures. Maybe, if they were really, really lucky, they wouldn't have to use the sandbags.

She could always hope the huge snowstorm predicted at the end of the week would fizzle out before it reached their little valley. She wouldn't care if the Memorial Day ski weekend was ruined. She'd even take a hit on the coffee shop business if it meant the house was safe from flooding.

"I need to get the boys home to clean up and to make some dinner," Rick said, closing the tailgate.

"I'll let them know you're ready." Cayme wished for a way to prolong his stay, but he promised to be back and he'd keep his word.

Rick hopped in the truck and started the engine.

"Give me your shovel," Ben said to Cayme, holding out his hand. "I'll put it away." He took her shovel and strode around the back of the house.

Before she reached the house, Adam and Joey opened the front door and hurried outside.

"You're done?" Adam asked. "We got all warmed up and came back out to help."

"Just finished," Cayme said. "Your dad's ready to leave." She pointed to the truck.

"'Kay!" Both boys took off running.

"See you later, Aunt Cayme," Adam called. "I'll probably be at the store tomorrow."

"Right," Cayme replied. After everything that had happened, she'd nearly forgotten about Adam helping at the store. "Bye." She waved as the boys climbed inside the truck.

Rick backed out of the yard. He stopped a few feet away and rolled down the driver's window. "I'll see you later."

She nodded, not sure what to say. They'd discuss the crazy situation with Ben and, hopefully repair any damage before it grew out of hand.

Rick looked at her for a long moment then rolled up the window and drove off.

He always seemed to be moving away from her. Cayme sighed and turned toward the house. What did it matter? She didn't have a claim on the man.

Ben stood on the front porch looking at her with an odd expression. Suspicion, maybe? He didn't say anything though, just turned and went inside.

She followed him, the warm air welcome after being in the chilly, wet rain. Regardless of the warmth, the knots in her stomach tightened as she thought about what she faced later that night. Sighing, she kicked off her shoes and slid them next to Ben's work boots, grateful he'd remembered to remove them before tracking mud through the house.

In the living room, the TV played a sitcom rerun. Ben walked over and picked up the remote. He turned it off. "What did Rick mean by he'll see you later?"

Heat prickled over her cold skin. She had to wait to tell her brother what had transpired at the store; it would be better if he heard it from her and Rick together. "Um… Rick has something he wants to discuss with us. He'll be over after he's fed Adam."

"Why didn't you just invite them to stay for dinner and talk about it now?"

"Because the boys were wet and cold. We're wet and cold. And I want to clean up first." She wished Rick could've stuck around, but he was right to protect his son. Adam didn't need to know about this confusing adult business. She headed for the stairs. "I'm claiming the first shower and then how about the leftover meatloaf for dinner?"

Ben watched her for a moment, then a look dawned on his face and he swore. "You're selling the house, aren't you?" His questions stopped her on the first step.

She stared at him, stunned to see the hurt on his face, like a big, wounded teddy bear. "I thought you didn't care if I sold? You told me to make the decision."

He ran his fingers through his cropped, wet hair. "I don't care. I just don't understand why Rick's over here helping fill sandbags and repairing the roof if you're selling."

"I haven't made up my mind yet."

"Then why is Rick coming over?"

A loud knock sounded at the door. A rush of relief made her sag against the banister. "Maybe he decided not to wait. That's probably him now." She crossed the living room, aware of Ben right behind her. She paused and took a breath, ready to face the music.

When she opened the door, the greeting for Rick died on her lips. "Mayor Nicholson!"

"Hello, Cayme," the mayor said. "I came by in

person to offer my congratulations."

She cocked her head. "For what?"

"Why for your engagement to Rick Morrison, of course." He beamed. "I just heard, and I couldn't be happier. May I come in?"

Chapter Nine

Rick set a plate of grilled cheese sandwiches on the table and returned to the stove to pull the pan of tomato soup off before it burned. After all these years of cooking for himself and Adam, he still had trouble maintaining the correct temperatures on the stove. If he wasn't careful, he'd have to put cooking pots on his birthday wish list. Maybe his sister would take pity on him and stock his kitchen. Again. He was down to his last soup pot.

Adam wandered in from the office where he'd been doing his schoolwork, away from the distraction of the bedroom toys. "Is dinner ready?"

"Just about," Rick said. "Did you finish your homework?"

"Yeah. The teacher didn't give us very much."

"Good job. Wash up. I'm setting dinner on the table now."

Adam crossed to the sink and turned on the water. At eight years old, his son was taller than Rick had been at that age. At this rate, his son would be shaving before he reached thirteen. He hoped not. Cracking voices, growth spurts, and that special teenage-boy odor were challenges Rick wasn't ready for. Not to mention mood swings, need for sleep, rebellion…and, oh yeah, girls.

Rick never had much luck in the girls category until he'd enlisted in the Army. Something about being away from home and on his own had made him want to search out female companionship. Prematurely as it turned out. The result was a twelve-month marriage and Adam. He wouldn't give up Adam for the world, but most days he wished an ex-Mrs. Morrison wasn't in the picture. Adam deserved a mother—not someone who barely remembered her son's birthday.

He still hadn't told Adam about Roxanne's plans to visit. He tried to put himself in his son's shoes. Did Adam need a maternal presence to sooth a void? He'd never really said much about not having a mother around. At least not to Rick. Maybe he'd said something to Roxanne during one of those rare phone calls. Was that why she suddenly showed interest in her son?

Her need to serve in the military was strong, maybe even stronger than his had been. It didn't matter that she'd been born with a trust fund assuring she'd never have to work a day in her life. Maybe she was getting pressure from her family to reconnect with her child. That image was as unpleasant as her impending visit. He had full custody. However, he also knew how important family was. For Adam's sake, he wished Roxanne was more like his sister, or even Cayme. A person who wanted kids and a family.

He pictured Cayme's face. Her kind eyes had brightened while Adam talked about working in the store. Rick had no doubt she would make a great mother. Then he recalled her stormy eyes after his stupid announcement. He had no idea how to clean up that mess. He knew he had to try. Later. Once he'd fulfilled his parental duties—a job he loved more than anything else.

He poured the soup into bowls and placed them on the table. The warm aroma of grilled bread made his stomach rumble. Then he stepped behind Adam and squeezed a sturdy shoulder. "Quit growing so fast, bud."

Adam gave him a crooked grin and tossed the towel on the counter. "If I don't grow up, I can't take over your business once you get old like Granddad."

Rick chucked the boy's chin. "Hey, it's a long time before I'm that old, and you can fill my shoes."

"Those boats?"

"Those boats can still kick your butt." He tapped Adam's backside to prove his point. "Now, let's eat."

They sat at the table and Adam scooped a spoonful of soup into his mouth then reached for a sandwich. "Did you think some more about me helping at the bookstore? Is it okay?"

Rick took a drink of water before answering. "I still need to make a decision, bud. I've had a few other things on my mind." Like how to make things right for Cayme and her brother after his wild announcement. "I'm curious why you went to the store for a book, instead of the library?"

"Um…" Adam stirred his soup, studying it as though it held the answer. "I just wanted to see if the store had any new books from the last time I looked."

"I didn't know you'd been in there before." He'd never worried about Adam after school. The safety in the small community was one of the things he loved about living in Blakely. The entire length of Main Street was less than a mile. Rick knew from personal experience it was hard to find mischief and not get caught. It didn't hurt that the chief of police was a good friend and would let Rick know if his son got into any trouble.

Adam looked up from his dinner. "I was there a couple of times with Devon. Mrs. Foster used to let him clean up the back to earn money."

"Doesn't Devon want the job anymore?"

"No." Adam's expression had a slightly guilty look.

"Why not?"

Adam's face turned a little red. "Umm…"

"Did Devon do something he shouldn't have?" Was his son running with a kid who had an inclination for trouble? Although from what he knew of Devon's parents, it seemed unlikely.

"No, Dad." Adam swallowed. "Devon's just afraid to go inside the store since Mrs. Foster died. I told him her ghost wasn't there, but he doesn't believe me." Adam looked down at his food again. "I didn't see anything spooky there today."

Ah. Now Rick understood. Eight-year-old logic and a fear of death. If Devon had known Rachel Foster, her death could be confusing—even frightening. "So, you went into the store to prove ghosts aren't real?"

Adam nodded and took a bite of his cheese sandwich.

"What'd you learn?"

Adam wiped his mouth, leaving bread crumbs in the corner. "Well, the store's not exactly the same as before. Aunt Cayme was there. She's really nice and gave me a root beer. Even though it was cloudy outside, it felt warm and sunny inside."

That last statement brought Rick up short. Adam had pegged Cayme perfectly, and he wondered if his little boy was crushing on a certain redhead. Not that Rick blamed Adam. He had trouble ignoring her attraction as well.

He wondered if he should put a bug in Cayme's ear about the kids' fear of ghosts then backpedaled. He couldn't always grease the path for his son. Better to let him figure out a few things on his own. "Maybe you should tell Devon you didn't see any ghosts. Then he won't be afraid to go into the store."

"I'll tell him at school tomorrow." Adam stirred his soup before spooning some into his mouth. "So is it okay for me to help? I really like that place."

"I'm thinking about it." Rick didn't see any harm in letting his son do a few chores for Skeeter and Cayme. In the meantime, he needed to untangle himself from a fake engagement from the first woman to spark his interest in years.

"Do you believe in ghosts, Dad?" Adam asked with an eight-year-old's persistent imagination.

Rick smiled. "I've never met one. I guess if I did, I'd have to believe in them."

Adam giggled. "Even if Mrs. Foster's ghost was still in the bookstore, she wouldn't hurt anyone. She was too nice."

"She certainly was." Rick pointed his spoon at Adam's bowl. "Now finish up. I've called Misty to come by for a couple of hours tonight. I need to go back over to Cayme and Ben's house and discuss some things."

"I don't need a babysitter," Adam said. "I'll be in fourth grade next year. That's like almost junior high!"

"All the more reason to have someone here. I don't want you to call a bunch of girls and have a party."

Adam's face turned red. "Dad!"

Rick couldn't tell if Adam's embarrassment was from hating girls or if he had a newly developed interest in the opposite sex. He tried to remember how old he'd been when he'd noticed girls as something more than to tease.

"I'll be home before you're in bed. Since your homework's done, you can play a video game." That bribe usually did the trick to keep the whining to a minimum.

"Can Joey come over?"

With that statement Rick knew his kid was still a little boy after all. "Sorry, bud. It's a school night."

****

Cayme gripped the handle on the front door, her knuckles growing whiter by the second. Night air filled the living room while she stared at Mayor Timothy Nicholson with a mix of horror and trepidation.

Ben rushed up next to her and glared at the mayor, who still stood on the front porch. "What are you talking about? My sister isn't engaged." When Ben went into warrior mode, his nostrils flared, and the muscles on his neck stood out, making him seem larger than life.

The mayor took a step back. "I guess it really *was* a secret." He gave Cayme a contrite look. "I didn't realize you hadn't told your own brother."

Cayme wanted to bury her head in the biggest hole she could find until this ugly mess washed away. But that wouldn't happen anytime soon. Instead of preventing a catastrophe, she was stuck doing damage control. Alone. Rick, the culprit who'd started this atrocious rumor, was nowhere around.

"I…" She looked at her brother.

Hurt and betrayal was clearly stamped all over his face.

She wanted to tell him the truth, but that would make Rick sound like a liar. He'd already spouted off the announcement in the bookstore. If the mayor knew, then the news could be all over town by morning. She turned back to Nicholson. "We've kept it a secret because it's too soon after Mom—"

Ben swore. Pivoting on his heel, he marched through the living room and thundered up the stairs.

It took all of Cayme's willpower not to call after him.

She offered the mayor an apologetic look and opened the screen door. "You'd better come in." Her tone was less than welcoming. She sighed. The man had caught her in a hard spot.

He offered a rueful smile and stepped inside. "I really am sorry. I didn't mean to cause trouble for you and your brother."

"I'll deal with it," Cayme said. "I'm sure you didn't drive over here just to offer congratulations." He'd surely come for one reason—to talk her into selling the property. She didn't want to discuss the sale tonight, yet from the grim look on his face, she wouldn't be able to avoid it.

"I have to admit your engagement was a more pleasant topic than the one I originally planned. Or so I thought."

Cayme closed the door and sighed again. "Come in and sit down." She led the way into the front room and gestured to a chair.

Mayor Nicholson removed the jacket proclaiming

his loyalty to the Boise State Broncos and draped it over the back of the chair. He'd dressed casually in jeans and a button-down flannel shirt. His graying hair was neatly trimmed above his ears. He was a handsome man by any standards. However, he was also the mayor and not only wanted her property for the city, he wielded enough influence with the community to affect the future of the bookstore.

She needed to tread carefully and not give him any reason to deny the store's business license when it came due for renewal at the end of the year. "Can I get you something to drink?" One of her mother's favorite sayings was that sugar attracted more bees than vinegar. The problem was sugar also attracted flies and ants. Both were less desirable than bees. Which was the mayor? A honeybee or a fly in her sugar bowl?

"A cup of tea, if it's not too much trouble," he replied.

Cayme raised an eyebrow at the request for the tame drink but refrained from saying anything. She walked into the kitchen, filled the kettle, and placed it on the stove. Surprisingly, the mayor followed her.

"Your mother made the best tea." He sat on the stool next to the counter.

"You had tea with my mother?" Cayme couldn't have been more surprised than if he'd announced he regularly had tea with the President of the United States.

Mayor Nicholson smiled again. "Don't look so shocked. She didn't hate me the way you do."

"I don't…" Cayme stopped and heat warmed her face. "I guess I've been a little stubborn with the city council."

His head tilted and a teasing look crossed his face. "Just a little bit, eh?"

She lowered her gaze. "Okay. A lot." Lifting her chin, she added, "But with good reason. Mom wasn't even gone a week when one of those vultures started twisting my arm to sign the papers."

"Councilman Peters." The mayor grimaced. "I'm sorry about that. I didn't realize what he'd done until you stormed into my office to complain. He had no business coming to your house so soon after the funeral."

"This visit is ahead of the deadline, too," she reminded him. "I've read the contracts. I have until the end of the month. I could use some space until I've made the decision."

He shook his head. "I'm not here to hassle you about the property. But if you have questions about the contract, and what we plan to do, I'll be happy to go through the details that I covered with your mother."

That statement gave her pause. "Then why are you here? And please don't say it's just to congratulate me." That would be worse, considering the engagement was a fake.

"No. Like I said, it did give me a good excuse to stop by." He looked uncomfortable all of a sudden. "This is more of a personal visit."

"Personal?"

He looked ready to say more, but the whistle on the teakettle blew at that moment, interrupting him.

Cayme pulled it off the heat. She set out the tea canister and selected a couple of tea bags. After pouring water over one of the bags, she handed a cup to him.

He took it and held it in his hands as if curling his

body around it for warmth. He suddenly looked lost…alone. "I miss Rachel. I wondered if I came by…" He didn't finish the sentence. Instead, he lifted the cup and stared into the liquid for a long time as though reading tea leaves that didn't exist.

Cayme nearly dropped the sugar bowl at his unsaid comment. "What are you saying?"

He looked up, his eyes bright.

She set down the sugar, walked around the counter, and sat on the stool next to him. "You? And my mother?"

Nodding, he said, "She was a good friend. She was there after my wife died last year. When I needed someone who understood what I was going through. She had amazing insight and compassion."

Cayme swallowed. "You and Mom…dated?"

"No." He shook his head. "I wanted to, but your mother… She said the gossip would compromise my position. In spite of that, she never turned me away whenever I stopped by for a visit. She was very discreet."

More than discreet. Her mother had never mentioned the mayor in any of her e-mails or phone calls.

When she took ill, Cayme had made arrangements for an extended leave of absence and came home at once. Those days were filled with hospital visits and caregiving. Many nights were a blur as she slept in the chair next to her mother's bed. No mention was ever made of Mayor Nicholson or his friendship with Mom.

The disease was devastating, the way it ate away at her mother's mind and sucked life from her body. The cancer took her so quickly, Cayme barely had time to arrange her mother's affairs before she was gone.

The mayor had come by to visit her once, but her mother hadn't recognized him, and he'd left.

The next time Cayme saw him was at the funeral. Most of the town had been there, so she didn't think it odd for the mayor to attend.

Cayme recalled the day he'd come to the house to visit and realized he'd seemed more upset than she'd expect from just an acquaintance. But she'd been so caught up in her own grief she'd chalked up his reaction to a failure to conclude his business before her mother passed.

But now…in retrospect… Cayme looked at him again.

"I loved her." He bowed his head slightly as he removed the tea bag and stirred in a spoonful of sugar. "She must have known about the disease or had an idea that something was wrong. She never offered a concrete explanation for refusing my requests to go out—even for an evening meal. Not that it mattered. I cherished her friendship. It meant as much, if not more, to me than anything else I've had for a long time."

"I'm sorry," Cayme offered. "I didn't know."

"You had your mother to take care of. You didn't need a grieving old man hanging around."

"Why are you telling me this now?"

He swirled the tea in his cup for a moment then looked over at her. "The town hall meeting is next week to discuss options for the new park. I expect you'll want to be there."

"Of course. What does this have to do with my mother?"

"It's likely some busybody will say something

about our friendship and make hints about something more…or worse. Some may imply that I took advantage of a sweet woman, with a heart of gold, in her final hours."

"Did you?"

"No. Never." He shook his head. "But I know how it will look. I wanted you to hear the truth from me. Not from some gossip that will twist our beautiful friendship into something ugly."

"I suppose I can understand that."

He took a deep breath and then sipped his tea. He seemed to savor it for a moment, then offered a sad smile. "Not as good as your mother's but close."

The mayor's charm and charisma surely garnered votes at election time. But his honesty was coated with melancholy and heartache at her mother's absence.

"She loved you, Cayme. You and Ben. She would never make you choose between what you wanted and what she wanted for you." He took another sip. "She wanted you home for a long time, and you were with her at the end. That's a gift not many people get in this lifetime. Cherish those moments and the memories you have of her."

"And yet, you—" She gestured toward him. "—the whole town wants me to give up the memories. This house is the one thing I—Ben and I—have left."

"Unfortunately, I'm afraid we're asking you to do exactly that."

"If I decide against selling, I'll be ostracized by the community. It'll hurt Skeeter and the business."

"I didn't say this would be easy. Only *you* can decide what's best." He took a final swallow of tea and then stood and walked over to the kitchen sink. He rinsed the cup and put it on the sideboard.

His movements made Cayme think he'd done it many times before.

When he turned, he gave her a smile. "Thanks for the tea. And again, congratulations to both you and Rick. Your mother would be very pleased."

Chapter Ten

Cayme closed the front door behind the mayor and took a deep breath. The revelation that he and her mother had been in a relationship seemed so improbable. After listening to him, it sounded as though the man had a bad case of unrequited love. She wondered if Skeeter had known about the pair. Had Ben known?

She glanced at the stairs where Ben had disappeared after the mayor's untimely arrival.

As if her thoughts conjured him up, Ben's bare feet appeared at the top of the stairs. He slowly descended until he reached the last step, where he stopped, waiting. "Is the mayor gone?" He'd changed into dry clothes.

Nodding, she stayed beside the door, unsure of Ben's mood and whether to confront him about the information she'd just learned.

"Did he tell you about him and Mom?"

She let go the breath she'd been holding. Okay, so Rachel and Timothy Nicholson were not news to her brother. "Why didn't you ever say anything?"

Ben shrugged. "No point. Nothing ever happened." He stepped off the last stair. "It's not like she was marrying him or anything. Like he told you, they were just friends."

"You were listening?"

He nodded and regret shone in his expression. "Look, when Nicholson congratulated you… I shouldn't have reacted like that. It just took me by surprise."

"Ben, I can explain about me and Rick—"

He held up a hand. "No. Let me finish." He clenched his fists then buried them in his front jean pockets, making his broad shoulders hunch. "I've done a lot of soul-searching lately, and I need to tell you something."

A shiver raced down her spine. "What?" She wasn't sure she was strong enough to take more bad news tonight and remained frozen in her spot beside the door. The entire living room separated her and her brother. She wondered if she'd ever be able to bridge the gap that had grown between them. Was it even possible?

Ben hadn't budged from the foot of the stairs either, as though he'd found an escape route he was unwilling to abandon. He took a deep breath. "I've been selfish to let you carry all the responsibility since Mom died. I'm sorry. I was shocked about the engagement, so I reacted badly. But honest, I'm really happy for you and Rick."

That was the last thing she expected to hear. She didn't know how to respond. Too many things chased around her brain. The mayor, her mom, and the not-so-small matter of Ben believing that she and Rick were engaged. "Look, Ben, the engagement is—" A knock sounded at the front door again. She started at the sound. "What now?" Exasperated at another interruption, she turned and flung open the door.

Rick stood on the porch.

She almost sagged in relief. Thank goodness. At least she could clear up one of her problems.

"Hey," he said. "Is this a good time?"

Ben hurried across the room. He joined Cayme in the doorway—a huge grin on his face. "Hey, man!" He opened the screen and shook Rick's hand. "Come on in, you sneaky dog! I hear congratulations are in order!"

Rick entered the living room, throwing an accusing look at Cayme, as if she'd deliberately chosen to perpetuate the farce he'd started.

She opened her mouth to deny Ben's words, but her brother was talking again.

"I just found out that you and Cayme are engaged. It sort of freaked me out at first. But honestly, man, I was just telling Cay that I couldn't be happier for you both. Everything is starting to take a turn for the better."

At seeing Ben's enthusiasm, Cayme's denial evaporated in her mouth. How long since she'd seen her brother genuinely happy? Months? Longer? How could she take that away by telling him the engagement wasn't real?

Rick's eyes narrowed and he looked over Ben's shoulder at her.

She shook her head, sending a subliminal plea to help her get through this without destroying Ben.

An expression crossed Rick's face that she couldn't quite interpret. He gave her a wink then turned his attention back to Ben. The smile on his face looked genuine.

Her tummy pitched in response.

He clapped Ben's shoulder. "Thanks, Bro. I'm relieved that you're not upset."

Oh dear. That was so not what she'd meant by her

silent message.

Ben grinned sheepishly. "Well, I have to admit when Mayor Nicholson stopped by and congratulated Cayme, I was upset at first. I still don't know how he knew before I did. But while he was telling Cayme about Mom, I realized how unfair I was to judge. Particularly, when I'd never said anything to her about Mom and the mayor. But you two…" His hand waggled between her and Rick. "I totally understand why you wouldn't want anyone to get the wrong idea so soon after Mom died." Ben turned to Cayme. "I'm really sorry I blew up. I'm still working on my temper. But it'll get better. I promise."

Cayme didn't know what to say. Her brother's good wishes and kind words stunned her. Shame and embarrassment warred with a fierce desire to keep Ben's happiness intact. If her feet hadn't been frozen to the floor, she would've raced out of the room, out of the house, and back to Seattle to avoid destroying that look of happiness on his face. Yet, after his candid revelation, it was unfair to let him believe she and Rick were engaged. She had to tell him the truth.

Rick stepped beside Cayme and curled his arm around her shoulder.

His warmth comforted her, but his spicy musk scent did something entirely different. A twist of longing rolled through her, and she swallowed hard. Twice now, in less than twelve hours, she'd found herself inside his protective, almost possessive, embrace. It felt good to let someone else bear the burden, if only for a second.

"Mind if I have a private word with your sister?" he asked Ben.

"Of course not! Take your time. I'll get out of your way."

Ben reached out and squeezed Cayme in a bear hug that took her totally by surprise. Maybe he really was improving.

"I'll start dinner," he said, breaking free and turning toward the kitchen. "When you two lovers are done, I want to hear all the details."

Rick started to lead Cayme toward a corner in the living room. Instead, she grabbed his hand, led him into the office, and shut the door.

"Haven't you had dinner?"

"Really? You want to discuss dinner? That's the least of my problems," she ground out with a hiss. "We have to tell Ben the truth." As much as she hated wiping the happiness off her brother's face, she hated herself even more for this deception.

"How did he find out? And what's this about Mayor Nicholson and your mom?"

"This entire night has been one mess after another." She rubbed her temples to ease the headache building behind her eyes. "Mayor Nicholson came by right after you left. The first thing out of his mouth was congratulations to us on our engagement. And of course, Ben was standing right there." She swallowed the sudden lump in her throat. "He lost it."

"The mayor congratulated us?"

"Us? There is no *us*." She shook her head. "And no. He came over to warn me about the town council meeting next week." She went on to tell him about the mayor's relationship with Rachel.

"Wow," Rick said. "That was some secret. Ben knew, but you didn't?"

"I had no idea." She paced to the other side of the office and leaned against the old desk her father had bought before she was born. She loved that desk, worn and used, and every fiber of wood was filled with memories of her parents. Right now, she just needed the support. "You've got to help me straighten this thing out."

"You saw him out there," Rick said. "What would it hurt if he believes if we're engaged?"

"It's a *lie*, Rick. That's what will hurt."

He seemed to be staring hard at her mouth again. She swallowed at the sudden dryness on her tongue and resisted the urge to moisten her lips.

"Are you seeing anyone?"

Cayme stiffened, as if she'd been shot. "Why would you ask that?"

He shrugged. "I need to know if I'm stepping on any toes."

"Wait. What? I've been working days at the store and nights here at home to keep up with my job back in Seattle." She pushed off the desk toward him. "I don't have time for a private life, let alone a social life."

His eyebrows disappeared under the lock of hair that constantly fell over his forehead, as though he was working through a problem. Then he crossed to the chair next to the desk and sat. "What about Seattle? Is there anyone there? You sure you're not involved?"

"Hardly." She snorted. "I barely have time to see my own family these days."

He cocked his head, studying her for a moment.

Feeling a bit like one of Adam's worms under a microscope, her heart gave a strange little bump. When he didn't say anything more, she lifted her arms and then dropped them in exasperation. "My last serious relationship was the bozo you met at the store today. And that ended five years ago."

By his crinkled brow and serious eyes, Rick was thinking hard on something.

She'd seen that look on his face before. The one she remembered most clearly was during his graduation ceremony. She'd sat next to her mother on the hardback chairs at Ben's and Rick's high school graduation, knowing in her heart this was the last time she'd have a chance to just stare at Rick, unobserved, for a very long time. The following week, he and Ben left for Army boot camp. She'd wondered if she'd see either of them again, given the war raging in the Middle East.

His expression cleared and his brown eyes grew warm. "What if we made the engagement real?"

Cayme reached for a chair and sat before her legs gave out. "Are you out of your mind?"

Rick laughed—a hollow sound in the little office. "Occasionally. I don't think so this time."

"Why would you want to perpetuate a fake engagement?"

"It wouldn't be fake if we made it real." His voice was as serious as his gaze.

She shook her head. "You're not really asking me to marry you. You don't love me." She stopped short of saying she didn't love him. She'd always had this stupid crush, and that wasn't real love. "Wait a minute!" She glared at him. "Is this about the property?"

"No." He blinked, looking confused for a moment. "No. Of course not. Why would you think that?"

Cayme splayed her hands open. "Because I can't

think of one good reason why you'd want to be married to me."

"Is it so hard to believe I find you attractive?"

That took the wind out of her sails. "Really?"

"You must not look in the mirror very often." He stood and stepped closer to her, forcing her to look up at him. "You're right. This isn't about some sudden, newfound love." He swallowed. "I just think, for now, an engagement could be a mutually beneficial arrangement." He placed a warm hand on her shoulders. "You've seen what it's done for Ben."

At his touch, some of the fight went out of her. He was right. Ben seemed so happy for them. Could this be the thing that would bring him back from his dark nightmares?

"He's my best friend," Rick said. "This is the closest to normal I've seen him since his last tour. I should have been able to protect him better, but then we were assigned to different units. After Adam was born, I didn't reenlist. I couldn't do anything about—"

"What happened to my brother isn't your fault. You can't blame yourself."

"I blame myself for convincing him to join the army with me."

Cayme shook her head, refusing to let Rick carry any guilt. "He made the choice. You didn't twist his arm."

"Of course not. He's my best friend and stood beside me while we took an oath to defend this country." Rick swallowed. "Now, I want to return the favor."

"So, you're doing this for Ben?"

"And for you."

She stood, forcing Rick to take a step back and let go of her. A chill took the place of his warm hand. "I don't understand. How does a fake engagement help me?"

"It's not fake." Rick sighed. "Not if you agree to make it real." A slight smile played around his mouth.

"You find this funny?" Nothing that had happened that night had any humor in it.

"Not funny. But I think I'll enjoy finding out things about you I never knew."

That statement didn't ease her apprehension. "Give me one good reason we should make this engagement real."

"Okay." He paused. "I'll give you three. First off, you can save face with Chase Peters. I picked up on the tension between you two at the bookstore. I don't know what happened for you to call off the wedding, but I'm fairly certain he wasn't the man for you. Besides, if the mayor knows, so does half the town by now."

She scowled. "And whose fault is that?"

At least he had the grace to look guilty.

"I never said I wasn't taking the blame. But you believe the town knows by now, right?"

That was an understatement, the entire county probably knew by now. If the park project wasn't on the table, no one would even care. She took a breath. Facing the good people of Blakely would be hard, but she'd deal with the fallout. "Everyone will think I'm a flake, but that's nothing new. I'm not running away again." She waved a hand between them. "You'll have to do better than that. What's reason number two?"

"The property."

She stiffened. "You said this wasn't about the

property."

"Hold on." He held his hands in front of him as if he was warding off an attack. "I'm not after the property. I've just had a feeling you aren't planning to sell. Am I right?"

"I don't know." The promise she'd made to her mom was becoming harder to keep, but she needed to do what she could if possible.

"Well, while you make up your mind, this will show the council that I'm on your side. Having me vested in you will keep them off your back. I meant what I said on Sunday. The decision is yours. Don't let anyone sway you—not even me."

"Wouldn't it be more likely that the town will think you've proposed just to get your hands on the land? They might start hounding you."

"I'm a big boy and pretty sure I can handle it."

She chewed on that for a moment. He didn't need to point out his manly attributes. She'd managed to spot those all on her own. "And the third?"

Rick nodded toward the closed door. "Ben."

That was the clincher. "He's really happy for us."

"Happier than I've seen him for a long time. Have you considered that maybe he's been feeling responsible for you?"

She jerked in surprise. "Not really. Just before you came by, he said he was sorry about all the responsibility he'd dumped on me. Before that, I thought he didn't care about the house."

"Well, I don't need any more proof that our engagement is a good thing for him. I don't want to take that away."

Neither did Cayme but she still couldn't see how

this arrangement was a good idea. "What do you get out of this?"

He seemed to hesitate before answering. Then he took a step closer and stared into her eyes. "I get a bit of protection, too."

"From what?" How could being engaged to her protect him?

"From my ex."

"Oh." Cayme knew very little about Rick's ex-wife. He'd gotten married, had his son, and then divorced, all before she graduated from college. The ceremony had been quick. His family had flown back east to witness the marriage. Sherry had told her how pretty Rick's wife was but that he'd only married her out of his obligation to the baby. At the time, Cayme had been proud that he'd taken responsibility for his child's mother. At the same time, she'd felt bereft—all hope of ever becoming Mrs. Rick Morrison was lost. And now look where she stood. If she pinched herself, would she wake up and find this was all some sort of bizarre nightmare?

A knock sounded at the door, making Cayme jump.

"Hey you two!" Ben called. "Are you staying the night in there? If so, just say the word and I'll toss in some pillows and blankets."

"We'll be out in a minute, buddy," Rick called. He turned back to her. "What do you say, Cayme Foster? Will you marry me?"

****

As proposals went, it wasn't the most romantic. But, like Cayme said earlier, this wasn't about love, simply a mutually beneficial arrangement. Rick hadn't exactly considered all the consequences before Ben sprung his congratulatory enthusiasm on them, yet the more he contemplated it, the more it seemed like they could make this deal work.

He couldn't deny his attraction to Cayme. She was pretty. More than that, whenever he was near her, that tightness in his chest seemed to unravel a little more each time. He was glad to learn she wasn't dating anyone. She was smart and seemed to like Adam. Of course, she'd make a great mother. If they took this engagement all the way and she wanted to have children of her own, he wasn't opposed to that idea. He knew her family and her background because they'd known each other since they were kids. In those few years he'd been gone, and she'd been away in Seattle, she'd changed from the girl next door to an incredible woman. And now, he wanted to learn more about that woman.

The idea of being engaged to Cayme Foster was definitely growing on him. And having a buffer between him and Roxanne wasn't a bad thing either.

"What do you say?" he asked again. "It's not like we're strangers. Our families have known each other for a long time. You're single. I'm single—" He left the statement hanging, waiting for her response.

Cayme blinked, as though she was returning from a long distance. "It won't work. Your sister and dad will know it's not real. Skeeter already knows you were just protecting me. We can't keep that truth from Ben. And what about Adam? This is a lie. We can't lie to your son. It will make things worse."

He considered her words, and the logic and truth behind them. She was right, of course. Except he couldn't shake the feeling that this engagement was a good idea. He took a deep breath and held it a moment. "Okay, you've got several valid points. I'll explain to Adam that we're dating and getting to know each other better. He'll understand that." He gestured to the door. "On the other hand, Ben's waiting, so why don't we just go out there and tell him we made a big mistake. You know what it will do to him." He shrugged. "I'll support you, whatever you decide."

She stared at the closed door. Indecision crept into her eyes, tinged with a touch of fear and sadness too.

That protective feeling washed over him. "Or how about this? How about we tell your brother the truth—that I foolishly jumped in with both feet to rescue you from Peters by announcing our engagement. And after discussing it over tonight, we realized this is a good thing for both of us. It may have started out as a fake, but it's real now."

Her gaze swung to his face. A tiny light of hope—of gratitude—gleamed in the depths of her blue eyes.

Stepping closer, he captured her shoulders. She quivered under his touch. He wanted to wrap his arms around her and shield her from every single worry in her world. He couldn't do that, but he could offer to bear some of her burdens. "Say yes, Cayme." He lowered his head.

When he left the house that evening, his intention had been to help Cayme with damage control after what happened at the bookstore. He'd figured they would need to smooth things over with Ben. But at this very moment, all he could think of was how soft her mouth would feel under his.

The kiss was brief. A tender pressure as he captured her gasp of surprise. Her lips were cool and smooth, and unexpectedly firm. Unlike his earlier kiss, a burst of need bloomed in his chest and he let his tongue brush the seam of her lips. She tasted like cherry bubble gum. She didn't open for him. If she had, they might not leave this room.

A spurt of pure male satisfaction filled him at the needy, lusty look in her eyes. It took all his control not to kiss the daylights out of her. Right there. Right then. He cleared his throat. "Ben's waiting. One way or another, we'll have to face him," he said softly. "I think we can make this work to our mutual advantage. What do you say?"

"Okay," she whispered. "On one condition."

He raised an eyebrow. "What's that?" he asked cautiously, not agreeing outright to any conditions.

"Engagements are trial periods," she said with a hint of cynicism. "That's how we'll approach this. I've learned from experience that a lot of things can go wrong before…the wedding." She swallowed. "So, no wedding date. No talk of a wedding at all. This is totally an engagement of convenience."

"No wedding. Got it. A trial period it is." That's all he was asking for. Just until Roxanne had tired of whatever game she was playing and was gone from his and Adam's life.

Cayme took a deep breath, straightened her spine as though she were going into battle, and then opened the office door.

Ben stood on the other side, looking concerned. His gaze bounced between Rick and Cayme, and his frown grew deeper. "Is everything okay?"

Cayme shook her head. "There's something you need to know about our engagement," she said. "Rick and I need to clarify what happened." She brushed past him and headed into the living room.

Ben stepped in front of Rick, blocking him from leaving the office. "What did you do to her?" He seemed to bristle, as if any spark might set him off.

They were the same age. Stood the same height. But Ben outweighed Rick by at least twenty pounds. Having recently returned from active duty, he hadn't lost all that hard muscle that came from day-to-day living in a war zone.

"It's okay, Ben," Rick said to calm him down. "I'll take good care of her. But like she said, we need to explain a few things." Rick held his ground and sidestepped around the man who'd been his best friend growing up. Hopefully they would still be friends after this. If Ben wanted to wipe the floor with him, it would be no contest.

Ben eyed him with suspicion but didn't punch him.

Rick crossed the living room to join Cayme on the couch.

Ben perched on the armrest of the recliner and stared at them like he was scoping out the enemy. "Okay, spill. Why don't you two look like a happily engaged couple?"

Rick picked up Cayme's hand. Whoa, it was ice cold. She was more worried than she'd let on. He silently vowed he wouldn't let her down. He cleared his throat. "Our engagement is a bit more recent than you think."

He relayed to Ben what happened at the bookstore, explaining that he couldn't help but step in to protect Cayme by telling Peters they were engaged.

"That bum." Ben stood, fists clenched, angry

muscles bunching under his shirt as he spat out a couple more expletives. "So, the engagement's not real?"

"Not then," Rick confirmed. "But I've made it real tonight. I just asked Cayme to marry me."

Ben turned his intense gaze on his sister. "Is this true?"

She nodded.

Her hand trembled in Rick's.

"Are you doing this because of your old crush on Rick?"

Rick stared at Cayme, watching her cheeks turn pink. How had he not known about a crush? Why hadn't his sister ever said anything? Surely, Sherry had known.

"I… no." She shook her head.

The expression in her eyes wasn't convincing.

"Because if it is, you're way beyond schoolgirl crushes, Cay." Ben sounded more like the older brother he was.

"Take it easy, Ben," Rick said. "I might be a bit slow when it comes to seeing a good thing, but I really like your sister."

"*Liking* isn't the same thing as loving," Ben said. "You're my best friend, Rick. I don't want to see you hurt any more than my sister. That doesn't make me the bad guy, does it?"

"No, you're the best brother a girl could have." Cayme gave Rick a tentative smile. "I like Rick, too. That's a better foundation than I had with Chase. I look back on that time and realize I was in love with the idea of marriage, not the man."

Ben swore. "I hated that guy. I still hate him. Why couldn't he just leave you alone?" He looked at Rick then at Cayme. "If he hadn't messed with you this wouldn't have happened."

"I'm past that," Cayme said. "Right now, we have to deal with the present. By tomorrow, most the town will believe Rick and I are engaged. Think of Rick's son. Adam won't understand the deception. Making this real is a good thing. For everyone."

"I don't know." Ben frowned at them. "I was really happy for you two. Now it just feels like a disaster waiting to happen."

"You can still be happy for us." She looked at Rick, her expression showing a firm commitment. "I've accepted Rick's proposal. We're engaged, that's all. We're not in any rush to plan a wedding."

Hearing Cayme's words, something foreign filled Rick's chest. Maybe not quite the love that Ben alluded to, but the swell of admiration and respect was something he couldn't ignore. His smile had almost as much relief as happiness. "Thank you," he whispered. "Like I promised Ben, I'll take good care of you." The words were simple and heartfelt.

They faced Ben again.

His gaze bounced between her and Rick, his expression softening. Finally, he turned to his sister. "Okay. You're engaged. I'll roll with that for now. But I know you. Even though you just made one of the biggest decisions of your life, you'll be up at the crack of dawn tomorrow, opening the store. No time for celebrating tonight." Suddenly, he broke out in a huge smile. Almost as big as the one he'd greeted Rick with earlier at the door. "I'm taking you both out for dinner this weekend to celebrate." He pushed off his chair and then scrunched between them on the couch, wrapping them both in a hug. "We'll do this up right."

Chapter Eleven

The couch barely held all three of them, but circled in Ben's arms, Cayme knew she and Rick had passed a major hurdle. Not only did her brother seem more at ease since first hearing the news, he seemed less tense in general. She saw a glimpse of the old Ben.

The tension eased at the base of her neck. If he could take this unexpected shocking news in stride, then he must be getting better. And he was in their corner. Maybe once everyone else learned she and Rick were taking things slow, any speculation about their sudden engagement would die down. In actuality, an engagement was too soon after her mother's passing. Plus, she wanted to protect Ben against the masses who might question him about her and Rick.

By making the outlandish announcement, Rick was once again offering protection. But he liked her—respected her. And that was more than she ever had from Chase.

Smiling at her brother's relaxed face, she took a deep breath. She could do this. Go out on a couple of dates to keep up appearances. Then when the time was right, she could break it off. Or Rick could.

He'd go back to his world. And Cayme…well she'd figure something out. This arrangement was for appearances. She wasn't about to march down the aisle into a loveless marriage. She'd faced that prospect before and had chosen to walk away. Once in this lifetime was enough.

Rick extracted himself from Ben's hug and stood.

Ben gave her shoulder another squeeze and stood too. He put out his hand and Rick shook it in that brother-in-arms way they had.

"Thanks for understanding, man," Rick said. "I'm glad you're onboard with this."

"I understand, all right," Ben said, grabbing Rick with his other arm. "But you understand this too. If you hurt her, I'll break both your knees." He let go of Rick and looked between them to show he was serious.

Rick glanced down at Cayme and gave her a wink. "We'll be fine."

Cayme's stomach gave a little lurch. She hoped Rick was right. Maybe a marriage based on mutual respect was worth more than one based on love these days. Not that they… No, they weren't really going through with it. She got to her feet. "Yes, we will be fine. Just fine."

Rick extracted himself from Ben's grasp and took her hand. "I know leaving right now looks bad, but I need to get home. I told the babysitter I wouldn't be long." His expression was somewhat subdued. "I should break this news to Adam tonight before he goes to bed. I don't want him to hear about it in school tomorrow."

A twinge of guilt sent a cold chill over her. Was any of this fair to Rick's adorable little boy? Surely Rick knew how his own son would react. "Tell Adam I said hello. And if there's anything you think I should do…whatever you think he needs, I'm here for him." She smiled and dropped her gaze briefly. "For both of you."

Rick studied her a moment, an unreadable expression in his eyes. "Thank you. That means a lot to me."

Those simple words rode an arrow straight to her heart. "He's a great kid." She let go of his hand and ducked her head to hide the rush of heat to her face. Crossing in front of the couch ahead of Rick, she said, "I'll walk you to the door."

Outside, they stood on the porch in an awkward silence. She didn't know what more to say or do. That kiss Rick had given her in the office replayed through her mind.

Their first kiss. No. Their second.

Still, the instant his lips touched hers she'd frozen like a statue. Inside everything seemed to combust— every nerve on fire. And yet, she hadn't been able to respond. What was wrong with her? And if he kissed her now would the same thing happen?

He gazed out over the yard and then looked up at the sky.

Stars peeked through the thinning clouds, promising a night without storms.

"I've been thinking I'll let Adam work in the store." He faced her. "If it's still okay with you."

"Of course." She shifted her weight from one foot to the other and clasped her elbows. "It will give us a chance to get to know each other better."

One side of Rick's mouth lifted in a crooked smile. "Right. A trial period all around." He brought his hand up to stroke her hair. "We can make this work, if we really try."

"It's a lot to get my head around. I wasn't even

sure I was staying in town until just this morning." She glanced back at the house. "I definitely can't leave now. This change in Ben is remarkable. I can't abandon him."

Rick frowned. "Since you stopped the sale of the house, I thought you'd decided to stay. Are you certain there's no one waiting for you in Seattle?"

She shook her head. "Just my job and my roommates. I guess it's time they found another roomie."

"I'm glad you're staying." With that, he leaned in and gave her a peck on the corner of her mouth.

It happened so fast she didn't have a chance to react.

A moment later, he was climbing into his truck. "See you tomorrow," he called.

The taillights of his truck disappeared around the street corner before Cayme snapped out of her stupor. She should have asked how she could help Adam deal with the engagement. Even more than Ben, she didn't want that little boy hurt by their decision.

For now, she faced more grilling from Ben. Somehow, this partnership with Rick gave her the strength to face just about anything. She turned and went back inside the house.

"Rick's a good guy," Ben said.

Cayme closed the door behind her. "Yes, he is."

"You could do a lot worse."

"I know." She grimaced. "I've already traveled that road. If this engagement doesn't work out, it won't be because Rick cheated on me."

"Is that what Chase did?" Ben's expression grew dark. "I always wondered what happened for you to break it off with him." He smacked his fist and palm together and headed for the door. "I ought to pay him a visit."

Cayme kept her back to the door, blocking it. "You're not going anywhere. And please don't say anything to anyone. *I* broke it off. That's all anyone needs to know."

"Did Mom know?" Ben asked, his temper quieting a little.

She nodded. "I needed her to understand why I had to leave town."

"You stayed away too long." Ben paced back to his chair but didn't sit.

"I know. I was selfish." Nothing she could do about it now. "I hope I can make it up to you some day for being away, even though it's too late to make it up for Mom."

"The person you need to please is you, Cay. Stop putting everyone else's needs before yours." Instead of dropping into his chair, he headed into the kitchen. "I hope that's not the reason you've agreed to this arrangement with Rick."

That's exactly what had happened. But she didn't want Ben to know that. "It's not." She joined him in the kitchen and set the table.

Ben stared hard at her.

She shrugged. "I'm pretty sure it's not."

After they finished dinner, Cayme stacked the dishes in the dishwasher and turned it on. With Ben no longer in therapy, the dirty dishes stacked up quicker. Since her brother had made dinner, she wiped the counter and tidied the kitchen. She was glad to share the duties—and conversation.

She found Ben in the living room, plopped in his chair, hands clasped behind his head, and looking as relaxed as she'd ever seen him. "With all this drama tonight, I forgot to ask about your job interview. How did it go?"

"Got the job." He gave a quick smile.

"That's great! When do you start?"

"Monday. I'm installing a new network in Rick's office."

Cayme let out a silent sigh of relief. Her warrior brother stooped over a computer circuit board was hard to picture, but she was glad he wouldn't be around the heavy equipment. "I.T. is a perfect fit for you. You did an amazing job setting up the Wi-Fi network in Mom's store."

"Like I said earlier tonight, things are really looking good right now." He actually smiled, bigger this time. He'd been doing a lot of that tonight.

With all the decisions she'd made that day, she hoped this engagement wouldn't be the thing that destroyed his happiness.

****

After driving Misty home from tending Adam, Rick pulled into the driveway. "Come on, kiddo, time to get inside and ready for bed." He hadn't wanted to break the news to his son until they were home and entrenched in their nightly routine.

"Can't I stay up a little later?" Adam asked, jumping out of the truck. "Misty didn't let me watch my favorite show, but we recorded it. It's only a half-hour."

Rick put an arm around the boy's shoulder. "Not tonight, bud. We have some important things to talk about."

Adam looked up at him. "Did you decide about the job at Aunt Cayme's store?"

Rick nodded. "I did. That's not all we need to discuss." As they went into the house, he tapped his son on the back. "Go get ready for bed and I'll be right up."

Adam raced up the stairs, leaving Rick to stare after him. He wondered how his boy would handle the news that was about to shake his world. A few minutes later, he settled on the chair by Adam's desk.

His son sat cross-legged on the lower bunk, scrubbed clean, no extra food on his mouth for a change, and dressed in his favorite baseball pajamas. He looked eager, waiting for Rick to talk.

Rick paused a moment, contemplating how to start one of the toughest conversations he'd ever had.

"Did Aunt Cayme say she didn't want me to do the afternoon job?" Adam asked. In typical little kid fashion, he assumed the worst, which was Rick's fault. When it came to his boy, silence was never a good thing. He should know that by now.

"Cayme is thrilled to have you help out." He put his son's fears at ease.

Adam bounced on the bed and punched the air with his fist. "All right."

"Settle down. We need to cover some ground rules, though."

"Sure, Dad. I already know I have to finish my homework first. But school's almost out and the teachers aren't giving us very much."

"Regardless of how much you get, I still want you to read a chapter in your book every day." Rick used his father-knows-best voice to make sure Adam knew what was expected. "You can go straight to the store after school and read there."

"What about summer vacation? Do I still have to read?"

"Absolutely," Rick said. "It took you almost all year to get caught up and you're not getting behind, again. Understand?"

"Okay." Adam nodded, undaunted by the summer homework. "I promise I'll read. I can't wait to tell Joey and Devon that I have a summer job."

"About that. No bragging."

Adam took a deep breath and let it go with a sage nod. "I guess that wouldn't be very nice, huh?" For an eight-year-old, he caught on quickly. "Is that all?"

"Not quite." Rick cleared his throat. "You know that Aunt Cayme isn't really your aunt, right?"

"Yeah. Joey said he calls her that because she's a good friend of his mom's. Aunt Sherry is my real aunt."

"Right." Rick took a deep breath, hoping what he said next wouldn't upset Adam. "Well, Cayme and I are…seeing each other."

Adam cocked his head and frowned. "Like you and I see each other with our eyes?"

"No…we're…dating." He didn't want to use the word engaged, yet. It still didn't feel real, even though he was the one who'd started the whole thing. "Do you know what that means?"

Adam scrunched his forehead. "Like a boyfriend and girlfriend?"

"Something like that." Rick swallowed, waiting for his son's reaction.

"Does that mean you have to kiss her?" He made a face. "Is it yucky?"

Rick's lips twitched and he tried not to laugh. "When you get older, you'll learn kissing's not such a bad thing." Kissing Cayme had been most enjoyable. When they'd said goodnight, it had taken all his willpower to place that little peck on the corner of her mouth, instead of hauling her into his arms and kissing the stuffing out of her.

"I dunno." Adam wrinkled his nose and shook his head. "I don't think I would ever like it."

"That's okay. You have a long time before you have to worry about it." Rick leaned forward a little. "I wanted to tell you about me and Cayme tonight because you may hear some things at school tomorrow."

"Like what?"

This was harder to explain than he expected "Things like, um, Cayme and me getting married or that she might come to live with us."

"Really?" Adam's eyes grew round. "That would be cool!"

"Well, it's not happening right away," Rick cautioned. *If ever*. "But I didn't want you to be worried."

"I'm not worried. I like Aunt Cayme." Adam squared his shoulders. "This is like man talk, huh?"

"Yeah, it's exactly like man talk. I think you're grown up enough to understand. Right?"

Adam nodded vigorously. "Right!" He leaned back on his hands. "If you get married, will Aunt Cayme be my mom?"

"She'd be your stepmom."

"What about my real mom?"

Rick's stomach sank. The next tough topic on his man-talk agenda. "Actually, your real mom might come to visit you soon. Would you like that?"

"Really?" Adam's entire face lit up. "She's coming to see me?"

All the hope in the world shone in his son's eyes. A two-ton beam lay across Rick's chest. He took a deep breath and let it out slowly. "She might be here in a couple of weeks."

"She could come to my baseball games! I can show her how good a catcher I am."

"Yes, you can."

Adam grinned. "I can't wait!" Then his smiled slipped and a frown formed between his eyes. "So if my real mom will be here, why doesn't she come to live with us instead of Aunt Cayme?"

And there it was. Rick's worst nightmare unraveling right in front of him. How to explain divorce to a kid who still believed in the tooth fairy and Santa Claus. Joey had spoiled the Easter Bunny myth this spring, after sneaking a peek at Ken hiding Easter eggs, and then sharing his revelation with Adam.

He'd tried to explain to Adam over the years why his mother didn't live with them. Until now, she'd only been a picture in a frame on his bedside, a disembodied voice on the phone, a gift in the mail—not a hope for the future.

"Come over here." Rick reached across the space and lifted Adam off the bed and onto his lap. "You're growing up, bud. But I hope you're never too big to give your old man a hug."

Adam obliged, squeezing Rick's neck tightly. "This is one of those complicated thingies, huh?"

"Yes, it is. You're a pretty smart kid, you know that?"

"I'm not too smart." Adam laid his head on Rick's shoulder. "I didn't get a 100 on my last spelling test."

"You have other smarts that are just as important." Rick stroked Adam's hair. Probably should make both of them an appointment for a haircut next week. "I hope you'll understand that even though your mom will always love you, she and I can't be together anymore."

"Does that mean Aunt Cayme will live with us instead of Mom?"

"I don't know," Rick said. "Cayme and I are getting to know each other better."

"She knows you already," Adam said. "She said she knew you when you were kids, like me and Joey."

"When did she tell you this?"

"Today. At the store." Adam squirmed and seemed to tense up.

What really prompted his son to go to the store in the first place? Rick wasn't sure he bought the-library-didn't-have-his-book or the ghost hunting excuses. But that was a conversation for another day. For now, he needed to help his son understand the nuances of adults a little better.

"When I was your age, I used to play over at Cayme and Ben's house." Since learning about her crush, he realized she'd done well hiding her real feelings for him. Even as a teen, he'd noticed if other girls were watching him. Not that he'd have done anything about it even if he'd known about Cayme's crush. She was Sherry's best friend—Ben's little sister. He'd never thought about her quite like that…until she returned last month. "Now that we're grown-ups, there are things I'd like to know better about her."

Adam settled against Rick's shoulder again. "Like

what?"

"Well…" Rick didn't want to explain to his eight-year-old son all the facts of life. "I like to know what her favorite things are now. I left town for a while, and when I moved back again, she was living in Seattle."

"I know where Seattle is. We learned the states this year. It's in Washington, right?"

"Right." Whew. Nice that his son redirected the conversation on his own.

"Joey's mom said Aunt Cayme came home because her mom got sick and died."

"That's right. She had to take care of things." Rick cleared his throat and changed the subject. "So, what do you think about all this man-talk stuff?"

Adam's sturdy little shoulders lifted in a sigh. "I guess I'm okay with it. But what if, when Mom comes, I like her better than I like Aunt Cayme?"

Rick smiled. "You don't have to choose between them. You can like them both the same, or different—they're different people so it's okay to like them however you want." Which, in Rick's case, was easier said than done. He hoped he could keep his own distrust of Roxanne from affecting Adam's perception of his mother.

Chapter Twelve

The next morning at the store, all hell broke loose for Cayme, starting with a seven a.m. call from Sherry. Not the most convenient time, right in the middle of an espresso order.

Skeeter handed over the phone and completed the order for a pair of late-season skiers getting an early start on the slopes.

Cayme reluctantly took the phone and turned away from the counter. "Why are you calling the store?"

"Because you're not picking up your cell." Sherry sounded determined. "I want answers. Right now."

"I'm a little busy *right now*." Cayme had wrestled all night with how to break the news to Rick's sister. She'd guessed he wouldn't say anything to her. He probably hadn't even considered how his sister would react to the situation.

"Tell me it's not real," Sherry begged. "Tell me you're not engaged to my goofy big brother."

"I can't." Cayme sagged against the wall wishing for a chair to prop her up. "We're engaged. How'd you hear about it so soon?"

"Well, not from my best friend, I can tell you that. How could you keep this a secret from me?"

Cayme winced at the hurt in Sherry's voice. "We kept it a secret from everyone." She sighed. "If Chase hadn't been so obnoxious in the store yesterday, Rick wouldn't have come to my rescue and spilled the beans." At least that much was the truth.

"How long has this been going on?" Sherry cried out. A small commotion broke out on the other end of the line. "Hush, baby, I'm talking to Aunt Cayme on the phone."

"You're busy. Go get Joey ready for school. We can talk later."

"Joey can get himself ready. He's almost nine. He can drive himself to school—this is more important."

"Whoopee! I get to drive."

A youthful shout echoed through the phone.

"Go brush your teeth," Sherry yelled.

Cayme held the phone away from her ear. When the commotion died, she said, "Stop being dramatic." Little wonder that Rick didn't want to talk to his sister. "Swing by the store once your morning settles down."

"See you in ten minutes." Sherry hung up.

Cayme slowly replaced the phone, and then grabbed a fly swatter, smacking it on the wall, hoping to slay her demons and an errant fly at the same time. No way Sherry would make good on her promise to be over in ten minutes, not when she had a kid to get to school. Regardless of the reprieve from not facing her best friend immediately, the day would be a long one. She rejoined Skeeter at the front counter. The line for coffee was almost out the door.

"You should get engaged every day." Skeeter rang up another sale. "It's great for business."

At least three members of the city council were in line to order drinks. And where was Rick? Probably at home with his sweet little boy eating the breakfast of champions. She sighed. If she were in his shoes, that's where she'd be.

"Can I take your order?" she asked Mazey Fredrick who'd stepped up to the front of the line.

The woman had been on the city council for years. Her permed blue hair and dark eyeliner made her look like Tutankhamun's mummified mother. Mazey had had her eye on the Foster property long before the city wanted to buy it.

"So, Cayme Foster." Mazey glanced at the line of people behind her. "The rumor must be true. What I want to know is if you're going through with it this time. Or will you leave the groom at the altar and skip town like last time?"

Most of the customers this morning had been well-wishers, wanting to congratulate her and Rick. Mazey was the exception. The mean blue-haired hornet was buzzing around looking for a bit of gossip to spread—the only thing she did with any vigor.

"Actually, Ms. Fredrick, I was thinking I'd wait until after the ceremony and spoil the marriage bed. Are you taking your lattes fat-free these days?" Cayme rang up the order. "That'll be three fifty-three, please."

"Well! What nerve!" As Mazey spun on her orthopedic shoes, a tuft of blue curls broke free, bouncing as she stomped out of the store.

"You go, Cayme girl," Skeeter cheered in her husky voice. "Give 'em all what for."

Right. One down, and fifty more to go. Good thing the town's population wasn't any larger. She turned to the next customer in line with a smile pasted on her face. "Hi, what would you like this morning?"

****

Two hours later, the crowd had thinned. The early

morning rush was over. Those straggling in were mostly tourists.

When Sherry finally breezed through the door, Cayme was refilling the caramel flavor pump.

Little Rachel bounced on her mother's hip, with an adorable pink headband bow over her blonde curls. A huge grin showed off a new tooth.

Sherry stormed up to the counter and plopped the baby down. "I need the biggest mocha you have. Whipped cream and make it a double shot." She dug through her purse and pulled out a sippy cup. "Oh, and some milk in this."

Skeeter came from around the counter and lifted the baby into her arms. "My goodness. Look how big you've grown." She smooched the chubby cheeks and then handed the baby back to her mother. "I got this one, Cayme girl. You go sit down. I'll bring the drinks in a minute."

Cayme hesitated at leaving the safety of the counter, unwilling to face Sherry's wrath.

Sherry jerked her head toward the reading nook. "What Skeeter said, Cayme girl. Let's duck in here for some privacy."

Cayme followed Sherry around the corner and found the reading nook empty for the moment. Thank Heaven for small favors. This wasn't a conversation she wanted to have. To have it in the main part of the store with spectators would be even worse.

Sherry settled on the couch and propped the baby on her lap. "Spill."

"Rick proposed. I accepted." Cayme sat gingerly on the edge of a chair. She wanted to move quickly if Sherry started one of her tirades.

"Rick proposed. I accepted." Sherry mimicked in a whiney, high-pitched voice. "Seriously? You think that will satisfy me? Come on. I'm your best friend. He's my brother! Why did you keep this a secret? *How* did you keep it a secret?"

Skeeter arrived with the drinks, giving Cayme a moment to gather her thoughts. Why on earth hadn't she and Rick taken time to get their story straight before she had to face all these questions today? She'd been stupidly shortsighted. Someone would out them and the whole engagement lie would break wide open like an overfull dam.

Cayme took a sip of her latte. Skeeter had made it just how she liked it, and it offered a bit of calm to this hectic day.

"You're stalling."

Sherry could read her like a comic book. "I know this seems sudden."

Sherry snorted, making the baby giggle.

Even Cayme smiled at the child's happy sound. Then she sobered to face her best friend. "It's too soon after Mom. We kept quiet because it would be inappropriate to say anything right now." At least that much of The Engagement Story was consistent.

Sherry's furious look softened. "I suppose that makes sense. But how did you two even hook up? Wasn't last Sunday the first you'd spent any time together? And that was in the company of our tribe. No privacy there."

"I've been back for over a month. Rick stops by the house to see Ben all the time." All of that was true. Although when Rick stopped by, Cayme was either working at the store or in the office spending time on her other job. She'd known Rick was in the house, but hadn't actually seen him. Sherry didn't need to know that. "It just sort of happened."

"You caved, didn't you?" Sherry frowned at her. "Does he know about your crush?"

"He does now." That much was true, too. She'd wondered what Rick thought after Ben brought up her old crush last night, only there'd been no time to discuss it. Maybe he didn't really pick up on it.

"So, have you set a date?" Sherry was nothing if not persistent.

"No." Cayme gave a nervous laugh. "I—we want to take things slow. You know what happened last time."

"Rick is not Chase Peters. He won't cheat on you." Sherry's voice rose to her outdoor volume.

"Shhh!" Cayme hissed. "You don't need to tell the whole world."

"The whole world ought to know what that womanizer did to you. Then you wouldn't have run away like a scared rabbit. Put *him* on the defensive for once."

"If the world knows he cheated, then what does that say about me?" Cayme voiced the insecurity that had haunted her for years. "That I couldn't keep a man interested, so he found another willing body?"

"You're loyal and faithful—to a fault, I'll admit. You see the good in everyone."

"I was duped. Gullible. I'm still gullible." Cayme took a sip of her drink, letting the hot liquid warm the icy spots she wanted to banish. "I never want to be hurt like that again," she murmured around the rim of the cup.

"Oh, honey." Sherry adjusted the baby on her lap and leaned forward. "Rick's a good guy."

"I know he is," Cayme said. "But what if—" She stopped. For this engagement to work, it had to look real. If she kept voicing her doubts, the whole thing would blow up in their faces.

"No doubts." Sherry said. "I love you like a sister. But if you hurt my brother…"

"I promise we're walking into this with our eyes wide open."

The other woman tilted her head. "You don't look like you're in love."

"I look like I've been up most of the night and then started here at six this morning with wall-to-wall customers."

"Then I'll let you off the hook this time. But I want you and Rick over for dinner this weekend."

"Ben's taking us out to celebrate." Cayme shuddered. A public appearance—together. She couldn't avoid them forever. "Maybe next weekend?"

"I'm holding you to it."

"I'll need to check my schedule…and with Rick too. But I'm sure we can be there."

Sherry heaved out a long breath. "I gotta go, and you've got to get back to work." She stood. "Sorry if I came on a bit strong. The news just took me by surprise, that's all."

"I know. It's not quite real for me, either. Easy to forget, until yesterday." Okay, she should stop talking now.

"Whatever." Sherry hefted little Rachel on her hip. She leaned in and gave Cayme a hug.

Cayme returned it and bent down to kiss her

goddaughter. "Be a good girl for your mommy."

"She's happy today. That first tooth finally pushed through."

****

Later that day, after the lunch crowd thinned, Cayme camped out on the store's floor sorting through the shipment of new romance books. Despite veiled slurs and snickering remarks, those books sold out on a regular basis.

Cayme's mom had loved reading anything but really gobbled up romances. Before the illness kept her bedbound, she and Skeeter had arranged scheduled distributions from some of the better-known publishing houses. Recently, Skeeter started placing orders from independent publishers too. The store's patrons showed their appreciation by forcing frequent restocking.

As much as Cayme's mother had loved a good romance story, she'd never remarried. The mayor's surprise visit the night before was the first Cayme had heard of her mom taking an interest in another relationship. She'd seemed to never recover after her husband was killed in a car accident.

Cayme's father, Matthew Foster, had been a master electrician. He'd owned his own business, and was often called out of town for long projects. Because he managed the contracts, he'd been free for fun vacations during the summer. He'd even coached Ben and Rick's baseball team for eight years in a row, from T-ball all the way into Little League.

On that fateful night, after doing a job out of town, Matthew had fallen asleep at the wheel while returning to the arms of his loving wife and family. Ben was fourteen. Cayme was twelve and had just started junior high. She wished she could permanently erase the entire year from her memory.

She reached inside the box and pulled out several paperbacks with loving couples on the cheerful covers. Like her mother, Cayme would indulge in the occasional novel. She loved a happily-ever-after, particularly because her own life seemed like a series of never-ending Greek tragedies.

This latest development was a prime example. Her engagement to Rick should have been a dream come true. It would have been, if they loved each other. Even though Sherry didn't voice her doubts about the engagement, Cayme had a hunch they were there all the same. She didn't blame her friend. She had doubts too, starting with the fact that the whole thing wasn't real.

The front door chimed and Cayme looked up to see the object of her thoughts walk in with his son. This would be her first encounter with Adam since the news. Would he be as suspicious and wary as Sherry had been?

She stood and dusted off the seat of her jeans.

Adam spotted her and came running over. Without warning, he flung his arms around her middle and squeezed. "Hi, Aunt Cayme." He pulled back and looked up at her. "Oops. I forgot. You're not my aunt. Dad says you're dating and maybe you'll be my stepmom. Do you want me to call you Stepmom?"

Nerves fluttered in her stomach. She looked at Rick for an answer.

He most helpfully shrugged his shoulders.

She could've punched him right then, except hitting her fiancé, even a pretend one, wasn't a good idea. Especially in front of his son. She and Rick *really* needed to talk. "Why don't you call me Cayme for now. Especially here at work."

Adam gave a nod, looking very mature. "That's because of Neapolitan."

Rick laughed. "Nepotism," he corrected.

Cayme lifted a brow. "Wow. Impressive. Did you learn that vocabulary word in school?"

"A conversation some young ears overheard the other day," Rick explained. He raised an eyebrow at his son. "Do you remember what it means?"

Adam nodded. "It means that family members who work together get in trouble."

Rick patted his son on the shoulder. "Close enough for now."

Adam gazed up at Cayme. "Will I get in trouble working here because you're dated to Dad?"

"Dating," Rick said.

"Of course not," Cayme said at the same time.

Adam dramatically wiped his brow. "Whew! I'm glad. So, what do I do first?"

"Your chapter reading comes first, remember?" Rick said.

"Your dad's right, homework or reading before you start the job." Cayme reminded her new employee of the rules they'd discussed.

Rick nodded his approval. "Sounds like my cue to get back to work. I'll pick you up at five-thirty, okay bud?"

"Sure." Adam gathered his backpack and headed for a table. "See you later, Dad."

Rick turned to Cayme. "I have some things I need to do right now. I'll call you later."

She supposed that was better than not talking at all.

"I'm off work at six. After I fix dinner for Ben and me, I'll have some time."

"Sounds good." Rick hesitated at the door, staring at her as though he had more to say. Instead, he turned and left, the chime sounding hollow in the mostly empty store.

Cayme stood for a moment, feeling as though something more should have happened. Like a kiss or at least a hug—from the dad, not the son. Maybe Rick was uncomfortable showing displays of affection in public. If that were true, it didn't explain his actions yesterday. Maybe she didn't know Rick as well as she thought. And that notion disturbed her. They *really* needed to talk.

She stopped by the table to make sure Adam started his homework.

"I think I'll like you for a stepmom," he said, pulling a book from his backpack.

His generous words spread warmth from the soles of her feet through the crown of her head. "I think you'd make a terrific stepson," Cayme had had a crush on Rick for years, but even with that, she wasn't sure she was in love with him. Not like with this little eight-year-old boy who'd already stolen her heart.

"Dad said my real mom might visit me this summer. She doesn't live with us because Dad and her are divorced." He leaned in and whispered, "That means they didn't stay married."

Suddenly Cayme felt as if she'd dropped into quicksand. The sinking sensation grabbed hold and she couldn't climb out. She didn't know anything about Rick's marriage or his ex. In fact, she couldn't imagine any woman voluntarily letting go of a family like Rick and Adam. Did the woman have any idea what she was missing?

Regardless of what ex-Mrs. Morrison was like, Cayme wasn't about to dis Adam's mom. If she wanted to clean up her karma, she needed to let go of the past with Chase Peters, and tread carefully here, too. "Are you excited to see your mom?" Cayme asked as neutrally as she could.

Adam bobbed his head and his eyes sparkled with excitement. "This will be the first time I get to meet her. I was just a baby when she left. But I have all the pictures she sent from Germany last year. She's in the army like my dad was."

"I bet she gets to see all kinds of interesting places." Was it a good or bad thing to encourage Adam to talk about his mom? Inside, her stomach was roiling at the possibility of meeting Rick's ex. Wasn't she the reason Rick wanted this engagement to be real? Entanglements with the ex sounded like a lot of drama. This engagement was becoming more and more of a bad idea.

"Yeah. She sends me stuff from all over the place for my birthday and Christmas."

"That's really nice of her." This was *not* a conversation Cayme wanted to have.

Adam cocked his head, his gaze curious. "Do you think you'd like my mom?"

Now she was in unknown territory. "I don't know. I would hope so." *Lie, lie, lie*. She was going to burn in Hell.

"My mom will like you," Adam said with all the confidence of an eight-year-old whose worldview ended at the city limits. "You're nice."

"Thank you, Mr. Morrison. It's kind of you to say so." She pointed to his books. "Now it's time to get started on your homework. We have chores for you to do later."

He beamed at her. "You got it!" Adam obviously got his work ethic from Rick. With school so close to being out, Adam had very little homework and diligently focused on his reading.

"You're a terrific kid, Adam." Cayme ruffled his silky hair. She was so burning in Hell for wanting this little boy to like her better than he liked his absent mother.

Chapter Thirteen

It took three days for Rick's announcement to spread through the town like a wildfire on gasoline. Cayme didn't know whether to be relieved or horrified that in those three days, the only times she'd seen her fiancé was when he came into the store before closing to pick up Adam. If they were truly an engaged couple, shouldn't they at least go on a date?

Admittedly, not finding time together was her fault. The previous week, she been worried about not hearing from her boss, then on the same night Rick proposed, she finally got a call from him. The project he'd sent kept her holed up in the office late every evening. The senior editor explained that the manuscript was the first of a three-book deal for the author. He wanted a complete read-through and pre-edit review done by Monday morning.

The long conversation she'd needed to have with Rick had been put off. That entire evening, and the next, were spent fine-tuning her notes and suggestions, advising that the story was indeed worthy of the three-book contract, maybe more. She'd e-mailed the final project notes late the previous night and hoped the author could deliver, because the book could go big. At least someone's life had a silver lining ahead, and she couldn't help but be a little envious that it wasn't hers.

Saturday was shaping up to be another busy day at

the store. Skeeter was scheduled to cover that afternoon so Cayme could leave early for the celebration dinner Ben wanted to give her and Rick.

Ben had mentioned the dinner six times in the last three days, making it clear she wouldn't get out of the date by hiding behind work. He seemed to be doing his best to influence that love-and-commitment angle he'd spoken of the night they talked with Rick.

In fact, Ben seemed almost back to his old self—leaving his dirty socks by the living room chair as well as teasing her for finally finding a boyfriend.

He had yet to pick up the guitar again. Cayme had a feeling it was only a matter of time. Regardless of how anxious she was about this dinner, she wouldn't jeopardize the evening by finding an excuse to duck out.

The downside of working all those evening hours was that she'd seen more of Adam than she'd seen of Rick. Not that seeing Adam was a bad thing; she just figured she should have seen more of his father three days into the engagement.

Saturday promised to be no different from the previous days, except her project was finished and Cayme was remedying her no-dating status that night. Nerves churned in her stomach at the idea of spending an evening in Rick's company, despite Ben's presence as a chaperone.

The store's door chime sounded and Cayme looked up to see Adam come in.

He'd been arriving alone since the first day but today, he had a friend with him. "Hi Cayme," he called.

"Hi yourself," she said. "How fun. You brought a friend today."

The boys crossed to the counter, weaving around a pair of customers getting ready to leave. The other boy was slightly shorter than Adam with reddish-blond hair and a smattering of freckles across his nose.

"This is Devon Cooper. I told you about him, remember?" Adam said.

"Hi." Devon looked at Cayme with wide eyes. "Mrs. Foster's your mom, huh?"

Cayme held out her hand. "She is… was. Nice to meet you, Devon." So, this was the boy who used to come in and clean for her mother and Skeeter. His little hand clasped hers quickly then let go.

"I told him that it was okay to come here," Adam said.

"Of course," Cayme replied. "Why wouldn't it be?"

"I was sort of afraid," Devon mumbled to his shoes. "Until Adam talked to me." His gaze lifted and skirted around the room as though looking for something.

"Afraid of what?" Cayme frowned. "Did something bad happen to you here?" She hoped he hadn't been bothered by one of their customers. For the most part, all their patrons were kind and courteous people; however, a lot of out-of-towners stopped in, especially during the extended ski season.

Devon shook his head. "Oh, no. Nothing bad happened."

Adam nudged his friend. "It's okay to tell her."

Cayme looked at the frowns on both boys' faces. "This sounds root beer serious. Why don't you guys find a table and I'll bring us something to drink. Then we can talk." She filled a couple of cups with root beer and grabbed her half-finished latte. She set the drinks on the table and pulled up a chair to join them. "So, what's this about?" She leaned forward with a whisper. "I promise I won't tell another soul."

Devon looked at her, a touch of anxiety in his eyes. "You promise?"

She nodded. "Cross my heart and hope to die." She made the requisite sign over her chest.

"Okay." Devon looked around again. "I was afraid to see your mom. That's why I didn't come back to work."

"My mother?" The unexpected comment caught Cayme off guard, and she swallowed the sudden lump in her throat. It had only been a little over a month, and the ache still cut deep.

He nodded.

"I'm sorry. She's not here anymore. She passed away."

Devon nodded again. "I know."

Cayme sat back in her chair. Oh. Devon was afraid of her mother's ghost. "I didn't know. I'm so sorry you were scar—worried about that." It must have taken a lot of courage for him to come in, and she didn't want him to feel embarrassed about admitting his fears. "My mom loved this store a lot, and I'm sure she was grateful to have your help. But you don't need to worry about her coming back to visit. She's in a much better place, and I know she's really happy there." Not wanting to upset the boy even more, she blinked to keep a tear from escaping.

"Are you sure?" Devon glanced nervously at the back room.

"I've been here every day," Adam said. "Except, I

won't be coming on Sunday. And I haven't seen Mrs. Foster once." He looked at Cayme. "That's why I wanted Devon to come in today. So I could show him nothing bad would happen."

"You're a good friend, Adam." Cayme gave the boy a fond smile.

Devon looked at her. "You're not mad that I stopped coming to work?"

She squeezed Devon's hand. "Of course not. I understand. I miss my mom terribly. Even I would be scared if I saw her tending the counter. Think of how hard it would be for her to make sandwiches." She mustered a wink to lighten the moment.

Devon and Adam laughed.

"That would be hard," Adam said.

"Are you upset that I gave Adam your job?" She wondered if that was the next order of business. Adam had only been coming in a few days, and she already looked forward to seeing him and asking about his day. Somehow, she knew if Devon wanted to come back, Adam would bow out.

Devon shook his head. "No. I'm helping at Mr. Anderson's sporting-goods store now. He asked my mom if I could help out when I turned nine, but I was already helping here. After Mrs. Foster died... I just went over there instead."

"That's good. It looks like this arrangement worked out the best for everyone." Cayme smiled. "I'm glad you came in and told me. That was very brave."

Devon grinned. "I'm glad too." He slurped the bottom of his drink. "I gotta go over to the sporting-goods store." He stood, grabbed his cup, waved good-bye, and walked to the door. "Thanks for the root beer,

Miss Cayme. See you later, Adam. Don't forget we have a game Monday night."

"Bye, Dev. Go Blackhawks!" Adam waved back then looked at Cayme. "That reminds me," he said. "Is it okay if I don't work on Monday? I have to get ready for my game."

"Of course," she said. "I totally understand."

"Will you come to my game?"

"I'd love to." She offered a regretful smile. "But I have to work, remember?"

"Yeah, but it would only be for a while. My games aren't that long."

Cayme glance toward the back room. "I'll check with Miss Skeeter, okay? She's covering for me tonight so I can go to dinner with your dad and my brother."

Adam's face lit up. "That's like a date, huh?"

"Sort of." If she could call it a date with Ben tagging along.

"How come just sort of?"

Her face grew warm. How did she confess that she'd like some alone time with his dad? A real date would be a good step in that direction. "Umm, sometimes when people are dating it's nice to be alone together."

"So you can do kissing and stuff?" He made a face.

She laughed. "When you're older, you might not hate kissing. But yeah, it's nice to have private time."

"Dad said I would like kissing when I'm big, too." He shook his head. "I don't think so."

Cayme smiled. "You have a long time before you have to worry about it."

Adam gave a dramatic sigh. "Good." He pulled out his notebook.

"You have an assignment? Today's Saturday. Didn't we get all your homework done yesterday?"

He grimaced. "I forgot that we're supposed to write a report on what we want to do this summer. The teacher says it's fun to read those at the beginning of the new school year to see if you did all the things you said."

Cayme liked the sound of that assignment. The teacher was obviously helping her students focus on staying busy through the summer. "That doesn't sound too hard," she said. "How long does it have to be?"

Adam scribbled his name on the top line. "A page. She said if we did two pages, then we'd get an 'A' for sure. I'm just not sure what to write."

"Well… you could write down that you're helping out here at the store, and have your worm business. What other things are you planning to do once school gets out?"

"Just baseball," Adam replied. "Dad says that he'll have to work extra hours this summer so we can't do any long camping trips."

Oh dear. What if Rick was forced to line up other contracts because he wasn't sure about the project to build the park? She suddenly realized how her decision about selling the property was having a ripple effect. Not just on the town as a whole but affecting the livelihoods of people she cared about very much.

A familiar tension crept up her neck, impossible to ignore. She closed her eyes for a moment and took a deep breath. She really needed to come to a decision. Maybe after the holiday weekend and things eased up at the store, she'd take the time needed to consider the contract.

For now, she focused on Adam. She'd promised Rick that Adam would do his homework before he started his chores. Even though he didn't finish it yesterday, she'd make sure he was ready for class on Monday. "What did you do last summer?"

He tilted his head to the side. "Lots of stuff, I guess. But that was last summer. I may not be able to do the same things this year."

"True. But you might do some things that were the same as last summer."

"Like baseball?" His eyebrows lifted. "I'm doing that again this year."

"Right." She nodded. "What else?

"I took swimming lessons." He grinned, showing oversized front teeth he'd soon grow into.

"It's a good bet you will this year, too."

He frowned. "But what if I don't? Then the teacher will think I lied on my report."

"Write down the ones you're sure of. And then write down the things you want to do."

Adam grinned. "Thanks, Cayme. This will be a lot easier than I thought." He picked up his pencil. "And I just remembered! My mom is coming to visit. I could write that down too."

The reminder of his mother's visit settled uneasily at the bottom of Cayme's stomach. She watched the excitement fill his face. Who could deny a little boy a visit from his mother? Not her. She took a deep breath knowing she couldn't change the circumstances in this child's life.

She left Adam writing furiously on his report and returned to her tasks behind the counter.

Skeeter walked over to stand next to Cayme and

straightened a stack of cups. "Looks like you've got a solid start on being a great mom. Good for you."

Cayme's breath hitched. Adam already had a mother. If things played out the way she expected, she'd never be his stepmom. All she could do was take one day at a time. "Adam is writing a report about his summer plans," she said, ignoring the comment about being a mom. "I think the hardest part about the assignment was figuring out where to start."

"Isn't that the case with most things?" Skeeter asked. "Sort of like what to fix for dinner."

Cayme nodded. "Too true."

She walked back to the table and saw that Adam had written half a page. "Wow, look at you go."

Adam looked up and grinned. "Thanks." He reached for his root beer and poked the straw in his mouth then set the cup aside and started to write again.

Twenty minutes later, he closed his notebook and took a final slurp of his root beer. He walked up to the counter where Cayme was filling a napkin dispenser. "That was easy!"

She squeezed his shoulder. "Well you certainly finished fast. I'll set the timer for your reading and when you're done, I have some boxes for you to take out back."

When the timer went off, Adam stuffed the book in his backpack. "I'm done, Cayme. Where are the boxes?"

She led the way to the back of the store and pointed to a corner where she and Skeeter had stacked boxes from the weekend deliveries. The stack wasn't too tall, but was threatening to tumble. If it did, it would block the back entrance.

"Don't they get in the way?" Adam asked. "How come you don't just put them outside?"

"We don't want them getting all soggy in the snow and rain. They're harder to break down if they're wet."

"Oh. So what do I do?"

Cayme showed him how to cut the box at the corner and side. "Be careful, because that cutter is really sharp," she warned. "Once you have the boxes cut, lay them flat. Then we'll bundle them up to be recycled."

"Recycling's a good thing," Adam said, putting his foot on one side of the box and straightening it. "Dad and I recycle stuff at our house, too. In school, we studied about taking care of the environment."

"I'm glad to hear that." Cayme smiled. "We want our world to stay nice for a long time. Even for your kids someday."

"I'm not having kids," Adam said.

"Not ever?" Cayme asked, amused at the bold declaration from the eight-year-old.

Adam flattened another box and put it on the stack he was making. "Well, not for a really long time."

"Not until you've finished school, right?"

Adam nodded vigorously. "Right."

She smiled, admiring how he got straight to the task. "You're doing great. I'll be right over here with Ms. Skeeter."

"'Kay."

Cayme let him work, keeping an eye out but also wanting him to feel she trusted him to do the job alone. When she was Adam's age, she'd never had responsibilities like a "job." It seemed eight-year-olds were a lot more mature these days.

About fifteen minutes later, Adam walked to the front of the store. "I'm done," he said to Cayme. "Want to see?

"Sure." She followed him and looked at the neat stack of boxes. "Perfect." She grabbed a roll of twine and tossed it to Adam.

He caught it in both hands.

"Nice catch."

"I'm playing catcher and third base." He grinned.

"I wouldn't want to hit a line drive to you. I'd be out every time."

Grinning wider, he held up the twine. "What do I do with this?"

She showed him how they tied the cardboard together in manageable stacks. Then she opened the back door and they took the stacks out to the recycle bin. They'd just dropped in the last stack and closed the lid on the bin, when Rick came up beside them.

"How's it going?" he asked.

Adam spun around. "Hi, Dad. Whatcha doing here? I thought you were working."

"I got off a little early and wanted to see how your afternoon is going."

"I did my homework, first," Adam said. "Cayme helped me."

Rick gave Cayme a long look. "She did, eh?"

Warmth rushed up her neck. "I helped with a suggestion for his report."

"Yeah," Adam said. "I even got two pages for the extra credit."

Rick's gaze softened. "Good for you." He nodded to the stack of cardboard in the bin. "Did you do all this by yourself?"

"Most of it," Adam said. "Cayme showed me how and then she had to go do other things in the store. I had fun."

"He did an awesome job," Cayme said.

She glanced up and found Rick staring at her with a strange expression on his face. Warmth shot through her middle. For a moment, she couldn't pull her gaze from his, and everything around them faded to background noise.

"Hey, Dad," Adam said breaking the spell. "I invited Cayme to my game on Monday. Is that okay?"

She jerked her gaze from Rick and looked at Adam's hopeful face. "I still don't know if I can get away from the store," she cautioned.

From behind her, Skeeter cleared her throat. "I'll cover for you, dear. You haven't had many breaks since your mother died."

"See?" Adam said. "Now you can watch me play third base." He turned to his dad. "Cayme said I'm a really great catch."

Rick raised an eyebrow.

Cayme heard the double entendre of Adam's words. "He catches really well," she said quickly.

"He's a great catch, too," Rick said with a wink. "So, will you come and watch the game?"

Adam looked from his dad to Cayme. "You can sit with Dad so you'll know somebody there."

Cayme knew Adam only wanted to help, but the energy crackling between her and Rick grew stronger.

Even Skeeter watched as though she sensed an electrical current too.

Feeling as if the world was holding its breath for her answer, Cayme gave in. "If it's not too busy at the store, I'll take a couple of hours off."

Adam punched the air. "Yes!" Then he gave his dad a high five. "We'll pick you up at four o'clock. I have to be there an hour early for warm-ups."

Cayme held up her hands. "Whoa… slow down. I don't think I should be gone that long. What time does your game start?"

"Five o'clock." Adam held up five fingers.

"How about I come over just before the first pitch?"

Adam looked a bit dejected.

Rick squeezed his son's shoulder. "Hey, buddy, not everyone has the afternoon free like you do." He looked at Cayme. "She promised she'd be there for your game. That's what you wanted, right?"

"Yeah."

No way would Cayme back out now and break this little boy's heart. "I wouldn't miss it. And if it rains, I'll bring my umbrella."

Adam laughed. "It won't rain. It's supposed to be sunny on Monday. Right, Dad?"

Rick took a deep breath and nodded. "Finally."

Cayme supposed the weather, as well as her not selling the property to the city, was wreaking havoc on Rick's business. "Then it's a date." As soon as the words left her mouth, she wanted them back.

Rick cocked an eyebrow and didn't say anything.

Out of the corner of her eye, she caught Skeeter's Cheshire Cat grin.

"Come on, kiddo," Rick said. "We need to head home and get you an early dinner." He draped an arm around his son's shoulder and steered him toward the truck parked in the alley. He looked over his shoulder and gave a wink. "Cayme and I have a date tonight."

"I know," Adam said. "We were talking about dates and kissing and stuff." Adam smiled and waved. "See you later, Cayme and Miss Skeeter."

"Later, gator," Skeeter called

"Bye, Adam," Cayme said at the same time, watching them walk away.

Adam jerked to a stop. "Wait a minute, Dad. I have to get my backpack." He turned and ran inside.

Rick returned to where Cayme stood. "Dates and kissing and stuff? Just what are you teaching my kid?"

"Gotta run," Skeeter said. "I think I hear a customer inside. Take care, Rick."

Rick's gaze never left Cayme. "You too, Skeeter."

Cayme's face flamed under the intensity of his dark stare, yet she refused to back down from his question. "You'd better know right up front, Rick, that I will never be less than truthful with Adam, unless the answer could hurt him in some way."

Rick took a step closer. "What about me? Will you be truthful with me?"

She swallowed, uncertain where he was headed with his questions. "Of course."

Rick nodded and stared at her mouth. "Kissing and stuff?"

"I told Adam our dinner tonight was sort of a date."

"Sort of?"

She gave a smile. Like father, like son. "That was Adam's question." She sighed. "Ben will be there tonight, and I told Adam that sometimes two people liked to be alone on a date."

"Ah. I see now where this conversation headed to kissing and stuff." Rick stepped closer. "Would you like to be alone with me tonight, Cayme?"

She swallowed again. "We haven't really talked since… that night. Shouldn't we at least act like we're engaged?"

"Maybe this will help." He slipped one hand around her neck and cupped the back of her head. In his other hand, he captured hers and pulled her near. Before she could take a breath, his lips were on hers.

The touch was so much more electric than that night in the office. His lips moved over hers with a hunger that sparked one of her own. Just as he was pressing for more, the door behind her slammed.

"Dad! I'm ready."

Rick lifted his head and Cayme jerked back. "Okay, buddy." His voice was husky.

"Are you kissing and stuff?" Adam made a gagging sound. "Yick."

"Not so much," Rick whispered, his eyes darkening with a need that probably reflected in her own eyes.

Her cheeks burned.

Rick backed away and caught his son by the shoulder. His expression shifted and he said, "Before I forget, the town council meeting is Tuesday night."

Cayme had forgotten about the meeting, even though Mayor Nicholson had reminded her earlier in the week. With everything that had happened between her and Rick, the meeting had dropped to the back of her mind. She grimaced. "Thanks for the reminder. I'll be there."

"Good. I'll see you and Ben in a while." He turned, and with his arm around his son, walked down the alley to his truck.

Chapter Fourteen

"If I hurry and finish dinner, can we play catch before you go to your date?" Adam fingered a couple of french fries and dunked them in his ketchup before stuffing them into his mouth.

Rick had driven to the fast food joint at the end of town and ordered takeout for Adam's meal. He normally didn't do the junk food scene, wanting his son to have every advantage, including healthy food choices. But that night, he'd made an exception—a treat to make up for his not being home on a weekend evening.

The reservations Ben set up were for seven p.m. Rick glanced at the clock, seeing he had about ninety minutes before he met Ben and Cayme at the restaurant. "We have a little time." He looked out the kitchen window. Clouds were gathering in the west. "Dress warm. It looks like another storm is headed in."

"Yeah. At practice this morning, Coach said it would rain tonight. But we'll still play on Monday. It's supposed to be a sunny day."

"That's good. What about all your rained-out games?" Rick asked.

"We'll have to make them up. I hate that it's rained so much this year. The season's almost over, and we've hardly played at all."

"Part of the challenge of living in the mountains."

"I like living here, though." Adam dunked another fry. "Once the weather's better, can we go fishing?"

"All summer, buddy. All summer."

"Good, cuz I wrote that in my report." Adam jammed more fries in his mouth and gulped his drink. He wiped the milk mustache off his lip and looked up. "Do you think Cayme will really come to my game?"

Rick glanced at his son's hopeful face, attempting to keep up with the change of topics. "I'm sure she'll do her best." He still had more to learn about the woman he'd asked to marry him. What he did know was that when Cayme Foster gave her word, she kept it. Which made exacting an engagement promise out of her all the more remarkable. Although, an engagement of convenience wasn't a good foundation for a solid, long-term relationship. He took a breath. Was he really considering that a possibility?

"I'm excited that she's going." Adam nodded, looking younger than his eight years for just an instant. "Oh, and I have another game on Wednesday. Will you have to work that day or can you come?"

Rick smiled. "Of course I'll be there."

"Cool!"

Rick wanted to be at as many events as he could, especially with just a few games left in the short season. Seemed like the snow barely melted before they started playing ball. Kids were out of school only a month before the season was over. Because the snow hadn't melted in the valley until the end of April, the season was even shorter this year.

"Is there any of Aunt Sherry's cake left?" Adam shoved the last of his hamburger into his mouth.

Rick looked at Adam's growing body. Was he

feeding his son enough? It seemed like he had two hollow legs. "You can have one piece. You know how you get if you eat too much sugary stuff before bed."

"But it's really good cake." Adam cleared the hamburger wrappers from the table and tossed them in the trash.

"One piece," Rick repeated and gave him a clean plate from the cupboard.

"Ooo-kay." Adam opened the drawer and took out a butter knife and fork. "If Mrs. Foster was a ghost, she'd probably be at her house, not the bookstore, right?" He cut into the cake and scooped a piece on his plate.

"What brought up the ghost questions again?"

"Devon came with me to Cayme's store. She was really nice to him about not working there anymore. She said Mrs. Foster couldn't make sandwiches for people if she was a ghost. That was pretty funny."

"Devon told her why he quit?"

"Yeah. Cayme said he was brave. But I still think he was scared." He brought the plate back to the table and took a bite of his cake.

"Sometimes it takes the most courage to do something when you're scared." Rick offered a bit of sage advice in a way he hoped Adam would understand.

"Were you scared in the army?"

By now, he should be used to the way his son's mind skipped from subject to subject, yet every now and again, it still took him by surprise. He paused to consider his answer. "Every soldier gets scared." He'd wondered when Adam would start asking questions about his service and hoped to satisfy his son's curiosity without causing nightmares.

"I wasn't scared of seeing Mrs. Foster's ghost." Cake crumbs clung to the corners of Adam's mouth.

Rick heaved a silent sigh. Thank goodness for short attention spans. "You're thinking too much about ghosts. What if you have bad dreams tonight?"

Adam rolled his eyes and shoved the last bite of cake into his mouth. "I don't get scared like Devon does."

Rick rinsed the morning's breakfast dishes along with the few dishes Adam used for dinner and put the last one in the dishwasher. "If you say so." He dried his hands. "Come on. Go get your mitt."

"'Kay." Adam ran out of the kitchen and thundered up the stairs. A few seconds later, he came pounding down again, sounding like a racehorse.

Rick grabbed his mitt and a hardball from the closet and met Adam at the door. They walked out into the yard together.

The days were growing longer with the promise of summer just around the corner. But that night, a chill hung in the air, and the impending storm would be cold enough to bring snow. Still, with the first of June just a couple of weeks away, snow wouldn't stay on the valley floor very long. The biggest threat was more accumulation in the mountains. Melting snow would flow into the rivers and streams, which were already bank-full in places.

And once again, Cayme popped into his head. If the river flooded, her property would become a lake despite the sandbags they'd prepared. Nothing he could do about it now. He'd ask Ben at dinner if he needed more help shoring up the bank. For the moment, he focused his attention on his son and tossed the ball to him. "By the way, you're staying at Aunt Sherry's tonight."

"Can't Joey come over here?" Adam snagged the ball and palmed it to throw back. "He hasn't spent a night in the bunk beds in like forever. Misty could watch us until you get home."

"I don't know how late my date will go." All of the evening's plans were up to Ben. Rick's main objective was to make sure Cayme and Ben had a good time without watching the clock. And maybe he'd even find some of that elusive alone time Cayme had alluded to. Kissing and stuff. Stuff he hadn't done in a long time.

The ball whizzed past his head, and he had to chase it. Not good for his mind to wander or he might show up with a black eye at dinner. He retrieved the ball from the damp grass and tossed it underhand to simulate a pop fly.

Adam had to jog forward and then lifted his mitt to let the ball drop into it.

"Nice catch." Rick said. "Way to keep your eye on the ball."

His son beamed. "Coach has been hitting them like that in practice. A lot of batters hit under the ball and make it pop like that. When I play third base, there're lots of fouls, too."

"Then we should practice more of those."

Adam threw another fastball that landed in Rick's mitt with a satisfying snap.

After thirty minutes of playing catch, they went inside. Adam hurried to pack his special overnight bag and then played his video game while Rick showered and dressed for the night out.

****

"I want details about your date tonight," Sherry said after Rick dropped Adam off before heading to the restaurant to meet Ben and Cayme.

"Then you'll have to get them from Cayme. I don't kiss and tell. I'm not gossiping with my nosy sister."

"Will there be kissing?" She arched an inquiring eyebrow, reminding him of their mother.

"Talk to Cayme."

"I could hold Adam hostage." The threatening look Sherry gave fell short when the baby stuck a finger in her mother's nose.

Rick laughed. "You could try. Both those boys have you wrapped up tighter than a Christmas package. You'd just give him back."

Sherry set little Rachel in her walker, and the baby scampered off to find the boys. She laid a hand on his forearm. "She's my best friend. But you're my brother. Something's not right about this engagement. I'm not saying I'm not thrilled to pieces. I just don't want to see either of you hurt." She gave his arm a squeeze to let him know she was serious.

"I get it, sis." He pulled her into a quick hug. "Cayme and I know what we're doing. Don't worry." At least he hoped they both knew what they were doing. He headed toward the door with Sherry on his heels.

"I'm a mom," she shouted. "I'm hardwired to worry."

"Save it for the boys." He jogged down the front steps and hurried to his truck under the drizzly skies. "I'll be by around nine in the morning to pick up Adam," he called and climbed inside.

Twenty minutes later, he pulled up to the upscale

restaurant. For a rainy Saturday night, the parking lot was full. As he pulled in, he recalled the last Saturday night date he'd had a couple of years ago. He barely remembered the woman's name. Some tourist who'd flown in for a week of skiing. It hadn't taken long for either of them to realize the evening wasn't going any further than a meal. She was too sophisticated for him, and he was too laid-back for her taste. A nice evening but no sparks.

There hadn't been sparks with any woman he'd dated since Roxanne, and those had faded as soon as she found out she was pregnant.

Cayme's face popped into his head. Definitely some sparks there. The night should be fun, even with her brother as a chaperone.

He found a parking spot on the last row, climbed out of the truck, and quickly crossed the lot to avoid getting too wet. As he reached the restaurant doors, he adjusted his suit jacket, and felt in the pocket for his tie. He hoped he wouldn't have to wear it but had grabbed it at the last moment just in case.

Pausing just inside, he gave his eyes time to adjust to the dim lighting. A romantic song played quietly through hidden speakers. The aroma of grilled steaks made him realize he hadn't eaten since breakfast. He gave his name to the host and was assured he didn't need a tie. Then he was led to a table set for three.

Ben and Cayme were already seated at the table. Too bad they weren't in a booth with Ben on one side, and him and Cayme on the other. He wanted to sit next to her, thighs touching. Or maybe not, with big brother watching.

As if she'd read his thoughts, she glanced up then

blushed and quickly looked down.

Ben stood and shook Rick's hand. "I was starting to wonder if you got lost."

"Had a hard time finding a parking spot." Rick looked around. Most of the tables were full. However, the spacing was discreet enough it didn't seem overcrowded. He couldn't have picked a better place for a real first date. Too bad they had a chaperone. Maybe he should have put Ben off another week so he and Cayme could have some alone time before tonight. He glanced at her.

She was still studying the napkin in her lap.

"I hope you weren't waiting too long."

She looked up, shook her head, and then went back to studying her napkin. "No."

Why did she suddenly seem shy? Rick pulled out a chair and sat, feeling more like a third wheel than Ben probably did. "This is really nice of you, Ben, to…uh…help us celebrate." He slid his chair closer to Cayme and laid an arm along the back of her chair, then gently stroked the soft skin along her cheek.

She raised her head, her expression a bit panicked.

He caught her gaze and gave a slight nod in Ben's direction.

Her eyes went wide and she seemed to understand his silent message. She offered a smile to her brother. "Yes. This is very nice, Ben. Thank you."

"It's the least I can do for two of my favorite people." Ben smiled. "Let's see what's on the menu. I'm starved."

At that moment, Rick decided whatever he and Cayme had to do to keep that smile on Ben's face was worth the effort. Even a fake engagement that went on forever.

****

For Cayme, the evening progressed like a blurry movie reel. The moment Rick touched her all cognitive brain functions short-circuited. Her mind backpedaled to his kiss earlier in the day and replayed it over and over and over again. What the man could do with those lips should be patented. No other man had ever sucker punched her with a kiss like that.

Rick was a drug, and she was addicted to him in a way she never imagined possible. This feeling went way beyond her youthful crush. She even had to bite back a groan when he'd removed his hand from her shoulder to eat his dinner. But after their coffee was served, he rested his hand there again, toying with the ends of her hair.

She had no idea if she'd contributed to the conversation between Rick and her brother. They'd probably talked a bit about Ben's new job, but she couldn't have repeated a single word that was said, even under oath. Chase had never made her feel like this—and Rick wasn't even trying. Most of his attention was on Ben. Except his hand. Oh, that hand!

Ben pushed back his chair and stood. "Okay…I'm out of here. You two are on your own for the rest of the evening." He winked at Cayme.

"Wait. What?" She came out of her stupor. "How will I get home?"

A wicked smile broke out on her brother's face. "Gee, I don't know. Maybe you and Rick can figure it out."

Heat crept up her neck and she felt it to the roots of her hair. She turned to Rick. "Are you ready to leave?"

"I've got all night." Regrettably, he removed his hand and looked at his watch. "However, the restaurant will probably close soon." He stood and shook Ben's hand. "Thanks for tonight."

Ben smiled and clapped Rick's shoulder. "My pleasure, buddy. I bid you congratulations, and good night. Drive safe." He leaned over and whispered in Cayme's ear. "I won't wait up."

Could her brother possibly embarrass her more?

After Ben left, Rick scooted his chair closer. "We have a few minutes to hang out if you'd like. What about an after-dinner drink?"

Cayme lifted her coffee cup. "I'll just finish this. Thanks." She swallowed the last of her coffee, then smoothed her napkin on the table in an attempt to compose herself.

She wasn't ready for the evening to end, unable to recall a weekend when she'd been free from catching up on her editing work. But that didn't mean she didn't have things to do. Boxes from the attic were stacked in the living room corner. And she wanted to read the contract for the property one more time before Tuesday's council meeting.

Still, the night had a magical quality to it—even with her chaperone brother. "We should probably leave, so you can get back to Adam."

The glint in Rick's eyes seemed to grow. "Adam's spending the night with Joey."

Just like that, Cayme overheated in spite of the chilly evening. Her imagination went places it had no business going. Even if they were making this engagement real, it had started on false pretenses. As much as she wanted Rick to put his arms around her and kiss her until she was senseless, that type of activity would lead to a place she'd never gone to with Chase.

And therein lay the dilemma. If she had put out for Chase, maybe they'd be married now. She shuddered.

"Are you cold?" Rick leaned forward and removed his jacket to place around her shoulders.

The scent of his aftershave hit her, and she closed her eyes and breathed it in. The warmth from his jacket surrounded her like a safe haven, and she wanted to curl up inside and never leave. "No, no. I'm fine." She gave him a shaky smile. "Just an unpleasant thought caught me off guard."

"It's too nice an evening for unpleasantness. Care to share? Unburden your soul?" He tugged on his ear. "I've been told I'm a great listener."

Who'd told him that? His ex-wife? A recent girlfriend? She knew so little about him yet also believed she knew all the important things. He was loyal, for one. Just look at how he'd stood by Ben during his therapy. And now he was possibly sacrificing a lucrative contract just to keep her brother happy.

Rick was also a wonderful parent, which meant he must be patient, kind, and interested in his child. That was a huge plus for Cayme. She couldn't marry someone who didn't love children.

Her mental list came to a screeching halt. She wasn't marrying Rick. This was a pretend engagement.

"What's really bothering you, Cayme?"

His question brought her attention back to the moment, the restaurant, and the man sitting next to her. She hated to destroy the evening but couldn't keep her doubts to herself. "Do you honestly think we're doing the right thing?"

He leaned back. "By right thing, I assume you mean getting engaged?"

She nodded.

"I think that if it wasn't the right thing in the beginning, we can make it right with a little effort."

Wow. That wasn't the answer she expected. "How?"

Rick tipped his head and looked at her. "We've already told the world. How much more real can we get? I'd like to get to know you better. I think there's something between us worth investigating."

She studied his face, the sincerity in his eyes. "I don't know what to say." She looked down at her hands clasped tightly in her lap, the whites of her knuckles almost glowing in the dim, romantic lighting.

One of Rick's large, calloused hands covered hers with a warmth that went straight to her middle.

"Relax, Cay." He tilted her chin up to meet his gaze. "How about we take it one day at a time? We're adults. We should be able to figure out if we're compatible."

On the man-woman scale, Cayme had no doubt they were compatible. She'd been crushing after Rick for too many years not to want to take this engagement to the logical conclusion. But on the husband-wife scale? Growing old together, mortgages, bills, raising Adam together—maybe even more children? Was she ready for that?

What about the hours she was putting in at her mother's store? She had a job in Seattle, at least for a while longer. What if she couldn't make things work now that she was home? She might need that job. And

Ben. She had to think about Ben.

"You look like you're attempting to solve the world's problems in one night."

Rick interrupted her runaway musings by placing a palm on her cheek.

"Stop it," he said with a low growl. Then he leaned in and placed the merest whisper of a kiss on her mouth.

Chapter Fifteen

When Rick's lips touched hers, Cayme's entire being vibrated as if it were a cornice of snow about to break free and avalanche down a steep slope. For just that moment, she let his kiss sweep her away, tumbling into the slide, leaving a path cleared of worries and responsibilities.

But an avalanche devastated anything in its path. And giving in to these incredible feelings wouldn't wipe away her cares. They'd become even bigger problems. She had too many unresolved issues to allow this selfish passion to take over—her job, Ben, and whether or not to give in to this wild desire for Rick. With a whole lot of reluctance, she pulled away.

Her mouth tingled. Her body withered in protest. She lowered her head and studied her hands clasped in her lap, marveling that she hadn't reached out and pulled Rick on top of her.

He seemed to sense the turmoil inside her and pulled back as well. "I should get you home."

His words came out in a rough croak, proving he'd been as affected as she'd been by the kiss. She nodded, her voice not quite working and glanced around the restaurant. Heads quickly averted, as though everyone had been staring. She gave a silent sigh. "The rumor mill will be buzzing again tomorrow."

"What fun is it to be engaged and not act like it?"

Taking Rick's offered hand, she stood and slid out of his jacket. "It's certainly fun for the audience." She reached for her purse and her own jacket on the back of the chair.

He leaned in and smiled. "Come on. You didn't enjoy that just a little bit?" His tone was teasing, but his expression was serious.

"Do you really need me to answer that?"

A satisfied smile split his face. "That good, eh? Then my time here was a success." He tugged on his suit jacket before holding her coat out for her.

She turned around, allowing him to slip it on, while at the same time hiding the small hurt at his comment. This engagement was a convenience for both of them, but the playacting would surely leave a few scars—at least on her. "You always seemed to land on your feet." She wrinkled her nose and shook her head at him. "No matter what you set your mind to."

"Don't tell my sister that. She thinks she's the one who rescued me once I returned to Blakely with a child and no place to live." He placed his large hand at the small of her back, and they made their way to the front of the restaurant.

Cayme paused at the door, looking at the rain that had started again, making the night cold and dark. "Sherry's had the mothering instinct all her life." She glanced at Rick. "I'm glad she was there for you."

He lifted his collar to prepare for the walk outside, and then looked over at her. "She was there for you, too."

She nodded, sensing Rick was referring to her unexpected exodus from town after she'd called off her wedding. "I know." She stared back at the rain outside, so different from the mist that hovered over Seattle much of the time. That time and place seemed so distant from this moment. "I had to deal with my problems on my own."

"By running away."

"By not leaning on others."

"We all need someone to lean on once in a while, Cayme." He took her hand and led her out into the rainy night. "Even you."

****

Monday morning, Rick woke up late. He'd slept poorly the past two nights. When he did sleep, he'd dreamt of chasing Cayme in a game of hide-and-seek like they'd played when they were kids. Except in his dreams they weren't kids anymore. When he finally caught her, they'd tumbled to the grass in a tangle of limbs and lips. After each dream, he'd roll over and pound his pillow with the taste of her sweetness on his tongue.

He wanted to blame Cayme for his sleepless nights; yet, it wasn't her fault he got an itch he couldn't scratch whenever he was around her. Even though Adam had spent Saturday night at Sherry's, Rick hadn't invited Cayme back to his house to extend the evening, despite how much he'd wanted to. And no way could they have gone back to her place with Ben there.

Instead, he'd driven her home—the windshield wipers slapping a mocking rhythm to the throb in the lower part of his body. They didn't even spend that much time parked out in front of her house. While they'd discussed the river levels and what to do if it overflowed onto her property, the cold made the windows fog. Rick chose not to linger, even though her warmth called to him. Neither of them needed more gossip while they steamed up the inside of his truck like a couple of teenagers.

With an ache inside, greater than any physical pain, he climbed out of bed to get Adam ready for school. Thirty minutes later he stood outside his house on a rare sunny morning, watching Adam walk down the street. Then he rushed back inside and put the breakfast dishes in the sink to soak. He gave the kitchen table a swipe with a damp dishrag and promised to do a better job before dinner, which would be late that night because Adam had a game.

Eight years ago, when Rick came home alone with an infant son, he'd committed to being the kind of single father who kept his kitchen clean. His time in the Army instilled a discipline that carried over into civilian life.

He rinsed out the dishrag and laid it on the edge of the sink to dry. If he and Cayme followed through to the inevitable conclusion of this engagement, they could share domestic duties. On the other hand, he wasn't entirely certain he wanted to follow through with a marriage. He'd already failed in that arena once before.

Unfortunately, errant images of Cayme filed through his brain like a platoon marching to the cadence of a drill sergeant. The accompanying headache was a result of sleeplessness and unfulfilled frustration. He was a grown man. Had withstood officers yelling in his face, his son's scraped knees, and the city council breathing down his neck. He could handle this attraction to a certain redhead with a firm grip on his emotions—even if it killed him.

He glanced at the time again and attempted to clear his mind. After taking a couple of painkillers, he climbed into his truck and drove to the job site near the river. The plan was to start on the north end of the park. They'd already broken ground on the project but were forced to wait for the city to reevaluate the situation if Cayme rejected the contract her mother had agreed to. Rick couldn't help but think that if Rachel had just signed the contract before she'd died, they wouldn't be stuck in limbo waiting for Cayme to decide whether or not she was selling.

While parking his truck, he surveyed the activity around him. Good, his crew had already dismantled the old, rusted playground equipment. The useable metal would be separated and sent to a recycling plant in Boise. The rest was relegated to a junk heap for the city dump trucks to take to the landfill.

Rick climbed out of his truck and was greeted by his scowling foreman.

"You're running late this morning, boss." Willis tilted his hard hat back, exposing thick brows and a buzzed hairline.

The older man had worked for Rick's dad. In fact, Rick had inherited most of the crew. They were all good men and accepted Rick as their new boss, even though many had more construction experience than he could ever hope to have.

"I didn't sleep well last night," Rick admitted. As if compelled by some magical incantation, his gaze was drawn across the expanse of the old park to Cayme's house.

"Well, it's bad enough that Foster woman is holding up the project, but you—" Willis poked a stubby finger in Rick's chest. "—Mr. Boss Man, better find a way to be here on time from now on. With the weather holding for a couple of days, we should have the ground cleared and leveled by this coming weekend. I'm not approving any overtime for the holiday weekend."

"I'll be here at sunup tomorrow." Rick was willing to pull his weight. "But I promised Adam I'd go to his ball game this afternoon."

Willis frowned again, his weathered face crinkling at the brows.

"All the schedules and duties are assigned. As long as we have a full crew for the day, we should have the place cleared like we planned."

"If we can remove the playground equipment—" Willis nodded. "—and get the concrete busted up, and stacked for the city to haul away tomorrow, we'll be ahead of schedule."

Rick gave the man an appreciative look. "I knew you'd be right on it." He liked his foreman and relied on his guidance in areas where Rick lacked expertise. His army job hadn't involved a lot of construction work, but he'd done plenty of grunt work setting up temporary housing during his time in the Middle East. He'd paid better attention then than when he'd been on his dad's job sites as a kid. It served him now in taking over his father's company. The last thing he wanted was to fail. He refused to disappoint his father or let down a great crew who relied on the work for a payday.

Building a park was different from erecting Quonset huts and temporary housing but prepping the ground was similar. At least this part of the job he knew well. He would rely heavily on Willis to install the new equipment and decide how to place the walkways around the perimeter. Part of their job was to make sure pedestrians and bikers weren't at risk if a Little Leaguer sent a foul ball through the air.

Rick, Willis, and the crew spent the morning going over the plans they had for the north side of the park. Even if Cayme refused to sell her home and land, there'd be a place for kids to enjoy the playground equipment. The planned ball diamonds and basketball courts couldn't go in without the extra property. The current area was just too small for all the projects the city had planned. Too bad the Foster's house was between the old park and the majority of the property the city needed.

If the city acquired the adjoining land, they could tear up the street, tear down the houses, and expand on the south end. The ball diamonds—four of them were in the plans, adjoined at the backstops and fanned out to look like a clover leaf—would be the focal point of the park. The playground was on the north end and the basketball and tennis courts on the south. A bike and walking path would circumnavigate the entire park and join with a bike path that ran north to the resorts. It would be an amazing community gathering place. If Cayme sold her property.

Rick tabled the what-ifs, knowing they'd never find another location that would accommodate the original design. Besides, the city owned the current parcel where the old playground was located. He'd already drafted alternate plans to show the city. Those designs illustrated viable alterations if Cayme didn't sell.

By one o'clock he was at his desk, having picked

up a burger at the fast food joint because there had been no time that morning to fix lunch. He'd been tempted to stop at Books, Bytes, & Brews to eat, but chose instead to walk the long way around to avoid the woman who had invaded his dreams. If he didn't avoid her, he'd probably never get back to work. Instead, he'd have the sweet torture of her company during Adam's ball game that afternoon. He hoped to resist the urge to touch her, taste her—well, he could touch—and look. But for some reason, she seemed skittish when he kissed her. Maybe they just needed to be completely alone—no audience, no interruptions—for her to finally let go.

A knock on his open door kept the thought from going further. He looked up as Mayor Nicholson entered the office and took a seat on the other side of the desk.

"Mayor, what can I do for you?" Rick looked down at the alternate plans and knew exactly what the man wanted.

"Do I have to ask?"

"No." Rick stood. "I suppose you don't." He leaned over his desk and spun the blueprint around for the other man to see. "I want to tweak a couple of things, but this is what I'll present at the meeting tomorrow night."

The mayor stood and looked at the design. He took his time reviewing the diagrams then gave a nod. "I like what I see. If we don't get the extra acreage, I think we can work with this."

Rick sighed. "It'll be a tight squeeze, but I'll make it happen."

"I guess that's all I can ask." The older man tugged at his tie. "That's not all I came to talk about." He settled back in his chair. "I talked with our Ms. Foster a few nights ago. I want you to know how happy I am for the two of you."

"Thank you. Cayme mentioned you had visited." Was that why the mayor looked uncomfortable?

"I didn't go over to strong-arm her, if that's what you're thinking." The mayor rubbed his palms along his thighs.

The gesture worried Rick. "You're too nervous, Timothy. Why don't you tell me what's going on?"

The persona of mayor seemed to disappear at Rick's question, and in its place, was a man. "Given the relationship between you and Cayme, I'm sure she told you about me and Rachel."

"She did."

A look of relief crossed Timothy Nicholson's face. "We didn't—" He cleared his throat. "—I mean we didn't have an affair, just a friendship."

"So why are you telling me this now?" Rick frowned.

The other man swallowed, and his "Mayor" look was back. "Because it's bound to come up at the meeting. Like I told Cayme the other night, I wanted her to hear it from me, not some catty gossip. I don't want it to look like I'm hiding something torrid."

"I didn't think that at all." The surprise was that the mayor had been closer to Cayme's mother than anyone suspected. Although Timothy Nicholson and Rachel Foster were single adults and free to get involved, Rick could appreciate wanting to avoid the community gossip mill.

"I'm glad she told you. I just wanted to tell you personally since you and Cayme are engaged. That's all." Nicholson stood to leave. "I'll look forward to seeing the tweaks at the meeting."

Rick stood too. "You make it sound like we'll have to implement them."

"I don't want to. However, I wouldn't be surprised if Cayme doesn't follow through with her mother's wishes to sell."

Rick shrugged. "There's a lot at stake for her."

"My point, exactly." The mayor held out his hand. "See you at the ball game?"

Rick took the offered hand. "I promised Adam I'd be there. I won't let him break his promises, so I'd best not break mine."

"You're a good dad, Rick." With that, the mayor left Rick's office, closing the door behind him.

Two minutes later, the office door opened again and Rick looked up to see Councilman Samuel Peters standing there.

"I saw the mayor leaving your office."

Rick closed the file he was reviewing. "Councilman Peters. What can I do for you?"

Peters glanced over his shoulder then stepped all the way inside the office and closed the door behind him. "Has that Foster woman come to a decision? Did you get the green light to start on the original plans? Is that why the mayor was here?"

Rick narrowed his eyes at the other man. "No, no, and it's none of your business."

Peters huffed. "Everything about this project is my business. When will that stubborn woman come to her senses?" He gave Rick a hard stare. "I'd tell you to do something about her, but she's about as unreliable as any person I've ever had the misfortune to know. I don't imagine she'd even listen to you."

Rick pushed his chair back and straightened to his full height. "You need to remember that's my fiancée you're talking about. If you're not here to talk about business, you need to leave."

The other man's face flushed a deep red and he took a step back. He seemed to pause with indecision. After a moment, he hefted a briefcase onto Rick's desk. With a flourish, he snapped it open, retrieved a manila envelope, and held it out. "I have a project I want to offer your company."

Rick folded his arms. "I'm not taking on new projects right now."

"I wouldn't be so sure you can afford to reject work, Morrison." Peters waved the envelope.

That was the only thing Peters had said since walking into the office that had any truth to it. Regardless, Rick didn't want anything to do with the rich resort owner, especially when he threw his weight and money around. Reluctantly, Rick took the packet and unwound the string holding the flap and pulled out the papers. After glancing through them, he stared back at the other man. "What is this?"

"You can read." Peters helped himself to the chair in front of Rick's desk. "But to be clear, that is a contract to develop a new golf course with an access bridge across the river from the new park to the clubhouse."

"The new park isn't a done deal. You know that." Rick dropped the papers on his desk. "I can't accept this contract, even if I wanted to. I'm booked for the year and can't take on another project." Not entirely the truth, but he didn't appreciate Peters walking into his office and expecting Rick to bow to his wishes.

"I have every confidence that the park will be a done deal. That Foster woman will have to sell to the city, or the city will take her to court for breach of contract."

Rick balled his fists. "And you're supplying the lawyer, I suppose."

"Bet your last dollar on it."

Rick picked up the papers to hand them back to Peters. "You need to go."

Peters stood, gave a nod at the papers then snapped his briefcase closed. "You keep those. In fact, make sure you look through them carefully. Pay particular attention to the bonus paid once the project is complete." He pivoted and strode out of the office, closing the door behind him with a decisive click.

What in the world was he supposed to think of Councilman Peters' bombshell? All he knew was a dung-pile of complications had dropped on his desk, and he was front and center with this land deal whether he wanted to be or not. What kind of fallout would take place at the town hall meeting the next night?

He'd have to watch Cayme face a room of merchants, parents, and concerned residents who wanted this park and the benefits it would bring the community. The proposed bike path was like none other in the state. The current path that ran for about five miles toward the resort was popular with a group of competition bikers. If the original plans went through, the bike path would stretch for nearly twenty miles and take the growing bike traffic off the road between Blakely and the resort to the north, reducing potential accidents and easing frustration for tourists forced to share the roads.

And now Peters was working some deal on the side to bring an even larger economic boom to the community.

Rick pulled open a drawer for his antacids and shoved a couple in his mouth before turning back to his designs. Somehow, he had to come up with something that would work for everyone. It looked more and more likely that someone would get the short end of the deal. And he couldn't help but wonder if it would be him or Cayme.

Chapter Sixteen

Cayme woke up early Monday morning without the alarm—a rarity. It felt so right that for a moment she couldn't quite put her finger on why she was so excited.

Oh, right. Ben was starting his new job this morning. And of course, she was taking the afternoon off. Another rarity. And Adam's ball game. She wasn't sure about spending more time in Rick's company—his last kiss was never far from her mind—but she wasn't about to let Adam down. Keeping her word to the boy was important.

But was her desire to keep her promise because Adam's mother had abandoned him or her fondness for the boy? Maybe both. It bothered her that this unknown woman hadn't only left her son, but a pretty terrific man, too.

Ultimately, Cayme's true reason for not breaking the promise didn't really matter. She'd keep her word. Even if it meant sitting close enough to Rick to smell his uniquely masculine scent, feel the heat from his body, and listen to his sexy voice encouraging his son.

By six-fifteen, after wishing Ben good luck on his first day, Cayme was at the store and setting up for the morning crowd. Unlike weekends at the store, which were less hectic, Mondays had a hurry-up quality to them. Everyone wanted a quick fix of caffeine to start the workweek on the right foot. She'd been working long enough to discern the patterns of each day and appreciated the predictability. She liked that same predictability in her own routine. Even though the last few days had taken on a life of their own, a new normal was taking shape and the change wasn't unwelcome.

She straightened the flavor bottles on the counter then grabbed a rag and started wiping down the surfaces. Hopefully the store would have a quiet afternoon that day so she wouldn't feel like she was abandoning Skeeter to the mercy of the customers. Never mind that Skeeter had handled several weeks on her own, with only part-time help, after Cayme's mother had taken ill and Cayme had stayed at home with her. The one time she'd come in was when Skeeter had needed help with the bookkeeping. That was her first chance to see how the store was doing. Things had looked bleak without her mother there to help.

At that time, Skeeter had assured Cayme that things were in the red because the slow season and the rainy spring weather had put a damper on business. But with the promise of a late Memorial Day ski weekend, and then the summer, things would pick up.

After the funeral, she'd thrown herself neck deep into getting the store in the black. They were making it now. But if they had a couple of bad summer months, things wouldn't look so good.

If only she had some savings tucked away to invest in the store. After the last few weeks of putting her heart and soul into helping it succeed, she didn't want the store to fail. Since deciding to stay in town, she'd told her roommates to look for someone to take her place. She'd pay her part of the rent until then.

Hopefully it wouldn't take too long.

A small, niggling voice whispered that if she sold the house, she'd have funds to dump into the store. The property was hers and Ben's, free and clear, except for the taxes. The city's offer was fair—more than fair, if she was honest.

She recognized now why her mother had planned to sell, probably intending to infuse money into the store just like Cayme was considering. But if she sold their home, she and Ben needed to find a new place to live.

Skeeter came in from the backroom, prompting Cayme to shelve that particular problem for later. "Hi." She greeted the other woman with a smile that wavered a little. As much as she had looked forward to the afternoon, she suddenly wasn't sure if she should leave.

"Hey, baby." Skeeter traded her jacket for an apron. "How was your night?" She headed into the pantry for items she'd need for the day.

"I must have slept well," Cayme answered. "I woke up this morning without the alarm."

"That's a good sign." Skeeter's voice came from inside the storage closet. "It means you're starting to settle in."

Cayme finished wringing out the rag she'd used to wipe the counters. "Skeeter, have you always been a morning philosopher?"

Skeeter closed the pantry door, dimples bracketing each side of her wide mouth. "Ah, darlin', you just bring out the mother in me."

"I think you'd make a great mother. How is it you never married and had kids?"

Skeeter's smile faltered a little. She swiped a hand

in front of her face like batting away a bad memory. "I guess that love bug never bit me like it did you and Rick." She gave Cayme a considering look. "Besides, I'm happy to fill in anytime you're missing your momma."

"And you do an awesome job. I think I'm finally doing okay." Cayme hoped her words sounded optimistic because the statement came out less enthusiastic than she wanted.

"Do you now?"

Okay, now she wasn't as sure as she'd been moments ago. She hadn't caused more problems than solutions for Ben, Skeeter, and the store by taking over, had she? "Haven't I done all right since I've been here?"

"You've done as well as your mother. In some cases, even better. Neither one of us wanted to handle the bookkeeping. Your accounting skills have kept us on track." Skeeter seemed to read her mind.

Cayme took a breath. "Things will be fine this summer, right?"

The other woman hesitated. "Of course they will. School's out. Some of the college crowd will be here to hike and camp. There'll be a little lull until the summer tourism picks up, but folks still like to grab an early cup and check out the news before they start the day. I think we'll see more kids looking to use the Internet, too."

Cayme looked around the store where she spent more time than in her own home. "I hope you're right."

Skeeter came up behind her and gave her shoulder a squeeze. "I'm right." She gave Cayme a little push. "Now let's get to work. You can help me stock up and arrange things so if it does get busy this afternoon, I'll have it all right here."

"I feel guilty about leaving you alone."

"Nonsense." Skeeter shook her head, making her long ponytail swish over her shoulder. "You wouldn't disappoint that little boy, would you?"

Cayme pictured Adam's face and the pleading look when he'd invited her to attend the game. "No." She swallowed, pushing down her own misgivings. "You're right. Let's get everything ready."

"Sounds like a plan. Don't want you disappointing that big boy either." Skeeter gave a sly grin and headed into the backroom.

****

That afternoon, Cayme pulled onto the gravel lot of the ballpark, turned off the engine, and sat in her car looking at the crowds gathering near the bleachers. Some people stared back. She recognized folks who'd lived there all her life. Other people were customers who occasionally stopped in the store. She would see many of these same people again the following night at the council meeting while she justified not selling her home. Despite the stares, the only person who directed a hostile expression in her direction was Councilman Peters. She took a breath and stared back, not wanting to be first to look away.

He gave her a scowl and moved toward the bleachers.

Maybe coming to the game wasn't such a good idea. Why put herself through the whispers and gossip until she absolutely had to? Skeeter would call her a coward for running away again, yet Cayme doubted her courage to face these people.

Had it not been for disappointing a certain eight-year-old boy, she would have found several reasons to leave the ballpark. Who was she kidding? The game wasn't making her anxious, neither was the crowd. Seeing Rick was. How could she hide her growing feelings for him? On one hand, she didn't want to hide her feelings, on the other hand, she was positive their engagement would end soon, and if she didn't keep her feelings in check, she'd be left holding a broken heart.

She caught a glimpse of Rick out on the ballfield playing catch with the kids. The rocks in her stomach started to roll. Why was she making herself sick about this? She had a right to enjoy the spring air and some baseball.

As she reached for the door handle, someone knocked on the car window. Her heart raced until she recognized her bestie. Thank goodness. Someone who wouldn't judge. She grabbed her jacket and climbed out.

Next to Sherry stood Joey and Adam wearing red-and-black uniforms over gray ball pants. They even had on matching long-sleeve shirts to keep the unseasonable spring chill at bay.

"You guys look ready to play for the majors." Cayme grinned at them. "What's your team's name?"

"We're the Blakely Blackhawks." Adam's little chest puffed out.

"Yeah. That's cuz we look like we're flying when we're running the bases." Joey flapped his arms like a bird.

Cayme laughed. "Is that so? Will I have to cover my head when your team is up to bat?"

Adam frowned. "Not if you sit behind the backstop. It's safer there and you can watch us at bat."

"Sounds like the perfect place to sit." She looked at his aunt. "Will you join me?"

Sherry attempted to hide a grin at Cayme's comment. "For as long as I can." She hitched her youngest higher on her hip. "This one doesn't sit still very long. I usually end up pacing behind the bleachers." She leaned in closer and nodded to where the councilman was sitting on the bleachers. "Looked like you were about to go into battle."

"Not talking about it here." Cayme extended her finger for little Rachel to take. A chubby gloved hand clutched on, and Cayme jiggled it to make the baby smile. "I can join you behind the bleachers, though."

Adam's face fell. "But then you might miss something. Aunt Sherry is always missing us when we hit the ball."

"Oh, I hadn't considered that." Cayme returned her full attention to the boys, the real reason she was there in the first place. "It must be hard to see the field from behind the bleachers."

"It is." Both youngsters nodded vigorously, their red-and-black ball caps bouncing in unison.

"Then I'll sit where I won't miss a single bit of action," Cayme said. Sherry's expression said she'd given the right answer. There'd be time for grown-up talk later.

"Yes!" Adam held his hand up and Joey gave him a high-five.

"Adam, Joey!" Sherry's husband called to the boys. He was wearing the same team hat. "I'm putting you at the end of the lineup if you're not over here in two seconds."

The boys' eyes went wide, and they scurried

toward the third base dugout, mitts clutched in their hands.

Cayme looked at the man towering over the team. "Ken's the coach?"

"Indeed, he is." Sherry grinned and waved to her husband. "Wave to Daddy." She took the baby's gloved hand and waggled it in the air.

"Ken's been Joey's and Adam's coach from the time they were old enough to play T-ball." Sherry started to walk toward the bleachers. "Instead of brains, the two of them have baseballs between their ears. Thank goodness I have a little girl or I'd go bonkers."

They climbed up three bleacher benches. High enough to see the game but easy for Sherry to climb down with the baby.

"I'm glad you're here. I wasn't sure about coming…"

"What are you talking about?" Sherry scowled. "You think the whole town feels like Peters?"

Cayme swallowed and glanced at the councilman all bundled in his expensive wool coat sitting on the top row. "I wonder… You know most of the residents think I'm stalling to get more money."

Sherry swiped at the air. "Nonsense. It's your home. Stop justifying yourself." She plopped the baby in Cayme's lap. "Here. Hold your goddaughter. I'm giving my man a good luck kiss. Life is better at home if they win." The exuberant woman hopped off the bleachers and headed toward the dugout.

The baby found a corner of Cayme's scarf and pulled it into her mouth and started sucking.

Cayme tugged her clothing free and replaced it with a pacifier just as Rick climbed up and sat beside her.

"Getting in a little practice?" He winked at her.

The Blackhawk red in his jacket really brought out the brown of his eyes. For a moment, she lost all thought. "Practice?" she repeated. She had no idea what he meant, unless he was referring to a time in the future when she might have kids of her own. Cayme gave him a sidelong look at his teasing tone. Her stomach pitched a little at the image of them making babies together.

He gave a quick shake of his head. "Sorry. Getting a bit ahead of myself."

She was tempted to pursue the comment, reminding him that they were only in a pretend arrangement, but Sherry returned just then. After handing the baby back to her mother, she turned to Rick. "How was Ben's first day?"

"It took him a couple of hours to settle in, but then he started the assessment of my network." Rick nudged her shoulder. "I'm glad I brought him on board. I had no idea how behind the times my computers were."

Cayme smiled. "I'm still wrapping my head around those calloused hands running over a keyboard. He surprises me sometimes."

Rick leaned even closer. "We made a good decision to make this thing work. I think it's taken a burden off him."

"I hope you're right." She settled in to watch the game, focusing on the kids instead of worrying about Ben, the property, or Rick's warm scent as his thigh brushed hers.

The visiting team was at bat first. Cayme cheered when Adam, who was playing third base, scooped up a grounder and threw it to first base to get the runner out.

"Wow. He's quite the player."

Rick's shoulders squared and he smiled with pride. "That's my boy."

As the game progressed, she couldn't stop herself from jumping up and cheering after Adam or his teammates made a great play or grumbling if the umpires made a bad call. Although, for the most part, the umps did a fair job for both teams. She had no idea she'd get so wrapped up in the game. Her concerns about sitting with Rick or what the townspeople thought of her seemed to disappear.

****

Rick loved coming to his kid's games, yet he couldn't remember one he enjoyed more than that day. Listening to Cayme yell out encouragement to his son, grumbling under her breath at a missed ball, and clapping for the kids on the team, had him seeing the game with fresh eyes. And seeing a different side of his fiancée.

Her physical presence was impossible to ignore. He was even more aware of her energy and enthusiasm.

In spite of how uncomfortable she must feel around the residents who wanted her to sell her house, she made the effort to enjoy the game. She didn't seem to notice folks whispering as they walked by. And more importantly, she'd kept her promise to Adam.

That tipped the scales for Rick. All of those things added to his growing affection for her. Definitely more affection than he expected. He was beginning to think this engagement deal was good for both him and his son. A cheer went up from the home crowd, drawing his attention back to the game.

"Come on, Adam," Cayme shouted. "You can do

it!"

His son was walking up to the plate, giving a thumbs-up to Joey on second base. Joey must have hit a double and Rick missed it while daydreaming about the pretty lady next to him. The scoreboard showed two outs at the bottom of the fourth inning. At Adam's age, a time limit instead of innings determined the length of a game. The game was about over, and the other team was up by one run. And his son was at bat.

No pressure there.

Rick scooted to the edge of his seat, sweat forming on his palms.

Adam stepped away from the plate and took a couple of practice swings then looked at his coach standing along the third base line and got the signal. He stepped into the batter's box and settled into his stance. Squaring up, he twirled the tip of the bat in the air, waiting for the pitch. When it came, he swung for the fence. But his bat missed just under the ball. Strike one.

Rick's heart pounded and a lump formed in his chest. More than anything he wanted to take the pressure off his kid. He didn't want Adam to be the one who was responsible for the team's win or loss. It didn't matter that the win or loss was the team's effort, everyone always remembered the last player at bat as the hero or the one who lost the game.

But Rick couldn't take this moment away from his son. Moments like these defined character. What kind of father would he be if he tried to protect his boy from all the bad things in the world? All he could do was prepare him as best he could and hope for an outcome that would shape his son into a fine man. The one thing any parent could do.

Suddenly, his arm was in a vise grip.

"I can't watch," Cayme said. "How do you stand this?"

He glanced at her and then at the empty space where his sister had been sitting. Sherry was probably off walking the baby. "You have to watch. If you miss his at bat, Adam will be disappointed." He placed a hand over Cayme's and squeezed. "That's how I do it. I have to."

She eased her grip on his forearm, and leaned forward a little, but didn't let go.

Neither did he, offering a steady hand when she seemed to need one. He liked the sensation of comfort that came over him with the simple gesture.

Adam took another practice swing and looked at the coach again. Almost the same signal. The opposing coach must have picked up on it, too. He yelled at his fielders to back up. The boys were only eight and nine years old. Did they have any idea what their parents were going through?

The pitcher wound up and gunned the ball at the plate. Adam didn't swing this time. And the umpire called a ball. The count was one and one.

The next pitch made it two balls, one strike.

Rick kept his hand over Cayme's and was surprised to find it a little cold.

She squeezed harder with each pitch.

When Adam had a full count on him, Rick was squeezing back, unable to hold in his nerves.

The pitcher took the mound and checked the bases. Joey was poised on second base, ready to head for home. At the next pitch, everyone seemed to hold their breath.

Once again, Adam swung for the fences, putting everything he had into his windup.

When the ball connected with a crack, the entire crowd rose to their feet.

Adam took off running.

So did Joey.

The ball never reached the fence. Instead, it landed just behind the right fielder. Joey had rounded third and was headed home by the time Adam reached first base. Instead of turning right to hold his position, he headed toward second.

The coaches were giving both Joey and Adam the go-ahead signals, while the right fielder scrambled to find the ball and relay it in.

As the ball reached the first baseman, Joey scored the tying run.

Unfortunately, the first baseman missed the ball and the pitcher who should have been backing up first was still on his mound shouting at the fielder. The ball struck the dirt. It took a bad bounce and rolled along the first baseline staying in bounds. The first baseman and catcher both took off after the ball.

By the time Adam reached third base, the coach was yelling at him to stay put. Adam either didn't hear him or was too caught up in the moment.

He headed for home, running faster than Rick had ever seen.

The pitcher rushed to cover home plate and yelled at the catcher to throw him the ball.

As Adam slid into the plate, the ball landed in the pitcher's mitt. The pitcher swung around to tag Adam but missed by mere inches.

The umpire threw his arms wide and yelled,

"Safe!"

Adam had scored the winning run!

A smile lit up Cayme's entire face, and Rick grabbed her and pulled her into a hug. "Did you see that? My boy hit a home run!"

"I know. I was so nervous for him. But he stayed with the play like he'd planned it all out." She hugged Rick tighter. "I'm so glad I got to see him play. He's great!"

"Joey, too!" Rick smiled over at his sister as she climbed the bleachers to join them. "Please tell me you didn't miss that!"

Sherry's smile was as wide as Cayme's. "I caught all the action just as Adam hit the ball. What a game." She winked at Rick, proving she caught more than the action on the field.

Cayme was still grinning. "No kidding. I was having a heart attack. I haven't had that much heart-pumping excitement since I got home." She reached out and grabbed Rick's hand.

Rick was surprised a little but held onto her.

Sherry laughed. "Girl, you have to get out more."

At the team's group cheer, they all turned to watch the winning team smack palms with the opposing team. Even the other team's coach pulled Adam aside and shook his hand.

Maybe any dad would feel pride for his son, but Rick's chest felt ready to pop.

The team gathered in the dugout to put the equipment away then headed to the grass to listen to the coach's instructions about the next game.

Cayme let go of Rick's hand.

He expected her to say goodbye and go back to the

store, instead she surprised him by hovering beside Sherry while they waited for the boys.

"Cayme!" Adam called. "Did you see us? We won!"

She grinned and flattened her palm for Adam to smack it. "I saw that double and the homerun. You guys are amazing!" She gave Joey a high five, too. "Thanks for inviting me to your game."

"We have two more before the tournament," Joey said.

"Yeah," Adam chimed in. "You should come. You're our good luck charm."

Cayme glanced at Rick.

Her hair caught the sunlight, making it glow like an angel's halo.

Looking at the boys, her smile grew even bigger. "I'm not sure I brought you luck today, but I'd love to come to your other games."

She faced Rick again, with a cute little shrug. He smiled back, feeling a burst of joy he hadn't felt in years.

Adam tugged on Cayme's arm, drawing her attention again. "Can you come with us to get ice cream?"

Her mouth opened and she glanced at Rick with wide eyes, then back to Adam. "I…"

"Please." Joey added. "You have to, cuz we won."

"You get ice cream even if you lose," Sherry teased.

"Yeah. It just tastes better when we win." Adam grabbed Cayme's hand and pulled her toward Rick's truck. "Come on. You can ride with us."

Cayme took a couple of steps with Adam, her

smile even bigger than before, then she stopped. "Whoa. Hold on there, kiddo. I can't just leave my car."

"Oh." Adam looked at where she pointed to the little blue compact. "Well, can you follow us so you won't get lost?"

"Cayme knows where the frosty stand is." Rick finally joined the conversation with a hand on her shoulder. "She won't get lost."

Adam gave her a curious look. "Really?"

Cayme brushed some home plate dust from his uniform.

Rick saw then and there what a great mother she'd make—a great stepmother for Adam.

She gave a final swipe at the dirt and said, "Well, I've been gone for a long time. But if the frosty stand is the same one, I know where it is."

"Cool!" Adam grinned. "I wanna ride with you. Can I?"

Chapter Seventeen

Cayme took a step back at the sudden emotion hammering in her chest. Adam's request to ride with her to get ice cream made her feel needed, just for being herself. How had this little boy wrapped around her heart so quickly?

Rick's face had gone still as if her answer to Adam's question was as important to him as to Adam. She opened her mouth then quickly shut it. What was the right answer? "If it's okay with your dad," she finally said.

Adam turned to his father. "Can I, Dad?" He jumped up and down. "It's just a short way."

Rick gave her a smile that nearly melted her right there on the dusty parking lot.

"I'll meet you guys there."

"Can Joey ride with us too?" Adam asked.

"Wait a minute," Sherry chimed in. "He wasn't invited."

"It's okay," Cayme said. "Of course, he can. Aren't you two joined at the hip?"

"Huh?" Both Joey and Adam looked at her.

Sherry and Rick laughed.

"Didn't take you long to figure that out," Sherry said.

Cayme joined in the laughter and placed hands on both Adam's and Joey's shoulders. "Trust me. It's a good thing."

Adam looked at her with a hint of maturity that took her by surprise.

"It means we're really good friends, huh?"

"That's exactly what it means." Rick gave Cayme a wink. "Friends of the best kind."

His wink curled her toes. Could she and Rick remain friends after this engagement sham ended? Could they be friends with the city project putting them on opposite sides of the fence? Was that earlier hug a reaction to the moment, or did he feel something more? With two little boys wanting ice cream, this wasn't the time to dig into those questions. "Come on, boys." Cayme waved her arm toward her car. "Let's go celebrate a Blackhawk victory."

The burger joint on Main Street was a short ride from the ballpark.

For years, Cayme had known it as the frosty stand. After family outings, her dad would take them to get soft-serve ice-cream cones dipped in hot fudge and covered with chopped peanuts. With the two boys in her back seat recapping the game, play-by-play, she had a sudden craving for those carefree days when all she had to worry about was keeping the ice cream from melting before she got all the chocolate shell eaten.

She pulled into a spot between Rick's truck and Sherry's car. They joined the others and placed an order for soft-serve topped with hot fudge. Just like when she was a kid, she licked the sides of her cone, pondering how her life had come full circle. Or was this just a quick stop down memory lane before she was forced to move on?

Unlike the days when her dad had brought her and

Ben here, she couldn't go home and play in the yard or ride her bike around the neighborhood. Or pretend she was all grown-up and ready for love. She *was* grown-up now, and instead of playing house with the love of her life, she had responsibilities. Her mom and Skeeter's store as well as Ben's future rested on Cayme finding a stable foundation going forward.

As if he'd read her mind, Rick looked over with a raised eyebrow. "Why so serious?"

She shook herself. Rick didn't need to be worrying about her struggles. "Nothing too serious." She checked her watch. "Although, I do need to get back and help Skeeter wrap up for the day."

"You've got a busy week coming up, right?"

She nodded. "We're prepping for the sunrise ceremony next Monday."

Sherry leaned over and joined the conversation. "Are you providing coffee and pastries like your mother used to?"

Cayme nodded again. "It's a tradition. I don't think it should stop just because my mom isn't here to carry it on."

"It's wonderful that you're doing it," Sherry said. "Do you need a hand with anything?"

Cayme smiled her thanks. "I think Skeeter and I can handle the preparations, but I'd love some help that morning." She nodded toward the baby reaching for Joey's ice cream cone. "Can you get away?"

"Ken will handle the kids for me."

"Ken will?" The big man wearing a Blackhawks ball cap stepped over to their table.

Sherry squealed and jumped up to give her husband a hug. "You won!" She kissed him with no regard for the staring crowd.

"Eew." Both Adam and Joey made faces. "Kissing." Joey made a gagging noise and Adam giggled.

"Enough, boys." Rick glanced at Cayme.

Her smile slipped a little at the heat in his eyes.

Then his gaze traveled lower to the front of her shirt.

She looked down and spied a vanilla drip over her left breast. Embarrassed, she grabbed a napkin and swiped it.

"So—" Ken sat at the table next to Rick and across from his wife. "—you're stealing my wife away for the Memorial Day ceremony."

Cayme winced. Was he upset at her return to town? She had been dipping into Sherry's time lately. "Only if it's okay with you."

Ken's laugh filled the room. "Like I have a say." He reached across the table and snatched his wife's hand. "I'll just have to manage the hoodlums on my own."

"Rick can help you." Sherry looked between the two of them. "And then both of you can bring the kids to the ceremony."

Rick shrugged. "I'll be there anyway. I'm helping the scouts with their part of the presentations."

Sherry beamed. "Then it's settled."

Ken scowled in a way that seemed more for show than real. "Guess I'm there as well."

Sherry stuck her tongue out at her husband and then offered baby Rachel another lick of ice cream.

Cayme sighed. If only she could have that same easy connection with a guy that Sherry had with her husband. It seemed like the men Cayme dated didn't want to take the time to know her before they tried to get in her pants. She wasn't a prude, simply wanted more in a relationship. She glanced at Rick again, and he gave her a conspiring smile. Right then, she realized Rick was different than any other man she'd known. Warmth gathered in her stomach in spite of the ice cream.

Maybe the engagement was becoming more and more real. She mentally backpedaled. Maybe that was a road she shouldn't explore right now. She stood and turned to Adam and Joey. "I'm sorry, I have to leave. Thanks for a great afternoon and for inviting me to the game. You guys played great."

"You have to come to the next game," Adam said.

"Adam—" Rick's voice held a soft warning. "—Cayme may not be able to."

"I'll come if I can." She ignored the tingle from the sound of her name on Rick's lips. "But I have to work, too. I can't always leave Skeeter like I did today."

Adam stood and gave Cayme a hug. "Tell Miss Skeeter thank you for letting you come to my game."

Cayme fought the burning behind her eyes at his thoughtfulness. "I will." She returned the boy's hug with a gentle pressure, not wanting to let go.

He stepped away and Joey, not to be outdone, ran up and gave her a hug too.

She laughed.

Sherry stood. "I think you have a couple of new boyfriends. Your new fiancé will have to watch out."

Cayme smiled. "I hope it doesn't turn into an awkward love triangle. I wouldn't want any broken hearts."

Rick's head jerked up and he looked like he was about to say something but brought his cone to his mouth instead and gave her a teasing wink.

Goodness, she needed to watch what she said, especially around the boys. This engagement was becoming all too real.

****

After Cayme left, Adam settled next to Rick. "Did you see my hit, Dad?"

Rick put his arm around his son. "I sure did. You about gave me a heart attack, waiting for the full count to pull out your save."

Adam grinned at the compliment. "I had fun. Even if it didn't go over the fence, that was the best hit I've had all year. I'm glad you were there."

"Me too, buddy. Me too."

An hour later, Adam had changed out of his baseball uniform and taken a shower. He joined Rick outside beside the grill.

The chicken for their dinner smelled great, but the little-boy smell mixed with the scent of soap brought back memories of Adam when he was just a baby and Rick used to give him baths. His son was growing up and didn't need his old man constantly reminding him to wash behind his ears. Soon he'd be shaving and thinking about girls—

"Dad, do you think Cayme is pretty?"

Yeah, he definitely thought Cayme was pretty. And maybe his son was thinking about girls *now*. He took a moment to turn the chicken, formulating an appropriate answer. "What makes you ask a question like that?"

Adam stood on his toes to get a better look at the chicken. "Well, I think she's pretty. I didn't know red hair could look like that."

"Like what?"

"Like a fireball from the sun."

Rick smiled. His son had a poetic soul. "I guess it does." He wondered if Adam was experiencing his first love. When he was Adam's age, he'd developed a crush on the new swimming instructor who taught that summer. Funny how he never noticed girls again until junior high.

Of course, Cayme and Sherry had been two years behind him and Ben. Even into high school, Cayme hadn't been on his radar other than another person to make up being short a player for a ball game. It didn't matter if they were playing baseball, football, or a pick-up game of basketball, she seemed to be available to make the teams even, and not one of the other boys seemed to think it odd. He certainly hadn't.

Now he wondered how she'd felt about it. They'd treated her like one of the guys, and when they didn't, she was just his sister's best friend. Someone in the background. Someone he'd noticed but never really wondered too much about.

"I think she's really nice," Adam said. "I'm glad you and her are dating. She knows lots of stuff about books too."

Rick slanted a look at his kid. "Since when are you interested in books?"

Adam shrugged. "We move them around and stuff in the store. Some of them look interesting."

"I'm glad she's letting you help. Reading's important." Rick reached for a bottle of water he'd brought out earlier. "If I remember right, she was pretty smart in school."

"Was she in the same grade as you?"

"No. But her brother was. Ben and I used to hang out together."

"Like you do now sometimes?" Adam walked over to the picnic table and sat down.

"Yeah." Rick twisted the cap on the water and took a sip.

"It's sad that her mom died." He looked curiously at Rick. "Does she have to cook for just her and her brother, like you cook for me?"

"I suppose she does."

"Maybe we should invite them over so you can cook for them too."

Rick laughed. "Maybe. She does keep busy with work, and she spends time with your Aunt Sherry."

"Her and Aunt Sherry are friends, huh?"

Rick nodded and turned the chicken again, then lifted his bottle for another drink.

"Were they joined at the hip, too?"

Rick sputtered out his drink and gave Adam a smile. "They were."

"That's funny. When Cayme said that, I remembered those girls we saw on the news one time." Adam cocked his head. "What were they called?"

"You mean conjoined twins?"

"Yeah. Them." Adam craned his neck. "Is dinner ready? I'm hungry."

Rick smiled to himself. Ah, to be a kid again where everything could be solved with a full stomach. He flipped over the chicken one last time then slid the grilled breasts onto a plate. "Ready to head into the house, buddy?"

Adam nodded. "I'm starved." He ran ahead and

held the door open for Rick.

As they settled into the kitchen to eat, the front doorbell rang.

"I'll get it." Adam slid off his chair.

Rick grabbed his son by the collar. "Hold on there, bud. Remember what we talked about?"

Adam stopped. "Oh yeah. I need to be careful and check to make sure it's somebody I know, right?"

"I wish it didn't have to be that way, but it's always best to be safe."

As they walked to the door, Adam trailed Rick. He checked through the peephole and his stomach dropped.

When he opened the door to the woman standing on his front steps, Adam scooted in front of him, his entire body jittery with excitement.

"I recognize you! You're my mom."

Chapter Eighteen

Rick stood in the doorway, staring at his ex-wife and crushing the cool metal handle under his hand. Even though she'd sent pictures to Adam in her annual Christmas cards, it'd been nearly eight years since he'd last seen Roxanne. A point in her favor, Rick conceded, to let her child know she was thinking of him. Or that she wanted him to be thinking of her.

She'd changed some from the first time he'd met her. Back then, even in her BDUs, she was a strikingly beautiful woman, making her all the more irresistible to a twenty-something kid away from home for the very first time. Here, on his front steps, stood a more mature, still beautiful woman with her long black hair loose about her face and shoulders and a hint of makeup to enhance her already stunning features.

Gazing at Adam, she said, "Hey there, Adam. How are you?"

"You're my mom!" He said it again and tentatively stepped closer to give her a quick hug.

She staggered backward a little, eyes widening at his reception, but she hugged him back.

Adam lifted his head. "Wow! You're here. Dad said you might visit. And you did!"

Rick swallowed the lump in his throat. Watching the hopes and wishes of his eight-year-old son coming true was almost more than he could take. Especially since he wasn't sure this was what he wanted for his little boy. Roxanne had broken Rick's heart once, and he was very much afraid she'd break Adam's as well, by simply walking back into his life.

Glancing at Rick and then back at Adam, she hugged him a little tighter. Her smile was as bewitching as it had been at their first meeting. "I started my leave sooner."

Seeing that she wouldn't disappear like a bad apparition, Rick stepped back and opened the door wider. "Why don't we all come inside?"

Adam slipped from her hug and tugged on her hand to lead her into the house. "When Dad said you might visit this summer, I thought you would come after school was out. It's so cool you're early. Come on, I want to show you my room and all my stuff!"

"Slow down there, buddy," Rick told him. "We just sat down to dinner. Maybe your mom would like to join us." He glanced at Roxanne whose bemused expression still looked as though she couldn't quite wrap her head around Adam's enthusiastic greeting.

"Oh, yeah." Adam pulled up short and looked at his mother. "Dad grilled some chicken. He's really good at grilling. Come on." Instead of racing upstairs, he headed for the kitchen.

"Somehow I pictured you living in a much larger place." She glanced around while his enthusiastic eight-year-old guided her through the tidy but homey living room.

Rick bit back the retort on his lips. The size of their house was none of her business. Instead, all he said was, "This is our home."

"It's perfect for us," Adam chimed in. He paused,

looking around the living room. "But maybe we should move and get a bigger place."

"Oh, no." Roxanne shook her head. "This is a nice house, very cozy." When they entered the kitchen, she seemed to take in the small table and functional appliances with the same critical eye.

The hair on the back of Rick's neck pricked, and his temper started to rise. Who did she think she was, arriving unannounced, interrupting their meal, and making presumptuous remarks about how they lived? Just because she'd been born with a silver spoon in her mouth didn't give her the right to judge the home he'd made for himself and Adam.

Adam went to the cupboard and pulled out a plate. Opening a drawer, he grabbed some flatware and carried it to the table. "Sit here, Mom."

"Uh…" She glanced at the place setting, then to Rick.

He pulled out the chair across from Adam's. "Yes. Sit down."

After giving Adam a small smile, she sat, rearranging the fork and knife next her plate.

Not noticing his chicken dinner had gone cold, Adam slid into his place at the table with a grin. "I didn't think when I got up this morning that you'd be here for dinner. It's too bad you weren't here sooner, cuz you missed my game." He looked at Rick. "I did really good today, didn't I, Dad?"

"You did great, son," Rick agreed, still processing his ex-wife's arrival. He hadn't seen her since Adam was a baby, and now she was sitting at his kitchen table. He placed a grilled chicken breast on her plate.

Roxanne grabbed her fork, her knuckles going

white as though she was gripping a lifeline.

Rick hadn't known her all that long before she got pregnant and they had rushed the wedding, but regardless of the situation, she'd never before seemed out of her element.

Only Adam acted as though it was perfectly normal for his eight-year-absent mother to show up for dinner without warning.

Rick slid the salad bowl toward her. "It's nothing fancy. We've had a busy day, and this worked up quickly."

Her hand shook as she took a bit of salad and slid the bowl to the center of the table. "Thank you for letting me join you. I know I should have called first, but I wanted to surprise you. Both of you."

Adam blurted out. "I'm surprised. Aren't you, Dad?"

Rick nodded. Surprise was not quite the word that came to mind. Emotions swirled inside and the hits were coming at him so fast, all he could do was take a deep breath and cut into his dinner. The chicken was cold and tasted like cardboard. He considered heating it up again, but the shock of his ex-wife's unannounced appearance made his appetite disappear.

While he poked at his food, dinner proceeded in an awkward, strained manner. Of the dozen questions he wanted to ask, the topics were completely out of bounds with his son sitting right there, chatting to Roxanne about his day as though she'd been part of the family for years. Thankfully, Adam seemed unaware of the strained undercurrent between him and Roxanne.

Adam finally finished eating and hopped off his chair. "Can I show Mom my room now?"

At Adam's question, Roxanne laid down her fork next to her untouched meal. She took a breath, seemingly relieved to exit the domestic scene. "I'd love to see your room." She pushed aside her plate and stood. "Which way?"

Adam glanced at Rick, looking for permission.

"It's okay," Rick said. "But then you need to get your schoolwork together for tomorrow. And since you didn't go to the store today, you still have reading."

The boy's shoulders drooped. "But Mom's here. Do I have to go to school tomorrow?"

"Yes." Rick's answer left no room for arguments. He was glad Roxanne didn't say anything. Not that he'd let her override his rules.

"Okay." Adam groaned but then waved for his mother to follow. "Come on, Mom. My room's upstairs."

Roxanne hesitated, looking solemnly at Rick. "Thank you." Then she hurried after Adam.

Rick pushed his half-eaten dinner aside, his stomach sour. He stood and put away the leftover food then loaded the dishwasher. It seemed a lifetime since he'd rushed out of the house that morning. And what a day it had been.

He'd had very little sleep with Cayme invading his dreams. Those visits from the Mayor and Councilman Peters had thrown him off, especially Peters' golf course proposal. Adam's baseball game had been a great way to push all of that to the back of his mind, until he'd nearly kissed Cayme right there at the ballfield. He still wasn't sure what had stopped him. Now with Roxanne's earlier-than-expected visit, he hoped Cayme would keep her end of the engagement bargain. An engagement would send a message that Rick wasn't pining for his ex-wife.

Whatever Roxanne wanted, she needed to know she couldn't just walk back into their lives.

Shoving the dishwasher door shut a little harder than necessary, he wished he could start the day over. He'd have taken Adam out of school and headed to Boise for the week. Anything to avoid facing his ex. He wasn't sure Roxanne's visit didn't come with a hidden agenda and was afraid of what would happen to his son when the dust settled. But he'd never run away from a challenge and he wasn't about to start now.

Adam's excited voice carried downstairs, proudly showing off his toys.

Roxanne's oohs and aahs followed.

The situation had a surreal quality to it. Like something out of a nightmare. Even though he'd been mentally preparing for her visit, her early arrival showed him he wasn't prepared at all.

Adam thundered down the stairs, followed by Roxanne's more sedated descent.

By her dazed expression, the situation must have had her head spinning. She obviously wasn't prepared for the real-life exuberance of an eight-year-old boy.

"Dad, Mom really likes my superhero toys. She said they were awesome." Adam's smile was wide and proud.

"I'm glad. But now it's time to hit your books." Rick hesitated to put a damper on his son's excitement, but routine was important. Maybe even more so now. He couldn't let this unexpected visit derail their nightly schedule. He took a breath. "Your reading is waiting, and your mom and I need to talk."

"Yick." Adam's shoulders slumped. "Do I have to? Besides, there's barely two weeks left of school and it would be okay if I missed one day. I could do double next time. Mom might not be here that long."

Roxanne touched her son's shoulder. "Reading is important, and I'm staying in town for a few days so we'll have plenty of time to be together." Her words were unsettling.

No matter what she wanted from this visit, Rick wanted her gone as soon as possible.

"That's awesome!" Adam surprised his mother with another hug. "I'll go read now, but don't leave tonight before I go to bed." He turned toward Rick's study and disappeared.

Roxanne watched him with an odd expression on her face, angling to see where he'd gone. "He doesn't do homework in his room?"

"He loves sitting in my chair in the study to read," Rick replied. "It's the same chair where I read to him when he was a baby."

A pained look crossed his ex-wife's face. "I've missed all those years."

Rick ground his teeth to keep from blasting her for all of the milestones where she was absent. In truth, if they'd stayed together, it wouldn't have been a good marriage. Yes, Adam had grown up without a mother, but raising his son in a dysfunctional family would have been worse. He pushed the greasy feeling down and gestured to the living room where they could talk. "Let's sit in here."

She followed and sat on the far end of the couch.

Rick sat in his recliner, facing her.

She scooted to the edge of her seat, looking

nervous, yet still hauntingly beautiful in her own way, and said, "So. How have you been?"

Rick wasn't in the mood for small talk any more than when Councilman Peters had cornered him in his office earlier today. Like pulling off a bandage quickly, he preferred to get straight to the point. "You said you'd call and let me know when you were coming to town." His words were uncompromising, setting the tone for the discussion.

She took a breath, an apology in her gaze. "I know." She glanced at the open door of the study. "And I can tell you're unhappy about me being here. But I'd rather not let Adam hear us argue."

He leaned back in his chair, clenching his fists. She was right about him being unhappy. But she was also right about Adam. For the first time in his son's life, his parents were in the same room together. The boy didn't need to overhear them arguing. Wasn't that why he'd let Roxanne have her way when she wanted to leave in the first place?

Rick still wanted what was best for his son and contentious parents weren't it. He'd agreed to take care of Adam so Roxanne could pursue her career. Now that she was suddenly back in their lives, how did he keep his son from feeling Rick's personal animosity toward her? He forced his hand open and tried to relax. "Then let's talk about how long you're planning to stay."

"That depends on you. And Adam, of course."

"What do you mean by that?" If the situation were up to him, Roxanne wouldn't even be there. Why weren't her plans more concrete?

"I have three week's leave, so I was hoping to stick around long enough to get to know Adam better."

"Three weeks! You've missed eight years. What do you expect to learn about your son in three weeks?"

A sheen of tears formed in her eyes, and she brushed them away with an impatient hand. "I know it's not long enough. But it's the time I have."

"Where were you planning on staying?" Rick suddenly knew the answer but hoped he was wrong.

Roxanne ran her finger along the arm of the couch. "Well, I hoped maybe I could stay here." She glanced around the living room again. "I assumed your house was a little bigger." She shrugged an elegant shoulder, her dark hair catching the lamplight. "There aren't a lot of options in town, and the resort is miles up the road. Even if I could find a room, with all the skiers in town the cost would be astronomical."

Rick frowned. She was right about the bad timing. Still… "Money's never been an issue with you before. Why now?"

The temperature cooled between them. "Nothing has changed in that regard. That silver spoon you hated so much is still there." She scooted farther to the edge of her seat. "But I've changed. I want to be closer to Adam. And like I said, get to know him."

Rick rubbed his jaw while he studied his ex. Something was up, and he wasn't sure how to get it out of her. He took a deep breath. "What's really going on Roxanne? What's changed? After all this time—"

"Dad! I finished my chapter!" Adam stepped into the living room, cutting off Rick's query.

He glanced at his son and the excitement shining in his eyes. Whether he wanted Roxanne in Adam's life or not, she was here now. At least he'd be present to mitigate any damage she might do. He sighed. "Then come on out here, buddy."

"Yay!" Adam crossed to the couch and sat next to his mother.

For the next few minutes, he fired questions at her like a machine gun, asking everything from what she did in the army, to all the places she'd visited. "I have all the postcards you sent in a box in my closet." Before either Roxanne or Rick could stop him, he jumped off the couch and thundered up the stairs. "Be right back!" he called.

Roxanne followed his progress with a bemused expression. "He sure has a lot of energy."

Rick gave her a skeptical stare. "That he does."

"And he's so well behaved," she said. "You've done a wonderful job raising him."

Okay, that was an unexpected compliment. Was she buttering him up for something? "Thanks."

Adam came back down the stairs carrying a box. "Here they are." He began pulling out postcards and asked Roxanne about each place and her experiences there. His son was beaming when he finally tucked the last one away. "I want to go see all those places someday. I can't wait to tell Joey and Devon all about them tomorrow."

Rick watched the interchange.

Roxanne seemed relaxed, talking and sharing stories, almost falling naturally into the role of Adam's mother. She didn't seem to realize she was even doing it.

Maybe he didn't have to worry about her hurting his son.

Bedtime for Adam was later than usual and a bit of a battle with all the excitement. He also didn't fall asleep as quickly as he usually did. But eventually, he settled down.

With all quiet upstairs, Rick felt safe to finish the discussion with Roxanne.

They returned to the living room and resumed their positions across from each other.

Rick took the hundredth deep breath for that night. "Why don't you tell me why you're really here?"

She tilted her head with a frown. "I did. Surely, you can see that I sincerely want to know my son."

"I see a woman who wants to connect with an eight-year-old boy. But I'm not sure I see a mother who wants to know her son." He cleared his throat. "If that was the case, you'd have been here sooner. So why now? Why after all these years?"

"You're right."

She had the grace to look guilty.

"I could have visited sooner. I wanted to several times." She glanced down, clasping her hands in her lap. "I didn't have the courage."

He frowned. That sounded all wrong. "You're in the military," he reminded her. "I know you've been in combat zones."

Roxanne nodded, still staring at her hands. "It takes a different kind of courage to face your past. To confront your own mistakes." She sighed and looked over at him. "I train for battles." She waved a hand toward the stairs, toward her son's room. "There's no training for this."

Rick had to concede that point. He'd certainly not known how to be a parent. No one had offered a manual for a squirming newborn. No instructions on what to expect between runny noses and baseball practice. For the most part he'd winged it, with the helpful advice from his sister and his parents. "I get that you were afraid. I was too. But you didn't stick it out. What's changed now?"

Roxanne paled. She seemed to swallow several times before wrapping her arms protectively around her middle. "I'm pregnant."

That was the last thing Rick had expected to hear. A dozen responses rose to his lips. He wanted to ask why she hadn't learned her lesson the first time. Was she planning to marry the father and stay married this time? Had she even told the father? "I…I don't know what to say…congratulations?"

"I'm not sure congratulations is the right word." Her voice was soft with worry.

"Does the father know?" Flashes of how he felt when he first learned he would be a dad filled his mind. He'd been glad, and proudly fulfilled his fatherly responsibilities.

"I haven't told him," she said almost in a whisper.

A spit of fury burned on behalf of the unknown man. He would have hated being kept in the dark. "He has a right to know. You need to tell him."

She seemed to shrink at his comment. "I know."

"Is he married?" For some reason, that wouldn't totally surprise him. Roxanne was a hard woman to resist when she went after something she wanted.

She shook her head, the worry evident in her face.

"An officer?" That would certainly put a damper on her career, and the father's, if he outranked Roxanne.

She shook her head again. "A civilian contractor. He's overseas right now."

"I don't see the problem." Rick leaned toward her. "You're both single. There are no regulations forbidding your relationship. Your careers shouldn't be that difficult to manage, even with a baby. Do you love him?"

"Yes." She nodded.

"Does he love you?"

"I think so."

Rick leaned back, exasperated. "Then what's the problem?"

Roxanne stopped clutching her stomach and leaned forward, a terrified look on her face. "I wasn't cut out to be a mother the first time, Rick. What if I'm not now?"

With that confession, all the pieces of her visit fell into place. She was scared, and facing the prospect of motherhood once again. She needed to see if having another child was worth whatever sacrifice she was considering now. She wanted a test run with Adam.

Should he be livid at her audacity or feel sorry for her and the unsuspecting father? Of course, this meant he would probably grant her request to stay at the house. He wouldn't toss a pregnant woman out on the street, even if she was his ex-wife.

Chapter Nineteen

Unable to sleep for thinking over the day's events and worrying about the upcoming council meeting, Cayme eventually gave up and went downstairs. She wandered the house and finally ended up in the room where her mother stayed her final days. She'd avoided the room for almost two months, going into it once to wash the bedding and tidy up.

The room was exactly how she'd left it. Ben obviously hadn't been in, either. He'd barely been able to be in the same room with their mother. Seeing the place where she took her last breath would have been hard for him.

Where medicines had once covered the bedside table, there was now a thin layer of dust. The book her mother had been reading before she passed still rested next to the small lamp.

Cayme lifted the book and opened to the bookmark on the last page, indicating her mother had finished the story before passing. A sad smile tugged at Cayme's lips. Her mother never liked to leave anything unfinished.

She returned the book to the table and opened the top drawer.

A journal was tucked inside, as though waiting for her mother to make the next entry.

Debating whether or not to look inside, her hand

hovered over the journal. These pages would contain her mother's most private thoughts. Looking inside would be an invasion.

But perhaps it contained the answers to the questions she should have asked while her mother was alive. Questions like why she hadn't wanted Cayme to sell the house, especially since she'd verbally agreed to sell to the city.

Cayme lifted the journal from its resting place. She needed those answers.

Turning out the light in the spare bedroom, she clutched the journal to her chest and crept quietly up to her room. After climbing into bed, she opened the journal with shaking hands and flipped to the final entries. Her mother's spidery handwriting had become less legible at the end, and Cayme leaned closer to the lamp, holding the book at an angle to read better.

I can tell my time is close. It's harder and harder to stay awake, and the pain...the pain is so bad, I can hardly think. I'm afraid this may be my last entry, and I don't even know what to say.

Cayme has been home for a few weeks, maybe longer. I can't remember. I just know she's home and I'm so happy. She's been such a blessing these days. Even Ben seems less anxious now that she's here. I want her to stay. I never want her to feel like she doesn't belong. This is her home. This will always be her home.

The entry ended. The following pages were blank. Flipping backward through earlier entries, she found reports of doctor's visits, notations of progress and then regression, and always the pain. Each entry was followed by an uplifting quote, some positive statement to close out the page. The obvious thing missing was a mention of the house, her decision to sell, or her decision to make Cayme promise to not sell.

This will always be her home.

Cayme's gaze returned to those final words. Tears burned behind her eyes and threatened to spill.

Was it really that simple? Had her mother feared that Cayme would leave again and never return? True, if she hadn't made the promise, she might have gone back to her job in Seattle. She was fairly certain Skeeter would buy her mother's share of the business—if asked. And Ben would be better off in a smaller place, where he didn't have to worry about the upkeep of this old house.

But that moment with her mother—the promise— changed everything.

The decision Cayme faced was so very difficult. Would she keep her promise, or allow the city to purchase her home?

Ben was getting better. Cayme loved running the store with Skeeter. She was becoming part of the community. Her sense of finally belonging wasn't because of the house, or even the plot of land. She'd always have a special place in her heart for this parcel of earth. But this little town, nestled in the lovely valley would always be home. Her home.

In sudden clarity, she made up her mind. No more indecision about the house. And she knew, without a doubt, her mother would understand.

Despite the heartache of giving up part of her life, Cayme was at peace. She *was* home.

****

The morning of the city council meeting, Cayme

woke early. Having come to a decision, she'd slept remarkably well. The nightmares about Ben and the rising river had stopped. In their place, were captivating dreams of waking up in Rick's arms and making breakfast for Adam before he headed off to school. Those dreams left her with a warm feeling of being needed and accepted.

But reality was different.

Although Ben was doing better, no way he was cured. His demons would probably be something he'd have to manage his entire life. Regardless of his challenges, he returned from work each night to cook dinner and had it waiting when she got home. It appeared he was truly on the road to recovery. Other than the threat of the rising river, things were feeling almost normal.

The storms were brewing again, promising to pound the mountains with a fresh blanket of snow. Local and visiting die-hard skiers alike were guaranteed amazing downhill runs. Oddly enough, the previous weekend had also offered great golfing in the valley resorts. The forecasters called it designer weather, and the tourists ate it up.

But the upcoming Memorial Day weekend was another matter. Because the flood danger was too high, the forest service hadn't opened the campgrounds near any of the creeks that fed the Blakely River. Most people weren't even planning to leave town for the first official camping weekend of the year because of the soggy conditions.

The previous night, Cayme had checked on the river, hoping the sandbags would hold. She'd never seen it seethe with whitecaps like that before. If the water broke through, she had no idea how she'd protect her property from flooding. When she described the river to Ben that morning, even he looked worried.

He put a plate of eggs on the table in front of her. "I'm getting off early tonight to fill more sandbags. We need to think about barricading the house, too, not just the riverbank."

She poked at her breakfast, the intense feeling from her pleasant dreams fading. "I'd come home and help, but I need to be at the city council meeting tonight." Putting down her fork, she inhaled the warm aroma of coffee before taking a sip.

At the stove, he finished filling his plate and turned to face her. "Have you made a decision about the house?"

She nodded. "I think so." Outside the wind blew, promising a storm later in the day.

He crossed to the table and sat. "And?"

She hesitated, not sure how her brother would react to her decision.

"You can't keep putting it off. What if the property floods and the town doesn't want it anymore?"

"We'll still have a home. If I sell, where will you go?"

"Don't worry about me. I'll be fine." He dug a fork into his eggs and scooped a hefty bite onto a piece of toast before sticking it in his mouth, showing that selling their childhood home wasn't messing with his appetite. "There'd be a windfall from the sale, and I have a steady job with Rick's company," he said around a mouthful. "I can put a down payment on a place around here, or a deposit if I decide to rent. Things look pretty good from where I sit." He brought his coffee to his lips and took a swallow. "What's bothering me is why you pulled back on Mom's commitment."

Cayme weighed the promise she'd given her mother against her brother's desire to understand her reluctance to sell. The longer she kept the secret, the harder it became to share it. She didn't care what the town or city council members thought of her. Hurting Ben was something she never wanted to do.

If she agreed to the city's contract and sold the house, Ben would never have to know she'd been keeping the secret.

"Cayme?" Ben's query brought her attention back to the breakfast table.

She glanced up from her eggs. "Yeah?"

"Where'd you go just now?" He'd finished his breakfast and cradled his cup in his large hands.

She bowed her head, wanting to tell Ben about the promise. He was getting better. What if the deception set him back? When she looked up, she said, "I'm thinking about how much better you are. I'm glad you want to get out on your own." Laying down her fork, she pushed her plate away.

"I'm a grown man, little sister." He put down his cup. "I should have been on my own long before now." He stood and gathered up her half-eaten breakfast and stacked the plate on his. "What aren't you telling me?"

She couldn't keep the secret from her brother any longer. "Mom made me promise not to sell."

He jumped, making the dishes rattle in his hands. "What?"

"I'm sorry. I should have told you sooner."

"Why?"

His question was simple, except she wasn't sure if

he was asking why she was sorry or why she'd kept the secret. She knew the sin of omission was as devastating as a lie in his eyes. "I realize I should have told you sooner. Mom couldn't possibly have meant for you to not know. At the time, I was keeping a promise to her."

He crossed the kitchen and put the dishes in the sink, before turning around. "I think you better start at the beginning." His body was still, but his eyes were bright with curiosity.

She curled fingers into her palm. "The morning she died, she made me promise not to sell the house." Cayme's voice broke. She swallowed and continued. "Of course, I said I wouldn't sell. Why wouldn't I? At the time, I didn't know about the plans she'd made, or her commitment to the city." She leaned on the table, praying he'd understand what she'd been asked. "I think she was afraid I'd leave again, and if I sold the house, I'd never have a reason to return."

"So, you're breaking that promise now." Ben's tone wasn't accusatory, however his words struck like a blow.

"If I had known she'd planned to sell the house I wouldn't have made that promise. I would have told her I was home to stay. Unfortunately, until Mr. Peters showed up on the day of the funeral with the contract, I had no idea. Mom hadn't actually signed the papers, but the implications were enough to prove she'd intended to sell."

"You could have asked me about it."

"I was afraid."

"Of what?"

"You were…" She hesitated. For her, Ben's PTSD was still a sensitive subject. Surely it was for him, too.

"Say it, Cayme." Ben squared his shoulders, though he didn't move away from the sink.

The time for cowardice and hiding was long over. She took a deep breath. "You were in a bad place. If you weren't already aware that Mom wanted to sell our home, I didn't want to make things worse for you."

"Why didn't you say something once you found out I knew about the contract?" His voice rose a little. "Why wait until now? The meeting is tonight."

She winced. "I've been keeping the promise a secret since Mom died. I was truly afraid to tell you. It's been horrible. I made a mistake by waiting. I'm so sorry, Ben. Can you forgive me?"

He faced the sink, his hands propped on the edge, shoulders tight around his ears.

"I'm sorry, Ben." She didn't care how many times she had to say it, she would repeat herself until he heard her. Really heard her.

When he turned around, the tension had loosened from his shoulders even though his expression was granite-like. "I won't pretend that what you did wasn't hurtful. But you're my sister. We're family. We're all the family we've got. We shouldn't keep things from each other."

"You're right. I'm sorry. I won't ever do it…"

He held up a hand. "You can't make that promise."

"I will to you."

"No. I may be done with therapy, but I'm a long way from being cured." He swore. "I don't think there is a cure. I just have to learn to live with this shadow war in my head." He paused. "But I do get that people hide the truth if they're afraid or think they're protecting someone. I get that you want to protect me,

Cayme, but I need to protect you, too. And I can't if I don't know what's going on."

She hadn't expected that response. "Okay. I think I know what you're saying."

He crossed to the table, sat next to her, and took her hands in his. "No. I don't think you do, but that's okay. At some point, I'll probably mess up and show my temper if I think someone is withholding something from me. I can't put it all in words. What I need is everything out in the open so I can deal with it—even if I deal with it badly. It's how I can push aside these demons that are always sneaking up on me."

That was something Cayme could understand. "I'll do the best I can from now on to include you in all the dealings of the house."

Squeezing her hand, he said, "I know I messed up, leaving you to make the decision. But I'm here for you, now, Cay."

Tears coursed down her cheeks. This was more of a heart-to-heart than any previous conversation she'd ever had with her brother. "Thank you, Ben. I'm here for you, too." The comfort of his hands covering hers was almost more than she could bear.

"So, what decision did you come to? Are you keeping the promise you made to Mom?" He squeezed her hands tighter.

She shook her head. "No. I believe the best thing for both of us is to sell."

"I think you're making the right choice, especially since you're engaged to Rick now."

"About that…"

He pressed a finger to her lips. "Shush. I know it's not the way you wanted to start a relationship, but I can see what's happening. It's been good for both of you."

Her heart pounded at his statement. "What do you think is happening?"

"Looks to me like love will win the day."

She pulled out of his grasp. "I don't think…"

"Stop thinking about things so much." He stood and placed a hand on her shoulder. "Get through tonight and then tackle the next thing on your plate."

She smiled up at him. "When did you get so smart?"

He gave a small chuckle and headed back to the sink to finish cleaning up. "All those therapy sessions had to be good for something, right?" He had his back to her so she couldn't see his face, but his tone sounded almost normal.

Her worry of keeping the secret from him faded, but concerns about the rising river outside their home grew. Time wasn't on her side. There would be a flood, but when? At least she would give the council her decision tonight, and that particular worry would be off her plate.

****

In spite of unburdening her soul to Ben that morning, a feeling of unease followed Cayme throughout the day.

Rick had called earlier to say Adam wouldn't be in after school. He wouldn't go into details on the phone but said they'd talk that night. He assured her that Adam wasn't sick or anything troublesome, but his tone seemed off.

She worried most of the day anyway. It hadn't taken long for her to look forward to seeing Adam in the afternoons, and when he didn't come to the store, she missed him.

A storm had blown in around noon, and it had turned cold. Snow fell as Cayme closed up before heading to the council meeting. The evening temperatures had dropped. However, the white stuff wasn't sticking to the valley roads. She bet the ski resorts were overrun with tourists enjoying the new spring snow totals, though. As much as she hated to see it, the snow was good for the resorts and surrounding businesses, including the store. The water tables were doing well after so many years of drought, even though the areas in the flood zones could be badly damaged with runoff.

She tugged on her coat and pulled her gloves on before locking the doors. The snow hadn't accumulated on the car windshield yet, but she let the engine run for a moment anyway. While waiting for the engine to warm up, she debated whether or not to keep the store open during Monday's Memorial Day flag-raising ceremony. With all the tourists in town for the last skiing of the season, it would be good for the store's bottom line to stay open. However, supplying refreshments for the ceremony had become a tradition her mother started once she and Skeeter set up the business, and Cayme wanted to continue that tradition. All she had to do was confirm with the mayor and city council that night if they still wanted her services. She hoped announcing her decision would make a favorable impression.

The drive from her store to city hall was short. In fact, she could have walked had it not been snowing. The old brick building was built in the late eighteen hundreds and took up the entire half of one block.

Decades of annual community gatherings, from Fourth of July barbeques to Labor Day picnics, were celebrated on the grounds outside the city hall.

She parked near the front of the large building and turned off the car. Without the heater blowing warm air, the car quickly grew cold and the windows fogged over. She barely made out shapes of people arriving for the meeting. It seemed most of the town had braved the sloppy weather. No point in delaying her announcement.

Cayme gathered the folder that contained the papers her mother had left her and opened her car door.

Skeeter stood next to the car with an umbrella. "'Bout time you showed up. I was beginning to think you'd chickened out." The sound of snow pelting the umbrella seemed to echo Skeeter's accusatory tone.

Cayme didn't take offense, knowing Skeeter was coming from a place of love. Still, turning tail and running sounded like a good idea, too. She took a breath and searched the stream of people headed inside the building. "Is Rick here?"

"Not that I've seen." Skeeter raised the umbrella to cover Cayme. "Come on in where it's dry and we'll find him."

They followed a group of people into the main hall where the unmistakable aura of a century-old building greeted them. A couple of corridors led to office areas that were now closed for the day. Ahead and to the right was a curved staircase to the second-floor offices. On their left was the entrance to the city council meeting room. Near the doorway was a sign-in table, and standing next to the table was Ben. Cayme smiled her relief that her brother had shown up for support.

He waved them over and handed her a pen to sign the register. "You made it."

She took the pen and signed her name on the line below Ben's. Between Skeeter's and Ben's comments, even the people closest to her must wonder if she was still a coward. She supposed she couldn't blame them. The last time she'd planned to face most of these folks in a gathering—her wedding—she'd opted to run away.

Laying the pen down, she turned, looking for Rick. He wasn't in the main hall, so that meant he was either inside the meeting room or hadn't arrived. She glanced at the clock above the entryway. Six fifty-five. Rick was never late, so he must already be inside.

Turning to Skeeter and Ben, she said, "Let's go face the masses."

The meeting room had folding chairs arranged in rows with an aisle between the left and right sides of the room. At the front, was a large, raised podium area, much like a judge's bench but longer and curved so the council members could view each other while they discussed city business. To one side of the podium were two long tables butted end-to-end for city committee member heads to sit. Rick was there, a hip propped against one of the tables, speaking to the Zoning and Planning Commissioner.

He glanced over at her, and his brow lowered, and he seemed to take a deep breath before turning back to listen to something the commissioner was saying.

After Rick looked away, Cayme's fragile optimism shattered, all her mental preparations for the meeting crumbling. She hadn't realized how badly she'd needed his support tonight.

Skeeter touched her arm and guided her to a seat

on the front row. With everyone staring at her, Cayme felt as though she was walking to her execution. Some gazes seemed accusatory, while other faces filled with pity. She sat with her back to everyone and tried to block out the stares and hostile energy directed at her.

"Relax, baby." Skeeter laid a hand over Cayme's. "You're not on trial. This is just a meeting to let people have their say. No one can make you do something you don't want to do."

"I know. It's just been hard to know if I'm doing the right thing."

On the other side of her, Ben leaned in with his shoulder. "Trust me, Cay, this isn't hard."

She looked at her brother and gave a small nod. He'd been through hell himself and had seen so much worse. She could be strong for him.

The meeting progressed through the minutes of the previous meeting and updates on old business. Plans were still on track for the Sunrise Ceremony on Memorial Day. And yes, after the ceremony, Cayme would supply coffee and pastries as previously arranged with her mother. When she glanced at the mayor, he gave her a small smile and nod of thanks.

New business was next on the schedule. The only item on the agenda was the new park expansion. Rick, who'd remained near the tables with the Zoning and Planning committee, gave an update on what they'd been able to do for the improvements while they waited for the final approval, or halt, on the expansion. A few murmurs of relief rippled through the audience. At least part of the project was proceeding as planned.

During his report, Rick glanced in Cayme's direction a couple of times. If only she could read his expression and know what he was thinking. She hated that she'd put him in this position—that *they* were in this position, facing an entire town that believed they were engaged to be married and now stood on opposite sides of a community issue. No one could possibly believe they were in love based on their actions. She bowed her head, ashamed she'd not shared her mother's promise with him.

"Ms. Foster." A sharp voice brought her attention back to the proceedings. Mazey Fredrick tapped her pen against the notepad in front of her, her bluish-gray hair glinting under the harsh fluorescent lights. "We will hear from you now."

Cayme swallowed and stood. Skeeter squeezed her hand, then Cayme stepped toward the microphone at the front of the meeting room. She clutched her speech as though it would save her from drowning. Even though the mic faced the podium, she would plead her case to the people behind her. She glanced at the papers, and the words blurred. She didn't know if she could say what she'd written. At the time, it had seemed so eloquent. But after hearing why young mothers wanted new equipment for their youngsters and why town folk wanted a place to enjoy a picnic inside the city limits and winter fun without the cost of resort prices, she wasn't so sure of her speech. Her delay had caused concerns for everyone.

She cleared her throat, blinking furiously to clear her vision to see the men and women behind the tall podium. Councilman Peters glared at her with the same hostility echoed in Mazey's eyes. Mayor Nicholson's expression was more sympathetic. The other two council members were people she didn't know well, however, their expressions seem more neutral. She glanced over at Rick.

For the briefest of moments, he smiled, his brown eyes turning to liquid cocoa.

She turned to face the podium. "Members of the council and those here tonight. Thank you for the patience you've shown regarding the sale of our property." She glanced over her shoulder at Ben.

He gave her a nod, offering support for what she had to say next.

She swallowed and turned back to the podium again. "A few days ago, I had prepared a statement to ask your indulgence while I wrestled with my decision to honor my mother's verbal commitment." She glanced once again at Ben. "You all know that before my mother passed, she'd planned to sell—" Her voice broke and it took a moment before she could continue.

"What you don't know is that before she closed her eyes for the last time, she asked me—" Cayme took a breath. "—she asked me not to sell the house."

A murmur arose through those assembled.

The mayor cleared his throat, drawing her attention back to the front.

He leaned forward with a gentle expression. "We can see how hard this must be for you, Cayme. This explanation helps us better understand why you stopped the contract from going through. But if that is the case, why not tell us you weren't selling? Why didn't you just cancel the contract?"

"Because at the time of the promise, I didn't know my mother had already committed to sell." She looked at Councilman Peters. "Then Mr. Peters came to the house with a copy of the papers. I…I didn't know what to do."

The room buzzed. Members at the podium turned to each other with whispers.

Only the mayor remained still. "Does this mean that you're not selling the property to the city?"

Cayme glanced to her brother who straightened in his chair and gave her a nod. With a deep breath, she faced the podium. "I don't understand why my mother would want such a promise from me…unless she believed I would leave town again if the house sold."

Her gaze darted to Rick, then she looked at the council members. "I'm not making any plans to leave. Blakely is my home. I'm not sure where my brother and I will live. But I want to do right by the city and honor my mother's original wishes to offer our property to expand the park. I also want to express appreciation for your patience and apologize that it took so long to reach this decision."

With that pronouncement, the room burst into chaos. As the gathering assimilated her final statement, the murmurs grew louder.

Someone from the back of the room shouted, "Look at all the time we've wasted because you were so wishy-washy."

Someone else hushed him, and the mayor slammed his gavel on the block, calling the group to order.

Cayme hurried back to her seat before her legs gave out. She didn't really hear any of the chaos, only the voices in her head. Unless the store began to make a bigger profit, she didn't have prospects for earning a living in this small town. Her boss in Seattle might be unwilling to let her continue working remotely. If he didn't, she'd be forced to find work elsewhere. But the town got what they wanted. She loved this town. She was falling in love with one of the residents.

And she wasn't running away again.

Chapter Twenty

After settling the crowded council meeting room, the mayor thanked Cayme for her remarks and her decision. The meeting's closing business took a few more minutes, with the mayor asking Cayme and Ben to stay afterward to set dates to review the contract.

The entire process moved faster than Cayme anticipated. Instead of climbing into her car, and then into a hot bath to soak away the traumatic night, she was stuck in the drafty city hall going over the logistics of the sale.

Skeeter gave Cayme a hug and whispered, "You didn't have to keep that secret alone."

"I realize that now." Cayme hugged her back. "I'm sorry."

"Baby, it's not me you need to apologize to." Skeeter stepped back and nodded to Rick. "I'll open the store tomorrow. Take all the time you need." After giving her and Ben another hug, Skeeter left.

The mayor directed her and Ben to a corner of the room to discuss the sale. Finally, a closing date of June fifteenth was set, and everyone shook hands to seal the deal.

Ben was withdrawn, but only Cayme seemed to notice.

Maybe he was finally realizing that she'd just turned over their childhood home to be bulldozed to the ground. And now they had to find a new place to live.

While Ben and Cayme were in their corner of the big room with the mayor, Councilman Peters pulled Rick into a conversation in another corner. From Rick's expression, he wasn't enjoying the dialogue. He kept glancing Cayme's way, as though sending some subliminal message.

She gave up attempting to interpret his message and opted to focus on her conversation with the mayor.

"I can't imagine how hard tonight was for you, my dear," Mayor Nicholson said. "It took tremendous courage to confess that promise to your mother in public."

"I shouldn't have kept quiet for so long. At the time I made the promise, I honestly hadn't known about Mom's commitment to the town." Cayme glanced at Ben. "But it's done now."

Her brother wrapped his arm around her shoulder. "It's time to move forward."

She nodded then looked at the mayor. "Is there anything more we—"

"What is *she* doing here?" Ben shifted suddenly, blocking Cayme's view of the front of the room.

"Who?" She peered around him to see who caught his attention.

A tall, dark-haired woman had entered the room.

She was beautiful, with striking features and a graceful stride that ate up the distance as she made a beeline for Rick. But what held Cayme's attention was Adam's hand in hers.

"That's Rick's wife," Ben said. "Roxanne."

"Wife?" Cayme's head swam. "You mean ex-wife, right?"

"Yes…yes, of course. Ex-wife." Ben shook himself and seemed to pull back from the stupor he'd succumbed to at the sight of the attractive woman. Cayme didn't know if her brother was acting strange because of the woman's stunning looks, or her unexpected appearance. "I wonder when she got to town?"

His question brought back the unsettled feeling Cayme'd had about Rick and Adam earlier in the day. No wonder Adam didn't want to come to the store. His mother was in town. And Rick's demeanor when she'd arrived at the meeting suddenly made sense. He must be experiencing all sorts of emotions at his ex-wife's surprise visit. Not unlike the way she'd felt after she'd encountered Chase a few days ago. But why hadn't Rick called her or said anything? Weren't they partners in this engagement?

Except the engagement was just a convenience. Even though Rick had used his ex as an excuse to get engaged, maybe after seeing her in the flesh, he wasn't as committed to the arrangement as he'd expected. And who could blame him? Roxanne had turned every head in the room.

"Cayme!"

Adam's shout startled her out of her thoughts.

He disengaged from his mother's hand and waved.

Cayme mustered a smile that she hoped didn't betray her shock and waved back. "Hi, Adam."

Rick glanced her way, his expression unreadable but certainly not as sour as it looked during his conversation with Councilman Peters.

Adam said something to his dad, and with a nod from his father, he hurried over to Cayme. "I'm sorry I didn't come to the store today." His face was filled with excitement, and he pointed across the room. "My mom's here."

Cayme couldn't pin down a single emotion. How could she not be happy for this little boy? The mother he'd longed to see was back in his life. How could she stop the green-eyed monster from churning in her chest? She didn't *really* have a claim on either one of these males who'd stolen her heart. After the night she'd just had, all she wanted was to crawl into bed and hide under the covers for a week and sort out her feelings.

She touched Adam's shoulder. "I'm so happy she came to see you." Cayme would be genuinely glad for this little boy, even if it killed her.

Adam tugged on her hand. "Come on. I want you to meet her."

Cayme attempted to pull back, perfectly happy to never meet the woman. "I'd love to, but I need to finish my business with the mayor."

The mayor touched her arm. "We're done for tonight. Go on."

It took all her willpower not to glare at Nicholson for abandoning her.

"I'll come with you," Ben said.

She glanced at her brother and shook her head. "No. I'll be fine." Some things he couldn't protect her from.

Something akin to pity shone in his eyes. "I'll see you at home." And with that, he shook the mayor's hand, gave Rick a hard stare, and then left the room.

"Come on, Cayme." Adam tugged her hand again.

As they crossed the room, Adam's mother frowned

at their approach.

Here comes the competition.

"Mom!" Adam let go of Cayme's hand and reached for his mother. "This is Cayme. Her and Dad are dating."

Oh, yeah…definitely the competition.

With such a bald announcement, loud enough for those in the room to hear, the gossip buzzards would be circling tomorrow. At least it would make for another busy morning at the store. That was good for business. Since she was planning to stay in town, maybe she should schedule a bit of drama once a week to keep the store in the black.

Even Rick winced when his son's statement had Roxanne's head whipping around to stare at him. Apparently, he hadn't shared his current relationship status with his ex-wife.

"Roxanne," Rick said. "Cayme Foster." He turned to Cayme. "Cayme, this is Roxanne Hardwick."

"Adam's mother." The other woman finished for Rick.

Rick's eyes narrowed at Roxanne's statement, but he didn't contradict her.

Had Adam's mom made the statement to mark her territory? Regardless, Cayme was definitely put in her place. She swallowed and reached out a hand. "Nice to meet you." As they briefly shook, Cayme didn't realize how cold her hands were until the other woman's warm grasp closed over her fingers.

"Likewise."

An awkward silence followed, so Cayme ventured more conversation. "Adam's been excited for your visit. He didn't mention it would be so soon. What a nice surprise." She was pleased her voice didn't sound weak.

"I thought a surprise would be fun." Roxanne ruffled her son's hair.

"It's been awesome," Adam chimed in. "Mom spent the night and made me breakfast before I went to school."

Cayme's smile froze. The dream she'd had the previous night shattered like broken glass at her feet. "How…nice."

Rick cleared his throat. "Cayme, it's not what you think."

Roxanne reached out to lay a hand on Rick's arm. "Rick, you should never assume what a woman is thinking." She turned to Cayme again. "I'm sorry. This must be uncomfortable for you."

You have no idea. "It's not been the best of nights for me." Cayme gave another smile that encompassed the entire family unit. "Very nice to meet you," she said to Roxanne. "I apologize for cutting this short. I need to follow up on a few things before I leave. If you'll excuse me." She turned toward her chair.

"I'll call you," Rick said.

Cayme looked over her shoulder. "When you can." Hoping she didn't look like she was running away, she walked over and picked up her coat. From the corner of her eye, she watched Rick gather his briefcase and put on his jacket. As he glanced her way, she averted her head. It took all her willpower to focus on straightening her papers and stuffing them back in the folder. She'd not even used the speech she'd prepared. It didn't matter now anyway.

"My condolences, Ms. Foster," Councilman Peters

said.

As the councilman approached, Cayme looked up to see a smug expression on his face. "I'm sorry?"

Peters gave a nod toward the doors where Rick, Adam, and Roxanne had exited. "Even I had a hard time watching that." He faced Cayme again. "But I have to believe you got handed your just desserts a moment ago."

"Do you have a point to make, Mr. Peters?"

He shrugged. "I'm wondering if you finally got a taste of what my son felt after you left him standing at the altar five years ago. How does it feel to have the love of your life ripped from your arms?"

The man had a lot of nerve. She was torn between running from the room to avoid the confrontation and wanting to drag her short fingernails through his eyes. She settled for a compromise. What did she have to lose? She'd already divulged one secret tonight. Why not get them all off her chest?

"I suggest you have a conversation with your son, Mr. Peters. I think you'd be surprised to learn that he wasn't as brokenhearted as he's led you to believe."

Peter's eyes narrowed. "I think I know Chase pretty well. And your lies don't interest me."

"How about a hefty dose of truth, then." Cayme took a deep breath, letting all the hurt and betrayal from that fateful night tumble out of her mouth. "First of all, I didn't leave Chase at the altar. I found out about his infidelity two weeks before we took our vows. When I surprised him that night, I didn't recognize the woman in his bed. She was probably some snow bunny he'd found on the slopes. It doesn't matter now. What matters is he'd taken a lover just fourteen days before I was supposed to be his wife."

She ventured a glance at the shock on Peters' face before she continued. "Yes, I broke the engagement and called off the wedding. But your son broke my heart. Not the other way around." She paused. "You know what? That's not true. I didn't leave town with a broken heart. I left to avoid the embarrassment and gossipy witches who probably knew more about your son's improprieties than I did. I was lucky to have avoided a marriage that was doomed from the start."

Peters took a step back. "I don't believe you."

Cayme tugged on her coat and picked up the folder. "You and your wife take pride in the longevity and sanctity of your own marriage. I applaud you for that. But it's really too bad you didn't raise your son to follow your example. So, you know what? I don't care if you don't believe me."

She pulled her hair out of the collar and swung her purse over her shoulder. "Ask Chase. Ask him why it didn't matter that I left. Ask him why he never called to coax me back. Ask him what he did with the engagement ring I threw at him that night."

"You better believe I will. And if I find out you're lying, I'll sue you for slander."

"Take your best shot." Cayme squared her shoulders. "Goodnight, Mr. Peters." She hurried out the doors of the council room and through the empty foyer of City Hall which was darker and colder than before the meeting.

Pushing open the big, paned-glass doors, she stepped into a whiteout. The sidewalk was covered with the heavy white stuff and crunched under her boots. The snow fell so thick and heavy she could barely see where she'd parked. She made a cursory brush of the windshield with her gloved hand before climbing into the car.

Then the tears started. She was one hot mess. Everything about the night hit her all at once. Giving up her home. Seeing Rick with Adam's mother. Even as much as she didn't like Mr. Peters, was it really her place to destroy his son's image? How would she feel if someone accused Adam of something so heinous?

Okay…that was a bit ridiculous. She didn't have a claim on Adam. He wasn't hers. Neither was Rick. She took a deep breath and brushed the tears off her cheeks.

Now, if she could only remove the ice that had settled around her heart since meeting Rick's ex-wife and seeing the sparkle in Adam's eyes when he looked at his mother. If Roxanne Hardwick wanted back into Rick's and Adam's lives, who was she to stand in the way of their family getting back together?

Chapter Twenty-One

"Ben?" The living room was dark as she stepped inside the house, and her voice echoed through the emptiness. She closed the door and slid her boots off and onto the mat. "Ben?" she called a bit louder to carry up the stairs to his room. "I'm home. Can we talk?"

A lamp clicked on next to the worn recliner, and light spilled into the corner of the living room. "No need to shout." Ben's voice was low. He sat in the chair with the guitar on his lap. The case was on the floor beside his stocking feet. His face held a quiet, contemplative look.

"Are you okay?" She couldn't begin to imagine what he must be thinking.

"I'm fine. What about you?"

His question was simple. The answer was complicated. "The night was harder to get through than I expected."

"No kidding." His head tilted, but the rest of his body remained still, his hands on top of the guitar as though he was afraid to move.

A part of her was thrilled that he'd come home and opened the guitar case again, even if he wasn't playing it just yet. She wished she could understand what it all meant. But asking that question now wouldn't resolve the problem that hung between them in the quiet living room.

She unzipped her coat, shrugged it off, and hung it on a hook by the door. Crossing to the couch, she sat and curled her legs under her. "We'll need to find a place to live." Cayme's voice broke. She swallowed and continued. "Maybe staying in town isn't the right decision. You could always move back to Seattle with me." She pulled her legs in tighter as though that would keep her from running away again. "I know I said I was staying, but…well…"

"You're not—*we're* not going anywhere." Ben shifted in the chair, lifting the guitar off his lap and placing it back in the case. After he snapped the lid closed, he sat back and looked at her. "It's been a long day and a pretty rough night. We aren't making any decisions tonight. You need some sleep and so do I." He pushed himself out of his chair and gave her a curious look. "When are you calling Rick? You two need to talk."

"I don't know." It hurt to think about Rick returning home with his son and ex-wife. The woman was staying in his house, sharing those intimate hours she longed to have. It felt like the situation with Chase all over again. This time, the pain cut much deeper. And it shouldn't. She and Chase had been engaged for real. They'd set a wedding date. Everything with Rick was just pretend. Well, mostly pretend.

Ben stood waiting for her answer.

She shook her head. "Not tonight. I may say something I'll regret. Like I did with Mr. Peters."

Ben stiffened. "Peters? What are you talking about? I knew I shouldn't have left you there alone. What happened?"

Cayme gave him an abbreviated version of her

encounter with the man who would have been her father-in-law. "Someone should have told him what a jerk his son is long before now. I shouldn't have been the one to do it, though."

"If not you, then who? That loser hurt you, betrayed you. I'd like to toss him in the river and rid the town of his sorry backside."

Cayme smiled. Her big brother truly wanted to protect her. How had she not seen that need in him before? "I've let it go. So should you. Pushing back only internalizes the anger, makes us hurt more. I need to move on."

"Doesn't make it right."

"Nothing'll make it right, Ben. But he's the one who has to live with what he did. I choose not to."

Ben stepped over to her and wrapped his arm around her. "You're changing, Cay."

She laid her head on his broad chest. "I don't feel any different."

"You've stopped running."

She felt the smile on his face and the burning love that radiated from him. He would be okay. *They* would be okay. "Thanks for being my big brother."

"Always, sis."

"You're right. We'll get through this, just fine." She gave him a squeeze.

****

"Sleep tight, buddy," Rick patted Adam's shoulder through the cozy blanket. "See you in the morning."

"Night, Dad." Adam lifted his head. "Night, Mom." He smiled at Roxanne who stood in the doorway watching the bedtime routine play out.

"Goodnight, Adam." She turned out the light and

stepped into the hallway.

Rick followed and closed his son's door behind him. As he led the way downstairs, he hoped the conversation he had to have with his ex-wife wouldn't get out of hand and carry to his son's room. Adam didn't need the drama. Neither did he, yet it appeared he was destined for it. When he reached the bottom step, he said, "I'm making some coffee."

"Now?" Roxanne spun around and stared. "Why so late?"

"Come in the kitchen." Rick's tone was hard, and he glanced up the stairs, sending a clear message he didn't want Adam listening in.

She looked up then closed her mouth and followed him through the living room.

At the counter, he set up the coffee to brew and pulled down two cups.

"None for me." Roxanne placed a hand over her middle. "I'm cutting back until this baby arrives."

Rick nodded, found a glass, and handed it to her. "There's milk in the fridge."

Roxanne grimaced but took the glass and opened the door. She poured some milk and sat at the table, frowning. "I'm sure I can guess what this is about. You have that look on your face."

"Good. Then my next question won't come as a shock. How much longer are you planning to stay?"

"I've been in town one day. Is it really so bad having me here?" Her hand shook a little when she picked up her glass and took a sip of milk.

Clearly, she was upset by his question. However, when she put the glass down, her face showed little emotion. Rick mentally rehearsed what he wanted to say. He took a breath. "Adam will start thinking we're getting back together."

She gave him a quizzical look. "Won't your *girlfriend* have something to say about that?"

Cayme. He turned his back on Roxanne and poured his coffee. The tension that had built across his shoulders during the council meeting increased. What must Cayme be going through right now? The bombshell she dropped at the meeting shocked a lot of people, including him. Why hadn't she said something? Shared that burden? He wanted to call her and ask. Instead he was stuck here with his ex-wife.

Without turning around, he said, "Cayme isn't my girlfriend. She's my fiancée. So yeah, she'd have a right to say something about you insinuating yourself into my life."

Behind him, the room went completely still. Then Roxanne's glass clinked on the table. He turned around.

The color left her face. Her dark hair was in stark contrast to the whiteness of her skin.

Was she going to faint? "Are you okay?"

She swallowed, her eyes going dark and wide. "I didn't see a ring."

His grip on the coffee mug tightened. The fake part of the whole engagement story reared its ugly head. "We were keeping it a secret. Her mother just passed, and it's still too soon to make it public."

"I'm sorry to hear that. She's Ben's sister, isn't she?"

Rick nodded.

"Does Adam know she's more than just a girlfriend?"

He shook his head. "No. We've been taking things

slow. Letting him get used to the idea."

If anything, Roxanne seemed to blanch even more. Perhaps she finally realized the cost of her past decisions and that someone else might take her place as Adam's mother. She took another swallow of her milk. "He seems to like her."

"Yeah. We both do."

From her seat at the table, Roxanne studied him, making him uneasy. "You don't act like a man in love."

"I…we…" He started to explain. "No. This conversation isn't about me. We're not discussing my love life here. We're talking about how long you plan to play 'mommy' before you drop the act and disappear like last time."

She let go a small laugh. "You're the one who brought up the subject. Discussing your love life seems quite relevant. And I'm not playing 'mommy'. I *am* Adam's mother, and I don't want another woman taking my place."

Rick choked on the coffee. "What are you talking about?" She was silent long enough for all sorts of strange images to roll through his mind. She couldn't possibly want to get back together. She was carrying another man's child, for Heaven's sake. Did she think she could move on but not him? Then another, uglier possibility struck him. Was her real motive to take Adam away from him? "You're *not* taking Adam!" His tone was hard and unyielding.

Roxanne shifted in her chair. "Maybe being with his mother is what's best for him."

Rick slammed his cup on the counter. "You've been back in his life exactly *one* day. You have no idea what's best for him." Keeping his tone as even as he could, he continued, "You don't even know him. There's no way that's happening. You can pack your bags right now. Send your lawyer to talk to mine."

Roxanne didn't move. Her mouth hung open, then she licked her lips and swallowed hard.

Several seconds passed, stretching into a long standoff, with the two of them staring at each other in stony silence. She obviously hadn't expected him to call her bluff.

She blinked first then looked down at her milk. "I'm sorry." Her hand shook as she lifted the glass and drained it. Setting it down, she glanced at him, tears in her eyes.

Tears from any woman tended to upset him, but he mentally held his ground, refusing to offer any sympathy.

She sniffled and reached for a napkin from the holder in the middle of the table. She dabbed her eyes. "It's not really an excuse. I'm just an emotional wreck." Her tone was less confrontational now. "When it comes to rollercoaster rides, the last couple of days have topped the charts."

He didn't reply, dizzy from the ups and downs himself.

"I couldn't take Adam from you. I won't. It would devastate both of you. You've done a wonderful job raising him. Alone. And you're right. I've had nothing to do with the wonderful boy he's become. I've failed as his mother." She touched her stomach and dropped her chin. "I'm just so afraid I'll fail with this child, too."

Rick refused to feel sorry for her, but he couldn't deny the truth. "You may have come to see Adam, but I believe the real reason is to see if you have what it takes to be a mother. That took some courage."

She looked up at him with a hint of respect and understanding in her eyes. "Are you saying that to be nice?"

He snorted. "The last thing in the world I feel right now is nice. You just threatened to take my son."

She took a deep breath. "I'm sorry, Rick. I was out of line."

"Yes, you were." He wanted her gone, but he still didn't have an answer to his original question. "How much longer are you planning to stay?"

"I'd like to continue my visit through the holiday weekend if I can. But I'll find a hotel. Staying here was a really bad idea."

Six more days. He bit down on the inside of his cheek. Way longer than he wanted to put up with. But Roxanne had missed almost eight years of Adam's life. He supposed he could give her a few days. As long as she stowed any threats in her duffel and didn't drag them out again. He nodded. "Fine. But you're right—you can't stay here anymore."

"I know." She took a deep breath and let the smile reach her eyes. "Thank you. You've been very generous."

"Don't think for a moment that I'm totally on board with what you're about. But I know Adam is glad you're here, so don't make me bar you from seeing him. Because I won't hesitate to do it."

With that issue settled for the time being, he hovered while Roxanne gathered her things and took them out to her car. The snow had stopped and the roads were only wet now. He brushed the windows and then helped load her things in the back of the car.

She closed the door and then turned to him. "I'd like to spend as much time with Adam as possible. Would it be okay if I came back for breakfast?"

Six days loomed ahead like a long dark tunnel. "He has to be at school by seven-forty-five."

"I won't be late."

After sending Roxanne on her way, he locked up the house, and tried really hard not to think about how weird the entire situation was. He wanted to call Cayme, to talk to her about tonight's meeting and explain why his ex was in town. The clock read midnight by the time he reached his room. Cayme had to be up early the next morning to open the store. He didn't feel right calling so late and put off the call until the next day. She'd understand, right?

Chapter Twenty-Two

Cayme descended the stairs to the aroma of breakfast and clattering dishes. Unfortunately, she lacked the energy to enjoy seeing Ben standing at the stove, scrambling eggs. Even though the situation was similar to the day before, her mental state was completely different. She had lain awake in bed long into the early morning hours, reading more of her mother's journal while waiting for Rick's call. She'd ached to hear his voice and his explanation of the things she'd seen after the meeting. The desire to understand what was going on with his ex-wife made sleep impossible.

The one thing that wasn't a burden any longer was her decision about the house. That weight was gone and she was glad to have finally shared the secret with Ben.

"You didn't get any sleep last night, did you?" Ben set a plate of eggs and toast in front of her.

"Is it that obvious?" She reached for the cup of coffee he'd thoughtfully filled a moment earlier, grateful for the caffeine hit.

"Oh, yeah." He sat across from her. "You won't stand a chance against the gossipmongers coming in for their morning fixes."

She grimaced. "And you said you wanted to protect me from all the bad things."

Ben grunted. "I'm not taking a bullet from Mazey

Fredrick for you."

Cayme couldn't stop the laugh that bubbled to the surface. She'd missed the teasing side of Ben. "I guess I can't blame you there. Maybe she'll actually pay for her drink this time around."

He set his fork down. "Seriously, Cay. You look like crap. Maybe you should call Skeeter—"

"Ouch! Thanks for the vote of confidence." She shook her head. "I'm facing the music today, brother. No point talking me out of it."

"It's your firing squad." He shrugged and finished breakfast.

She gave a wry smile. Indeed. But at least she had her brother on her side.

****

Halfway through the morning Skeeter came into the backroom where Cayme was grabbing more cups to restock the counter. As expected, the day had started out busy, but by mid-morning, the crowd had finally thinned to a couple of customers. "You're needed out front." She took the cups from Cayme and shooed her through the door.

When she saw Sherry waiting for her, Cayme's steps slowed. All morning, she'd been hoping to see Rick, except he'd been a no-show. Would he call her? Or was he reconciling with his ex-wife?

Sherry shifted baby Rachel to her other hip and offered a sheepish grin. "I know my timing is bad. I couldn't wait to see you."

Skeeter stepped beside Cayme and glanced at the two customers in line. "I got this. Just don't be too long in case the crowds return for an early lunch."

Cayme would never be able to repay Skeeter for

constantly covering for her. "I promise to be quick."

Sherry blew a kiss at Skeeter. "I'll make her keep that promise."

Skeeter just rolled her eyes and took the next order.

Cayme led the way to the book alcove, grateful the little nook was empty for the moment. Without waiting for her friend to sit, she said, "Have you heard from Rick?"

"No. I haven't talked to him. But I've heard who his visitor is." Sherry sat on the couch, perching the baby on her lap and giving her a teething ring to gnaw on. "I'm so sorry."

Cayme sat next to her. "Why? Because you haven't heard from your brother or because he's getting back together with his ex?"

"I'm sorry I don't know what's going on. I can see how much you're hurting." She touched Cayme's arm. "I'm also sorry that I didn't really believe you loved him enough to be engaged. I can't imagine what Roxanne's visit is doing to you."

Cayme hated that the hours of worry and sleeplessness showed on her face. "Did you know she's staying at his house?"

Sherry nodded. "Not until last night. I was putting Joey to bed. He said Adam was so excited his mother was staying with them. It took all I had to not blow a gasket right then. Once I got him tucked in, I went outside and screamed into a dishtowel. Ken had to lock me in the house so I didn't go over there and kill my brother."

"Looks like we were both blindsided. I found out last night, too. She showed up just as the city council meeting ended. Several people witnessed the whole thing."

Sherry tipped her chin toward the front of the store. "Explains the boom in business today."

"You have no idea."

Sherry squeezed Cayme's hand. "I can tell you this much. Rick's not getting back together with his ex. He's been over her a long, long time."

"They've been apart for years. Maybe he sees her differently now. Adam is over the moon." She swallowed at the sudden ache in her heart. "I know I'd do anything to make that little boy happy. Why would his father feel differently?"

"Stop that. Right now." Sherry gave her hand a shake. "Rick isn't doing anything rash. He's not a bundle of impulsive emotions."

"Maybe he would." There was his outlandish announcement that they were engaged. If that didn't prove he could be impulsive, she didn't know what did. "You know what? I'll be okay with him getting back with his ex. If it's what he really wants. It might be a good thing for both him and Adam." As Cayme said the words, she realized that no matter how much it would hurt, she would step aside. "This engagement was a trial period, right? It's not permanent."

"You'd give him up?" Sherry leaned back in shock. "You'd give up my brother? You're not fighting for him?"

Cayme took a deep breath. Time to stop keeping all her secrets. "I can't fight for something I never had. The engagement isn't real."

Sherry frowned. "Of course, it is. You should see your face when you talk about him. And I haven't seen Rick this happy for a long time. Why would you say such a thing?"

She told Sherry about the events that led to Rick's proposal and her agreement to make it convenient for both of them.

"Then it's real. If you accepted his proposal, it's real."

"We aren't in love." Cayme forced the words to come out evenly.

Little Rachel took that moment to start fussing and tossed the teething ring on the floor. Despite attempts to quiet her, the little girl's cries grew louder. Sherry stood, bouncing the baby on her hip until she calmed down a bit. "You'll never convince me you two aren't in love." She picked up the teething ring and stuffed it in her purse. "I've seen the way you look at him. The way he looks at you. Maybe you don't know it, but I do. This is way beyond your high school crush."

Cayme stood and reached out to brush the tears from the baby's cheek. "I wish that Rick did love me, and he didn't want to get back with his ex. But I can't change the facts in front of me. If I care for him, then letting him go is the right thing to do."

Sherry huffed. "You're pathetic." She bounced the fussing baby again. "And I have to get this tyrant into her crib for a nap." She gave Cayme an awkward hug. "I'd come over tonight and talk some sense into you, but I can't. There's a ball game. And don't forget Adam and Joey are expecting you to be there. You're their good luck charm."

"I don't know…Rick and his wife—"

"Ex-wife."

"How am I supposed to face—"

"If you really care for him… If you really love

him, and you're willing to let him go, what difference does it make? This is a small town. If you're right, and they're getting back together, you can't avoid running into them."

The baby let out another cry, preempting anything Cayme might have said. It didn't matter anyway. Sherry had made her point.

"Tonight," her friend called then carried the squalling child out the door. "Be there."

Cayme walked back to the counter.

"She's right, you know," Skeeter said.

"I know. It's just not as easy as it sounds." Cayme shrugged.

"You're made of sterner stuff than you think." She wrapped a sandalwood-scented hug around Cayme's shoulder. "You can show 'em. Show the whole town what you're made of."

And that was her biggest fear—that the town would find out exactly what she was made of. "Sterner stuff" was pretty low on the list. Cayme laid her head on Skeeter's shoulder, drawing strength from the older, wiser woman. "What would I do without you, Skeeter?"

"Let's hope you never have to find out. Now get back in the storeroom and prep for lunch. Then you can stock up before you leave for the ball game."

****

The snow from the previous night was nothing but a memory. By midmorning the sun had melted everything on the valley floor, and the forecast called for a hold in the weather. Even though it would be a cold afternoon, Adam's ball game was on.

Rick had no choice but to take Roxanne to the game. He couldn't deny his son the pride of showing off his ball skills to his mother. Adam had talked of nothing else from the moment he'd gotten home from school. At least he'd remembered his responsibilities at Cayme's store and had called her to explain why he wouldn't be in that day.

On the ride to the ballpark, he said. "I told Cayme that Mom was staying through the holiday. She said it was okay that I didn't come in and to enjoy my visit with Mom."

Roxanne, sitting in the front seat of his truck, turned and smiled at Adam. "How very responsible of you, sweetheart." When she faced forward again, she smiled at Rick. "Such a good boy."

Rick glanced in the rearview mirror and saw Adam beam. He didn't know whether to be relieved or worried. He should have called Cayme himself. He'd intended to call her the moment he got to work. But Councilman Peters was waiting for him at the job site. They'd holed up in his on-site office, reviewing the plans for the golf course for several hours. Now that Cayme had agreed to sell her property, her neighbor, old Mrs. Jones, had signed her contract that next morning. Councilman Peters was getting everything he'd asked for, even gloating that he didn't have to resort to twisting Rick's arm to get his fiancée to sell.

After Peters left, the rest of the day was full of meetings with the crew, reviewing the original plans to expand the park onto Cayme and Ben's property. He didn't even have time for lunch. At least he'd gotten off work early for the game.

Sometime that night, after the game, he'd call Cayme. Explain everything. At least Adam had informed her that Roxanne's visit was only temporary.

He was grateful for that small favor. He couldn't imagine what was going through her mind with his ex-wife's sudden appearance. Did she think he and Roxane were getting back together? Or did she trust him enough to know that he wouldn't even consider a reconciliation?

As he pulled into the ballpark, he spied Cayme's car and his spirits lifted. Good! He didn't have to wait until that night to see her or hear her voice. He'd have the chance to explain what was going on and put his guilty feelings to rest.

"Look!" Adam pointed at the little car. "Cayme's here! She remembered to come and be our good luck charm."

Roxanne frowned and whipped around to stare at her son. "Good luck charm?"

Adam bounced against his seat belt. "Yeah, Mom. She came to our last game and I hit a home run. The very first home run I ever hit! I told her she was our team's good luck charm, and she had to come to all our games." He took a deep breath. "I was afraid she would forget or be mad at me because I wasn't at work."

"Cayme would never be mad at you, son," Rick assured him. At the statement, he felt Roxanne's stare burn the side of his face. It didn't matter what she was thinking. He'd confirmed his relationship with Cayme the previous night, and nothing his ex said would change his mind. He found an open spot next to Cayme's car and parked the truck. Turning to face Adam, he said, "You did a good thing, calling her today."

Adam nodded. "Yeah. And it's even cooler she came like she promised."

Rick smiled. "It sure is." He tilted his head toward the door. "Grab your gear and let's go say hi before you warm up."

"Yay!" Adam grabbed his ball bag and popped open the back door.

Rick climbed out, shrugged on his jacket, and walked around to the passenger side of the door to help Roxanne down.

She'd already hopped out, pulled her coat on, and slammed her door. "I'll just sit over here while you visit with your girlfriend."

Rick shrugged and locked the truck. "Suit yourself." He didn't look back, and instead, followed Adam over to the bleachers. By the time he caught up to his son, Adam was wrapped around Cayme in a big hug. She was even wearing a Blakely Blackhawk jacket in support of his son's team. The sight made Rick's heart clutch and nearly brought him to his knees. This woman had come to mean so much to him in such a short time. The long-overdue phone call to explain things didn't seem like such a hurdle now that he saw her. Getting engaged to Cayme was one of the best decisions he'd ever made. Even if it wasn't real in the beginning, having her in his life was real now.

As she met his eyes, the smile that had been so warm for Adam clouded.

Rick took a deep breath. Maybe that hurdle was still there—and larger than he'd anticipated. But they'd get through it. "Hi."

She gave Adam one more hug and tweaked his cap. "Go get 'em, champ."

"I'll hit another home run just for you, Cayme." He straightened his cap and smiled. "See you after the game." He turned and waved at Rick. "Bye, Dad." Then he turned and ran back to Roxanne. "Wish me luck, Mom!"

Both Rick and Cayme watched Adam give his mother a hug before he joined the team on the field for warm-ups.

Rick turned back to face his fiancée, who glanced between Adam and Roxanne with a pensive expression. "Hi." He was repeating himself, but he suddenly wasn't as sure about their relationship as he'd been a few moments ago.

"Hi." She gave Roxanne another glance then took a deep breath and faced Rick. "Can I talk to you? Privately?"

He saw the direction of her gaze and smiled to ease her worry. "Sure. I was hoping we could talk. The game's not starting for another fifteen minutes." He gestured to a corner of the field currently unoccupied by ballplayers and spectators. They could hold a conversation without being overheard, even though everyone at the ballpark, except the kids, was probably watching them. "I owe you an apology for not calling sooner."

"It's okay. I understand." She lifted a shoulder as though shrugging off the elephant between them. "I'm sure you've had a lot on your plate. I used the time to think about things."

"Things?"

"Us." They reached the fence line next to right outfield and she stared across the grass. "I've been thinking about us."

He smiled. "Good. I have, too." She wasn't looking at him and missed his smile.

Instead, her gaze had moved to where Roxanne sat on the bleachers with Sherry.

Sherry glared in their direction.

He couldn't quite tell what his ex-wife was thinking, but her eyes were locked on them as well. What he'd give for complete privacy right now.

"Rick, I'm releasing you from our engagement."

He jerked his gaze back to Cayme. "What?"

She cleared her throat. "I've come to realize I care too much for you and Adam to stand in the way of your reconciliation. He's so glad his mother's back. And I see the three of you all together…you make such a lovely family unit. I won't stand in the way of that."

"You care for me?"

If anything, she looked even more morose. "Don't make me say it."

Frowning, he reached out to tilt her chin until she looked at him. "Say what?"

She licked her lips. "Please, Rick."

"Say what, Cayme?" he repeated.

She swallowed and dropped her eyes. "I've fallen in love with you. For real this time, not that stupid crush from high school."

It felt as though fireworks exploded in his chest. Then her other words found a way through the joy. He let go of her chin and rubbed a spot between his eyes. "I don't understand. If you love me, why are you saying I need to get back with Roxanne?"

"*Because* I love you. I don't want to stand in the way of your happiness."

His eyes widened. "And you think I'd be happier with Roxanne?"

"Adam is over the moon because his mother is

back in his life. I would do anything for him, just like you would. How can you deny your little boy his mother?" Her smile was sad and she shook her head.

"I certainly can't."

"Let me get this straight. You love me, so you're breaking up with me?"

She let go a short laugh that held no humor. "We aren't breaking up. We were never together. You know the engagement wasn't real. I can't even believe we attempted to convince everyone we were in love enough to be engaged." She swallowed. "To get married."

He was still reeling from her confession of love. His heart thundered in his chest. "But you love me. You just said so."

"I do. Except you don't love me. Everything you've done has been out of obligation—some sort of chivalrous code of coming to my rescue." Her back stiffened. "I don't need you to rescue me. And I'm not standing in the way of you making your family whole again."

A bubble of anger churned in his chest. He couldn't believe he was having this ridiculous conversation. "So, this is the 'I love you so much I'm breaking up with you' speech?"

She shrugged. "I guess."

"What if I love you back?"

Her head tilted and her eyes grew wide. "Oh, come on, Rick. We haven't even been on a single date." She raised a bare-fingered left hand. "We're not really engaged. If you loved me, you would have called last night. You would have called this morning. We would have found a way to be alone together these past few days. That's what lovers do."

"I'm not totally to blame in that department, you know."

She started. "What do you mean?"

"When have you had time for me?"

She grew quiet then nodded in acknowledgment. "You're right. I haven't made time, either."

"Then how do you know you love me?" Was he lashing out from hurt or finding some hidden truth they both had missed? "Maybe you want out of the engagement for yourself. Maybe seeing Chase Peters made you realize what you lost the first time around. He's certainly a better prospect than me."

She shrank away from the accusation.

But Rick couldn't withdraw his words. Years ago, he'd been rejected by his ex after she'd given birth to his child. Now, Cayme, a person he believed to be sincere and honest, was rejecting him in the name of love.

His chest hurt. He was losing the one person in his life who would bring it meaning. He needed to make her understand what was really happening. "Roxanne isn't staying around. We're not getting back together."

"What do you mean?"

"She's only in town for the week. She came to spend time with Adam. I don't know if she'll come back again. Ever." Although he suspected now that Roxanne had made inroads with Adam, she'd be less of a stranger. But that didn't mean she would be a permanent fixture in their lives.

Cayme stared at him with a glimmer of light in her eyes, like hope flaming to life. Then it extinguished as quickly as it came. "No! You need to do something to keep her here. I don't know what happened the first time you split up, but she's back now. Please don't let her think you don't care. It's not fair to leave her guessing like you did me."

Bile rose in his throat. "You're damn right, you don't know what happened. You don't know that she up and left me with a baby to care for. She was selfish and didn't think twice about abandoning her child and husband."

Cayme winced. "That must have been awful for you." Then she glanced over to where Roxanne sat. "But she must be having second thoughts, or she wouldn't be back now. Adam is so very happy. How can you deny him his mother? A chance to be a family?"

Their conversation was going in circles. Cayme wasn't listening to what he was saying, or she was choosing not to listen. He should stop rescuing women. His personal code of honor had gotten him in this mess—time to get out. "You know what? I obviously can't change your mind. Maybe you're right and this engagement was a bad idea. I'm sorry I put you through it." He took her left hand and rubbed the bare spot where he should have put a ring.

Her hand trembled.

"I hope someday you'll find someone who makes you happy." His voice broke slightly.

"I want you to be happy, Rick. You and Adam."

"I don't think you know what will make me happy. If you really loved me, you'd know that." He dropped her hand. Facing the ballfield, he leaned on the fence. His breathing was shallow and quick, and the buzz in his ears wasn't from the noise in the park but from the blood pounding through his veins.

After several moments his head cleared, and his heart knew the truth. He was being stupid. He couldn't let Cayme go. He turned to face her.

She'd already slipped away, heading back to the bleachers. Her shoulders hunched forward, and she clutched her middle.

Feeling as though the bottom had dropped out from under his world, he trudged back to the bleachers. "How will I ever fix this?" he whispered to the breeze.

Chapter Twenty-Three

Sitting through Adam's baseball game was harder than returning that stupid engagement ring to Chase Peters. Excruciating couldn't begin to describe the experience of being so close to Rick yet separated by this emotional turmoil.

She perched on the bench next to Sherry, doing everything she could to ignore Rick and Roxanne on the other side of her best friend. After every great play, one or both of them cheered, like parents should at their son's ball game. She wanted to be more vocal herself but was afraid to make any noise that drew attention to her. If it hadn't been for her promise to the boys, she'd have left after the first pitch.

Through most of the game, Cayme sensed Rick's stare as though he was sending some subliminal message. Even Sherry seemed to be aware of the awkwardness, returning to her seat quickly after attending to the baby, as though she wanted to block the tension.

After the Blackhawks lost, Cayme took a minute to congratulate Adam on making the final out of the game. She wanted to console him for the loss, but she was ready to explode from the strain of the situation with his father and mother. As soon as she could, she waved goodbye and headed for her car. She was about to start the engine, then Sherry pounded on her window.

Cayme rolled it down and her best friend unleashed her fury.

"Don't you *ever* do that to me again."

"What?"

Sherry rolled her eyes. "You know what. The waves of tension rolling off you and Rick were like a tsunami." She smacked her hand on the top of the little car. "You two need to straighten things out or I'm staging an intervention."

"There's nothing to fix. I told Rick he should make things work with his…with Roxanne." Cayme tried to lower her voice hoping Sherry would do the same. "And I told you this morning the engagement wasn't real."

Sherry tossed her head back and barked out a laugh. "Says you! For two people with nothing between you, you act like the world is ending." She glared into the car. "And speaking of things breaking, you'll break a little boy's heart if you don't work it out. Adam's my nephew and I won't stand by and let you hurt him." With that, she stomped off to where Joey stood next to his dad, looking dejected about losing the game. Sherry gave them both a hug and they climbed into their minivan.

Adam was already in the truck with Rick and Roxanne. He waved wildly through the window at Cayme, his smile never dimming while they drove away.

Cayme mustered a return smile and waved back. As soon as they were out of sight, she dropped her head onto the steering wheel. The entire afternoon had been a disaster. For the boys, the stinging loss would fade with the help of an ice cream cone. But Sherry was right. If she and Rick didn't at least act as though they liked each other, Adam would suffer hurt along with them.

He was young and resilient but also intuitive and sensitive to the feelings of others. He'd eventually understand that people who dated didn't necessarily marry. But at the moment, his age limited his understanding.

After learning that Roxanne had abandoned Adam and Rick, Cayme had paid closer attention to the other woman's actions.

There was no doubt Adam enjoyed having his mother around.

And when Roxanne looked at her son, her face shone with as much pride as Rick's. It seemed as though they'd become a perfect family, if they just gave it another chance.

Cayme was sure Rick would see how great it would be for Adam to have his mother around. Every boy deserved that kind of happiness, and Rick couldn't deny his son.

Cayme sighed. Regardless of where everyone's feelings fell along the spectrum, she'd done the right thing by ending the charade of the fake engagement. In a way, she was relieved to stop the pretense. If only she wasn't feeling like the one who'd struck out today.

She finished her day at the store and then drove home. The moment she stepped inside the house her cell phone rang. She held her breath, thinking it might be Rick. Instead her boss's caller ID flagged on the screen.

He started the call by thanking her for the edit review she'd recently turned in and agreed with her suggestion that their company should represent the new author. Then he asked again when she planned to return to work.

No time like the present to break the bad news. Taking a deep breath, she offered her verbal resignation. "I know I said in our last conversation that I expected to only be another month. But things here have changed. I've decided to stay. I'm not returning to Seattle."

"Oh. I see." He cleared his throat. "That's too bad. You have a great eye for spotting writing talent, and I don't want to lose that." He paused. "You've already proven you can work remotely. How about I counter with a suggestion? Would you like to work remotely on a permanent basis?"

"Wow. I didn't expect…I don't know…" She swallowed. This was more than she had hoped for. "I'm working full-time at my mother's coffee shop. That's a lot of hours now, and the reading I've done for you has been part-time. I'm not sure if I can keep up a full-time reading and editing schedule."

"What you've done for me part-time has been a great help." He cleared his throat again. "I know I don't say it often enough, but I've appreciated your work. Even part-time you do more than some of the other assistants I've had."

"So, we'd amend my employment to part-time?"

"If you agree to it. Do you still want time to consider it?"

"Yes…I mean, no…I mean, I accept." The extra income would help. And who knew? Maybe by the end of the summer she and Skeeter could afford to hire someone for the store, and Cayme could edit full-time again. Or not. She really enjoyed working in the store.

"Perfect. In the meantime, would you review another manuscript?"

She let out a short laugh that held no humor. Since she'd broken up with Rick, she had nothing to keep her from working late into the night. "Sure."

****

By the end of the week, Ben had cleared most of the old stuff from the shed and had various piles for keeping, donation, and the landfill. He seemed to embrace the change in routine, regardless that, in less than a month, they would no longer live in their childhood home.

Cayme had found a three-bedroom apartment in a new complex on the south end of town and suggested they move in together. But after reviewing the details of the contract and assessing the windfall they would receive from the house sale, her brother said he wanted his own place.

She was disappointed that she'd not have as much time with him. This change meant she'd have to live alone. Was she ready?

"Are you sure you want your own place?" she asked Ben again on Sunday evening after they'd finalized the paperwork to give to the city for the closing in the middle of June.

"Absolutely. With the final check from Mom's life insurance, we'll have a lot more money than we expected—even after we split the proceeds from the sale. I don't have a problem with you living nearby, but it's time I made a go of it alone." He kicked back on the recliner, the guitar resting in his lap.

She'd yet to hear him do more than tune the instrument since he'd picked it up a few weeks ago.

Maybe he wasn't ready to play it in front of anyone. She chewed on her lip. "I wasn't expecting us to live in different houses."

"Are you okay with that?" He thumbed a string while twisting the tuning knob. The twang was strangely mesmerizing.

"If it's what you want." She shrugged. "I'll make it work." She scooted to the edge of the couch. "Since we're splitting the funds, I'll look for a smaller place. Maybe I'll find something above one of the old businesses in town. I'd like to be close to the store. Then I can invest some of my money back into the business."

"Isn't the store doing okay?" He laid the guitar in the case next to his chair. "If you need more money, we can still move in together."

She appreciated his willingness to make the sacrifice, but if he wanted independence, then she wanted it for him. "The store is doing well. I ran through the numbers again on Friday. We should make a tidy profit from this final holiday weekend rush. I was only speculating that an investment might be a good idea for if times get a bit lean."

"Have you always planned ahead like this?"

She gave a wry smile. "No. I don't think I have. But it makes sense."

"You've really committed to sticking around. Even when our roots are disappearing, you're finding ways to make a home."

He smiled—a genuine grin that lit up his entire face and made her feel warm as if he'd given her a big hug.

"I'm so proud of you."

She was proud of him too, of his progress, and his support. "I wouldn't have gotten through the last few days without your help. I'm stronger because I can lean on you."

"Now you're just getting sappy."

She smiled and pushed down the tears. "Too bad, big brother. I'm your sister. That means around you, I get to be sappy all I want."

He bent down and snapped the lid closed on the guitar case. "Well, I'm off to bed before it gets too deep in here." He glanced up. "Don't we have to be up with the birds tomorrow for the Sunrise Memorial Ceremony?"

She took a deep breath. "We do."

"Sherry will be there to help, right? She didn't back out after you and Rick broke up?"

Cayme shook her head, but her heart still ached for the hurt Sherry must feel. "Friends to the end. I don't know what I'd do without her."

"I'm sorry about what happened between you and Rick. I know your engagement didn't start on the right footing. I was positive you two could make it work."

"As long as it isn't affecting your relationship with him, I can live with the fallout."

"I haven't seen a lot of him the last few days. Seems the moment you announced you were selling the property, the construction timeline ratcheted up. He's been buried in his office all week with either Peters or Mayor Nicholson. The best thing about this is that the entire town has rallied around you."

"Maybe." Once she got through the closing things would get easier. "It has been nice to be crossed off the pariah list."

Ben stood with a laugh and carried the guitar to the corner.

Cayme finally gave in and asked the question that burned inside whenever she saw him with the instrument. "Will you ever play that thing again?"

He paused, his entire body going completely still. Then he took a deep breath. "Maybe. Someday." He propped the case in the corner. "Abel has started a new band. They've been doing gigs at the bars near the resort. He's asked me to sit in with them."

Cayme clapped her hands. "You totally should."

He shrugged. "I don't know. Right now, I'm headed to bed." He pointed at her. "You should too. Five a.m. will arrive soon enough. We need to be completely set up by six, right?"

She stood. "Yes." She walked to the front door, checked the lock, and then headed up the stairs. "Night, big brother."

"Night, Cay."

****

When Cayme's alarm went off the next morning, she was sure it was still midnight. Sleep hadn't come easily, and it seemed she'd just dozed off. Reaching over, she turned the alarm off.

Forty-five minutes later, she was at the store, arranging boxes of pastries and making coffee. She wanted gallons of fresh coffee in the large, pump-style thermal carafes for the crowd they expected.

Skeeter arrived at Books, Bytes, & Brews about ten minutes after Cayme and Sherry trailed in behind her.

"The gang's all here!" Sherry called.

It took thirty minutes to finish the last-minute prep and load the back of Skeeter's pickup truck. As they drove to the cemetery grounds on the southeast end of town, the sky grew lighter. A glow ahead of the sunrise colored the sky with pink and purple hues—a hint that the storm they were expecting was still on the day's agenda.

The outside temperature wasn't quite cold enough to snow, and Cayme hoped the weather would hold until the ceremony was over and they'd returned everything to the store. They arranged the coffee and pastries on tables the Veterans of Foreign Wars members had set up earlier.

Rows of chairs faced the podium that stood beside the flagpole. Cayme counted the seating and did a quick calculation. Unless the ceremony was standing room only, they should have enough coffee and pastries for everyone.

A crunch of gravel and flash of headlights drew her attention to the parking lot, where Rick and Adam were climbing out of his truck. She glanced past Rick and saw Roxanne step out and close the passenger side door. The knot that had started to unravel in Cayme's chest suddenly tightened. Taking a deep breath, she pushed aside her own desires. This was what she wanted for Rick and Adam. Their happiness was what mattered most.

And to hammer home the point, Adam beamed as he took his mother's hand. Then he spotted Cayme and waved.

She waved back, unable to help the smile that pulled at her lips.

When he saw her, Rick seemed to hesitate. He didn't smile, but an odd expression crossed his face.

Cayme wished she could read him better, wished

she knew more about the man. But she'd had her chance and chose to end their engagement. No point in wishing for things that could never be.

Several more cars pulled into the cemetery, drawing her attention back to her task.

As the townsfolk got out of their cars, they gathered in little groups. Many greetings were subdued in deference to the upcoming event. When Mayor Nicholson approached the podium, people wandered toward the chairs, but no one sat. Instead, everyone remained standing and waited for the ceremony to begin.

If Cayme hadn't been watching closely, she would have missed the signal from the mayor.

Behind her, a lone bagpipe player began the mournful sound of "Amazing Grace." The musician moved forward in a slow march. He was followed by the local Boy Scout Troop.

The lead boy strode forward, bearing the United States flag. Another boy carried the state flag. The rest of the troop followed in two columns of boys ranging in age from Eagle Scout all the way down to Cub Scout.

Cayme spied Adam and Joey toward the end of the line.

As they marched, their little chests puffed out, proudly wearing their dark-blue uniforms.

The flag bearers reached the front, and with the final note of the hymn, the mayor stepped to the podium. He invited the group to participate in the Pledge of Allegiance, which was led by one of the scouts. After the Pledge of Allegiance, the flags were secured in posts on either side of the podium, and the audience took their seats.

Remaining at the back near the coffee tables, Cayme still couldn't relax. Her heart pounded at the sight of those boys. She was so proud of the respect they had shown for the flag and the ceremony they'd been in. She was especially proud of Adam and Joey and had to swallow several times at the lump forming in her throat.

At the podium, the mayor pulled a speech from his jacket.

When he looked out at the crowd, Cayme saw tears in his eyes too.

He cleared his throat and began thanking those who'd served to protect their country and families. One by one, he called names of those gathered in the crowd who'd served, asking them to stand and be recognized. Ben, Rick, and Roxanne were among the dozen or so men and women standing.

Then he did a roll call of community members who'd served but had passed on.

When he called out her father's name, the tears she'd struggled to hold back spilled down her cheeks.

Skeeter wrapped her arm around Cayme's shoulders, offering silent comfort.

After the mayor finished speaking, he asked the audience to stand once again. Two reserve servicemen stepped forward with a folded flag. To the sound of "Taps," they fixed the flag to the rope on the flagpole and unfurled it, ceremoniously raising it to the top of the pole, and then lowered it again to half-staff. As it reached the middle of the flagpole, the sun crested the east peak of the mountain range.

Although the ceremony was a simple tribute to those who'd served and sacrificed for their country, both past and present, Cayme couldn't remember seeing anything so moving.

After the ceremony, Cayme and Skeeter stood behind the tables and prepared to serve those who wanted to stay and mingle.

As the sun peeked in and out of the clouds and began to warm the crowd, the solemn mood lifted. Old-timers shared stories and laughter with each other. Some flirted with Cayme and Sherry. But when Mr. Morrison, Sherry's dad, gave an especially fulsome compliment on the spread, Skeeter blushed.

Cayme did a double take. Was there a budding romance starting between Skeeter and Gary Morrison? Naw. Not Skeeter and Gary. They'd been friends for years.

Just then, Adam came running up to the table. "Hi, Cayme. Did you see me help with the ceremony?"

She leaned down and straightened Adam's collar over his neckerchief. "I did. I didn't know you were a scout. Is this your Eagle Scout uniform?" she teased.

Adam laughed and snagged a pastry. "No, silly. I'm a Cub Scout. I won't be an Eagle Scout until I'm older."

"Is that so? Well, you'll make a great Eagle Scout in a few years."

"Thanks. I have to do a big project, but not until I'm like, fourteen." He finished the pastry and handed Cayme his napkin. "Can you throw this away for me? I want to find Mom and Dad."

Cayme took the napkin. "Sure thing, kiddo." She swallowed down the sting in her heart and watched Adam race off to join his parents.

Taking a deep breath, she looked around the

cemetery at the veterans and those who were still serving but had made it home for the long weekend. She was glad Ben was there to receive the honor offered by the community. Now that the rush had thinned, she turned to Skeeter and Sherry. "Can you hold down the fort for a moment? I want to make a visit before we head back to the store."

"Sure thing, baby." Skeeter reached into a box under the table and handed Cayme two bouquets. "Say hi for me."

Cayme took the flowers, sending Skeeter a grateful smile. "I will." Then she wandered past the small groups toward the plot where her father and mother were buried.

Approaching the graves, she noticed the small flag stirring in the light breeze on her dad's resting place. She wanted to stay strong, but as she placed a bouquet on each side of the shared headstone tears threatened.

"He shouldn't have died so young."

Rick's voice floated over her shoulder. She straightened, somehow not completely surprised that he'd found her there. "I know." She wiped her eyes. "We had a tough time for a while, but we got through."

"Your dad was a special guy." He moved to stand beside her. They both gazed down at the plots.

"Ben missed him a lot. They used to go fishing and hiking together all the time."

"I remember," Rick said. "I tagged along on some of those trips. Your dad loved the outdoors. He taught us both to fish."

Cayme smiled, the melancholy welling deeper. "Dad liked having you along. I remember one time after your outings he shared every antic you and Ben pulled.

I swear he enjoyed getting into as much mischief as the two of you."

"Your mom never seemed to mind."

Cayme had a hard time looking at the unsettled grass around her mother's resting place. "I think Mom loved the child in him as much as she loved the man."

As she looked at her mother's name that had recently been added to the shared headstone, raw grief bubbled to the surface. She should have come home more often during those last few years. All that time lost—time she'd never get back.

Rick placed his hand on her shoulder.

The warmth of his palm penetrated through her jacket and dispelled the cool morning chill. She shivered under his touch, unsure if she could handle the support he offered. She wanted something more. Something he couldn't give and she shouldn't want. But just for a moment she gave herself to the comfort—to the strength he provided without even being aware of it.

"I'm sorry I didn't make time for us, Cayme," Rick said softly. "I know you think breaking our engagement is the right thing." He cleared his throat. "And given the way it started, you're probably right. Even though we're not a couple anymore, you need to know I'm not getting back with Roxanne, either."

She turned to him. He didn't drop his hand, and she found herself in a light embrace. "I don't know what to say."

His eyes grew dark and his carefree, boyish expression vanished. The intensity of his look burned deep inside her. "I know you're carrying a heavy burden and things are tough right now. But you don't have to do it alone."

"I..." He wasn't offering anything more than friendship. And that was more than she deserved. She swallowed the lump of regret that rose in her throat. "Thank you."

He dipped his head and brushed his mouth across hers.

Shock kept her rooted. She couldn't move. Her heart was pounding so hard, she was sure it would beat out of her chest and drop right into her lurching stomach.

He lifted his head, yet his dark eyes showed that the brief kiss had affected him too. Without a word, he pivoted and walked back toward the gathering, his back straight and stiff as though he were punishing himself for giving in to a weakness.

Cayme stared after him. What had just happened?

Chapter Twenty-Four

"That was a lovely ceremony." Roxanne removed her jacket and draped it on the back of the kitchen chair. She gave Adam a smile. "You did a great job, son."

"Thanks, Mom. We practiced at our Cub Scout meetings. Then we got to meet with the older scouts." Adam looked at Rick. "I was glad to see Cayme there, but she looked sad."

Impressed with his son's perception, he said. "She was probably remembering her mom and dad. Sometimes it's sad to remember people who have passed on."

Adam nodded. "Yeah. I guess it hasn't been too long since her mom died. Even I still miss Grandma sometimes."

"Exactly." Rick missed his own mother, too. "This is a special day set aside to help us remember family and loved ones who aren't with us anymore."

"But you said they are always in our hearts, right?"

"That's right," Rick agreed. "Always."

Roxanne put an arm around Adam's shoulder. "You're a special boy, you know that, sweetheart?"

Adam grinned. "Thanks, Mom." He gave her a hug and then let go. "I need my mitt. Joey wants to play ball."

Rick grinned at his kid's mood changes. "Change your shirt and hang it up so it's ready for the next meeting."

"'Kay," Adam yelled and raced out of the room.

Rick walked over to the counter and lifted the coffee pot. He really didn't need more caffeine but wanted to keep busy, to keep from thinking of Cayme's sad face.

"Your girlfriend did look sad." Roxanne's comment made it clear she wasn't letting him off that easy.

He lifted the pot and poured half a cup. "It's what I told Adam. She and Ben just lost their mom. Their dad died a few years back. I'm sure the ceremony really hit home."

"That may have been part of it." She moved to the table and pulled out a chair and sat. "But I think there's more than that. She broke up with you, didn't she?"

Rick slid the coffee pot back onto the hotplate a little harder than he needed to. "Yes."

"Why?"

A bit more forcefully than he'd intended, he swung around and stared at his ex-wife. "Why do you think?" He gestured at her. "She has some crazy idea that I'd be happier with you. She believes she's doing the noble thing by stepping aside."

"Surely you set her straight." She glared at him.

"I tried. I don't think she believed me."

"Oh my God! Why not?"

"The engagement was a bad idea from the start. It's probably for the best."

Roxanne stood. "You idiot! You're in love with her, and you're just letting her go?"

"So what if I am?" He took a sip and winced at the cold, bitter brew. "She rejected me. I guess I'm finally clueing into the fact that I'm not cut out for relationships."

"What?" Roxanne's mouth hung open.

"Nothing." He heaved a sigh and dumped the coffee down the sink.

"Wow." She blinked several times as though still processing what he'd just admitted.

He couldn't believe he'd said that out loud. To his ex-wife, especially. Everything with Cayme had messed with his head, and he definitely wasn't thinking straight.

"You're not saying you wanted to stay married to me, are you?" Roxanne cleared her throat. "I thought our divorce was a mutual agreement."

"Well, you thought wrong. You'd just had my baby and suddenly you didn't want either one of us. The writing on the wall was clear. I wasn't sticking around where I wasn't wanted."

"But I wasn't *rejecting* you. I was giving you your freedom. If we'd stayed together it would've been disastrous. And I couldn't even begin to imagine how it would've affected Adam."

Rick held up his hand to stop whatever Roxanne intended to say next and walked to the entry to the living room. "Adam?"

"I'm about ready!" Adam called from the top of the stairs.

Rick breathed a sigh of relief. His son hadn't accidentally overheard anything. He turned back to Roxanne. "Save your confessions until he's gone."

At that moment, Adam came thundering down the stairs with his mitt. "I hunged up my shirt. Can I go over to Joey's?"

"Grab a jacket. It's supposed to rain later," Rick said. "And I don't want you going anywhere else. Only Joey's house."

"'Kay." Adam gave his mother a hug. "See you." He pulled his jacket off the hook, opened the back door, and hurried out, letting the door slam behind him.

Silence followed the whirlwind that was his kid—an unsettled, uncomfortable silence. Rick faced Roxanne with a raised brow. His heart pounded and an anticipatory chill snuck under his skin.

Roxanne had paled a little, perhaps with the realization that sharing her reasons for abandoning him and Adam would shape the rest of their lives. He certainly felt as though his life was about to shift on its axis.

"After I had Adam, all I wanted to do was hide. So I ran away." She swallowed and some of her color returned. "I was afraid of the responsibility. I was afraid of failing. But I certainly wasn't rejecting you."

"You didn't even try to be a mother and wife. Why would you think you'd fail?"

"Don't you think I know that? That's why I'm here now. I'm still scared. But I have to face this child. I'm not running away this time."

At least she was honest. "Did you love me at all?"

She went completely still then slowly shook her head. "Not in the way you deserve. Not the way I think Cayme loves you."

His heart stalled for a moment. Cayme had said she'd loved him, but then she'd called off the engagement. What in the world was he supposed to think? "She has a funny way of showing it."

"She loves you enough to give you up." Roxanne

gave a humorless laugh. "Trust me. I'm not that honorable or self-sacrificing."

He frowned. "I don't think that's true. Not anymore."

She smiled and cradled her stomach. "That's very generous of you. I hope I can change." She looked up. "Our relationship failed because of me. My fault, not yours. You stepped up and did the honorable thing. I didn't even give you a chance. That's on me."

Her confession settled in his brain for a long moment. A wound he'd been carrying for eight years seemed to close up, easing the sting. He couldn't quite get a bead on the subtle sensation, letting the feeling wash over him for a long moment. "Thank you for that," he finally said.

Roxanne gave him a half-hearted smile.

****

As the store's front door chimed, Cayme glanced up. When she saw who entered, she wanted to run the opposite direction. Instead, she pasted a smile on her face and watched Roxanne approach the counter. "Welcome to Books, Bytes, & Brews. What can I get you?"

The other woman glanced around at the mostly empty room. "Is there a place we can talk?"

"I really shouldn't leave the counter." The last thing Cayme wanted was a heart-to-heart with the woman who was probably taking her place in Rick's life, regardless of what Rick said.

"Please."

The single plea seemed sincere and Cayme couldn't find the words to be rude. She nodded and pointed toward the book section. "I think it's quiet over there." She called into the backroom, "Skeeter, I'm stepping away for a few."

Skeeter walked up to the counter, seeming to assess the situation at a glance. "I'm right here if you need me, baby."

"Thanks." Cayme moved around the counter and led the way to the book corner.

Roxanne followed and then paused as though assessing the little sitting area. "This is nice." She took a seat on the edge of the couch. "Thank you for taking time to talk to me."

Cayme glanced at the clock on the wall. "I don't have much time. Our lunch crowd will be coming in soon."

"I won't take too long." The woman's smile slipped a little. "This is harder than I expected."

What could be hard about asking her to stay away from Rick? Cayme remained quiet, allowing her nemesis to follow through with what she needed to say.

"I'm leaving town tomorrow," Roxanne started.

That made Cayme sit up straighter. Rick had said they weren't getting back together, but she really hadn't believed it. "Why? Aren't you here to stay?"

Roxanne shook her head. "I'm just here to visit. My reason for coming here is personal, but I realize I need to share that reason with you."

"I don't understand."

"I'm having a baby."

Cayme's cheeks grew cold. "Oh." She blinked. "Con…congratulations."

"Obviously, the baby isn't Rick's." Roxanne cradled her stomach. "I let go of my family eight years ago. I was selfish and irresponsible. But I've been given another chance to make it right with a man I desperately love. I came to town to make amends and to see…" She paused and swallowed hard. "To see Adam. And to see if I had what it took to be a mother."

Cayme frowned. "Adam is an amazing little boy. You can't just walk into his life and then leave. That will crush him."

Roxanne sniffed. "He won't be alone—he'll have you. I'm leaving both Adam *and* Rick in your care."

"But Rick and I…"

"Have some things to work out. I know. I have faith that you two can do it." She reached for Cayme's hand.

Her fingers were icy. Almost as icy as Cayme's.

"You have to take care of them. Love them."

"You don't understand," Cayme said. "Rick and I were never really engaged."

"Then make it real." Roxanne squeezed harder. "I believe Rick needs you more than you realize."

Cayme sat back, pulling away from the other woman's grasp. If only what she said was true. And what about Adam… "I can't take your place. You'll always be Adam's real mother."

Roxanne's expression grew serious. "Make no mistake in what I'm saying. I'm in town to visit, but I also won't be a stranger any longer. However, you're the person who'll be in his life every day. You'll be the mother he sees each day, and the one who tucks him into bed every night."

Cayme shook her head. "Rick and I aren't even together."

Roxanne stood. "You should be—no, you have to be. I want you to know that I trust you with my son."

"But you don't know me."

"I know that my son loves you. That's good enough for me. I'm pretty sure his dad does too." She gave another watery smile then stood and walked out of the room.

Roxanne's words made Cayme's thoughts spin, then the door chimed closed, snapping her out of the stupor. She got up and wandered back to the counter.

Skeeter took one look at her and moved to the latte machine. "You look like you could use a drink."

Cayme blinked. "I think I need something much stronger than coffee."

The older woman held up a scoop. "I'll make it a double espresso. Best I can do until later." She started the latte. "I tried to eavesdrop, except you were both talking so quietly, I couldn't hear anything."

"I'm thankful we weren't overheard." Cayme looked around, grateful no one else had come in while she and Roxanne had been talking. "Rick's ex-wife isn't staying in town. In fact, she's given her blessing to me and Rick." She tilted her head, unable to believe what Roxanne had said. "And permission to be Adam's stepmother."

Skeeter almost dropped the cup. "Wow." She glanced at the closed door as if attempting to see through it. "I gotta say I didn't see that coming." She turned her attention back to the drink, capped the cup, and handed it to Cayme.

Cayme automatically took the drink but didn't bring it to her lips. "Nor did I." A million thoughts swirled in her brain, the emotional hit from each one digging a bit deeper into her soul. Quickly rising to the surface was the conversation she'd had with Rick at the ballfield, and then his kiss at the cemetery that morning. Just a week before, she'd told him she loved him. He'd said he'd be there if she ever needed a friend—nothing about love.

She wanted more than a friend. She wanted Rick. And she'd blown it. What was she supposed to do now?

"Are you all right, baby? You look like you've seen a ghost," Skeeter said.

"I have to fix things." Cayme shook her head. "I need to find Rick."

Skeeter grinned. "That's my girl." With the backs of her hands, she shooed Cayme on her way. "I've got you covered here. Don't come back until you've squared it away with that man of yours."

Cayme was glad she didn't have to explain her urgency to set things right. "I so owe you." She grabbed her purse and coat and hurried out to her car.

Chapter Twenty-Five

Rain was falling again, and low clouds hung over the mountains. However, the temperature reading on the car's display indicated the air was too warm for snow, even at the highest peaks. The pounding rain was adding to the potential snowmelt, making floods imminent.

Cayme should be worried about the threat to her home. But at the moment, all she wanted was to find Rick. She had to undo the damage she'd caused...if he'd let her.

As she reached his house, she slowed the car. Through the curtain of rain, she couldn't see his truck in the driveway. But another car was there—Roxanne's.

The other woman climbed out of the car and a man joined her on the sidewalk. Together they started toward the front door.

Instead of driving past, Cayme braked and pulled to the side of the road.

Roxanne and the man glanced over curiously.

Making up her mind that confrontations seemed to be the order of the day, Cayme turned off the engine and got out. She strode toward the pair, somewhat reassured by Roxanne's smile.

"Cayme. What a nice surprise."

"Hi." Cayme tugged the collar up on her coat to keep the rain from seeping in, wishing she'd grabbed her umbrella.

"Why don't you come in?" Roxanne gestured to the house.

Cayme shook her head. "I'm looking for Rick. Is he at work?" She didn't think he worked on holidays. But if he wasn't at home, where was he?

Roxanne gave another smile. "I see you're taking my advice to heart. He went over to Sherry's to pick up Adam." She nodded toward the man who stood beside her. "This is Brad Hamilton. He's…" She paused, suddenly looking uncomfortable.

Brad draped an arm around Roxanne, pulling her close and placing a kiss on her damp hair. "I'm the man who's finally putting a ring on this lady's finger."

Roxanne beamed and laid her head on his shoulder.

"I guess congratulations are in order." Cayme gave Roxanne a pointed look. "Have you told Adam?"

"We're waiting for Rick to bring him home. They'll be back any minute."

"Oh." Cayme swallowed the cold seeping into her stomach. "Then you'll want some family time. This is an important moment for all of you."

Roxanne frowned. "For you, too. You should stay."

Cayme shook her head. "Things aren't settled between me and Rick." She wasn't sure how Rick would feel if she bared her soul. He may not want her around after all the things she'd said the other day. She inched backward toward her car. "I'll stop by later…when you've all, um, you know." She waved her hands uncertainly. Taking another step backward, she pivoted and climbed into her car before they could persuade her to change her mind.

"Congratulations," she called, then closed the door

and started the engine. Without looking back at the happy couple, she pushed her dripping hair out of her eyes, put the car in gear, and headed back to the store.

Leaving was the right thing to do. She wasn't part of that family, not yet. Maybe not ever. Adam was about to learn that his mother was marrying someone who wasn't his father, and that he would soon have a baby brother or sister. That was exactly the type of situation where he needed his parents—his real parents—to help him deal with whatever his imagination conjured up. She just hoped that he'd take the news well, because right then, her heart ached for the little boy whose world was about to be knocked on its side.

****

After leaving Rick's house, she returned to help Skeeter with the lunch crowd. Not that she'd been much help. She went through the motions, grateful she'd been working in the store long enough to not make too many mistakes while her mind was elsewhere.

They'd chosen to close up early because the crowds had been small, which Skeeter had attributed to the downpour keeping everyone indoors. The rain had also likely ruined the skiing that was supposed to have been amazing during the last day of the holiday weekend. Even though the day's proceeds were dismal, the impending sale of the house would keep them flush through the summer.

Later, as she unlocked her front door, the stillness of her own home hit her hard. Ben was with his friend, Abel, and wouldn't be home until after six.

Alone, Cayme let the events of the day wash over her. Like the raging river outside, she was tumbling downstream with nothing to catch her.

She glanced at the old clock on the wall showing half past five. It had probably been long enough that she could reach out to Rick again. The longer she waited, the harder it would be to rally courage for the difficult conversation. Poor Adam, hopefully he was doing okay with all the news he'd received that day.

A knock sounded at her door. She looked out the front window. Wow, had the little boy standing on the front porch materialized from her imagination? She opened the door wide. "Adam. Let's get you out of the rain."

His chin was buried in his jacket, and water dripped off the bill of his baseball cap. "'Kay." With slow, sloppy steps he walked over to the couch. He sat heavily, as though the weight of the world rested on his back.

Cayme swallowed. Chances were good he hadn't taken the news from his mother very well. She crossed the living room and sat next to him. "Want to talk about it?"

He heaved a sigh. "I'm just sad."

She laid a hand on his back, not caring how wet his jacket was. "Would you like to tell me what you're sad about?" Letting him say it all out loud, in his own words, might help. At least in theory it sounded reasonable.

"My mom is leaving in a few days and she only just got here."

"I'm sorry to hear that. I know how excited you've been to see her. I'm sure she'll visit more, though."

"Yeah." He nodded. "She said she's quitting the Army, so she won't be traveling all the time. She's visiting again next month."

"Well, that's a good thing, right? You finally get to spend more time with her." Roxanne resigning her Army commission was a bit of a surprise, but if she was having a baby, it also made sense.

"And she's having a baby." Adam heaved another sigh.

"Does that make you sad, too?" Oh dear, what would his young imagination make of his mother having a baby from a man who wasn't his own father?

"I don't know. When she does, I won't be her kid anymore."

"That's absolutely not true. You will always be her kid. You're her son, and she loves you very much." At least Cayme could assure him of this fact. Good thing Roxanne had filled her in on the situation.

"Yeah. She and Dad both said that. Even that Brad guy said I'd always be her son. No matter what."

Cayme took a breath of relief. Thank goodness the adults in this little boy's life were all about making him feel wanted. "So, you don't have to feel sad about her not being your mom."

"I know in my head I shouldn't, but my tummy feels different. It feels sad."

She closed her eyes. How was she supposed to fix the tummy, or more accurately, the heart? She tipped his chin up to stare into his eyes. "Does your tummy understand that you get to be a big brother?"

"Like Joey?"

She hesitated. Sometimes Joey didn't like being a big brother. But the fun and not-so-fun times were all part of the package. "Yeah, like Joey."

Adam tilted his head slightly. "It would be cool to

have a little sister like Rachel."

Cayme squeezed his shoulder. "See? Maybe being a big brother won't be so bad."

He shrugged. "But she won't live with me like Rachel lives with Joey."

"That's true. But when she comes to visit, or you go to visit her, think of all the big brother things you can teach her. She'll always look forward to seeing you. I'll bet Rachel hates how Joey bosses her around all the time."

Adam smiled. "Yeah, sometimes." He frowned again. "What if the baby is a boy?"

"A little brother might be even more fun. You could teach him to play catch. A baby sister might want to play with dolls."

"I could still teach my sister to play catch."

Cayme smiled. "You could indeed."

Adam scooted farther back on the couch, his expression brightening. "I'm glad I came over. I was afraid you wouldn't want to talk to me."

A chill slid along her arms. "Why would you think that?"

"'Cuz you and Dad aren't dating any more. I was hoping you would be my stepmom and we could talk all the time. Now that won't happen."

She searched for the right words to help Adam understand where she and Rick stood. "Your dad and I are still friends."

"But he's knocking down your house. That's not being a friend." Adam's eyes looked sad again. "Where will you live?"

She stood. This conversation would take some careful explaining and she needed reinforcements. "I promise it isn't as bad as it sounds. Let's go into the kitchen and make some hot cocoa. I'll tell you all about what's happening with my house."

Adam glanced around. "I like your house. I don't want my dad to tear it down."

Cayme started to unzip Adam's jacket. "Really. It's okay. Let's make—"

A loud pounding sounded at the front door.

She glanced up with a frown. "Why don't you go into the kitchen and warm up," she said to Adam. "I'll see who's at the door and then join you in a minute."

He took off his jacket and handed it to her. "'Kay." He headed into the kitchen.

She hung Adam's jacket next to hers on a hook then opened the door. "Mr. Peters!" She stood back to let him in.

The councilman shook the rain off his umbrella and set it upside down just outside the door then stepped inside.

"Thanks. I wasn't sure of my welcome." He shut the door behind him then glanced around at the homey furniture.

Oh, the snooty thoughts he must have about her humble home. "Why are you here?" She wanted to sound less hostile, except this man wasn't on her list of favorite people. Especially after she'd spilled the beans about his son, regardless that it'd been the truth.

"I came to offer you an apology." He spoke quickly, as though he'd rehearsed what he'd needed to say and didn't want to get it wrong. "I spoke with Chase." He cleared his throat. "I eventually got the whole story out of him."

Cayme was speechless, barely processing his

unexpected admission. "I-I don't know what to say." She motioned him farther into the house. "Would you like to come in? Adam and I were about to make some cocoa."

"Cayme! The river!" Adam's voice came from the back door.

She turned to see the boy sprint out onto the back porch. "Adam?" She faced Mr. Peters. "Excuse me." Hurrying through the kitchen, she caught a glimpse of Adam jumping off the porch and running toward the river. She raced through the back door, her heart pounding, her breath stalling in her lungs. What was he doing?

By the time she got to the porch and caught sight of him again, he was climbing the wall of sandbags. "Adam! Stop! What are you doing?"

"The sandbags are slipping," he shouted. "Your house will flood." He tried to push a sandbag back into place.

Even from where she stood, she could see the sandbag was too heavy for him to move alone. Behind her, she heard Mr. Peters come onto the porch, but she didn't turn around, keeping all her focus on the little boy perched precariously near the raging river. She ran down the porch steps toward the stack of sandbags. "Adam, come down!"

"I don't want your house to flood. Where will you live?"

If she didn't do something fast, he would fall into the river. She was drenched by the downpour by the time she reached the sandbag wall. "Adam, it's okay if the house floods, Ben and I are moving anyway."

"No!" Tears joined the rain streaming down his

cheeks. "I don't want you to move away, too."

At that moment, the top sandbag slipped under his weight, and he started to fall.

Cayme reached out and caught his arm.

Then his weight shifted, and he teetered to the other side.

She had to crawl onto the sandbags to hang on. He was caught by the river's rushing waters, throwing her off-balance. Instead of pulling him up, she tumbled into the cold, raging river after him.

As the icy water took her breath, she heard Peters shout. Not taking time to respond, she thrashed around, searching for Adam.

She spotted him bobbing in the current a few feet away, getting farther away by the moment.

She swam hard, battling the cold that threatened to take her under. "Adam," she called. "Swim this way."

He turned his head, his arms flailing while he struggled against the current to reach her.

Kicking harder, she stretched her fingers, caught his hand, and grasped it tightly. "Hang on to me." She pulled him close to her and kicked again. Struggling to hold both their heads above the water, she guided them beyond the sandbag wall toward the river's edge. She kicked with the current, grateful that this part of the river took a bend toward a sandbar and was shallower with fewer rocks.

Although still strong, the current at the bend wasn't as fast as in the center of the river.

As they rounded the bend, she spotted the big cottonwood tree just in front of them. The same tree she'd fallen out of when she was ten. Boards were still nailed to the trunk. "See that tree?" She struggled to speak, the effort to reach the shore draining more and more energy the longer they stayed in the cold water.

"Yeah." Adam coughed. "I see it."

"When we get close, reach for those boards. Grab on and climb up."

Water swirled around the trunk, and her feet touched the river bottom. She stood in chest-high water, fighting the current that wanted to drag them downstream. Pulling Adam to her, she lifted him to grab the first board. "Got it?"

Adam's hands, red with cold, grasped the board. "Y-yeah." His body started to shake.

Cold was seeping in quickly, and she needed to get him out of the water until help arrived. "Climb up. Hurry." She braced against the current and held him until his feet were on the first board.

He reached for the second board and then pulled himself up.

Cayme held onto the tree trunk, wanting to take a breath of relief that Adam was out of the water, but relief wouldn't come. She was shivering and losing feeling in her legs with every passing second in the cold water. She had to get out of the river, too. Looking up at the tree, it seemed to stretch forever upward, reminding her of her scare on the ladder a few weeks ago.

"Cayme," Adam called down to her. "D-don't leave me."

"I won't. I'm staying right here."

"Climb up h-here with me!" He patted the limb with hands that were still red and angry looking with the cold. "It's big enough to h-hold both of us."

"I know." As the cold seeped deep under her skin,

she started to shiver. Where was Mr. Peters? She glanced toward the house. Surely, he'd seen them fall in the river. Was he calling for help? She knew the man didn't like her, but would he leave her and Adam to drown without lifting a finger to save them?

Another shiver wracked her body. She might not drown if she stayed in this water, but hypothermia would kill her just as dead. The house wasn't that far away. She could slosh through the water for help. Adam should be okay as long as he stayed on the limb. No. She promised she wouldn't leave him, and she wasn't about to break that promise.

"C-Cayme." His voice had a scared tone. "Are y-you c-climbing up?"

Looking up at the shivering boy, she made up her mind. "I'm coming up." She reached for the first board.

"Yeah, Cayme. J-just like that. You can do it."

Now that her feet no longer touched the muddy bottom, it took more courage than strength to pull herself up to the second board. Desperation to get out of the water gave her the determination to continue. If she could at least get warm again, regain some strength, she could eventually climb back down and carry Adam to safety. When she reached Adam, she grabbed him and held him tight. "We'll be okay, just hold on to me."

He gave her a sad smile. "I'm sorry. I-I didn't mean to fall in."

"I know you didn't."

His chin dropped. "I just didn't want you to l-lose your home. I don't want you to leave me, too."

Too? "You thought I would leave like your mother?"

"I know you won't be my stepmom, but we're still

friends, right?"

A bit of the chill left her heart. "Always." She hugged him fiercely as if to pull him physically into her heart.

He shivered so hard that his body almost slipped off the limb.

Cayme tightened her grip even more. She scooted close to the trunk, keeping Adam next to her. Their soaked clothing dripped water into the river below.

Even though the rain hadn't let up, the branches and leaves protected them a little from the pelting drops. But without the sun, dusk was closing in early, and with it, a bitter cold night loomed. At least they were safe for the moment.

One way or another she'd get this precious boy to safety. And she wasn't letting go of him until then.

Chapter Twenty-Six

A splashing sound, out of sync with the rhythm of the river, drew Cayme's attention to the back of the house. Mr. Peters was sloshing through the water in their backyard toward the tree where Cayme and Adam had taken refuge. The closer he drew, the deeper the water became. By the time he reached the old cottonwood, the water was almost at his chest level.

"Cayme," he called. "Are you and Adam okay?"

She glanced down at him, grateful he hadn't abandoned them after all. "Yes, we are. But please. Would you come and get Adam and carry him to safety?"

"I can do you one better." He pointed to the side of the house where a crowd had started to gather.

Sirens wailed in the distance, getting closer by the moment.

In the lights of a truck that had been parked at the back side of the house, she saw Ben and Rick wade into the floodwaters pushing an inflatable raft.

Cayme's heart pounded with relief at the sight of her brother and the man she loved coming to their rescue. "Adam. Look, there's your dad."

"W-where'd he get the boat?"

"It's mine," Peters called up. "As soon as you fell in, I called your dad. Then I set to work getting my raft out of the trunk of my car."

"W-wow!" Adam said. "Now Dad can save us."

"Yes, he will." She gave Adam a squeeze, holding in her own shivers to radiate soothing reassurance to the boy. "Are you ready to climb down?"

He nodded.

"Okay, here we go." While she clung to the trunk, she helped Adam climb over her. "Slide around the trunk and then use the boards to climb down."

"Okay." He started creeping along the limb. When he got to the trunk, he stopped. "Do you want to go down first?"

She shook her head. "I'm not leaving this tree until I see you safe with your dad."

Adam turned back to her with the sweetest smile. "I'm s-so glad you saved me."

Her heart melted with those sweet words. "I think you saved me even more." She would have perished in the cold water if it hadn't been for this little boy's pleas to join him in the tree. But more than that, he'd shown her how important both Adam and Rick were in her life. If she could face the fear that had paralyzed her all her life, she could make amends to Rick. She owed him that much.

Rick and Ben reached the tree, and Mr. Peters helped them tie the raft to the trunk. Then Ben and Mr. Peters held it in place while Rick held out his arms to Adam.

"Climb down, son."

"I'm coming, D-Dad." Adam's little body shook, but he slid across the trunk and reached for the boards.

Cayme held her breath, afraid he'd slip back into the river.

But as he reached the lowest board, Rick grabbed

him around the waist. "I've got you."

She smiled at the words, recalling he'd said the same thing to her when he'd helped her off the ladder. No three words ever meant more—then or now.

Rick gently placed his son in the raft.

Ben draped a wool blanket around the little boy's shoulders then ruffled his sopping hair.

Adam rubbed his nose. "I lost my h-hat in the river."

"We'll get you another one," Rick said. He looked up at Cayme. "Your turn."

She hesitated, gripping the tree trunk tighter. Yeah, right. Her turn.

"Do I have to come up there and get you? Again?" Rick's tone was teasing. The concern in his eyes told another story.

As much as she wanted the comfort of his presence—his warmth—she had to do this herself.

"It's okay, C-Cayme," Adam called from the raft. "It's not hard. Don't be afraid. My dad will catch you if you f-fall."

Rick's gaze was intent on her. "I will. Always."

With those words, warmth infused her entire body. She took a deep steadying breath. Her arms and legs seemed to move on their own. Each step was sure and steady under Rick's watchful eye. She descended the tree until his warm hands grasped around her waist, heating her to the core despite her sopping cold, wet clothes.

As Rick guided her into the raft next to Adam, Ben wrapped another blanket around her. She gathered Adam close while Rick and Ben pushed the raft to safety.

A cheer rose from the crowd who'd gathered to watch the rescue.

In that moment, Cayme knew without a doubt that she'd finally come home.

****

Rick shook the water from his coat before sliding off his fishing boots. He placed them beside Cayme's back door, knowing he'd be demolishing this house sometime soon. The knowledge heightened emotions that were already at a peak. This place held so many memories. As his hand closed over the door handle, every single memory flashed through his mind, some wonderful and priceless. Others less forgiving.

One image he'd never forget was finding Adam clinging to the branch of that old cottonwood tree. He'd nearly lost his mind. The thing that kept him calm was seeing Cayme's arms wrapped around his son as though she'd never let go.

She'd saved Adam. She'd risked her life to rescue him from drowning. She'd braved her fear of heights to get him out of the icy water and keep him safe.

He owed her. More than he could ever repay.

More of the community had arrived to shore up the sandbag wall to stop the floodwaters from reaching the house, giving him a break to check on his son. Their efforts wouldn't save the yard, but once the rain stopped and the water receded, the foundation would dry out. They'd saved the house so Cayme and Ben could continue to live there for the next few weeks until they were ready to move.

Rick closed the kitchen door, muting the sound of the rushing river. Voices drew him toward the living room. There, he found Adam curled up on the couch between Cayme and Roxanne. Adam had refused to leave Cayme's house, so she'd given him a hot bath then dressed him in a pair of her old flannel pajamas while his clothes dried. A pair of oversized socks dangled on his feet, and the pajama legs were rolled up past his ankles. But he didn't seem to mind the pink panda print at all.

Adam looked at Roxanne with a concerned frown. "So, Mom, I thought you were leaving with Mr. Brad. Did my accident make you stay here?"

"In a way." She brushed a lock of hair away from his eyes. "Brad and I talked it over, and we're staying in town for a couple of weeks. He wants to get to know you better. And we both want to make sure you're okay."

"I'm glad you're staying longer."

She gave him a smile. "Me too. My visit was too short."

"Whew!" He wiped his brow. "And now you can watch my game tomorrow. I just know I'll hit a home run."

Rick smiled to himself. "You'll have quite a story to share at school tomorrow, that's for sure." His son was just fine. His capacity to bounce back was amazing.

As he spoke, the women glanced up. They'd been so engrossed with taking care of Adam they hadn't heard Rick enter.

"Dad! Did you fix the sandbags?"

"It's just about done." He gave Cayme a sympathetic look. "Unfortunately, we didn't catch it in time to prevent the water from reaching your house, but it's diverted enough now it should keep things from flooding more."

Her eyes clouded over for a moment then cleared. "It's okay. We'll be moving things out at the end of the month." Giving Adam's shoulder a little squeeze, she reminded him, "And I'm just moving up the street. I found a place behind the store that's just perfect."

Adam grinned at her. "That's good. I didn't want you to move away."

Rick glanced at his watch. "Come on, bud, it's time we got you home and into bed."

Adam groaned. "Do I have to? I don't want to leave."

Cayme stood and smoothed her sweatshirt over her jeans. She'd showered and changed too, looking freshly scrubbed and good enough to eat. "You've had a big day, kiddo. You need your rest."

"What Cayme said," Roxanne added. "I'll see if Brad is ready to go." She grabbed her jacket and headed out the back door.

Cayme moved toward the laundry room off the kitchen. "And I'll grab your clothes. They should be dry now."

As she started to walk past Rick, he said, "Let me help." He turned to follow her.

"It's okay. I'll only be a moment."

He trailed her into the laundry area. "Cayme…" He'd wanted to speak privately with her since the whole ordeal unfolded, and now was his chance.

She held up a hand. "Don't say it." Turning her back to him, she opened the dryer door.

He frowned. "Say what?"

She straightened with a bundle of Adam's clothes in her arms. "Whatever you're thinking."

"How can you possibly know what I'm thinking?"

"Because your emotions…my emotions are right on the surface. I don't want this situation to make either of us say things we're not sure of."

"I believe I'm pretty sure about what I'm feeling."

"And I think what you're feeling is an overwhelming sense of gratitude that may make you say something you'll regret later."

That made sense on one level. On another level, giving in to his emotions is what he should have done when she declared her love the other day. Unless she didn't really love him. Could that be why she didn't want to talk to him? "What if I ask a question?"

She clutched the clothes tighter and swallowed. "What?"

"Do you still love me?"

She gasped, clearly not expecting him to call her out.

"Do you? Or were you just playing the I-love-you-so-much-I'm-letting-you-go card to get out of the engagement?" He hoped his tone wasn't as harsh as the words sounded. He really, really wanted to know the answer. Everything hinged on her reply.

"I wasn't lying. I told you the truth." She took a step toward him. Looking him in the eyes with a brightness that defied the storm clouds outside, she said, "I loved you then. And I still love you now."

With her declaration, a tightness in his chest eased.

"There's more." She clutched Adam's clothes even tighter.

"I'm listening."

She licked her lips. "I've been a fool. I owe you an apology."

He frowned. "For what?"

"For making assumptions…accusations really, about you and Roxanne. I should have known better."

"So you no longer think I'd be happier with her?"

"I think you'd be miserable with a woman who is in love with another man."

"Sounds like the two of you have been talking."

Cayme nodded. "I was wrong about her. She wants to get to know her son…and I can't fault her for that. Adam's special."

"And he's alive. Thanks to you."

"I could never let anything bad happen to him. I'm so sorry he was in that situation to begin with."

"You can't blame yourself. You need to know that I don't blame you, either."

She took a breath, letting it out slowly. "Thank you for that. I'm not so sure I'd be that generous."

"You can't always know what's going on in an eight-year-old's mind."

"But he was distraught when he first came over. I shouldn't have left him alone."

"Stop it. Stop right now. It's water under the bridge, pardon the pun, and we both need to move on from here."

She swallowed and nodded slowly. "I can try." Relaxing her hold on the clothes, she dumped them on the top of the dryer and began folding Adam's little shirt.

He turned her to face him and took the shirt out of her hands. "Come home with us tonight."

She stared at him. "What? Why?"

"I want us to talk, to work things out. I don't want you to be alone tonight."

She chewed her bottom lip. "I won't be alone. Ben's here. And he may need me after all this."

"Maybe I need you more." His heart pounded, waiting, wondering, hoping her answer would be the one to set his world right.

"You need me?"

"I love you, Cayme." He tossed the shirt on the dryer and held out his arms. "More than you can possibly know. Tonight just drove the feeling home. And that's where I want you. Home. With me and Adam."

Cayme hesitated a moment then threw her arms around his neck.

He gathered her close.

When she lifted her head, she smiled. "Kiss me."

He obliged, putting everything he'd left unsaid into the kiss.

"Dad?" Adam called from the doorway. "Yick! Are you guys kissing again?"

Cayme pulled away just a little.

Breaking off the kiss, he looked over at his son. "Better get used to it, bud."

"Does that mean Cayme will be my stepmom?"

Rick gazed at Cayme's face, his heart pounding with the question. "If she'll agree to marry us."

Adam shuffled over in his floppy socks and looked up at her. "Will you marry us, Cayme?"

She knelt and gathered Adam into a hug. "I would love to marry both of you."

Epilogue

For a moment, a cloud slipped in front of the sun and dimmed the bright August sky. Even though most of the summer had been dry, Hawks Peak had remained green from the late snowmelt. At the base of the mountain, Blakely River ran at normal levels, adding a soft shushing sound to the quiet of the new park. The air was warm with the scent of summer and wildflowers strategically placed next to rows of chairs for the guests. For Cayme, the day couldn't have been more perfect.

As she said, "I do," sunlight burst through the clouds and shone on the three happiest people in the world.

Adam beamed, unable to prevent his enthusiastic punch in the air. "Yes!"

Rick pulled him close and then gathered Cayme to him for a toe-curling kiss.

A cheer went up from those gathered in the renovated pavilion centered in the original park, welcoming the newly formed family to the community. Her cheeks warmed, but her smile never dimmed, even through a touch of embarrassment.

As the three of them made their way up the aisle, Ben propped his guitar on his knee and strummed out the notes of the same upbeat 60s love song that played at their own parents' wedding.

She remembered their folks dancing to that song and sharing a hint of what had made them fall in love. And the miracle now was her brother playing that same song.

Several miracles had occurred since that fateful day she and Adam fell into the raging river. The miracle of Rick returning her love. And that he'd still wanted to marry her after she'd made a mess of their engagement. Adam had generously accepted her as part of his life. And of course, she assured him he'd never feel like he had to choose between her and Roxanne.

Now, as she reached the end row of the chairs, with Rick holding one of her hands and Adam holding the other, she had never been more complete. All day, her mother's presence seemed to hover, as if she had orchestrated the whole thing. This was her mom's way of making sure her children would be okay.

Cayme knew without a doubt her mother forgave her for not keeping her promise. Not keeping that promise had led to the best thing that had ever happened to her.

Rick and Cayme smiled through the congratulations in the short reception line. When Mr. Peters stood in front of them, she offered a hand.

He took it with genuine warmth, nodding toward the flattened landscape that was once Cayme and Ben's property. "I'm sorry you don't get your honeymoon until this project is finished. But I'm holding off on my golf course until next year, so you don't have to wait any longer."

Rick's smile faltered a little. "You don't have to hold off because of us. My company can take care of things just fine."

"Of course, they can. But you know I insist on the best, so I want you there supervising. By the way, your bonus is already in your account." He gave a conspiring wink. "This way, you can both enjoy the time you deserve."

Rick glanced at Cayme then back at Peters. "Sir, I can't accept a bonus for work not even started."

"Nonsense. Believe me, you'll earn it." He took Rick's hand and shook it. "Congratulations." Then he moved on, ruffling Adam's hair as he passed.

"Can you believe that?" Rick squeezed Cayme's hand. "Looks like we can take that trip after all."

"We still have to wait until fall," she said. "And what about Adam's school? We can't take him out just as it's starting."

"I get to go on your honeymoon?" Adam excitedly jumped into the conversation.

"I don't think so, young man." Sherry approached them with the baby propped on her hip. "You get to have some quality time with your Aunt Sherry and Uncle Ken."

Adam glanced between the adults with a frown. "A honeymoon trip sounds more fun."

Rick leaned over and whispered in Adam's ear.

The boy's frown deepened. "Really?"

Rick straightened with a nod. "Afraid so."

Adam sighed. "Then I guess I'll stay at Joey's house."

Rick squeezed his son's shoulder. "Good plan."

"Can I go now?" Adam asked. "Joey brought his mitt and mine's in the truck."

Rick grinned. "Go. Just make sure you keep the ball away from our guests."

"'Kay." With that, Adam took off running across the fresh green lawn.

Cayme stared at her new husband. "What did you tell him?"

Sherry cocked her head with curiosity. "I'd like to know the answer to that as well."

Rick smiled, his dark-chocolate eyes wicked with mischief. "I told him there'd be lots of kissing and stuff on our honeymoon." He took Cayme's hand and brought it to his lips.

"Okay, then," Sherry said, switching the baby to her other side. "That's my cue to go find my husband." She gave Cayme a hug. "Welcome to the family, sis-in-law."

Cayme gave her best friend a hug back. "Thanks. We're related, now."

Sherry grinned with a wink. "Are you thinking that's a good thing?" Before Cayme could respond, she wandered off to find her husband.

With a deep sigh Cayme laid her head on her husband's shoulder.

"Happy?" he asked.

She nodded, more content than she'd ever felt her entire life.

"Me, too. You know, I totally owe Adam for stopping by the store that day to look for my birthday present. Even then, you were stepping up to be a part of our lives."

Cayme gave a short laugh, remembering Rick's wild engagement announcement. "That day wasn't the most auspicious of beginnings, but we made it work."

"I wouldn't have it any other way."

She turned in his arms and smiled. "Me either." As

she looked across the street where her house once stood, her warm smile faded just a little. The physical reminder of her past was gone, but the memories would always be in her heart.

"I'm sorry you have to see that eyesore on your wedding day. We could have held the ceremony at my dad's house."

"No." She shook her head. "This is perfect. So much of our past is right here. And today starts our lives as a family." She pulled her attention from the house and gazed into her husband's eyes. "I have you and Adam. I'm home. And that's all I'll ever need."

A word about the author…

After a taste of life on both U.S. coasts, Stanalei now resides near the beautiful Wasatch Mountains with her husband. Together they enjoy the open road, visiting museums, exploring ghost towns, and our National Parks.

Visit Stanalei at:
>www.stanaleifletcher.com
>http://www.stanaleifletcher.com/

Thank you for purchasing
this publication of The Wild Rose Press, Inc.

For questions or more information
contact us at
info@thewildrosepress.com.

The Wild Rose Press, Inc.
www.thewildrosepress.com

Milton Keynes UK
Ingram Content Group UK Ltd.
UKHW010644140324
439439UK00015B/1485